Thornton's Gold

Also by F. H. Masters

Blackthorn
The Night Hawk
Thornbrook (A Blackthorn Mystery)

Thornton's Gold

F. H. Masters

Thornton's Gold

Copyright © 2017 by F. H. Masters

This is a work of fiction. All of the characters, names incidents, organizations, and dialogue in this novel are either the products of the author's imagination or are used fictitiously.

To my husband, Quincy,
who has been my biggest supporter
even though I didn't name this book
Like Doodlebug Fishing.

Chapter One

It was March and spring had come early to Northeast Florida. Everything was coming alive and Ada Tanner was glad to see the end of winter. She walked outside and stood drinking in the late afternoon, loving the sights and sounds of this time of year. Trees were blooming and the countryside was dotted with wild flowers and snowy hog plum trees. The yellow jasmine and wild honeysuckle were beginning to climb on everything, and the air was a profusion of birdsong.

The warm sun made Ada feel a little lazy and so did the soft hum of a bee in the wild azalea bush that was blooming nearby. She leaned against the old rail fence and closed her eyes, thinking of nothing in particular. Her thoughts were as lazy today as she felt.

As she stood there, a sound interrupted her somnolence and she opened her eyes. Her father was sitting in the shade of a giant live oak tree and she turned to look at him. He was making a cast-net and it was the sound of his shuttle as it wove and knotted the net that had nudged her to wakefulness. She immediately walked to where he sat and stood beside him, watching as he made the net that he would take to the river to catch mullet.

She was standing there when Mr. Harris' wagon came into view. He was coming up the road, his old mule, Patty, plodding along nonchalantly. Ada stepped up to the bottom rail of the fence and leaned over it for a better look. She waved as he stopped and then she called out a greeting.

"Hello, Mr. Harris," she said and he tipped his hat.

"Howdy, Ada," he pleasantly replied. He wrapped the reins around the wagon's brake and then he stepped down. He was a man in his sixties, short and thickly built, his hair was gray and his shoulders were rounded and stooping. He stepped up to the fence and put his hand on the top rail, and when he looked over it, his expression was sober and serious.

"Well, Fred, I see we're gittin' a new neighbor," he announced.

"You don't say," Fred answered. The shuttle was in his right hand and it paused in mid-air.

John nodded solemnly, and Ada leaned farther over the rail, not wanting to miss anything. The property that lay next to their small farm was up for sale and every man in the area had dreamed of owning it. There were thirty-five hundred acres of land in that section and no one had the kind of money it would take to buy it, but it didn't keep everyone from wishing—not even her father who had not the money to buy the twins a new pair of shoes, much less thousands of acres of land.

"I was at the post office," John went on to explain. "Heard a man talkin'. He said a surveyor had come in to buy supplies. Said he was surveyin' for the new owner."

"News to me," Fred said, but his brow creased ever so slightly. "Anyone we know?"

"No. I heard 'em say he was from New Hampshire or one o'

them New England states."

"I knew it weren't no southerner," Fred dryly stated. "No honest southerner, anyhow."

John agreed with a grunt that said more than any words could have. He looked over his shoulder at the surrounding property and you could see the disappointment in his eyes. He was not a young man anymore, but he had had his dreams the same as everyone else, but fantasy or not, he felt cheated by this sale.

"I reckon I'll go," he said. "Mary's not feelin' well and I gotta feed up."

"Stay an' have some coffee," Fred offered, but John declined.

"Another time," he promised. "I only come by to tell ya' the news."

He left and Ada stepped down from the rail and walked back to her father. He had picked up the shuttle and had already begun weaving the net again.

"I knew it was comin'," she said, "but it makes me rather sad."

Ada was eighteen years old and like everyone else, she had her dreams. They were not the same dreams that Mr. Harris or her father shared, but somehow, the buying of the surrounding property seemed to shatter them.

"It's the change," she went on to say. "Everything's changin', and I don't like change."

"Change c'n be good," her father pointed out, "but I know what ya' mean. We'll roll with the punches, though, just like we always do."

She looked at him and wondered about that. Fred Tanner was in his mid-forties and still a handsome man. He had the rugged good looks of a man who had spent his life in the outdoors. His body was lean and strong, his arms long and sinewy, but his once light brown hair was now prematurely gray. It gave his dark, suntanned face a unique appearance, especially with his cerulean blue eyes.

Ada had those same eyes. They were large and as blue as sapphires, but her hair was dark, almost black. She wore a simple handmade skirt and blouse, and her shoes were old and rundown, but not even that could hide her natural beauty.

"I wonder when they'll get here?" Ada mused, more to herself than to her father.

"Maybe never. Sometimes folks just buy things for an investment. Maybe that's what this feller's done."

But three weeks later, the Tanners received word that the new owner had arrived and that lumber was being delivered for a house he planned to build.

"It sounds like he's here t' stay," John said to Fred. His farm was southeast of the Tanners and he often took the long way home just to stop for a brief visit. "There's lumber enough there for a fair sized house."

"Where's he buildin'?" Fred asked.

"Not far from the ol' Hampton place," John replied. That could have meant anywhere from Sink Hole Branch to the St. Johns River. Well, if he was building too close to the branch, he would be sorry. The ground was dry now and it appeared solid, but after a good rain, Sink Hole Branch would turn into quicksand and swallow anything around it, including his house if he was foolish enough to build there. He would have to learn the hard way, though. No one was going to tell him.

"He's gonna build fences, too," John added. "There's enough bales of wire been delivered to stretch from here to Jacksonville an' back."

"Ya' don't say."

"I do say, and that ain't all. I heard his name today and it's gonna int'rest you. They say he's Wade Thornton, Jr."

Fred's head came up. It did interest him.

"Same as Cap'n Wade Thornton?"

"I reckon. It'd be too mucha coincidence not to be."

Well, that was more than just interesting. The War Between the States had been over for seventeen years, but the Tanner's memories were long and they had not forgotten the young Union captain who had recuperated in their home. He had been shot not far from the Bellamy Road and he and his squad had been running for their lives when they had come upon the Tanner's farm. After that, they just weren't going any further.

There had been only Mrs. Tanner and her two little girls on the farm at the time. Fred was fighting in Pennsylvania so there was no resistance. The Union soldiers simply came in and took over.

But the soldiers didn't stay long. They were nervous and under a great deal of pressure to get to the landing at Bay Yard Point. The story was; they carried gold, a Union payroll of gold coins that had first been stolen from a train by Confederate forces and then later recovered by Captain Thornton's men. A squad under Thornton's command was given orders to take the gold to the landing where fresh troops would take it up the river and then north to a more secure location. It was a good story, but Fred had never believed it. For the first time, he wondered.

There had always been one point of the story that Fred found curious, and it was the only point that could have given the story credibility. The squad of soldiers left Captain Thornton at the Tanner's farm and for some reason, they had gone south instead of going northeast to the landing. The story went that it was to bury the gold. What other reason could they have had for going one way when they should have gone another?

The answer to that question was destined to be a mystery. The squad had been completely wiped out and Captain Thornton was not talking. If there had been any gold, no one had found it.

Captain Thornton had stayed at the Tanner's farm for three days and after that, southern soldiers had taken him away. He spent the remainder of the war in a confederate prison of war camp near Jacksonville, and he never divulged the details of his orders—nor verified the existence of the gold.

In spite of this, the story of the buried gold had grown with time and so had its value. Legend had it that fifty thousand dollars' worth of gold was buried somewhere to the south-southeast of the Tanner's farm. Even a few hundred dollars would have been tempting, and trust people to look even when the odds were impossible. The ground had been turned up everywhere from Tanner's property to Sink Hole Branch, but nothing had ever been found. It was curious, though. Who better than Captain Thornton's son to know where to look? And why, out of all the places he could have bought, did young Wade Thornton choose this very piece of property?

"It's right pecul'r," John said, but he never commented further. It was not necessary. Everyone knew what he meant.

"He's camped out over at his place," John went on to say. "Him and several other men. They look like a rough lot."

"You've seen 'em?"

"No. That's what I've been told."

John picked up his hat and after he left, Fred walked to the house. He had too much to do to worry about other folks' affairs, but something about all this bothered him. Maybe there was gold, after all. It caused him to pause in wonder. What man wouldn't want fifty thousand dollars' worth of gold? The lure of it had never before reached Fred, but now he was thinking of what even a portion of it would mean to him, and to his wife. He looked toward her and a pang of regret stabbed him like a knife. She had worked hard her whole life and time had not been kind to her. She looked old, older than her forty-two years. Her black hair was white and her once smooth dark skin was now faded and wrinkled. She deserved better, he was thinking, and the regret hit him again, but it didn't last long. Things like this never did in Fred's case.

Two tow-headed boys dashed past him, interrupting his thoughts. They threw the door back and let it close with a slam as they raced into the house.

"See here, boys!" Fred warned them. "That ain't no way to enter the house. Show your ma some respect."

"Sorry!" Silas apologized and he and his brother, Paul, skidded to a stop.

They looked exactly alike. Both were blonde and blue-eyed and their skin was tanned, their faces round and peppered with tiny freckles. They wore identical overalls, right down to the patches on their seats and the holes at their knees, and their feet were bare.

"They're tough as lighter knots," Mr. Tanner had often said, and it was the truth. No two boys were more rough and tumble nor more daring and energetic than these two scamps. What one could not think of doing, the other could, and they had tried it all.

In spite of this, Paul and Silas were a lovable pair. Their mischief was without malice and their pranks mostly directed at each other. There was not a job they wouldn't tackle nor a friend they wouldn't help, and they loved their sister, Ada, better than anyone else in the world.

"We come to git Ada," Silas explained.

"What for?" Fred asked, curious about the excitement they were showing.

"To go over and spy on that new feller. He's at the west corner of our property, justa lookin' around."

"See here," Fred said. "You boys stay away from him, an' I mean it!"

"Ah, Silas, I tol' you not to tell anyone but Ada. Now look

whatcha done!"

But Fred was not listening anymore. He walked outside again and looked across the pasture toward the west, but he could not see anyone. He wondered what Wade Thornton was doing at the corner of his property. He gave it some thought and at last he shrugged it off. There were many reasons and the most likely was he was just scouting the land, planning where his fence would set and at the same time, getting a feel for things.

Or could it be more? Was he looking for landmarks? Was there something in particular that drew him to that corner where the two properties met?

Something burned inside Fred and he knew what it was. It was the lust for treasure and the thrill of the reward it would bring. He had never had it before, but the coming of Wade Thornton, Jr. had kindled it in him.

It kindled something else within Fred Tanner, too, something he thought he had overcome years before. With a start, he realized he was still as jealous as ever.

He heard his wife's soft voice as she hummed a familiar tune and he looked over his shoulder in her direction. She had been a beautiful woman when she was young, but Fred had not realized how much that had caused him to distrust her until he had learned of her care of the Yankee captain she had nursed in their home.

When Fred had returned from the war, Esther Tanner was a different woman and she had never been the same since then, although no one seemed to see this change except Fred, himself. In his opinion, it was because of Wade Thornton. Fred grunted in disgust, and the fire inside him burned hotter.

Chapter Two

"You two get outta here," Ada said, scolding the twins as they made tracks across her freshly mopped floor.

She picked up the broom and made a playful swipe at them as they ran through the house and skidded to a stop on the porch.

"Now, see here," Paul admonished her. "You know, if you beat us with a broom it'll make us lazy," he told her.

"Yeah, and after we wuz gonna ask ya' t' go to the spring with us, too," Silas added.

"It's too cold yet," she pointed out, but at the same time, she felt a wistful longing to go there. The spring was a beautiful spot with clear water running under a bank of white sand, and moss laden live oak trees spreading leafy arms across the spring head, shading the deepest part of the pool. The runoff had made a wide ditch where the water flowed toward the creek and she and the boys had cleaned it out and enlarged it until it was a fine place for swimming.

It was also a good place in which to escape when Ada wanted to be alone. She had often walked down to the spring and sat there, simply enjoying the solitude. That longing that came over her just now and she knew she was going to give in to the twins even before she opened her mouth.

"Not f'r fishin', it ain't," Silas pointed out.

"Have you done your chores?" Ada asked, not wanting to appear too anxious.

"We're all done."

"Well, then help me empty the mop buckets and I'll walk down there with you."

The boys whooped with glee and cheerfully took up the pails of water and ran off the porch with them. Mrs. Tanner came into the room, drying her hands on her apron as she walked.

"What're they up to?" she asked with a smile.

"They wanna go down to the spring. I told 'em I'd go with 'em."

She nodded as if that was no surprise.

"Be careful," was all she said. "Snakes 're movin' around. They like the warm weather—and the water."

"We will," Ada promised.

It was a pleasant day, warm and sunny when the three of them started out for the spring. They went out the gate on the back side of the yard and walked down the well-worn path that led through a tangle of woods.

The trail was sandy and covered over with reddish brown pine needles, but as they emerged from under the tall pines, the white path twisted through a more complex forest, a mixture of pines, oaks, black cherry, and sweet gum that gradually merged with bays, magnolias and stands of sabal palms. The undergrowth changed, too. The patches of saw palmetto gave way to shrubs and short trees and as they progressed, to ferns, mosses, seedlings and a variety of herbaceous plants.

The spring was in a clearing where the trees abruptly stopped. A narrow glade separated the old hardwood forest from the spring on one side and a large stand of sabal palms on the other, and in between were a variety of woody plants, wax myrtle and mallows, as well as several types of grasses.

Ada and the twins had cleared away most of the brush surrounding the spring and had enlarged the runoff ditch until it was a wide pool. It gleamed in the sunlight. The water was almost turquoise in color, changing to deep blue where it narrowed and ran through bunches of tall grasses, down a sandy ditch, and on to the cypress pond in the distance.

It was a beautiful spot. Near the head of the spring was a giant live oak tree with spreading branches that reached for the sky as well as the ground, and its shadow made a shade over the head of the spring. That was where Ada always chose to sit. In the hot summer, it was a cool spot. She was protected from the sun overhead and cooled by the water from below.

The boys ran ahead so Ada was the last to arrive. They were already running around the bank, gesticulating excitedly by the time she got there. She stopped on the edge of the bank and calmly looked down into the water.

It was not more than four feet deep even here where they had worked to enlarge it and the water was crystal clear and icy cold. The sandy bottom was white and sparkled like diamonds when the light hit it.

"You be careful," she warned as they began pushing and shoving each other. "You'll scare the fish."

Ada knew they didn't really want to do any fishing, but she

went along with the ruse anyway. They were like her in many ways so she understood them. It was just the need to see the spring and to be here after a winter of infrequent visits. She knew that was how they felt, because she felt it, too.

The twins had laid their fishing paraphernalia on the ground near the trunk of the old oak tree, and they were just sizing up the place. While they walked around, talking to themselves, Ada found her favorite sitting spot and took a seat. She immediately felt the cold air coming off the water and she smiled when it caused a slight shiver to run down her spine.

She supposed she loved this spring better than any other place. It had been a place of entertainment and of refuge and its primitive beauty was unparalleled in the surrounding countryside.

Her seat was located in a place where she could easily drop her feet into the water, but today, she sat curled up on the bank, her feet tucked under her. The water was too cold and the days not yet warm enough, but in a couple of months, she would welcome that cold water on her hot feet.

"I did not!" Paul suddenly exclaimed, breaking Ada's reverie.

"You did too!" Silas insisted, giving Paul a violent shove.

"You take that back!"

"Will not!"

"I'll bust your nose!"

"Just try!"

Suddenly they were pushing and pulling and before Ada could get to them, Paul had hit the water. The resulting splash wet her from the waist down.

Silas was laughing and pointing but Ada was not amused.

"Get outta that water!" she angrily shouted, the cold shower washing away her good mood. "Get out right now!"

"Here, I'll help you," Silas said and when he reached over to take Paul's outstretched hand, he was pulled into the water, too. They both began laughing and it was plain to see they had orchestrated the whole episode.

"You little scamps! Get out right now or I'll tell daddy."

"Ah, Ada. You're as grumpy as an ol' woman," Paul bemoaned as he stood up. He knew what it would mean if she complained to Mr. Tanner. They'd be put on restriction and not allowed to go to the spring even when the weather turned hot.

But they could not resist a few gags before leaving the water. Silas shot a spray of water at Paul, but he dodged it with practiced ease. The water, however, took Ada right in the face and she gasped as the chill took her breath away. The boys gasped, too, the seriousness of what they had done taking their breaths away as surely as the cold water had done to Ada. Their faces took on a comical relief and as she recovered, Ada could not help but notice. They were frozen, eyes stretched wide and their mouths open in a silent scream. Silas had one hand outstretched as if to catch the escaping shower, but Paul was as rigid as a pole, just standing, staring in horror.

She released the air with a long sigh and then she began to laugh. When she laughed, the boys wilted with relief and then they laughed, too, and that was what they were doing when the angry voice shouted at them from the woods on the far side of the pool.

"Hey! What're you kids doin'?" he demanded.

Paul and Silas stood up and turned, wiping their too long hair back from their eyes and the water from their faces. Ada gasped, startled by the sheer unexpectedness of the man's harsh voice.

He was a stranger. None of them had ever seen him before, but Ada could imagine who he was. He stepped forward, a scowl on his face and his hands on his hips, arms akimbo. He was a man of middle age, not tall, but of average height. He wore a hat that hid his eyes, but under the brim, you could see his mustache and a well-rounded chin.

"You're on private property," he warned them.

"Come here, boys," Ada said, drawing the boys to her with beckoning hands. They waded out of the water and stood shaking with cold beside her.

She had not even thought about it. The spring had always been theirs for the using and she had given no thought to the fact that it now belonged to Wade Thornton. She looked at him and she didn't like what she saw. He was arrogant, but more than that, he was belligerent. She had expected as much, but still, it surprised her.

And she was saddened. The beautiful spring was his and it was hard enough letting it go without having to release it to such a hateful man.

She lifted her chin and gave him an icy stare.

"Forgive us for intruding upon your *private property*," she said with an imperiousness that would have done a queen justice. "We didn't suppose it was hurtin' anything by us bein' here."

"Well, you'll learn," he harshly said. "We won't have you people trespassing."

"Trespassin'?" She was indignant. What an overbearing snob he was. She had never hated anyone in her life, but her feelings for Mr. Wade Thornton were frightfully close. "Come along, boys," she said, turning them toward the path that led home. "*We people* wouldn't want to be *trespassin'* on this man's *private property.*" She cast him an incensed look and then she turned away, herding the boys before her.

She was so outraged she could not think, but when she got home she told her mother what had happened and then the story was repeated to her daddy once he came home.

Fred had been at the river and he arrived with a mess of mullet. He unloaded the back of his wagon and set the barrel of fish on the ground as he listened. He had never seen Ada so worked up, and he had to admit, it flew in his face, as well.

But like it or not, Wade Thornton had the legal right if not a moral one to put them off his property, and if the spring belonged to Fred, he knew he would be inclined to selfishly guard it, wanting to keep it only to himself.

"Well, I'm sorry, Ada," he said after she finished her tirade. He picked up the barrel of fish and walked to the side of the shed where he always cleaned his catch. She followed along, just a step behind him. "It's a shame, but the spring's his."

"We've always played there," she insisted as if that was justification for possession. "An' we weren't hurtin' anything.

He could've told us nicely that he didn't want us there, but no, he was rude and hateful."

"It's some folk's way," Fred said. He dumped the fish and began setting things up for cleaning them. "I was hopin' he'd be civil. I reckon not."

Was that all he had to say? Ada thought. *Could he not see the injustice and be at least a little outraged*?

"Oh, daddy, you aren't goin' let 'im get away with this, are you?"

He stopped what he was doing and gave her a curious look.

"What d' you think I c'n do?" he asked. "I'd a bought the place if I coulda. It's his. He c'n do as he pleases."

"But he insulted us. *You people*," she said, lowering her voice an octave to imitate him while at the same time she put her hands on her hips just like he had done. "*You people are trespassin' on my private property*. His private property? He has no right to it. It just isn't fair."

"Right or not, he bought it. It's his," Fred said. He dumped a bucket of water on his scaling bench and began scrubbing it off. "I'm thinkin' he'll learn a few things the hard way, especially if he treats everyone like that. It's hard to live in a community if you're cut off from everyone."

That was no consolation. Ada wanted concrete retaliation, not some wistful speech about vague justice in the sweet bye and bye.

"We'll stay on our side o' the line and he can stay on his," Fred went on to say. "I know that's not what you wanna hear, Ada, but that's what we've gotta do."

Ada was not satisfied. She walked to the house and joined her mother in the kitchen. It was time to start supper so she set to work, hoping to distract her own thoughts.

The afternoon passed quickly and the sun was just setting as they finished eating. Fred took his pipe to the porch and sat down to smoke it. He had just lit it when he heard the horse approaching. Skippy, his big yellow dog, began baying the arrival and Fred quietly scolded him.

A man in jeans and a faded red shirt rode up to the front of the house and stopped his horse at the gate. His outfit was more western than southern. He wore a black Stetson and a leather vest, and boots with a pointed toe. Likewise, his saddle was sturdy with a large horn and a low cantle.

"Light 'n set," Fred called from the porch and the man stepped down.

He was a young man with dark hair and eyes. He stood one inch less than six feet tall and he walked with a military air, straight and purposeful. His face was lean and smooth and he wore neither a beard nor a mustache. There was nothing to hide the perfection of his handsome face except a tiny scar on his chin that dared to mar his fine features. He stepped onto the porch and removed his hat, and then he held his hand out to Fred.

"Mr. Tanner," he began, "I'm your new neighbor, Wade Thornton."

Fred eyed him through the drifting smoke of his old pipe and he neither spoke nor took the outstretched hand.

Wade made a gesture that was full of resignation. He

19

turned his hand palm up and looked at it as if examining it for the offense it must have caused. He didn't give in to the rebuff, however, but he did withdraw his hand. He gripped his hat with both hands and looked down at Fred.

"I've come to introduce myself and to apologize," he said. "I was hoping to have a cordial meeting with the family who cared for my father while he was convalescing, but I understand one of my men unnecessarily provoked your children. I've reprimanded him and I've come to apologize on his behalf."

Ada had come to the door and was looking out. She had seen the fine looking young man as he had walked across the yard and had climbed the steps to the porch, and she had wondered who he was. When he spoke his own name, her shock was obvious, but her anger was not quelled by his apology.

He spoke with fine sounding words and long sentences and she wondered if he was purposely being condescending. She made a derisive sound and stomped away from the door, but not before he had taken a look himself. He looked and then he looked again, and for just a moment, he stared. Ada stopped only once and that was to cast a look of contempt his way, and then she went out of sight into another room.

"So that weren't you," Fred said and Wade's eyes swung back to him.

"No, it wasn't," he said. "I'm sorry your children were rudely handled and I promise you, it won't happen again."

"Have a seat," Fred said and Wade gratefully took a chair beside him. He supposed that meant his apology had been accepted and he didn't want to make another offense. He sat down in the ladder back rocking chair and placed his hat in his lap, but he could not help casting one more look over his shoulder toward the door where the face had appeared and then just as quickly had disappeared.

"I hear you're buildin' a house and puttin' up fences," Fred commented. He puffed on his pipe and a cloud of blue smoke rose up between them.

"Yes, sir. I've heard stories about this country my whole life so you can imagine my excitement when this opportunity presented itself. I'm building a small house on that oak hill just north of Sink Hole Branch."

Fred grunted a response. He could imagine a lot of things and some of them were the subject of the stories Wade must have heard his whole life. He had probably been drilled from childhood about the gold—if there was any gold, and Fred was quickly becoming a believer.

Ada had retreated into the house but she had not gone so far that she could not keep an eye on what was happening on the porch. The man they had met at the spring had not been Wade Thornton, after all, but that didn't make her feel any better about her new neighbor. He was still a condescending snob, in her opinion, and she could not like him.

"Why don't you take the men some coffee?" her mother asked. Mrs. Tanner had quietly walked into the room and she had noticed Ada's intense interest.

"I'd rather not," Ada replied, lifting her chin defiantly.

"It'd give Mr. Thornton a chance to apologize to you in person—and he's a right good lookin' man," she pointed out.

"Who cares," Ada flippantly remarked. "Listen to him talk. He thinks we're hicks and won't understand all his big, fancy words. Well, I've had an education. As poor as we are, you saw to that, so I understand 'im quite well. I also understand how he has condescended to come here, at all. I don't like him, and I don't want him apologizin' to me."

Mrs. Tanner was quiet for a moment and then she spoke in her soft, knowing voice. "His daddy was a good man, I think. In another time and another place, we coulda been friends. He was a gentleman and I imagine he raised his son to be one, too."

Ada flashed her eyes at her mother. "I don't care," she insisted. "He c'n drop dead for all I care."

She didn't really mean that, but she was upset, and the trouble was, it was not so much about the man himself. It was the spring that brought about these strong feelings of animosity. The spring was their spring or that was how she had always felt and the thought of losing it hurt so deeply that Ada was stricken with both mental and physical pain. She could feel the loss like an ache in her heart and a gnawing in her stomach. It almost made her nauseous. She was frustrated with the futility of her desire and Wade Thornton was now the object of that frustration.

In reality, Fred felt hardly better about his young neighbor than his daughter felt, but he had a motive for hiding these feelings. Rather than show his frustration, he chose to cultivate Wade's friendship. If there was animosity between them, how would he ever have the opportunity to look for the treasure?

No, he had to keep a good rapport so the probable

locations of the gold wouldn't be cut off from him.

The thought caused Fred to consider the fence. He noticed Wade had not commented on it even though he had been quite thorough with his explanation about the house. He removed the pipe from his mouth and waited as the smoke dissipated.

"Where's the fence goin'?" he bluntly asked.

Wade shifted nervously in his chair.

"I'm fencing the whole thirty-five hundred acres."

Fred whistled long and low. "That's quite an ambition," he said. "Folks ain't gonna like it. You'll be cuttin' 'em off from routes they've been takin' for years. It'll mean goin' the long way around to get to some places."

"It's not my intention to make a hardship for people," Wade said. "Nor to bar anyone from my property. I'd be willing to put in gates at strategic points if that would help, but I'm bringing in cattle and I want them to stay on my property."

"Cattle? You don't say," Fred exclaimed. "Ya' gotta know what you're doin' to run cattle in Florida. Rough woods like yours, it'll take about thirty-five acres for just one cow. The folks with cattle 'round here, let 'em free range, 'cause o' that reason."

"I'm not plannin' a big operation. I spent some time on my uncle's ranch in Texas and I found I loved the life. I just want to see fat cows growing on my own property."

Fred could understand that. The only cow he had was Hettie, the milk cow, but he liked the look of lazy cows grazing on green pastures, and he would have had it, too—if he could have afforded it.

"It seems you're quite knowledgeable," Wade said. "I could use a man like you."

Fred looked up in surprise. He had not expected that. It gave him a moment of intense excitement, but the feeling quickly passed. Fred was a peculiar man where work and money were concerned. He often mourned the fact that he was a poor man and would have liked to have all the resources he needed or wanted, but at the same time, he had no desire to pursue a career that meant obligating himself to any commitment. He would much rather do what he enjoyed—fishing, hunting, working his small farm, and taking time off when he felt like it. He could do what he liked whenever he wanted, and he answered to no man. To Fred, that was worth more than the value of the gold supposedly hidden on Wade Thornton's property, although, he was beginning to consider the independence that gold would give him. He could be free to do all the things he had always wanted to do if he had it.

But Fred Tanner was not burning any bridges behind himself, either. He quickly considered an answer and cautiously replied.

"Happy to help out—onct 'n awhile." He thoughtfully puffed on his pipe and then expertly shifted it to the corner of his mouth. "Seen anything unusual up on the hill?" he suddenly asked. His eyes were squinted against the smoke and he was indifferently looking off into the distance. "Not that I take stock in such things, but folks're always sayin' how they see things over there. It's the place all them soldiers were buried, you know."

"No, I didn't know," Wade said, giving that some thought. "What do people see?"

"Nuthin', I don't reckon," Fred said with just a hint of impatience in his voice. "Nuthin' what cain't be explained. You know how some folks are."

Wade could not remember his father ever explaining what had happened to the men in his squad after they had been killed, but it made sense that they would have been buried on the spot.

"Exactly where are they buried?" Wade asked.

"Don't know. Nobody knows, I don't reckon, but there's a place just this side o' the saplin' thicket where nuthin' but pearpads and beargrass grows to this day. Folks say that's the place they were all buried—even their horses."

Wade would check out that place as soon as he had time, not that looking at it would tell him what was beneath the surface, but he was thinking that he would certainly hate to dig up a skeleton or disturb the resting place of his father's lost squad. He wished Fred could be more specific.

The sun had set and shadows were filling the woods. The evening was growing cool and Wade knew it was time for him to go. He moved, drawing his feet back in the first step of rising from his chair, but he hesitated, suddenly reluctant to leave.

He realized with a bit of surprise that he had been hoping the girl at the door would come out and meet him. He glanced over his shoulder again and wondered about her, while at the same time, he admonished himself for his interest.

He had no right to be thinking of anyone but Angela. She

was his girl, the one waiting for him in New Hampshire. There was an understanding between them, but there was more than that, too. It was what everyone expected, and Wade supposed he was comfortable with that. Besides, Angela was like him. They came from the same social background and had been raised in the same area, with the same customs and beliefs. He was not a bigoted man, but at the same time, he understood what it meant to cross those lines.

But still, the face at the door had prompted a response he had neither expected nor invited. It was curious, especially when Wade Thornton was a practical man.

He immediately left, but he took the image with him. The next morning, the same image prompted him to make a trip to the spring. He got up early and left, walking, even though it was a little more than a mile away. It would give him a better education of the area, and there were things Wade Thornton wanted to know. He arrived about an hour after sunup, coming suddenly upon it. He stopped abruptly some distance away, and he simply stood and stared.

The spring was in a beautiful little glade surrounded by indigenous, vine covered trees. The sun was dancing on the surface of the water and a patch of phlox was blooming in a sunny spot behind it. The wind stirred the moss in the old live oak tree and the flowers nodded their pink heads. A cardinal was singing in a nearby tree and the dry fronds of a cabbage palm rustled loudly in the gentle morning breeze. In the distance, a gray cloud was on the horizon, the tall green trees of the cypress pond standing out in relief against it, and as he looked, a formation of pond scoggins sailed across the sky, their long, white bodies clear against the dark background.

He had to admit, he was enchanted. The place had that effect on everyone who saw it, except maybe for Jim, his employee who had found the spring and the children all at the same time the day before. Jim was a cantankerous man who seemed to walk through life with blinders on his eyes, but for all his contentiousness, he had been a great help to Wade.

There was a sentimental side to Wade Thornton which could appreciate a place like this so he understood the loss the Tanners must feel. He considered what he should do about permanently cutting them off from the spring, and he quickly decided that just like everything else, the spring had to be fenced in. If he let himself be taken in by every queer notion from his neighbors, his holdings would shrink to a meager lot.

Besides, he had to keep his thoughts moving in the right direction, and the Tanners were a subject that was leading him the wrong way and down a precarious path. It was the girl who upset his equanimity. He had been told her name was Ada, but it was a name he knew he should forget.

But even as he thought this, his eyes looked around, searching for the path that led to the Tanner's property. It was well defined and easily found. They had come to this spot a lot.

When Wade returned to the campsite, he stopped at the edge of the clearing and looked around. Everyone was busy and the work was progressing nicely. He pushed his hat back and studied them, wondering if he had made the right decision.

He was twenty-three years old, but he sometimes felt older.

He had worked hard all his life, but it had not been out of necessity. Wade's father was a successful businessman, and that position could have been Wade's if he had wanted it, but the idea of working behind a desk or managing a mercantile was the nearest thing to hell he could imagine, and Wade Thornton could imagine a lot.

That was why he had left home at eighteen. He had joined the army but he had stayed with that only a couple of years before taking a job on his uncle's ranch in Texas. Curiously, it had been with his parents' blessings. Looking back, Wade could understand why that blessing had come so quickly and so easily. They had thought he would find the work too hard and ranch life too demanding, and that he would return home, satisfied to take over his father's holdings, but that was not what had happened.

Wade had loved the hard work of ranch life, and as it turned out, he also had a natural aptitude for the job. After just six months, he had made up his mind to have his own ranch one day, and at the time, he imagined it would be someplace in Texas just like that of his uncle's ranch. He never figured that such an unlikely place as Florida would ever figure into his plans, but it had.

Wade had been in Texas for only a year and a half when his father had fallen sick at work. The doctor had told them it was a stroke and that Wade Thornton, Sr. would never be able to work again. Wade immediately returned home, and he had stepped into his father's position without resentment or complaint.

His father had slowly recovered, but it was an illness that had taken its toll. The right side of his body no longer functioned properly and it didn't appear it would get any better with time. After six months, Wade, Sr. announced his intention of selling out, and his son would have been lying if he had said he had not been relieved.

At that time, Wade Thornton, Jr. had a decision to make. His parents were in a stable position, but he felt an obligation to them. He didn't feel that he could just run off again to Texas and leave them. He had also renewed his relationship with Angela and she was expecting things from him that required his presence right there at home. He was in a quandary, not knowing exactly what to do, but realizing that whatever decision he made was going to impact him for the rest of his life. It had to be the right decision.

Surprisingly, it was Angela who set him on his present course. Her father was a retired Army major and it was he who had first heard about the property for sale in Florida. Like Wade, she had heard the story of Captain Thornton's campaign her whole life. He had talked with great animation about the wild beauty of Florida and its mild temperatures, and he had often hinted that he would have liked to return under more favorable circumstances, but the story of his last campaign had been a disappointing one and Captain Thornton grieved the loss of his men with such passion that he knew he would never return to the place of their deaths.

Angela had heard all this, so it seemed to her that it was almost too much of a coincidence that the property where this demise had come about should come up for sale. It was as if fate was dealing a hand in Wade Thornton's future. Destiny was surely directing him. His father felt it, too, and it was he who actually purchased the land. When he turned the deed over to Wade, there was no doubt in either of their minds that this was the direction he should take.

And here he was. He had brought seven men with him and they were all working out better than expected. Jim was the only man who had come all the way from New Hampshire with Wade. Four of the men were recommended to him in Green Cove Springs and he had hired them on the spot, but Rusty and Powder Keg Smith were friends from Texas. Wade never knew why they called the latter Powder Keg. It had been suggested that when he became angry, he exploded like a powder keg and that was how he got his name, but Wade had never seen him even mildly upset. A more even tempered man he had never known.

They had moved onto the place and set up just as if it had been a Texas cow camp. It was something Wade was familiar with and with which he felt comfortable, so Smith drove a chuck wagon in and took over the job of camp cook and the rest of them picked up the remaining jobs. They would be camping out until the house and bunkhouse were finished so that was the job getting the most attention right then.

Wade was still standing there when he heard the horses approaching. They came cautiously, with hesitant, pausing steps, and Wade was too well versed in the approach of guilty men not to recognize trouble. He moved to the edge of the clearing and was standing there when the four horsemen appeared.

They came slowly, just like they had been coming all along, and when they stopped, they bunched together in a tight little knot.

Not very smart, Wade was thinking. They obviously knew very little about fighting or strategy or they would have spread out.

"What's the idee? What're ya' doin' here?" one of the riders demanded. He was a young man, hard of eye and stern of face.

Wade pushed his hat back and looked up at the four men.

"I'm Wade Thornton," he announced. "I own this property. What I do with it is my own business."

The youth looked around in shocked surprise.

"You don't say," he finally said. "I thought this was gover'ment property."

"No, it's mine."

"You don't say," he repeated, his eyes scanning the area with thoughtfulness.

"I do say," Wade said. "And you boys are welcome if you've come friendly, but if you haven't, you can beat it out of here right now."

The boy's eyes jerked back to Wade and there was no friendliness in them, at all.

"You tellin' us to leave?" the boy asked, his voice soft, almost a purr.

"No," Wade said, not intimidated by the menacing tone of his voice. "You heard what I said. If you're friendly, you're

31

welcome."

The boy didn't say anything. The four of them sat their horses and stared soberly at Wade. After a minute, the spokesman turned his horse, and then he glanced over his shoulder, looking once more around the campsite.

"I'm Logan Spencer," he said as his comrades crowded around him. "An' I neither run nor scare easily. You c'n bet, I'll still be here when you're long gone, an' I don't reckon that'll take too long."

They spurred their horses away then and Wade looked after them for only a few seconds before turning around. His men had stopped working and they were all standing there, rifles in hand, staring at Wade.

They had his back, and it gave him a warm feeling to know that, but the meeting with Logan Spencer had left him thoughtful.

"There's trouble if I ever saw it," Rusty Gavin said as Wade walked back to the foundation of the house they were building. He was a young man, only nineteen years old, but he was old in the ways of life. He had been doing a man's job since he was fourteen years old and he was steady and capable.

"Yeah," Wade agreed, "but I won't hunt trouble."

"You won't have to. It'll come to you."

He was right. Two nights later Wade and his men were awakened by loud yells and gunfire. A small herd of scrub cattle were rushed through the camp and only the attacker's unintended warning had saved them.

Wade jumped to his feet and ran for the safety of the trees, yelling for his men to do the same thing. Rusty was already there when Wade slid to a stop behind a large oak.

"I told ja," he said, and then he mopped his brow. "Whew, for a second there, I thought I was back on the trail an' in the middle of a stampede. Lucky f'r us it was only five mangy cows."

It had been more than five, but Wade had no time to consider that. He saw the fire as it sprung up and he shouted in disbelief at no one in particular. Logan Spencer and his cohorts were burning the foundation of his house.

A couple of Wade's men got off some shots and the attackers disappeared without a trace, but it was too late for the house. Two days' worth of work and materials were burned to the ground.

The next day, Wade went to town and ordered more materials. He was not going to be run off his own property, and anyway, today he was wiser than he had been the day before. He would rebuild the house and from now on, armed guards would be keeping watch.

Besides that, he planned to get the fence started. The sooner he could get it up, the easier it would be to keep the likes of Logan Spencer off his property.

Curiously, the idea of barring Logan Spencer prompted the thought that Ada Tanner would be fenced off from the spring, and he felt a stab of conscious. He told himself he could not go soft where the girl was concerned and to prove to himself that he could be stern and unmalleable, he decided the line between him and the Tanner's property would be the first piece to be fenced. The surveyors had done their work and so nothing was left but to hire the men to do the actual job. He hired them that very day, and a few days later they arrived in an open wagon, tools and camping gear along with them. They set up a temporary camp near the southwest corner of Tanner's property and started building the fence, going east, directly past the spring.

Chapter Three

Ada watched her parents and the twins leaving and she sighed with contentment. She was alone, which was something that didn't often happen, and Ada liked to be alone—sometimes.

Today was one of those days. She stood on the porch and listened to the quiet all around her and it was a comforting thing. The house was perfectly still. There were no distractions so that every sound in nature was heightened. Ada hummed contentedly as she walked into the house.

With no one around, she could do as she pleased and today it pleased her to take a book and sit under the white oak tree to read. She had done this before so the stool she used to sit on was there, waiting for her. She threw a pillow on the stool and sat down and she had just opened the book and begun reading when she heard the rider approaching. She closed the book with a sigh and peered toward the road, trying to see who it was that had disturbed her solitude.

She had to admit, she was quite perturbed, but only because this was her special time. She actually liked to have company—just not today, but when Ada saw who had arrived, she almost dropped her book. It was Wade Thornton, and Ada could not imagine a more unwanted guest.

"What is *he* doin' here?" she said to herself.

With a start, she wondered what she should do. Several things crossed her mind, but the foremost thought was that she should simply ignore him. No one was in the house and he would find that out soon enough. She would just stay right where she was and keep her presence a secret, and he would leave without ever knowing she was hiding in the yard.

But curiously, he didn't leave. He knocked on the door and he even called out a, "Hello! Anybody home?" to the empty house. No one answered him and he walked to the edge of the porch and stopped there, calmly looking around.

Ada sat very still and from her hidden spot, she watched him. He scanned the yard and the surrounding area. He appeared to be looking for something in particular, but Ada could not imagine what. He looked into the distance, standing like a statue, his head slightly tilted as if he was listening as well as studying his surroundings. Suddenly, he stepped off the porch and furtively looked around before turning and walking directly toward her.

She stood up with a start and in that moment he saw her. When he did, he came to an abrupt stop.

"What're you doin' here?" she demanded.

He looked guilty. Maybe it was because his man had ordered her off his own property just a week before and he was now faced with the same prospect, or maybe he was snooping around and knew he had been caught in the act. Ada could only guess, but then she had to ask herself why he would be snooping around their property. They had nothing worth stealing and little else.

"I was looking for your father," he said, but Ada knew he was lying.

"He isn't here," she flatly stated.

"Oh," he calmly said while at the same time, he removed his hat. His dark hair fell over a wide brow and she could see his face more clearly. He had smooth, dark skin and a straight nose. His cheekbones were high and his eyes were large and dark and without question, he was a fine looking man.

Ada imagined that his handsome face had gotten him out of more than one tight spot, and she supposed he figured it would get him out of this one, but she was not inclined to be influenced by him. His eyes were appraising her in a beckoning, alluring way, but she had seen men give her sheep eyes before. She thought to herself that he should have saved himself the trouble, because she was neither interested nor impressed.

But Wade Thornton had no such thoughts, had Ada known. He could not help the look in his eyes. It was a natural reaction to his impression of her which had again caught him off guard.

"You'd better go now," she said.

He moved at the sound of her voice as if suddenly awakened and then he nervously cleared his throat.

"Yes, of course," he said, but he didn't leave. "Uh . . . Look, I'm sorry about the thing with the spring," he said. "I really am."

"You needn't worry about it," she icily remarked.

He nodded. "Okay," he agreed. "But I really am sorry." He replaced his hat and looked closely at her. "Tell your father I'm sorry I missed him," he added and Ada nodded.

"I will," she said, thinking that he had hit the nail on the head with his repeated use of the word sorry. It was a perfect description of him, in her opinion. She watched him walk away, her expression frosty and just a little hostile.

He walked around the house and stopped beside his horse. He paused there for just a moment and then he swung up into the saddle with an easy, fluid motion. As he sat there, he pushed his hat back for a better look around before turning his horse and leaving. He cantered down the road and as he passed, he looked in Ada's direction, his face solemn and his expression unreadable.

Now, what was that all about? She asked herself.

She sat down, but the book in her hand was suddenly forgotten. If Ada had not known better, she would have guessed that Wade Thornton was looking for something on their property, but what could interest him on their sorry property? And then she thought of the gold.

Was he looking for the gold or could it be, he was looking for a landmark that would point him in the right direction?

She stood up again and this time, she looked to the southeast where Wade Thornton's property bordered their own. It had been seventeen years since the gold had been buried and in that length of time, the landscape had changed a lot. She wondered if he was looking for something specific that perhaps could only be seen from this vantage point. After all, his father had never left their property. If he had chosen landmarks and given directions, wouldn't they be visible only from this direction?

Ada was suddenly excited. She was convinced he was looking for the gold and now she was also convinced that he needed more information than he had in order to find it.

The thought caused her to scan the area. What could have been the landmark Captain Thornton had chosen to lead him back to the gold one day? It would have to be something more permanent than a tree. Trees grow and change appearances, and then they die either naturally or by storms or lightning. But what else was there in this Florida landscape to mark a hiding place?

Ada could see nothing. Everything looked generally the same, and she suddenly wondered what the land had looked like seventeen years ago.

The pine forest would have been much shorter, and Ada had heard that before her father had gone to war, he had cultivated a lot more land than he now farmed. She could imagine how the property between here and the Thornton's property must have looked back then and what she saw in her mind's eye was a clearing all the way to the southwest corner of their property. In that area, only one thing stood out to her. It was the big oak.

Trees had grown up all around it, but the big oak was the only old tree on that section of land. Everything else had grown up in just the past twenty years. Not only that, but the big oak was beside the line that separated the two properties.

Ada's excitement grew. Had she unraveled the mystery of the gold? She could not wait to see. She dropped the book and walked out of the yard, going past sheds and over the garden fence. When she got to the back corner, she crossed the fence again, and made her way to the old live oak tree.

When she was a child, she had climbed all over this tree, and now Paul and Silas did the same thing. Ada and her older sister, Carrie, had played here while their parents had worked in the nearby field and like the spring, it was a refuge she had often taken to when she needed to be alone.

But never had she visited the old tree with thoughts like the ones she had today. She looked around. It was a secret place under the spreading limbs of the giant tree. The branches came down to the ground all the way around, making a circular wall that hid the base of the tree and everything under it. The ground was sandy and dry with roots that spread away from the tree like groping and gnarled fingers, and Ada looked around, wondering what she should be looking for.

In her opinion, this was not a good place to bury a treasure, but then, what did Yankees know? The ground was hard and full of roots but perhaps the very inappropriateness of the location made it the perfect spot to hide the gold, and she had to admit, there were definite advantages. They would be protected while digging. No one could see them once they were under the spreading limbs, and foregoing some unusual event, the tree was going to be here for a hundred years or more.

There was just one thing that shot down Ada's theory. The tree could be seen from a great distance and it was right on the border of Wade Thornton's property. There was no need for him to come to the Tanner's house. All he needed to do was walk up to the tree from his side of the line and do all the searching he wanted.

Ada considered that and decided that the big oak was not where the gold had been buried, after all, but, perhaps, it was still important. Maybe it was the first landmark in a line of landmarks, and the only way to line it up was to stand in the Tanner's yard and make a siting.

That made more sense, but Ada wondered what long, enduring marker could be beyond the old oak. While she considered this, she pushed through the tangle of limbs that swept the ground on the far side of the tree, and stepped out right where their property met Wade Thornton's.

Ada gasped as she saw the long line of fence running in both directions, west to east, as far as she could see. She looked to the east and grimly realized what this meant. The spring would be fenced off. Well, Wade Thornton had wasted no time, she thought, and her heart hardened just a little more.

She walked back to the house, determined not to be distracted from her investigation. She stood near the white oak tree and she looked toward the old oak tree. She moved and looked from different angles, but there was nothing she could see that would have been there seventeen years before, nothing that would mark a location for a hidden treasure.

There was simply no permanent thing in which to make a reference, so Ada had to ask herself a question. What was Wade Thornton really doing here this afternoon?

She looked around the yard and wondered. It presented a mystery that was exciting. She had to admit, though, it was also a little disturbing. If Wade Thornton wasn't looking for the gold, then his reason for being here was strange, indeed.

Ada grunted derisively and set her hands on her hips with a gesture of frustration.

Well, what was he really doing?

Chapter Four

"Thanks for coming with me," Wade said.

"Tell me again what we're doin' here," Rusty dubiously asked as he looked toward the church. It was a long wooden building with a high pitched roof. There were windows down each side, two doors at the front of the building and two doors at the back, and a cemetery behind it. Rusty was skeptically eyeing it.

"If you want to get acquainted in a new community, you go where the locals go—their meetings and their church."

"Okay," he said, turning his head to follow the steps of a young woman as she passed by. She looked back and he smiled, not feeling so unhappy anymore. "Well, let's do it then."

They walked inside and Wade paused just inside the door to get his bearings. The service had not yet begun and people were still milling around, talking in hushed tones. He recognized a number of people, John and Mary Harris, Cody Wells, the Maraquettes, and the Tanners. Ada was sitting on a pew near the front of the church and beside her was Logan Spencer.

"Well, I reckon that explains that," Rusty whispered as he saw them together. "No wonder she ain't got any use for us."

Wade cast a glance her way and solemnly nodded an agreement, wondering when Rusty had met her to even have the opportunity to be thwarted by her.

His thoughts were interrupted when Aribella Bailey approached them, welcoming them to the church.

The door opened again and a large family came in. They were quickly introduced. It was Mabel and Harvey Allen and their six children, and then the organ began to play, hurrying everyone to their seats. Wade chose a pew not far from Ada and as he sat down, he saw her look over her shoulder. The look she gave him was first surprise and then a cool stare. It didn't take long for Logan to see her interest and turn his head, as well.

His faced flamed red and he started to rise, but Ada put a hand on his arm that stopped him. She said something to him and then the service began. Logan slowly came to his feet along with everyone else, and after what seemed like a long time, he looked forward, taking the songbook Ada thrust at him. After a few seconds, he began to sing.

Logan had no singing voice, but Ada was quick to notice the lovely timbre of Wade's voice. It was distracting and unexpected and she found she could not concentrate on the service with him so closely behind her. Throughout the whole service, she was consciously aware of herself in a way she had never been before. She sat very still and tried not to even turn her head although she ached to reposition herself on the hard pew. When the service was over, she had no clue as to what the sermon had been, and she scolded herself for letting Wade Thornton cause her such distress.

As soon as the benediction was said, Logan came to his feet and Ada was quick to caution him.

"Not here, Logan," she said. "Don't start trouble here. It'll only arouse sympathy for them."

He wisely listened and calmed down, and then he waited beside her while most of the congregation slowly filed out of the church, Wade and Rusty among them.

"What's the idee, do ya' suppose?" he quietly asked as he watched them go out the door.

Ada shrugged. "Who cares?"

"Well, I reckon, I do."

"Just let 'em be, Logan. Makin' trouble for them'll only get you in trouble."

He derisively chuckled. "Ya' think so? That bunch 's a pack of skunks. They ain't got no fight in 'em."

"Well, just the same," Ada said. She looked after Wade and wondered about that. She somehow knew he was a tough man even though he had the easy appearance of a gentleman about him. "Let's go out to the dinner," she sagely said, taking Logan's arm and guiding him out of the church.

When they got outside, she saw Wade Thornton surrounded by a knot of people. He was making friends, and that bothered Ada. She had hoped he would remain an outsider, unhappy with his new home, and then give up and go back to the place from which he had come. It didn't look like that was going to happen, though.

There was a church service only once a month when the circuit riding preacher made his rounds and so the community took full advantage of the situation. There was preaching in the morning followed by a dinner on the ground and then singing

45

in the afternoon. The Tanners didn't get home until the day was almost gone and Logan always came with them.

It was something he did almost every Sunday, church service or not, and Ada was used to him in an apathetic, comfortable sort of way. They had known each other their whole lives but they had not always been friends. As they had grown older, though, their relationship had grown. If you had asked Ada, she would have told you she was in love with Logan Spencer, and she imagined that one day she would marry him, too, but the idea neither brought about anticipation nor excitement although it was a perfectly acceptable idea.

After all, Logan was the most eligible bachelor in the community. All the girls found him handsome and Ada was no exception. She liked his boyish good looks. His tanned face was wide across the cheeks and his chin was square. He had unruly brown hair and green eyes that he habitually squinted. There was not a girl around that had not at one time or another tried to win his favor and then possibly his hand in marriage, but he had never seriously considered any of them, although he was not averse to playing around if the opportunity presented itself. Ada never knew how often that scenario had been played out or how many girls he had left with a broken heart.

But she did know she was his steady girl, and everyone else knew it, too, and Ada liked the prestige that gave her among her peers, so she imagined she was in love with Logan Spencer, and her future was snugly wrapped up with him.

The afternoon was quickly waning and she and Logan walked outside. He sat down on the top rail of the pasture fence and she stood beside it. It was a scene that had been repeated every Sunday for so long that until now it was simply something done out of habit. He would sit there and they would talk and then when he was ready to leave, he would jump to the ground and kiss her goodbye. That was the way it always happened and Ada had always been comfortable with the predictable routine.

Today was no different. Everything played out the same until he jumped to the ground.

"Ada," he said instead of kissing her, "You ever wonder what it'd be like to be rich?"

Well, who had not?

"Shore," she answered. "But it ain't likely to happen."

He turned his eyes slowly to her. "It might," he said. "I gotta hunch about that gold."

So had she, but selfishly, she had kept her ideas to herself.

"What kinda hunch?" she asked.

"Well, I been thinkin' about Wade Thornton's choice for a house site," he said, "an' an idee came to me when I heard he'd brought in big equipment to drive a well. What if that buncha Yankees hid that gold near Sink Hole Branch? We both know what woulda happened to it, but they prob'bly didn't. It woulda sunk down to the hardpan."

"If that's the case, then it's gone forever," Ada pointed out.

"Maybe not. Mr. Allen told me Thornton brought in a rig to drive a well, but he was curious about something else they brought in. He said they were crazy Yankees with fool ideas, but you know what I think? I think they know where that gold is and they plan to dig it up usin' that machine."

47

"What kinda machine is it?" Ada asked, trying to imagine anything that was able to dig up a treasure from Sink Hole Branch.

He shook his head. "I ain't seen it, but it's somethin' used in well drillin', I hear. Only, I think it ain't water Wade Thornton's lookin' for."

Ada had to admit, that was a good theory, but if it was true, then only Wade Thornton could get to the gold. Logan didn't have a chance and she told him so.

"I know," he said with a knowing grin. "That's why I'm gonna let him dig it up. Findin' it and keepin' it are two different things, ya' know."

"You'd steal it?" she asked, aghast at the idea.

"It ain't stealin'," he insisted. "It ain't his gold. It's government gold and I've got as much right to it as he does." He paused for a moment and then he added, "If he had the chance, he'd take it from me. This ain't no different."

It was and Ada knew it was, but she was not thinking about the right and wrong of it just now. She was thinking that if Wade Thornton found the gold, then he might take it and go away and she liked the way that thought made her feel. Surely if he could afford it, he would want to live anywhere but here.

At the same time, it occurred to Ada that he appeared to have money. He had bought the huge tract of land that no one around here could afford, and he had bought supplies for a house and fences, and now well-drilling equipment. What did a man like him need with a small treasure? He already had a treasure of his own.

Or maybe not. There was the possibility that he had borrowed heavily in the hopes of gaining the treasure. If that was so, then if he lost it, he might lose everything. She turned to Logan with hope in her eyes.

"Take it, Logan," she said with passion. "Take it if you can!"

Chapter Five

It had been too quiet around the campsite and Wade was beginning to worry. It had been two weeks since Logan and his friends had paid them a visit and that boded more trouble than all their pranks put together.

After the night they had burned the foundation of the house, they had come back and stolen all of the work tools that were lying around and had thrown them into Sink Hole Branch. Three nights later, they returned and shot up the camp, sending Wade and his friends diving for cover, and then the next night, they had cut the fence. Wade had been expecting that, but he was disappointed when he saw a half mile of it lying on the ground.

Another night, they managed to get to the horses and they drove them off. It took Pat all day to round them up and get them back to camp, but after that, things had been relatively quiet. Wade knew they were overdue for another visit.

He doubled the guard and he sat up himself, rifle across his knees, ready for anything, but nothing happened. His men were getting worn out from lack of sleep and he was feeling the effects more than anyone else.

Rusty began wearing his pistols. They were .45 Colts in a tied down holster, the kind that was popular in Texas. On some men, guns like that would have looked cumbersome and bulky. They would have stuck out all over them like they were wearing a hundred guns, but that was not so with Rusty. It looked so natural that Wade didn't even notice Rusty was wearing them until the next day. He decided it was not a bad idea, so any time he went scouting, he buckled on his own pistol.

"What do you suppose they're up to?" Jim gruffly asked as he thought about Logan and his friends. "Have they run out of ideas or have they just given up?"

"Neither, I'm afraid," Wade answered. "I think they're waiting on something."

"What?"

"I don't know, and that's what has me worried."

"Well, you know me. I'd take the fight to them."

"Where? They're a bunch of boys who live around here and not together. Where do I take the fight?"

Jim spat on the ground. "They've got to come together somewhere. I'd find out where."

That was a thought, but Wade didn't want to do that. He was in the right and if it came down to a legal fight, he had done nothing wrong. He would wait, but he had to admit, the waiting was harder than fighting.

And then that night, Wade was awakened by a strange sound. He sat up and looked into the darkness, wishing he could see into the distance. It was an eerie sound and he found himself thinking of the ghosts of the lost soldiers who were buried somewhere nearby.

"Owls," Cody Spicer said. He was standing guard and had

seen Wade aroused from his sleep.

"Owls?" Wade asked, thinking that it sounded like a congregation of people talking—or arguing.

"Yeah, a whole parliament of 'em, sounds like. It's the time o' year."

Cody was one of the men Wade had picked up in Green Cove Springs, and he was familiar with the sights and sounds of Florida. Wade lay down again, but he was not one hundred percent convinced even when one of the owls hooted with a familiar sound, corroborating Cody's story. He could not get the image of a ghostly group of soldiers, arguing over gold, out of his mind. He decided to check out that clearing near the pine forest at his earliest opportunity, but when morning came, the thought had left him. He had things to do and substantial problems to deal with. The whereabouts of the soldier's graveyard was not as important in the morning sunlight.

"How's the well coming?" Wade asked Jim as they stood looking at the rig at the side of the almost finished house.

"Good. You'll have water in another day."

Wade nodded. Everything was going slowly because of the constant vigilance, but he had an idea. He thought that some of the local boys might want jobs and if he hired them, it would create good will in the community. He had been thinking about it ever since Sunday when Mr. Allen had given him the hint and besides that, he needed the extra help.

Mason's Corner was the gathering place for all the folks around and Wade decided to go there and make inquiries. There were also a few things they needed that he could pick up while he was there, and he hoped to have a letter from home.

Mason's Corner was just a cluster of buildings at an intersection of roads—one going north to south and the other east to west, and nearby was a railroad track. Everyone sooner or later went to Mr. Mason's store. It was a small operation with the basic goods for a rural community, but it was also the post office and the depot. It wouldn't hurt for Wade to introduce himself to Mason, and he decided tomorrow was the day.

Just after breakfast the next morning, Wade saddled his horse and left for Mason's Corner. There had been no road to Wade's campsite when he had arrived—not even a good horse trail, but after all the traveling back and forth, there was now a clearly defined road. He followed it for more than a mile and then it abruptly stopped where it intersected with an older road.

This road was hardly more than a wagon trail. It was just two well-worn ruts separated by a grassy center. On both sides of the road there were trees growing right up to the ruts and in some places there were thick stands of saw palmetto bushes that were as high as Wade's head.

It was not far to Mason's Corner from here. It was just a mile east, or so Wade had been told, so he turned to the right and set a cantering pace down the narrow road. Before he knew it, he was riding into a clearing where a few rough looking buildings rose up beside a railroad track.

He stopped before Mason's store and stepped down from the saddle. He tied his horse to the hitching rail and carefully looked around. There were three main buildings here, the store, a blacksmith's shop, and a section house. The ground was hard packed sand and the only trees were some oaks and a few scattered cabbage palms.

The store was a wide building with a false front. Lettering at the top said "Mason's General Store" in faded red letters.

Wade stepped onto the porch and as he did, he removed his hat and gently beat it against his leg to remove any dust. He walked inside and paused to let his eyes adjust to the shaded interior of the store.

It was a wide open room full of merchandise. On one end was a counter and behind the counter was a short, balding man in his mid-fifties. He had a round face and he wore spectacles that were as round as his face, but he was a pleasant man and when Wade walked in, he leaned against his counter and nodded agreeably.

"Welcome," he said as Wade crossed the room to him. "How c'n I help ya'?"

"I'm Wade Thornton," he said, stretching out his hand for Mason to shake. "I've bought a place west of here and I've come to buy supplies and to introduce myself."

"Heard o' you," Mason admitted. "Heard about that fence you're buildin', too," he went on to say. "Is it still up?"

Wade smiled. "Most of it."

An old man was sitting on a turned up keg at the back of the store. A game of checkers was laid out on another barrel beside him. He appeared to be playing it solitaire, but at Wade's comment, he laughed with a high pitched he-he-he that brought him to Wade's attention for the first time.

"I figured as much," he said. "You puttin' it back up?"

"I am," Wade emphatically declared.

The old man nodded. "Figured that too. Well, good luck."

Mason pushed away from the counter. "What c'n I do f'r ya'?"

Wade placed a small order, just a few things they were running low on like coffee and beans, things he could carry on his saddle.

"I'm looking for extra help at my place," he said. "I thought you might recommend a couple of local men."

Mason looked over his glasses at Wade. "Men? Or boys?"

"It's a man size job," Wade said. "But a boy can do it if he's strong and determined."

"The Larkin boys could use the money. An' they're good workers. Never seen a job they wouldn't tackle nor one they couldn't do."

"How do I find these boys?" Wade asked.

"They live up the road there about two or three miles. I see 'em onct 'n awhile. I'll pass the word along."

"There's gonna be a get together at the schoolhouse Sat'rdee," the old man on the upturned barrel pointed out. "Be a good place to find a couple o' boys."

"I hadn't heard," Wade admitted. "Is it open to everyone?"

"That it is," Mason said. "An' Pappy's right. The Larkins'll be there along with ever' other young man in the community."

"I'll go there," Wade said. He reached in his pocket and pulled out a twenty dollar gold piece. He threw it on the counter

55

and picked up his supplies.

Mason stared at the money as if he had never seen gold before, but then he picked it up and gave Wade change from a rusty tin box behind the counter. Wade walked out, tied the supplies behind his saddle, and turned his horse's nose toward home.

Inside the store, Mason and Pappy looked after him, not saying anything until they heard his horse ride away.

"Didja see that?" Mason asked.

Pappy had stood up and now he walked across the room, still staring out the door.

"You know what this means, don't you?"

"Yeah," Pappy drawled. "He's already found the gold!"

Chapter Six

Ada was in the chicken yard, feeding the chickens when Logan arrived. It was early morning. The sun had just cleared the horizon and the air was still and cool. She looked up in surprise, but then she went back to her chore while he approached.

Logan put his hands onto the wire fence, curling his fingers through the octagon shaped openings as he looked into the yard. The ground was sandy and chickens were gathered around Ada's feet, pecking and scratching where she had thrown down the feed.

"Hey," she said. "What're you doin' here so early?"

"I wondered if you'd heard."

"Heard what?"

"Thornton may have found the gold."

"What!" She dashed the remaining feed on the ground and walked to the fence. "How d' you know?"

"He's been flashin' twenty dollar gold pieces around," he said, which was not exactly the truth. Wade had paid with one at Mason's store and that was the only one that could be proven he even had, but it was enough to start the rumor.

"What're you gonna do?" she asked, remembering his boast to take it.

"I haven't decided—yet."

"I wonder how much was there," Ada mused, thinking that the exact amount of the treasure had always been in question. "It's a whole lotta money, no matter what," she added. "He'll likely take it to the bank in Green Cove. He may already have."

"No. I don't think so."

"Where'd he find it? Did he use the well drillin' rig?"

"I don't know. All I know is he's got money and he's spendin' it. Mason showed me the twenty dollar gold piece he used to buy supplies at his place. It was minted in 1863."

"Oh, Logan," she sighed. "It must be it. He must've found the treasure."

"I want you t' do somethin' for me," Logan suddenly said. Ada had been musing about the gold, a myriad of thoughts running through her mind, but the tone of Logan's voice cleared her head. She looked sharply at him. "I want you t' make a trip over to his camp."

"What? No! I'm not goin' over there."

"Just hear me out," he said. She had gripped the chicken wire much the same as Logan had done and now, he moved his hand, affectionately cupping his over hers. "They've all taken to fence buildin' and none uv 'em's around durin' the day. You could go over there and have a look and even if they found you there, they'd think nuthin' uv it."

"No," Ada emphatically declined, pulling her hands away from his.

"Oh, come on," he said in a coaxing voice. "I c'n do it, but if they ketch me there, there'll be trouble. That young Texan's out t' git me anyway. He wears two tied down guns and I hear he knows how t' use 'em."

He did know. Guns were a tool that every man in the area used daily and with good reason, but most of the men carried rifles. The idea of the fast draw was new to Florida, but it had been witnessed by several reliable sources in Rusty's case. He had stepped off his horse and right into the path of an already provoked diamondback rattlesnake. The snake coiled to strike just as Rusty's foot touched the ground.

Nobody saw Rusty's hand move, nor the pistol leave the holster, but as the snake struck, his head disappeared in a blossom of red, and Rusty was standing there, a smoking gun in his hand. That was what Logan was thinking as he stood there gripping the chicken wire fence.

"Please don't go over there," Ada begged him. "It isn't worth it."

"It ain't worth it? Are you kiddin'? He's got fifty thousand dollars in gold. Fifty thousand dollars, Ada!"

It was a lot, but what was a man's life worth—or a woman's, for that matter?

"I don't want to, Logan," she said. "He'll think I'm runnin' after him. All the girls are runnin' after him and he'll think I am, too."

Logan jerked at her observation. Before Wade Thornton and Rusty Gavin had come along, he had been the object of every girl's infatuation, and he had not only liked the notoriety but had taken full advantage of it.

"Then I guess I'll do it," he said with pathos, turning loose of the fence and stepping back. It was a calculated move and one that had worked for him in the past.

"No, you can't," Ada insisted. She quickly went to the door of the chicken yard and let herself out. "You'd be crazy t' go over there," she said as she approached him.

"Maybe so, but I'm gonna do it—unless you will," he slyly added.

He gave her the look that had won him hearts in the past—including Ada's, and then he fondly reached out and gripped her arm. He pulled her to him.

"Stop it, Logan," she said, casting a fearful look toward the house. "Mama'll see ya'."

"Will ya' do it, Ada? For me . . ."

Ada thought about it for a few seconds. She knew she was going to say yes even before the words left her mouth. He had a way of making her do things she didn't want to do and it always began this same way.

"I'll do it," she miserably said. "If it'll keep you from doin' it."

He grinned from ear to ear. "You'll be glad you did this, Ada. When we get the gold, you 'n me'll git married and we'll shake the dust of this lousy place."

Lousy place? Ada liked it here. She didn't want to leave, but if Logan left, she would go, too. She told herself she could be happy anywhere as long as it was with the right man.

But was Logan that man? She shook away that idea. Of course, he was. He was the catch of the county, and he was hers. Of course, he was the right man.

"It's probably in his house," Logan said.

"What am I lookin' for?" Ada asked. "A trunk? A sack o' gold? More than one sack o' gold? I don't know what t' look for."

"It could be anything, but I figure it'll be in a trunk or something. Sacks woulda rotted away by now. Look in the house and then in the barn. There's also a bunk house in the back yard. It's a long buildin' with a porch across the front. It looks like there're four or five doors to it and the gold could be there, although I doubt it. Thornton'll probably wanna keep it near 'im."

Ada nodded, taking in all this with a frown.

"Go over there and hail the place," Logan said, giving instructions. "If nobody answers you, then you're okay. They've been stayin' at the fence 'til almost dark ever'day, and they won't be comin' in to bother you."

"Are you sure?"

"Yeah. You'll be okay. When you get there, if anybody *is* there," he continued, "just act like you're visitin'—be neighborly, you know."

Ada nodded again. She really didn't want to do this, but at the same time, she began to be curious about Wade Thornton's place. His house was finished and so were several other buildings including a barn and a bunkhouse. She wondered what kind of a place a man like Wade Thornton would build.

Paul and Silas ran across the yard just then and they whooped like a couple of Indians causing Logan to turn with a start.

"I gotta go," he said as if the distraction had prompted his decision. "Do it soon, Ada," he said. "Before he has time to move the gold."

She agreed with a nod of her head and he turned and walked away.

"Hey, boys!" he called out as he passed the twins. They lifted imaginary rifles and shot him, something that brought no response at all from Logan. He calmly walked to his horse, stepped into the saddle and rode away.

Ada picked up the now empty feeding pan and walked toward the house. The twins were in the yard, standing where Logan had left them.

"Why d' you put up with him, Ada?" Paul asked when she came abreast of him. His brow was wrinkled and he was giving the retreating figure of Logan Spencer a serious look. Ada didn't say anything, she simply looked after him, too. "He ain't got no imagination, a'tall," Paul went on to say as if that was reason enough for his feelings. "An' I don't like 'im."

"That's no way t' talk," Ada scolded him. "I'm gonna marry Logan one day, and then he'll be your brother."

"He won't be my brother," Paul insisted. "An' why wouldja wanna go off an' do a fool thing like that anyway?"

"You're too young to understand," Ada said, and Paul made a scoffing sound.

"That's what grownups always say, but you ain't old enough to try that tactic on me," Paul said. "Besides, I understand more'n you about some things, Logan Spencer included."

"Ada! What's takin' so long?" Mrs. Tanner called from the house so Ada patted Paul affectionately on the top of the head and walked away.

"She's in love," Silas jeered in a singsong mocking fashion.

"Or thinks she is," Paul wisely stated. "I ain't never liked that Logan Spencer."

"Yeah, me neither," Silas agreed.

"It's up t' me 'n you t' see she falls outta love with 'im, Silas, and that right quick."

"How d' we do that?"

"I don't know, but we gotta think o' somethin'," Paul said. "She ain't gonna marry Logan Spencer if I c'n help it and that's a promise."

Chapter Seven

It was midafternoon when Ada found an opportunity to get away. It was like her to slip away sometimes, so it was no surprise to anyone when suddenly she was nowhere to be found.

The sky was full of clouds. None of them looked threatening, but Ada wore her daddy's wide brimmed hat anyway. She walked down the road until she came to the cutoff to Sink Hole Branch, and as she stood there in contemplation, the sun came out from behind the clouds, shining brightly for a brief moment. The way was well defined and the tracks fresh in the new road. The sun seemed to highlight it as if a divine direction was being given, but just as quickly, the sun disappeared behind a cloud and the light went dim. Ada hesitated, not wanting to go any further. Finally, she summoned her courage and stepped into the road.

"I can do this," she repeated to herself over and over again. There was no reason to be uneasy. She was a neighbor, making a friendly visit, and there was no reason to expect trouble. In fact, she didn't expect to see anyone, or that was what she hoped.

But the thought of going through someone's house without their permission was offensive to her. She continued on her way, thinking that if she did this, then Logan wouldn't try to do it himself. It never once occurred to her that he was manipulating her. Her only thoughts were about keeping down confusion, but had she known, his thoughts were a lot more complicated.

It was two and a half miles to Sink Hole Branch, but Wade had built just north and east of it. Ada followed the road and came upon the clearing quite suddenly.

More than twenty acres had been cleared except for the old live oak trees. There were three of them, all of them giants and their massive limbs all covered with dry, curled up resurrection fern.

The house had been built under the largest of these trees. During the summer, shade was needed to cool the house, and Ada was impressed that a Yankee would know that. The bunk house was similarly situated between the two smaller trees, but the barn was behind them at the back side of the clearing. She stood at the edge of the yard, looking at the buildings with their freshly milled wood, standing out bright against the dark green background. Wade and his men had done a lot of work here, permanent things that made Ada wonder about him and his real motives. Quickly then, before she had time to reconsider, Ada walked up to the house and knocked at the door.

No one answered, just as she expected.

"Hello!" she called out, but there was still no answer.

Everything was quiet. Nothing stirred except the horses in the corral. One of them looked over the fence at her and made a friendly nicker, but other than that, there was no sign of life anywhere around her.

Ada looked over her shoulder and then back at the closed door. She knew what Logan wanted her to do, but she found it harder than she had expected to open Wade Thornton's door and go inside. She tried it, hoping it was locked, but it opened easily under her hand and moved quietly on its hinges.

"Hello," she said again. "Anybody home?"

Still, there was no answer.

Ada cautiously stepped inside. The room was small and rectangular with two windows on one side that was letting in a cooling breeze. The smell of fresh lumber was strong, but there was also a sweet smell of honeysuckle on the air.

The room was bare. The only furniture was a round table and a solitary chair. There was no place to hide a treasure so Ada walked to the door across the room and opened it.

It was Wade's bedroom. There was a single bed against the wall under a wide window and the bed was clean and neatly made. In the corner were some clothes, hanging on a rod that had been driven into the adjoining walls. Under it was a trunk.

Ada took a deep breath. This could be it. She quickly walked to the trunk and opened the heavy lid. It was nearly empty. There were just papers and mementos in the bottom of it, and a photograph of a pretty girl with light colored hair. Ada stared at the picture, wondering who she might be and thinking that she must be important to Wade. Her picture was on the very top of the pile.

Ada was looking at the picture when a sound outside brought her head up with a jerk. Quickly, she replaced the photograph and closed the lid to the trunk. She turned to leave and then she saw it—a shiny circle under the corner of the bed, a twenty dollar gold piece just lying there as if it had been accidently dropped and then forgotten.

She picked it up and looked around. Where was the rest of the treasure? Surely, this was part of it.

There was nothing in the room, no other place to hide anything, but Ada was sure now that Wade Thornton had found the lost gold. But where would he hide it? She considered that and decided that if it was in the house, he would have locked the door, which he had not done, so she asked herself what she would do with a treasure if she needed to keep it safe until she could get it to a bank, and a crazy thought came to her mind.

"I'd stow it away in the feed barrels," she said aloud and then she almost laughed at her own revelation.

With that thought in mind, she walked out of the house, taking the gold coin with her. This time, she didn't hesitate, but without pause she hurried across the yard to the shed beside the corral.

The friendly horse bobbed his head and stretched his neck toward her and Ada took a moment to pat his velvety nose. He was a lovely animal and he seemed to be lonesome so she talked softly to him as she looked into the dark recesses of the open shed.

There was straw on the dirt floor and Ada could see the corner of a bale of hay just inside the door. After a parting caress for her equine friend, she stepped across the threshold and into the dimly lit room.

It was dark enough inside that Ada had to pause at the doorway until her eyes adjusted. There were bales of hay stacked high to the side of the room and at the back, there were barrels for corn and grain. Swiftly, Ada started across the narrow room. Her focus was on the barrels, her mind on piles of gold that must be hidden there, but, oddly, she never made it.

Suddenly and without warning, something slammed into her and she felt herself falling. She fell forward, tripping over a bale of hay, and hitting the straw covered ground just beyond it. She cushioned the fall with her hands, coming down hard on the soft sand. Immediately, rough hands turned her over and then those same hands grabbed her wrists and pinned her to the ground.

It was Wade Thornton but Ada's surprise was no greater than his own. Her hat flew off her head and her hair fell down, and he recognized her too late to stop his attack.

"Ada!" he exclaimed in horror. He abruptly turned her loose, pulling his hands back as if she had burned him. He straightened up, shock all over his face.

"Did I hurt you?" he anxiously asked. "Are you alright? Ada, are you alright?"

When she didn't immediately answer, he became anxious and he leaned forward again, peering into her face. He touched her gently, looking for an injury, but he didn't find anything.

She was stunned and a little dazed from the fall, but she was not hurt. She blinked her eyes but when the room rocked behind Wade, she closed them until her equilibrium balanced.

"I thought you were someone else," he went on to explain. "Honest—I didn't know it was you!"

"I'm alright," she managed to say and she felt him wilt with relief.

"What are you doing here?" he anxiously asked, and in her confusion, she immediately began to reply with honesty.

"I was looking for the—" She abruptly stopped talking, realizing just in time what she was about to say.

She felt Wade's posture change. He tensed and then his weight shifted as he repositioned himself. Ada's eyes flew open, her mind suddenly perfectly clear.

He was curiously looking at her, his brow furrowed and his jaw set, and then, very carefully, his eyes went from her face to the hand where she held the gold coin. Without warning, he reached up and gripped her wrist.

Ada tried to pull her hand away, not wanting him to know what she held, but he was insistent and wrestled with her until her hand involuntarily opened and the gold coin fell out. It rolled across the hard packed dirt floor, toppled over, and came to rest among straws of hay.

They both watched it but Wade was the first to look away. He brought his attention back to Ada and there was no warmth in his dark eyes.

"So, what does this mean?" he asked, but she knew she could not explain. She looked up at him, guilt all over her face and more than just a little regret.

"I found it," she said and then, with contempt, she added. "I wouldn't have kept it."

"No, I didn't think you were a thief."

Her face flamed red. She was shocked that such a word would even come up between them. He had not accused her, but obviously, the thought had crossed his mind.

"Let me up!" she demanded, the shame of what she had done made her angry. She pushed him, and when she did, he grabbed her by the wrists and pinned her to the ground again.

"What were you looking for?" he asked and she stopped struggling to give him a blank stare. He wryly chuckled. "Don't give me that look," he said. "You said you were looking for something. I just want to know what it is you're looking for."

"I was dazed from the fall. I didn't know what I was sayin'," she honestly said.

He simply looked at her, his expression incredulous and just a little condescending, but slowly, his expression changed, awareness of Ada causing him to look at her with new eyes.

They were both sizing up the situation, each in their own way, but Ada's thoughts were becoming increasingly disturbing. She was acutely aware of Wade's compromising position against her, and the smell of his body, all warm from the outdoors, but not unpleasant, and the way he looked in the dim light filtering in from the open doorway. She knew each time his heart beat and every breath he took. It made her self-conscious of her own breathing which had curiously increased as she studied him. She closed her eyes to erase the thought, but it persisted, in spite of her effort.

Wade was having his own battle. He wanted to kiss her. He wanted to kiss her so badly that he was struggling with himself on every level. Here was the girl that had upset his own equilibrium and the one who had come unbidden into his thoughts so often that this situation seemed almost heaven sent. The trouble was, he knew why she had come. Logan had sent her and he could imagine that she would scream or slap his face if he kissed her. He didn't want either of those things to happen, and besides, there was Angela to consider.

Curiously, their thoughts concluded at the same point and they both sighed almost simultaneously. Very carefully, Wade released the hold he had on her and deliberately he pushed himself up to a sitting position. Ada truthfully admitted to herself that she was a little disappointed, but she mentally scolded herself and she never let him know.

Wade stood up and when he reached down and offered her his hand, Ada accepted it, letting him pull her to her feet.

"I'm sorry, Ada," he apologized and he sounded truly repentant. He looked around for her hat and when he found it, he leaned over and picked it up. "It was the hat that threw me off," he went on to say. "It's a man's hat."

Ada was brushing herself off and pulling loose pieces of straw from her hair, but she stopped and took the hat.

"It's daddy's hat," she explained.

"We've been having trouble and when I saw the hat, I thought I'd caught the man who'd been doing it."

Ada gave him a cool look. She had never been mistaken for a man before, and the idea was mildly sobering.

"Not that you look like a man," he quickly amended. "It was the hat. It threw me off—you aren't hurt, are you?"

"No," she quickly answered. "And I'm not a thief, either."

They both looked toward the coin on the floor and then just as quickly, they looked back at each other.

"I guess I know why you're here," Wade soberly said. "Tell Logan I said not to send a helpless girl next time. Tell him to come himself."

Ada lifted her chin defiantly. "Tell 'im yourself," she said, offended even though everything Wade had said was the truth. She was embarrassed and the embarrassment made her angry. "If you aren't afraid to face him," she hatefully added.

Wade's expression changed and his eyes narrowed ever so slightly. "Me? Afraid to face him?" he said with more than a little incredulousness. "Do you want me to go looking for him? I've considered it," he admitted. "The only reason I haven't faced him is because he's been painfully shy about showing himself. Tell him to come out in the open and fight like a man, and I'll be only too happy to face him."

He regretted it the minute the words left his mouth, but he didn't try to recall them.

Ada stuffed the hat on her head and with a huff, she turned toward the door. Wade let her go. He even followed her outside, where the brightness of the day after the dimly lit shed made them both squint into the light. The friendly horse thrust a hopeful head over the corral fence, but neither of them seemed to notice.

Ada paused to let her sight acclimate to the change and then she began walking.

Coming here had been a bad idea, just like she knew it

would be, and it had accomplished nothing. She was wrong to let Logan talk her into it and now she was angry with him as well as herself. Oddly, she was not at all angry with Wade Thornton. In fact, she was thinking about him in ways she had not thought before, and that made her angry, too.

He was a nice man, she realized with a start. He had had the opportunity to take advantage of her if he had been so inclined, but he had not. It provoked her to think that he had behaved as a gentleman—well, mostly, she thought. But the fact was, she knew Logan wouldn't have been so obliging had the shoe been on the other foot. She knew what Logan would have done—or tried to do.

At that thought, she looked over her shoulder and saw Wade standing at the corral fence, watching her. She was self-conscious again, uncomfortable about her appearance with him looking at her.

She made a huffing sound of exasperation and pulled the hat tighter against her head. She wouldn't let him provoke her, she thought, as she stomped angrily down the road.

Wade watched her go and had Ada known, there was no reason to feel self-conscious. He was thinking only complimentary things about her—the graceful way she moved, the pleasing way she looked even with the old, floppy hat on her head. He was also thinking about other things, too, things that he knew he should just forget, things like how she had felt lying so close to him, and the desire she had stirred in him.

He told himself to get such thoughts out of his head. It was an argument he had had with himself more than once lately, but today, he lost the argument. Today he dwelt on it and he envied Logan Spencer more than just a little.

The friendly horse spoke to him over the corral fence and Wade dipped his head with an affirmative nod.

"Yes, I know I'm a fool," he said as if the horse and he could understand each other. "She's Logan's girl and if that doesn't tell me a thing or two, it ought to."

The horse shook his head and blew as if in contempt, then he stamped an exasperated hoof and walked away.

"So, you're deserting me too," Wade said as he watched the horse go. "Well, maybe I should just do what I came here to do and get out." He huffed much the same way Ada had just done minutes before. "I'm a fool, I know, but I like it here, and I like most of the people. I don't want to go, and, you know, I don't think I will."

Chapter Eight

"So, why're ya' mad at me?" Logan demanded as Ada scolded him.

He was waiting for her when she arrived home and he excitedly stopped her before she could get to the house, knowing where she had been.

"Because it was stupid and I was stupid to listen to you."

Logan looked toward the house and then back at Ada. "Come on," he said. "Let's walk out here so we c'n talk."

He led her to their spot by the fence, but he only leaned against it, too excited to wait. "What happened?" he quickly asked. "Did you find the gold or see anythin' that would give us a hint?"

"No, Logan, I didn't find anything. I didn't have a chance."

"What d' ya' mean?"

"Wade caught me."

"Well, I toldja howda handle that."

"Yeah, well, I didn't have the chance. He took me by surprise."

"What? You mean, you didn't get to check out anything?"

"Logan, listen to me. Wade caught me snoopin' around and he knew what I was doin'."

"Nah, he's just a stupid Yankee."

"He isn't that stupid," Ada said, remembering how quick he

was to come to all the right conclusions. "He isn't stupid, at all."

Logan gave Ada a curious look. "Maybe you better start at the beginnin'," he said.

For no apparent reason, Ada's heart began to pound. She was ashamed of her roll in this scheme but she was more ashamed that Wade had caught her at it. She didn't want to tell Logan what had happened.

"I've toldja what happened," she said, hanging her head as she spoke. "There ain't nuthin' else to tell."

Logan didn't immediately respond and his silence was more menacing than any of his words. Ada apprehensively looked up. Logan was staring at her, his eyes squinted and a frown on his face.

"What happened when he caught ya', Ada?"

It was Ada's turn to hesitate with an answer. She looked at Logan and she felt her face burn. She knew guilt was written all over it. His back stiffened, and then very carefully, he reached out and removed a straw of hay from Ada's hair. It was stuck under the hat, almost hidden below her ear. He held it between them like a condemning finger and Ada could only stare at it. Logan's nostrils flared and his lips tightened in anger.

"What is this, Ada? Did you take a roll in the hay with that Yankee?"

Ada slapped his hand aside. "How dare you accuse me of such a thing!"

"I ain't necessarily accusin' you," he pointed out. "But I wouldn't put nuthin' past that Yankee—and you ain't exactly tellin' me what he did when he caught you."

"He just talked to me," she lied. "He somehow knew what I was doin' there and he knew you were behind it, too."

"How so?" Logan asked, stiffening with indignation. "You didn't tell 'im?"

"No, I didn't have to. He told me."

"So, where'd this come from?" he asked, holding up the condemning evidence of the straw.

"I was in the shed. There were stacks of hay all over the place. I musta brushed up against one of 'em."

"Oh? I thought you didn't have time to check out anythin'," he suspiciously said.

"I didn't. Wade came along just as I got started lookin'."

"I gotta feelin' you ain't tellin' me everything," Logan said, a scowl on his face. "Are you sure that Yankee didn't do somethin'?"

"Yeah, he did somethin'," Ada smartly remarked. "He made me feel as small as a mouse, ketchin' me snoopin' around like that."

"If you'd 've handled it right, he never would've suspected."

"Me? Handle it right? I told you not to send me over there."

"Yeah? Well, maybe you were right," Logan agreed. He continued to stare at her, his expression judgmental. "He's a right good lookin' man—or that's what I hear ever'where I go, but we both know he ain't got no honest intentions where the girls around here are concerned. He thinks he's too good f'r any uv you."

"I ain't fooled by 'im," Ada said and Logan casually nodded. "In fact," she went on, thinking that she knew exactly how to get Logan's mind off his present obsession. "I told him he wasn't man enough to face you."

"No foolin'?" Logan asked, pleased, just like Ada knew he would be. "What 'id he say?"

"It upset 'im," she said, thinking that there was no reason to tell Logan everything he had said. "He didn't like it."

Logan smiled and then, he chuckled. "Well, come 'ere, girl," he said, pulling her to him. He embraced her, squeezing her in a bear hug that was so tight that it was actually uncomfortable. "I guess that showed 'im somethin'," he bragged.

Ada supposed it had. She returned Logan's hug, gripping him tightly as she buried her face against his chest. She was no fool. She knew about Wade Thornton and she knew he was nothing more than a condescending snob. She wouldn't be taken in by him. Besides, he had all but called her a thief, she remembered.

She told herself she knew her place and it was right here with Logan. She looked up at him and smiled, but he didn't notice. His mind was miles away and on another subject. He was thinking about the gold and wondering what he should do next and nothing else mattered to him, not even Ada.

Chapter Nine

Rusty swung down from his horse and let the reins trail. He had ridden into the yard only minutes after Ada had left and he found Wade in a still, thoughtful mood.

Rusty was hot and sweat beaded his brow and wet his shirt. He immediately stripped down to his waist and walked to the pump where he vigorously worked the handle until a clear stream of water ran out and flowed down into the trough beneath it.

He splashed the water on his face and washed his body, shivering as the water cooled his sweaty body.

Wade watched him, thinking that he had known Rusty a long time, but he didn't really know much about him. He knew he was an orphan and he knew he was a hard-working man with a good, if not derisive, disposition. He was young, only nineteen. He had a full head of iron colored hair, more blonde than red, but an unruly crop that framed his wide face and often fell over his dark green eyes. He was not what you would call a handsome man, but he was attractive, his features quite appealing to the opposite sex, even to the habitually quizzical look in his eyes. He seemed always to be contemplating some perplexing but profound subject of a highly ironical nature, giving him a pleasant, but constantly amused expression.

There was not much else that Wade knew about Rusty, but looking at his lean, hard muscled body and seeing the two scars low down on his side told Wade something he had not known until then. Not only did Rusty know how to use a gun, but it looked like one had been used on him.

"What's up?" Rusty asked noticing that Wade's eyes kept returning to the narrow road. It was the road where Ada had just disappeared, but Rusty didn't know that.

"We've had company," Wade readily answered.

Rusty gave a start. He imagined the worst, but at Wade's nonchalant attitude, he quickly relaxed and curiously looked at him. At least one man was always left on the place to stand guard while the others built fences. It was necessary, they thought, especially after all the unusual things that had happened in the past few weeks. Rusty picked up his shirt and walked toward Wade, thinking about all the sleep he had lost and the reason why.

It had all begun with the owls that had awakened Wade that night a couple of weeks before. It was as if they were a bad omen and had somehow awakened an otherwise sleeping phantom. Unexplainable things began to happen and unusual things were seen and heard. Even Powder Keg Smith was unnerved. Now when he arose early to start breakfast, he laid a double barreled shotgun on the tailgate of his chuck wagon and he never moved very far away from it, although if what they imagined was true, a shotgun would hardly have any effect.

But Rusty didn't believe in ghosts. He figured he knew exactly who was behind all the weird and unusual occurrences.

It was Logan Spencer and his friends. They were having a real good time resurrecting the dead soldiers supposedly buried nearby, and then scaring the wits out of Rusty and the others, although, he uneasily remembered the one night he had awakened to a cold mist seeping quietly through the camp and the figure of a man standing on the edge of the clearing. Rusty knew it had to have been one of Logan's men. Logic told him the reason in that, but his imagination told him otherwise. It was heightened by the full moon hanging low in the night sky, directly behind the still, poised outline of the man, making an ethereal illusion. Rusty had sat up for a better look just as the moon disappeared behind a swiftly moving cloud, taking with it the ghostly apparition. It was the only time in his life Rusty had doubted his own eyes. He could have sworn the man was wearing a Civil War uniform.

Rusty instinctively knew, though, that today's company had not been an unwelcome guest, and when Wade explained, Rusty gave him a knowing smile.

"It was Ada Tanner," Wade said.

Rusty looked down the empty road again, and then he turned back to Wade. "You don't look very happy. What happened?"

"Well, nothing good," Wade soberly admitted. "I had been watching the place and I got restless. I decided to take a look at that barren ground near the pines," he said, tilting his head toward the south. "You know, that place where the soldiers are reported to be buried. I returned, coming up behind the corral, and I saw someone standing on this side of it."

"All I could see was a man's hat. It disappeared and I knew he'd gone into the shed so I came around the corral and followed him, thinking I'd caught one of Logan's men, but as it turned out, I'd simply caught Logan's girl."

Rusty raised a questioning eyebrow and smiled.

"What was she doin' here?" he asked.

"Logan sent her."

"Are you so sure?"

"I'm sure."

Rusty shook his head, but he continued to smile derisively. "What for?"

Wade had been resting his arms on the top rail of the corral fence, but he pushed away from it and gave Rusty a direct look. "She had a twenty dollar gold piece in her hand," he said.

Rusty didn't immediately answer, but his habitual profound quandary reflected in his eyes as he considered this.

"They're convinced I've found the treasure," Wade said.

No explanation was needed as to what he meant. Everyone had heard the rumor and some of his own hired men were as sure as the local people that Wade Thornton knew more than he was saying about the gold.

"I told her to tell Logan to come himself next time and not to send a helpless girl. She called me a coward—among other things."

Rusty grinned. "I'd liked to have seen that," he said.

"Yeah? Well, if I had ever entertained the idea of being friends with her, I can forget it. She was pretty clear on that subject."

Rusty was still grinning. "That's too bad," he said. "Then you won't mind stayin' behind Saturday night so we c'n all go to the shindig over at Sand Hill."

Wade returned Rusty's amused grin. "She isn't the only girl in these woods," he said, his grin turning into a broad smile that ended quite abruptly. "Laying all jokes aside," he seriously said. "I wanted to be friends with the Tanners, but not because of Ada. I've a girl waiting for me in New Hampshire—Angela. We have an understanding."

"Is that all?" Rusty asked. "Just an understanding?"

"It's enough," he answered, but oddly, it didn't make him happy to consider it.

"So, you're planning to go Saturd'y?" Rusty asked and Wade nodded.

"Yeah. I want to hire a couple of local boys. Mason suggested I go there and talk to some of them. Jim'll stay behind and I think Powder Keg will, too. The rest of us can go."

That suited Rusty. He liked to socialize and he liked pretty girls. Since coming to Florida, the closest he had come to satisfying these needs was when he had gone to church with Wade, so he was expectantly looking forward to Saturday night.

The school house was at a place called Sand Hill, just northwest of Mason's Corner. Wade and Rusty rode there together, but when they arrived, they went their separate ways.

Rusty was looking for a girl and Wade had no doubt he would find one—or she would find him. He caught more than one hopeful eye himself as he moved among the crowd.

There were at least fifty people at the gathering and so

most of them were outside the small building. A fire was burning in the back yard and Wade heard a fiddle playing somewhere nearby. He walked around and looked over the crowd, realizing after a minute that he was not just studying the group but actually looking for someone. He saw her at last. Ada was near the fire and she was with Logan Spencer.

Well, that was no surprise, he thought, but it gave him a still, solemn feeling to watch her having such a good time while she stood there beside his antagonist.

He could have admonished himself, but he didn't. He could have gone somewhere else and not have looked at her, but he didn't do that either. He stood under the branches of an ancient cedar tree and he indulged himself in a moment of pleasurable observation.

He didn't understand his own infatuation. Ada was a pretty girl, but he had seen prettier. She was not dressed in the latest fashion nor did she have the polish and poise of sophistication, but she had an innate quality of grace and beauty not unlike that of a wild animal, although Wade would never have compared her to anything so uncivilized. She was more sprite-like. He could imagine her as a fairy dancing barefoot around a fire—no, she was too sublime for a mere fairy. She would be the gypsy girl, her dark hair hanging to her waist as she moved with undulating grace.

Wade was ashamed of his thoughts and for the first time tonight, he scolded himself.

"What're you doin' standin' alone, here in the shadows?" a feminine voice coyly asked him. Wade turned with a start. A girl was standing there, giving him the eye and she was neither reluctant nor bashful. He smiled and she smiled back.

"I was just looking," he honestly said. Her eyes casually glanced toward the fire and then back again. There were a lot of people standing there and she could only guess which one he had been studying.

"I'm Mattie," she said, taking a step closer to him.

"Wade Thornton."

"Yes, I know," she said. "I saw you at church. I was hopin' you'd be here tonight."

"Thanks," he said. "I'm trying to get to know the community. Joining in on the social functions seems the quickest way."

"I'll introduce you around, if you like," she quickly offered.

He looked closely at her before accepting. She was a fair girl, blonde and blue-eyed, and right away, he saw she was older than most of the single girls here. Girls married young in this area, some of them no more than fourteen or fifteen years old, so she was a bit of an oddity. She could even have been older than he, although Wade didn't pursue that thought.

"I'm looking for a couple of boys," Wade said. "Maybe you could point them out for me," he suggested.

"Who?"

"The Larkin boys."

"They're here," she said, looking around. "Come on. We'll find them."

He followed her out from under the cedar tree and as they crossed the sandy yard, Ada looked up. The smile left her face as if she had reached up and wiped it away, and then she gave him an odd look. It was not cold or even unfriendly, but it didn't invite any interaction between them either.

Neither did Logan's look. His side was turned to Wade and Mattie, but as they approached, his head slowly turned and then his whole body followed. Repeatedly, there had been hot words between his men and Wade's, but Wade was hoping that wouldn't be a problem here. He cautiously approached, not taking his eyes off of Logan, but instead, studying him, watching his reaction for any sign of trouble.

Logan's eyes met Wade's and for just a second, there was a challenge in them, but curiously, the expression changed and changed quickly. He looked at Mattie and then right back at Wade and for just a moment, there was anger in his eyes. He masterfully replaced it with a bland expression and he even nodded in acknowledgment when Mattie introduced Wade to the group standing by the fire, but he never said anything. Wade noted, though, that he kept looking at Mattie, and the look he was giving her was either warning or hatred, and Wade was not sure he understood why.

But that was not entirely true either. To Logan, Wade was the enemy and so he probably viewed Mattie's courtesy as a kind of treason. She didn't appear to care. She neither acknowledged his look nor responded to his warning. In fact, she took Wade by the hand and walked away with him unconcerned that Logan followed them with his eyes until they were both out of sight.

"You're making some people uneasy," Wade cautioned her.

"Who? Logan?" she flippantly asked and then she laughed. "It'd be good for him t' be brought down a notch or two. He's gotta inflated opinion of hisself."

She would get no argument from Wade on that subject, but he didn't let on that he agreed with her. They had stopped near the front corner of the school house and while they stood there, Rusty suddenly appeared at Wade's side.

"Hey, come here," he said, pulling him aside.

"I'll be right back," he said to Mattie and then he followed Rusty. "What's wrong?"

"I've heard some talk. I think Logan's gonna try somethin' tonight while we're all here."

Wade looked across the yard. Logan was standing by the fire, but his jovial mood seemed to have vanished with Wade's arrival.

"Do you want us to go back?" Rusty asked when Wade didn't say anything.

"No. If you're enjoying the party, stay. He may just want to spoil our good time," Wade pointed out. "Anyway, what can we do that Jim and Powder Keg can't do?"

Rusty shrugged. "The more eyes, the better."

"Just let it go for now. I'm going to find the Larkin boys and talk to them and I plan to ride back after that anyway."

"You want me to go with you?"

"No — not unless you'll be ready to go."

"I won't be," Rusty proudly assured him and Wade smiled.

"Stay as long as you like."

Rusty nodded and then he hurried away. Wade looked back

at Mattie. She was standing where he had left her and she was waiting for him with a rather expectant look on her face. It was time to break away from her, he was thinking, before she got any ideas.

"What about those Larkin boys?" he asked as he rejoined her. "Somthing's come up and I've got to leave."

"Ah! No," she exclaimed with genuine regret. "You've only just got here."

"I know. Can you point them out to me?"

She nodded, but rather reluctantly. She scanned the yard and then pointed a finger toward the side of the school house where a small group had gathered.

"That's Jess Larkin," she said, indicating a young man with curly blonde hair and a mustache. "I don't see Daniel nowhere."

"That'll do," Wade said and he immediately began walking in that direction. Oddly Mattie didn't follow him and Wade was not sorry, although she had been nice and helpful. He had enough problems with his unsolicited thoughts of Ada without adding another girl to his thoughts.

He walked right up to Jess and introduced himself. "I know this is a party," he quickly said, qualifying his next statement, "but I want to talk business with you. May I have a minute of your time?"

"Shore," Jess said, but he cautiously eyed Wade.

"I need a couple of men to work for me. I've been told you and your brother are good, reliable boys. Are you interested in a job?"

"What kinda job?" he wisely asked.

"Hard work," Wade said. "Working around my place. You may be asked to do anything from feeding the animals to building fences."

"I heard about that fence," he said. "Don't seem right to fence folks offa the land they've always used."

"I have plans for that land," Wade said. "What would you do if it was your land? Would you never do anything with it just because it would inconvenience everyone else?"

He hesitated as if in thought. "No, I reckon not," he finally answered. "But folks 're takin' it hard. The fence's like a slap in the face to some."

"Who are these people? I'd like to know so I can talk to them. I'd like to make things right between us. I'm not above compromising a little."

"You might not wanna do that," he warned. "But if you're serious about makin' things right, me and Daniel'll go with ya'. We know how ta talk to 'em." He paused and grinned. "That is, if we really got a job with ya'."

"It's yours. You can stay right there on the ranch if you like. I've got accommodations enough for twenty men and only seven men working for me."

"Thanks," he said. "We'll consider that. When do we start?"

"Tomorrow is Sunday. How about Monday?"

"I'll talk to Daniel. We'll show up as soon as we can."

"Fair enough," Wade said.

He backed away from the group after talking to Jess and it was in his mind that he should get his horse and leave, but he looked around one more time, wondering about Ada. He wanted to talk to her. After she had left his place, Wade had thought of a dozen things he wished he had said to her. One of them was about the spring. He had fenced it off, but he now regretted being so hasty. He wanted to tell her she was welcome to go there. After all, what was it hurting for her and her brothers to go there? The spring was so far from his house, he wouldn't even see them.

Wade pushed through the group and returned to the fire. She was not there, and neither was Logan. He looked in the school house where some lively dancing was taking place, but she was not there either. Her parents were there, though, and Wade spoke briefly to them. There were quite a few people inside and he was stopped repeatedly before he could get outside again. They were older folks with friendly smiles and courteous words, and before Wade knew it, he had stayed longer than he had planned.

Once he was outside again, the only thought on his mind was that of getting to his horse and getting back to the ranch. He walked down the path that led to the small enclosure where he had left his horse, and as he hurried along, he heard an argument taking place off to his right. He stopped, not meaning to eavesdrop, but concerned when he recognized Logan's voice.

Logan was talking to a woman, and Wade guessed it was Ada, although he could not be sure. It was dark and he could not see them, and the girl spoke so softly that her voice was just an indistinct whisper in the night.

"Don't give me that," Logan harshly warned the girl. "You know you won't go through with it."

She said something and Logan laughed sardonically.

"Listen here, Ada," he said. "You're my girl but you cain't tell me what t' do."

She spoke again, but, still, Wade could not hear her. Logan's response, however, was loud and clear.

"You ain't gettin' soft on that Yankee, are you? I'll wring your pretty little neck," he warned her in a voice that was deep with emotion.

She said something and Wade almost winced at the acrid tone of her voice. He was almost glad he could not distinguish the words.

"I gotta go," Logan suddenly announced. "You git back to the party."

"No, Logan!" Ada said and Wade stiffened, finally hearing her voice. "It ain't right an' you know it."

Wade heard the sound of creaking leather as Logan mounted his horse. He was leaving and Wade knew he should go, too, but he didn't.

"Turn loose," Logan said and Wade could imagine Ada clinging to Logan as he was trying to get away. "The boys are waitin' an' I gotta go."

"If you leave now," Ada said. "Then don't bother to come around no more, Logan Spencer. We're through!"

He didn't immediately answer and Wade could only imagine what he was thinking.

"You don't mean that and you know it," he finally said. "But I ain't got time for this jus' now. You let go. We'll talk about this t'morro'."

She must have let go. Wade heard the horse leaving. He knew Ada would be coming toward him on her way back to the party, so he leaned his shoulder against the bole of a nearby tree and he waited.

It took Ada only a minute to appear on the path. She didn't see Wade until she was a few feet from him and when she saw him, she gave a little gasp and abruptly stopped.

"Hello, Ada," he softly said, the words coming out with more calmness than he felt.

"Mr. Thornton," she said in genuine surprise. She glanced over her shoulder and Wade knew she was looking for Logan.

He pushed away from the tree and took a step toward her.

"What're you doin' here?" she quickly asked. "Are you leavin'?

"It looks like it—if I'm going to catch up with Logan, that is."

She flashed a startled look at him, her eyes catching the moonlight and shining for a second.

"Where's he going?" Wade asked, but Ada didn't answer. "He's a fool," Wade then said, thinking that it was true for more than one reason.

"You don't know anything about 'im," she snapped, coming to Logan's defense.

"I know I wouldn't be out running around the country, playing war games, if I had a girl like you to be here with."

Ada caught her breath. She thought that he should not say such things and that she should be offended that he had, but strangely, his words pleased her and she could not find it in herself to be offended no matter how hard she tried. Nevertheless, she was determined not to like him and the remark she made in retaliation stemmed from that determination.

"It's just like a Yankee to think ill of us Southern girls."

Wade had not meant it in a derogatory way and he was sorry she had taken it wrong.

"I only meant—"

"I know what you meant," she said, interrupting him. She started to push past him, but he caught her arm and stopped her.

"You've got me wrong. I know I'm a Yankee and I know I don't understand your Southern ways and your unique etiquette, but my transgressions have all been unintentional."

"Good manners should be universal, Mr. Thornton."

"Wade," he said. "My name is Wade."

"Yes, I know," she coolly said. She shrugged out of his hold and took a step away from him.

"Wait a minute, Ada," he said. "Tell me where Logan's going."

Her eyes jumped up to his. That same look was in them that had been there the day he had accidently tackled her.

"You're a smart man. You can figure that out for yourself."

"So, he's going to my ranch, is that it?"

Ada shrugged indifferently.

"Thanks," Wade said, and without another word, he walked away from her.

"Mr. Thornton," she called after him, her tone a little

apprehensive.

"Wade," he said as he turned. "Please call me Wade."

"Wade," she said. "He's really not a bad man. He thinks he's in the right."

Wade stopped with his hand on the gate. "When a boy sets out to play a man's game, it doesn't matter whether he's good or bad and sometimes whether he's right or wrong."

She made no reply but, instead, she turned and walked into the shadows, making her way back to the school house.

Wade wasted no more time. He caught up his horse and rode out of the school yard and when he was well down the road, he ran the horse all the way to the turn off to his ranch.

He told himself he should not have stayed and talked to Ada, but if his thinking was correct, he still had time to get to the ranch before Logan could meet with his buddies, make his plans, and get there, too.

He rode into the yard and swung down even before the horse had completely stopped moving. A door slammed and Powder Keg spoke to him from the porch of the bunk house.

"That you, boss?" he asked.

"Yeah. It looks like we're in for some trouble."

"Logan Spencer?"

"Yeah."

"What's 'e up to?"

"I don't know, but he left the party just before I did. He was going to round up his friends. I couldn't find out what they had in mind."

"I c'n tell ya," he soberly said. "They'll try t' burn us out agin."

"What?" Wade said, but even as he said it, he knew it was true. He looked at the buildings and it grieved him to think of them burned to the ground. Everyone had worked so hard and not only that, Wade was running low on money. If they burned him out, he didn't know if he could afford to rebuild and still have enough left to stock his ranch with cattle.

Wade threw his hat down in anger and then he kicked at a bucket, sending it flying across the yard. His horse sidestepped cautiously and Powder Keg watched from the porch in stunned amazement. Wade picked up a bottle and threw it, smashing it against the side of the building. A tin can followed right behind it.

"They won't run me off!" he vowed, shouting in anger. "I'll stay here if I have to live in a palmetto shack! Logan Spencer'll never run me off!"

"What the devil?" Jim said, coming out to see what was going on. "Well, I'll be," he said as Wade kicked at nothing in particular, everything that could be moved gone in his tantrum. "It's about time he got mad."

Powder Keg chuckled while nodding his head in agreement. "Yep. Just about time."

"Get your rifles," Wade said, his face flushed and his eyes hard and steady. "Powder Keg, you take that corner. Jim, cover the road. I'm gonna stand right here. They ain't gonna burn us out."

Powder Keg and Jim moved quickly and without questions. They caught up their rifles and stuffed their pockets with

95

ammunition and then they took up their posts. A few minutes later they heard horses coming down the road. All of them waited in poised anticipation.

It was Pat and Cody returning early from the party.

"What's up?" Cody asked when he saw the three of them armed and ready.

"We think Logan's on his way to burn us out," Wade quickly explained.

"Well, glad we came back. At least we'll get a little bit o' excitement. Cain't say the same about that party. It was sure a bust."

They took care of their horses and then Pat took up a station at the back of the barn. Cody, on the other hand, suggested a high point for better observation and Wade agreed, letting Cody choose his own lookout. He climbed to the top of the bunkhouse roof and sat down beside the chimney. His body merged with the shadow and he was all but invisible at his post.

And then they waited.

Chapter Ten

Cody heard the horse long before anyone else. He looked toward the east and tilted his head to the side for better hearing. It was coming fast and straight for the ranch.

"A horse 's comin'," he called down to Wade.

Wade stepped into the yard and looked toward the road. He could hear it, too, coming fast, a hard ridden horse.

In another minute, Bart Baker rode into the yard and slid from his saddle. He hit the dirt and rolled over with a groan. Wade ran to him and so did Powder Keg and Jim. Cody stood up and looked down from the roof.

Wade rolled him over. "They cut the fence," he mumbled through broken lips.

He had been beaten. His nose was smashed and there was blood all over his face and clothes. A cut ran across his cheek and one eye was swollen shut. Wade was mad enough to pick up a horse and throw him if only he had had the strength to do so.

"They're comin'," he went on to say.

"It's okay," Wade said. He and Powder Keg helped him to his feet. "Let's get you inside so you can lie down.

"I wouldn't," Powder Keg said. "If they set fire to the bunk house, we might not git 'im out in time."

"I'm okay," Bart mumbled. "Just give me a gun."

He could hardly stand on his own two feet, but Wade understood the drive in him. To deny him a weapon would be a further degradation.

"Get him a rifle," Wade said.

"What!" Jim exclaimed. "He needs a doctor not a gun. He'll shoot one of us by accident."

"He won't," Wade firmly stated. He looked at Bart. "Can you walk?"

Bart nodded. "A little ways anyhow."

"Can you make it to that tree?"

Wade pointed to the giant live oak tree at the corner of the house and without answering, Bart began walking toward it. He stumbled more than once, but he made it and then he sat down beside it with his back against the trunk.

Powder Keg arrived with a rifle and a box of shells and he set them down beside him.

"Tell me what happened," Wade said.

"I was comin' back from the party . . . an' they caught me," Bart said. He stopped and wiped his bloody mouth with the back of his hand and then he continued. "They dragged me to the fence . . . said they were gonna hang me on it. I thought not."

He was struggling to tell the story, but his simple words painted a picture they could all see and understand.

"They held me . . . Two uv 'em worked on me . . . the others watched an' laughed . . . They threw me down and cut the fence . . . said they were gonna wrap me in the wire and hang me to the post . . . Got away when they turned their backs. They

98

thought I was unconscious."

Powder Keg exploded. Suddenly there was no mystery as to where he had gotten his nickname. He blew up like a stick of dynamite. Wade's little tantrum had been nothing up side of this. He swung at the air and cursed Logan and his boys for every vile thing he could lay his tongue to and then he swore a terrible vengeance.

Everyone stared in mild shock and then Cody whistled from the rooftop.

"He ain't got no temper atall," he lazily said. "Not none atall."

"A fair fight's one thing!" Powder Keg said. "But this! Those yeller-bellied dogs. Just wait 'til I git my hands on them — — — ."

"All done?" Wade asked as he calmed down and Powder Keg nodded. "Anybody else feel the need to let it out? Now's the time, but be quick about it."

"Too late," Cody said from the rooftop. "Here they come."

Everyone ran for cover and Bart jacked a shell into his rifle. The sound was significant in the following stillness.

Logan stopped a good distance away, but Cody could see him from his vantage point on the rooftop.

"They've held up and 're talkin'," Cody softly said down to Wade. "They're just settin' there."

After a minute he added, "I don't think they know we know they're out there."

"Good," Wade replied. "Let 'em keep thinkin' that."

"Uh-ho," Cody said. "Wait a minute. I think I see a flame.

Someone's playin' with matches."

"Wait for my signal," Wade called out as he ran to the corner of the building, his rifle in hand and ready.

They all came forward at once, burning sticks in their hands. They came fast and with great confidence, thinking they had the element of surprise.

They kept coming and Wade waited. Only Cody could see them until they came to the clearing at the back side of the barn. It appeared to be the intended target and only Pat was there to stop them, but as they came into the clearing they suddenly broke rank and spread out, each one taking a different building.

"Now!" Wade called out and all his men opened fire at once.

A startled yelp preceded the scattering of Logan and his men. Most of them stopped and dropped their firebrands, but some of the men fell to the ground alongside the stick they had just dropped. Others turned and ran, the fire fluttering in the wind as they spurred their horses in a hasty retreat. Logan, however, dropped the burning stick he held and then he turned his horse around and ran for a short distance before stopping. A couple of his friends pulled up beside him. They had just caught their wind when a voice accosted them from the dark and the sound of a pistol being cocked brought their hands up.

"Move and I'll start shootin'," Rusty said.

"We ain't movin'," Logan said. "'cept to go home—if you'll let us."

"Let's see what the boss has to say," Rusty said. "Get down

from your horses."

They reluctantly did as he said.

"Start walkin'."

Rusty herded them toward the ranch, picking up a couple of unsuspecting stray raiders on the way. He rode into the ranch yard with five men ahead of him.

Wade met them in the middle of the yard. His eyes were hard as he stared, but Logan had an insolent look on his face that showed he still had no idea how serious the situation was for himself.

"What's the idee?" he asked in mock surprise. "Firin' on us."

"What did you expect?" Wade asked. "You were asking for it."

"Us? We were just ridin' home—mindin' our own business."

His statement made Wade mad all over again. He felt the hot molten anger rise up in him just as it had done earlier, but this time, he carefully controlled it, harnessing it, the energy giving him a new strength.

"If your business is cutting fences and beating up innocent men," Wade stated.

"Who said we did that?" Logan demanded.

"I did," Bart said from the deep shadow under the tree.

Logan whipped around and peered into the darkness, and then he did something no one expected. He snickered and then he laughed. He didn't know he was seconds from dying until he heard Powder Keg Smith pull the hammers back on his double-barreled shotgun.

He stopped laughing with such haste that he made a croaking sound in his throat as he cut it off.

"I'm gonna ki' ya' like the mad dog ya' are," Powder Keg said, but Wade stopped him.

"Wait a minute," he said. "I have a better idea."

Every eye turned to him.

Logan's men were standing in a tight group. Rusty was still astride his horse and he had them covered with a pistol. Powder Keg, Wade, Jim and Pat were standing beside them, all of them armed. Cody was watching from the rooftop, keeping his position a secret. Only Logan had a weapon. The others had lost theirs somewhere along the way, but like Rusty, Logan had begun wearing a pistol in a holster. It was still in place, the thong over the hammer the way he wore it when riding.

"So you like to fight with your fists," Wade said.

"If you're talkin' about Bart, it was a fair fight."

"Fair fight! Like hell! One against one's a fair fight, you bunch a cowards!" Powder Keg exploded.

Wade raised a cautious hand up to Powder Keg.

"Who did it, Bart?" Wade calmly asked.

"Logan."

"Who held you?"

"None o' these. Some o' the others."

"Take off your gun," Wade told Logan.

Logan was looking around, his eyes darting from one side of the yard to the other. He was calculating his chances of getting away if he ran, but he was smart enough to know that

102

Powder Keg would take him down before he could get clear of the yard.

"I won't do it," he said.

"Take it off! Or we'll take it off for you," Wade said through clenched teeth.

Logan slowly and carefully let the gun belt fall to the ground.

"You kill me and you'll have the law down here on you. They'll hang you."

"I'm not going to kill you," Wade said as he handed Powder Keg his rifle. "I'm going to beat the daylights out of you."

Logan's eyes went wide and then he smiled.

"Shore," he said with some relief. He imagined he was more than Wade's equal when it came to a fist fight. He was heavier and taller, his reach longer, and he had won every local fight he had ever had.

What he didn't reckon on was Wade's muscle hard body, tough from years of backbreaking, hard work, nor his experience in a Texas cow camp where the type of fights Logan was familiar with would have been considered a quilting bee in comparison. Not only that, but Logan had no stamina for a long fight, whereas Wade had endurance.

Everyone eased back into a circle, giving Wade and Logan the center. Logan stepped up with confidence, the insolence still on his face. He expected a quick end to this and then he would be on his way, one more victory under his belt against this Yankee, so he circled carefully and darted in, striking the first blow.

He gave it all he had. He put everything he could muster into that blow and it hardly even fazed Wade.

It did bring first blood, though, and all of Logan's men cheered.

But Logan was not feeling the triumph he had felt just seconds before. He knew that was the best he had, and he knew it had always been the deciding factor in his past wins, but Wade was not even affected. The shock of it was as much the reason for leaving himself wide open for Wade's attack as was his lack of fighting skill. Wade hit him and lights exploded in his brain. He fell to the ground and he had no desire to get up, but Wade pulled him to his feet and slapped him a ringing blow from one side of his face to the other.

It infuriated Logan and he lashed out, jerking himself free from Wade's hold while kicking and swinging at the air, hitting nothing in the process. He had gone a little crazy, the sheer madness of his onslaught at last making contact with the side of Wade's face, and then Wade hit him in the stomach.

Logan felt like he had been hit with an axe handle. He had never imagined a man's fist could do such damage. He doubled up and Wade's fist took him under the chin, snapping his head back with such force that he hit the ground again.

"Get up!" Wade said to him, but Logan had no intention of doing it. "Get up! You sorry excuse for a man!"

Wade reached down and pulled him to his feet. There was no fight left in Logan. He was out of breath and he held his hands up in defeat, but Wade hit him anyway. When he fell to the ground, Wade jumped on him and hit him again and then again. He was so angry he could not stop himself and it was Pat and Jim who pulled him off.

"You'll kill him!" Jim warned as he hauled Wade to his feet.

There was shock and horror on Logan's friends' faces. They were solemnly staring, fear in every eye.

"Who's next!" Wade shouted at them, but no one moved or said a word. "Then take your sorry excuse for a leader and get out of here."

They cautiously stepped forward and took Logan by the arms, dragging him to the side where they worked on reviving him.

"And remember this. It's war now. If I see any one of you on my property, I'll shoot first and ask questions later."

Rusty rounded up some of their horses while they were trying to get Logan up. They mounted, a quiet group, not saying a word, and then they rode away.

Wade stood looking after them, the taste of blood in his mouth and satisfaction in his heart. That had felt good. He suddenly laughed and all his men turned and looked at him.

"What's so funny?" Rusty asked.

"Man, that felt good!"

Chapter Eleven

Ada sat solemnly on the porch steps, looking down the road where she expected any minute to see Logan riding toward her. She had waited for him at church that morning much the same way, standing instead of sitting on the church steps, but he had not come. She had stood there until Wade and Rusty had ridden into the yard and then she had turned and had gone inside.

Not before she noticed the bruise on the side of Wade's face, though, and the scab in the corner of his mouth. He had been fighting. She was afraid she knew what that meant. Logan's absence seemed to solidify her fear and she immediately wondered what he looked like after seeing Wade's battle wounds.

She and Logan had argued the night before, but that was not on her mind as much as the thought of Wade Thornton. She kept thinking about the way he had looked standing in the moonlight, waiting for her, his voice soft in the night as he spoke her name. She also remembered what he had said to her, the line about being with her rather than fighting.

A Yankee remark, she told herself, but she still could not make herself feel the offense. It bothered her more than she wanted to admit.

Paul and Silas came around the corner of the house. Their

heads were together and they were talking quietly to each other. They didn't notice Ada until they were practically upon her and then they stopped, the chatter between them quickly hushed.

"What's the matter?" Paul asked and Ada sighed heavily.

"Nothin'," she lied. She was thinking there were plenty of things the matter, but she didn't want to discuss them with Paul.

"You heared what happen'd last night, didn't ya'?"

"No," she answered, suddenly interested. "What happened last night?"

"Logan got the stuffin's beat outta 'im, that's what," Paul said with satisfaction.

"Wade?" Ada asked, knowing the answer without asking.

"Shore was," Paul said. "Didja see 'im this mornin'? Hardly a scratch on 'im!"

"What about Logan?"

Paul snorted with contempt. "He ain't around, is he? That should tell ya' a thing or two."

"So that's the kinda fello' he is," she said, angry all over again. "I bet it wa'n't no fair fight—not against Logan. Wade Thornton ain't never seen the day he could whip Logan in a fair fight."

"So you say," Paul said. "It was a fair fight, but they're sayin' what Logan gave Bart was nowhere near fair nor right. From what I hear, Logan got what he deserved."

"Where'd you hear this?" Ada demanded.

"At church this mornin'."

"Wade and Rusty are hardly reliable sources," she said,

thinking they were the only ones there who could have told the story. It would have been one-sided and slanted to make them look better.

"They weren't my source," Paul scoffed. "An' yore as blind as a bat, Ada. I could tell ya' a few things about Logan, but you'd only git mad."

She gave Paul a serious look of consideration. She might not get mad. Paul was a sharp little boy and she didn't completely dismiss his opinion.

"Why don't you like Logan?" she asked him and his shaggy head came up with a start.

"'Cause I know too much about 'im," he honestly answered.

Ada sighed again. She leaned her head against the porch post and said to herself that Logan would come and he would tell her everything, but he didn't come, not that day nor any day the next week. It was Saturday when Ada finally saw him and by then, her anger had cooled and the argument they had had seemed long ago and not important. He rode into the yard and walked up to the porch. Ada met him there and stared in disbelief at the marks that were still on his face.

The swelling was gone, but his eyes were discolored and there were cuts that were almost healed all over his cheeks and around his eyes. He looked like he had been mauled by a panther and Ada told him so.

His eyes turned ugly and he gave Ada a hard look of disapproval.

"He didn't ketch me at my best," Logan said. "I'd already been in one fight. One o' his men—Bart, they call 'im, and I was worn out. He took advantage of the situation—had that gunslinger there with a gun on me while he beat me."

"I knew it was somethin' like that," Ada said and she immediately fell back into his good graces. "What about the gold?" Ada then asked. "He's had time to move it, so I guess it's gone."

"I don't think so."

"Maybe there isn't any gold," she suggested and Logan gave her a look of disbelief.

"Are you crazy?" he said. "There is, but you know, I've been thinkin'. Maybe he hasn't found it, after all."

"What makes you say that?"

"I heard this past week that he's runnin' short o' funds. If he'd found the gold, he'd be spendin' it."

"Where'd you hear that?"

"Daniel Larkin told me."

"How would Daniel know such a thing?"

"He's workin' for 'im."

"Daniel?"

"Yeah, and Jess, too."

Ada was surprised, but she didn't know why that surprised her.

"That'll make him more popular with everyone," Ada pointed out, although she was thinking that he was well liked even with his imported crew.

"You don't know the half," Logan said. "He's goin' 'round, talkin' to differ'nt ones, makin' out like he's gonna give easements and right-o'-ways to folks who need 'em."

"Is it a lie?" Ada asked.

Logan shrugged. "We'll have t' wait 'n see. My guess is, he's gonna appease his neighbors 'til he c'n find the gold and git out."

"If that's his reason, why would he care?" Ada flippantly asked.

Logan shrugged again. "You know," he said, his voice soft and serious, "he tried to kill us the other night."

Ada considered that, looking curiously at Logan while she thought about it.

"I toldja not to go over there," she reminded him. "What did you do when you got there?"

"We were just horsin' around," Logan said. He had been sitting at his favorite spot, but now he jumped down from the top rail of the fence and landed on his feet beside Ada. "He's real touchy about folks bein' on his property—afraid, maybe, they'll git to the gold b'fore he does. They scattered us with rifle fire and then that young gunslinger got the drop on some o' us. He's gonna make a mistake one o' these days and I'll ketch 'im without those fancy guns 'a his."

"Who? Rusty?"

Logan gave her an odd look. "You're right familiar with these boys' names," he said. "Wade? Rusty?

"Ev'rybody knows their names," she said. "I ain't never heard Rusty called anything besides that."

"I reckon not," Logan agreed. "I'm gonna git him," he then declared, his thoughts going back to his original subject. "That's a promise."

"Just leave 'em alone, Logan," Ada said. "I wish they'd just get the gold and get out. If ev'ryone'd let 'em be, maybe he could find it and we'd be done with him forever."

"That's wishful thinkin'," Logan said, "but I was wishin' the same thing—'cept about 'im findin' the gold. I'm gonna find it, Ada. Wade Thornton thinks he can run me off and I'll hide like a yeller dog, but he don't know nuthin'."

"What're you plannin'?" Ada asked, seeing the seriousness of his declaration.

"He's told us it's all-out war," Logan admitted. "So I reckon, I'm goin' to war."

Chapter Twelve

Jim moved up beside Wade and as he did, he removed his hat and wiped his sweaty brow. The month had begun hot and humid, the air still and sultry, and Jim was uncomfortable.

"Whew!" he exclaimed. "If it's this hot and it's only June, what's it going to be like in July?"

"Hotter," Wade replied.

"Yeah, that's what I was thinking," Jim said with pathos.

But that evening, the sky turned dark and it rained almost all night. The next day, the sky was blue and the temperature had dropped. It didn't reach any higher than seventy-two degrees that day nor the next. Wade and his crew worked feverishly, taking advantage of the favorable weather, but still, they were little more than half finished with the building of the fence when the air grew hot and humid again.

There had been no sign of Logan since the Saturday night he had taken a beaten from Wade. It caused the crew to fall into an apathy that Wade didn't share. He had a feeling that Logan was biding his time and that at the right moment, he would strike again. He imagined the fence would be the object of his next prank, because it was long and unprotected, and he was right. Two weeks later, Daniel and Jess came upon the cut barbed wire. Almost a half mile of it lay on the ground, along with many of the posts.

It slowed the work even more, but Wade kept at it, determined now more than ever.

Little did Logan know that he was doing just the opposite of what it would take to run Wade off. After everything that had been done, Wade wouldn't have left even if he had wanted to. Which he didn't. The longer he stayed in Florida, the better he liked it, and despite Logan and his friends' harassment, Wade liked the people of the area.

That's why he had been making the rounds, visiting his neighbors, trying to make peace with them over the building of the fence. Wade's property was a huge tract of land, comprising more than five miles squared and until he had bought it, the local people had used it for everything from hunting and fishing to building roads that connected farms and settlements. Many of them had legitimate complaints and Wade was determined to be fair even though it made his job of fence building all that much harder.

The thought of all this brought him around to the Tanners. He had deliberately put off going to talk to them about the spring. There was more than one reason for this decision, but mainly it was because he didn't know exactly what he would say to them. The fence was already up. The separation was there, and he didn't know if he should even mention it now.

He found himself riding toward the spring before he even realized what he was doing. It was Sunday afternoon and he and his men always took Sundays off from work. The crew was lounging around the ranch so Wade was free and restless.

He rode out of the yard and turned east, cutting across the flat, tree-shaded landscape where there were no trails. He had come to know his property and he needed nothing to show him the way. He rode with ease and confidence right up to the clearing where the pool of bright water gleamed in the sunlight.

It always made him pause in wonder. There was nothing to compare to its beauty and more than once, he had considered relocating just to have the spring nearby. His eyes wandered down the path that led to the Tanner's property, knowing he would never do it just because of them.

He was sitting there giving thought to such ideas when he saw movement on the trail. Two tasseled-headed boys came into sight and Wade sat up straighter for a better look. They walked up to the fence and with ease, they slipped through the strands of wire. Wade immediately looked beyond them, down the path they had used to get there, but no one was with them. Ada's dark head didn't appear and Wade felt a moment of disappointment.

He stepped down from his horse and tied the reins to a sturdy bush. He didn't want to scare the boys away, so he advanced on foot, hoping to get to them before they saw him. There was no need to worry, though. The boys pulled off their shirts and pants, and jumped into the water and a marching band could have walked up to them after that and they would never have known. Wade's silent approach gave them no hint of his presence until he was standing beside the water, looking down at them.

"Hey, boys," he quickly said. "How's the water?"

They both stopped playing and then they looked at Wade in wide-eyed surprise.

"We ain't trespassin', are we?" Paul asked.

"No," Wade was quick to answer. "You can come here anytime."

Silas pushed the wet mop of hair out of his eyes and squinted toward Wade. "You mean it? We was told you'd shoot us for trespassin'."

"Well, I forgot to bring my gun," Wade said. "And the two of you could probably overpower me. I thought it would be wise to be agreeable."

They both laughed, knowing he was being facetious. They had seen Logan's face and neither of them doubted Wade Thornton's ability to take care of himself.

"Just the same," Wade went on to say, "maybe you need some supervision." He looked around, his eyes going to the path. "Is your sister coming?"

"Who, Ada? Nah, she ain't no fun no more. She'd tell pa if she knew we wuz here."

"Well," Wade said as he began pulling his shirt out of his pants and then unbuttoning it. "I guess it's up to me."

He pulled off his shirt and then he sat down and took off his boots. When he stood up again, he removed his belt and then he stepped into the water. The icy cold almost took his breath away.

Both boys stared with eyes open wide and mouths agape. The last thing they expected was for Wade Thornton, their Yankee neighbor, to go swimming with them in the shining pool.

It took them only a few seconds to recover and when they did, both of them saw the potential for fun. They exchanged mischievous glances and then they attacked. They dunked Wade and he went under, the cold chilling him to the bone. He came up amid the laughter of the two scamps, catching his breath as soon as he reached the surface. Paul and Silas were clinging to him and he flipped them backwards, taking them into the water as he went under again.

They all came up laughing and then the real battle began. A half hour later, Wade pulled himself out of the pool and fell on the ground beside it, exhausted and spent. He was smiling. He had not had that much fun since he had been a boy himself.

"Hey, you ain't quittin', are ya'?" Paul asked in dismay.

"I'm afraid I have to fly the white flag. I'm beat."

"Whoopee!" the two boys yelled in unison. They jumped up and clasped their hands in the air over their heads, laughing in good-natured glee at their success. "We've brought down the Yankee scourge," they said and Wade raised his head to give them a curious look.

"The Yankee scourge?" he said. "You'll make this a matter of honor and then I'll have to fight to the death," he said and the boys laughed all the harder.

Wade gave no indication of doing anything except lying in the sunlight and warming his ice cold body and soon the twins joined him. They pulled themselves out of the water and crawled across the lawn, flopping down beside Wade.

The sun was shining hot and they lay there on their backs,

soaking up the warmth.

"So, why isn't your sister here with you?" Wade suddenly asked.

"Ada's mad. She won't come here no more 'cause it's yore spring."

Wade folded his arms behind his head and looked up at the sky. White puffballs of clouds were moving slowly against a blue background, a gentle wind pushing them along. He silently watched them while he wondered how to ask about her. Nothing came to mind so he slowly sat up and reached for his boots.

"I have to go," he said. "But I demand a rematch. How 'bout next Sunday?"

"You mean it?" Paul asked, grinning from ear to ear.

"I mean it." Wade looked around at Paul and then he added. "Tell your sister she's welcome to come with you. I know the spring means a lot to her."

"She won't come," Silas said. "Fact is, she du'n't like you."

Wade smiled derisively. "Yes, I know. But tell her she doesn't have to like me in order to take advantage of the spring. That would be cutting off her nose to spite her face, wouldn't it?" he said as he came to his feet. He picked up his shirt and put it on but he didn't button it. He just let it gape, catching the breeze.

"I'll tell 'er, but she won't like it."

Wade grinned. "Okay, boys. Next week, then."

He walked away and both Paul and Silas came to their feet and watched him. He caught up his horse and stepped into the stirrup, swinging easily up to the saddle. He raised a hand in parting, waving at the two of them before turning the horse and riding away.

Paul watched him, a look of deep thought in his young eyes.

"You know," Silas said as he watched Wade disappear into the distance, "for a Yankee, he ain't half bad."

Paul looked at his brother. "No, he ain't," he agreed.

"Was it my 'magination or did he seem orful int'rested in our sister?"

"It weren't yore 'magination."

"Well, that's too bad—since she hates his guts. I'd rather have him for a brother than Logan Spencer."

"My thinkin' exactly," Paul said. He turned to his brother with a grin. "We could do it, you know. We could git Wade and Ada t'gether and they'd never even know how it happ'ned."

"An' then good-bye Logan Spencer," Silas sang out.

"Yeah—and good ridd'nce!"

Chapter Thirteen

The fence builders' camp was temporary, always moving as the barbed wire stretched into the distance. Monday morning when Wade rode into it, he could see Mason's Corner just a short distance to the east.

There were three men in the group that stayed with the fence, the rest were Wade's crew. They were working well together, and Wade was thinking that if he could keep Logan from cutting the fence, it might be finished by the end of summer.

"Why don't you get the law out here to them?" Pete had asked after the last stretch of wire had been cut and left on the ground. He was the foreman of the fence builders, a man from town who relied on the law when there was trouble, but things were different out here and Wade was quick to discern this. If he was going to live in this rural community, Wade had to prove something to the people who lived here. Bringing in the law was not going to prove anything except that he could not fight his own battles. It seemed that was important to these people and more than anything, Wade wanted to earn their respect.

"Not yet," Wade had answered. "Let's not throw in the towel just yet."

It was a hot morning. There was a fire burning in the camp where breakfast had been cooked and a pot of coffee was still simmering on the coals. Wade stepped down from his horse and let the reins trail.

"Where exactly did you want the gate?" Pete asked when Wade walked up to him.

"In line with Mason's," Wade answered. In the distance, a train whistled and Wade looked toward the north from where the sound had come. The sound was foreboding in the still morning air and Wade shook his head at the sense of dread that suddenly came over him.

"I'm going to Mason's," he announced and with that, he walked toward the small store with its weathered siding and its faded sign.

Pappy was sitting on the upturned keg just as he had been before, but Mason was sweeping the floor when Wade walked inside.

"Mornin'," Mason genially greeted him. "I reckon you're here for mail. Got some for ya'."

He laid the broom aside and walked to the counter in the back corner. Wade followed him.

"I see the fence is within sight," Mason said as he handed the letter to Wade. "I never realized how close your property was to us."

"I didn't either," Wade admitted. "I'm putting in a gate right behind your store. We aren't fencing you out."

"Didn't reckon you were," Mason said.

Wade looked at the letter and he immediately recognized Angela's fine script. He turned it over in his hand, reluctant to open it. The dread was on him again, and he had a feeling the letter was the reason.

Wade thanked Mason and then he walked outside, the letter still in his hand. He looked toward the tracks where the train had gone by just minutes before and then he looked around the little settlement. The ring of the blacksmith's anvil was distinct and clear, and he could hear the men working on the fence behind him. He stood there listening as he continued to hold the unopened letter in his hand.

He knew he should feel differently about the arrival of a letter from Angela, and he scolded himself for immediately thinking of Ada. It made him angry with himself and he stomped off the porch and tore at the letter as he walked toward the shade of a nearby tree.

He leaned his shoulder against the tree and read the letter, and then his mouth dropped open in surprise. Angela was on her way to Florida! She would be arriving with her father in just two days. They had reservations and would be staying at the newly built Magnolia Springs Hotel just north of Green Cove Springs.

Wade crushed the letter in his hand without even thinking of the damage he was doing to it. He stared down the railroad tracks to the north as if he could see all the way to Green Cove Springs and beyond to the hotel where they would be staying, but he was actually not looking at anything.

The last thing he wanted was for Angela to come here, but it was too late to stop her. Wade knew that was why she had waited to send the letter. She knew that if he had known she was planning this trip, he would have stopped her and Angela was not a girl to be talked out of anything once she had set her mind to it.

Two days! That was not much time, but then Wade asked himself why he needed any time, at all. He relaxed. Maybe this was going to be a good thing. He would have Angela here and she would make him remember his duty and his rightful place. It would get his mind moving in the right direction again, and Wade admitted to himself that he needed something to put him back on the right track.

But he could not shake the dread that had settled over him. He somehow knew a disaster was about to happen, but he could not see from which direction it was going to come.

He made up his mind to be happy about the Major and Angela's visit and he stood there in the shade of the tree until he had convinced himself that he was happy, and then he walked back to the fence.

"Bad news?" Rusty asked when he arrived.

"No. Good news. My girl's on her way. She'll be in Green Cove Springs in two days—she and her father."

"What?" Jim exclaimed. "You mean the Major's coming here? And Angela?"

"That's right."

Rusty eyed Wade curiously, that ever present cynicism in his eyes. He saw the crushed letter in Wade's hand and he divined what no one else seemed to notice, but he didn't say anything. He smiled derisively and went back to digging post holes.

Wade waited until the third day before making the trip to

Green Cove Springs. His reasons were sound and no one guessed he was being reluctant. He knew schedules were sometimes unreliable and he didn't want to arrive before Angela and the Major, and even if they arrived on time, they would be tired and the extra day would give them time to unpack and rest before he joined them—or that's what he told everyone.

Wade took the steamboat up the St. Johns River. It was a good choice for travel and Wade was interested in seeing the scenery from the viewpoint of the wide and beautiful river. The shoreline was green and thick with trees and brush. It was difficult to see into the interior except for a few places where the land had been cleared, but he stood at the side of the boat and looked over the railing anyway. The monotony lulled him into a somnolent state and he arrived at the hotel's six hundred foot pier before he realized it was time to be there.

The grounds were beautifully shaded and a promenade led from the pier, past a couple of cottages, and on to the hotel itself which was a magnificent building, square with corner towers and porches that ran the length of the building. It was luxurious and boasted a lovely view of the St. Johns River. Wade stopped at the row of steps leading up to the first floor and he looked around, admiring it while at the same time thinking that the hotel was Angela's choice. She had a taste for the opulent and the extravagant. He smiled, wondering what she would think of his tiny three room house.

Two women passed him. They were carrying rackets and were dressed for playing on the lawn, and as they stepped down the stairs where he hesitated, they gave him bold and approving looks.

"Do you need help?" one of them asked.

He was deep in thought and the question woke him from his musings.

"No," he said, giving both girls a friendly smile. "I was just thinking."

A girl suddenly appeared at the top of the steps. It was Angela. She had heard his voice and had quickly come to meet him.

"Wade!" she called out in excitement. She started down the steps and he began to climb them. They met in the middle and Angela took his hands. "Wade, it's so good to see you. And look at you!" She pushed him back for a better look. "You're as dark as an Indian. What has this Florida sun done to you?"

"Disappointed?" he asked.

"Hardly," she assured him. "It's very becoming."

She was dressed in a fashionable gown and her blonde hair was completely hidden beneath a hat with a broad brim all covered with tulle and feathers. He immediately compared her to Ada with her simple dress, so appropriate for the Florida weather, and her daddy's old battered hat. Angela saw the change in his expression and she tilted her head to one side and eyed him curiously.

"What? No return compliment? Have I then become a disappointment?"

Wade smiled. "No man would view you as a disappointment," he assured her.

"Well, I know that I'm not properly dressed for this steamy weather, but I'll take care of that as soon as I can find a shop. Here, let's find papa. He'll be unhappy that I haven't brought you immediately to him."

She pulled him up the steps and onto the porch. The Major was on the walkway, looking toward the river. He was standing military straight, with one arm tucked behind his back and the other at his side. He was smoking and as Wade and Angela approached, he reached up and removed the pipe from his mouth.

He genuinely liked Wade so the smile he gave him was sincere. He held out his hand and Wade gripped it, giving it a hearty pump.

"Hello, sir," Wade said. "So good to see you."

"And you," the Major said. "Quite a place this Florida," he went on the say. "You've really chosen a remarkable land."

"Yessir. I think so."

"You would," Angela said. She was fanning herself and sweat had made an unladylike bead over her lip. "I'll admit, it has a wild beauty about it, but mostly it's just bugs and heat."

"And this is only June," the Major pointed out.

They laughed as if it was a wonderful joke, but Wade only smiled. He had known all along that Angela wouldn't like Florida, although she was suited for the life of a tourist, playing on the lawn with the girls he had passed on the steps, or motoring down the St. Johns River with them, all of them wearing big hats to shield their delicate skin from the sun.

"How long will you be staying?" he heard himself asking

and the Major quickly answered.

"We're in no hurry," he said. "We want to see your ranch and do a bit of exploring while we're here."

"I want to visit Palatka," Angela quickly interjected. "I've been told it's absolutely marvelous and the boats make regular trips there. You'll take me, won't you, Wade?"

He had not expected the question and it took him a few seconds to reply. "I'd love to, Angela," he said, "but I have work to do. I can't be running off to Palatka just now."

"Oh, Wade, really! You can take some time off for us. After all, if I'm going to live here," she said with a gentle reminder to Wade of the promise they had made to each other. "I have to see the area."

"It's your place I'm interested in," the Major said and then he gave Angela a look of fatherly admonishment. "And that's what you should be interested in, too, young lady."

"There isn't much to see at the ranch," Wade said. "I'm afraid you'll be disappointed."

He knew Angela would be, but he was not so sure about the Major. Wade's house was just a small three room structure, but he had built it with the idea of adding on to it as soon as he was able. Just then, he thought of the spring and what it would be like to build a really nice house near it. As soon as the thought came to him, he cringed, thinking of Ada and how it would affect her.

"I'm anxious, just the same," the Major said. "I know you, and I can hardly imagine being disappointed by anything you are involved in."

"Thank you," Wade said, deeply moved by the Major's confidence in him. He looked at Angela. "It isn't set up for a lady, but the Major and I can stay in the bunk house and you can have the house. It's quite primitive, but if you're game . . ."

"I am," she assured him. "I wouldn't miss it for the world."

As it turned out, the Major and Angela wouldn't be coming out to the ranch for several days, but Wade had to return the next day. He took a room at the hotel and spent the night there and the three of them took advantage of the opportunities it offered. After dinner that night, Angela excused herself early and Wade was left alone with the Major. They sat down on the veranda, and a cool breeze blew in from the river while the night sounds softly serenaded them. Fireflies were dancing over the lawn and a yellow moon was high in the sky. It was a peaceful setting, but the Major had noticed that Wade's eyes were not reflecting the simple harmony of the evening.

"Is everything going well at the ranch?" he asked. "I can't help but notice you have a troubled look in your eye."

Wade had been staring toward the river, but he quickly turned to the Major.

"It's not gone as well as I'd hoped," he admitted. "We've had some trouble with a few of the local boys. One of them in particular has made it difficult to complete anything."

"I wondered. You've been distracted all evening and your urgency to return home . . .well, I put two and two together and figured you'd had trouble."

"A lot of the people resent me taking possession of the property, but most have been agreeable. They're a peculiar people in some ways, but I find I like their straight-forward, simple outlook. They're a gracious people and even if they don't like you, you won't be turned away if you visit their homes."

"I can't imagine anyone not liking you."

Wade could. Regretfully, he immediately thought of Ada.

"I haven't won everyone over, although, I've tried. Logan Spencer and I have had more than just words."

"A fight?"

Wade nodded. "He asked for it."

"I didn't suppose you went looking for it."

"I didn't."

"You're worried about taking Angela out there, aren't you?"

"A little. She isn't going to like it."

"She's tougher than you think," the Major assured him. "She may surprise you."

Wade gave that some thought. It would surprise him. Angela was a city girl, liking luxury and easy living, but she was also the Major's daughter and she had been in rough places before. He had to remember, too, that Florida had been Angela's idea. She had started the whole affair that had brought Wade here to begin with, but Wade knew she had her reasons, and he was afraid he knew what they were. It was the gold again, and something inside Wade turned over with sickening effect.

He suddenly looked at the Major. Was that why they were here?

"It's getting late," Wade suddenly said. "I'll be getting an early start tomorrow so I should be turning in."

The Major came to his feet when Wade did and he held a hand out to him. "Good night, Wade. It really is good to see you, and don't let Angela worry you." He stopped and cleared his throat, and then he chuckled softly. "In all honesty, she's anxious to get you to the altar—we all are."

Wade gripped the Major's hand and he held it tightly while he considered a response. Wade was not in any hurry to marry Angela, but at the same time, he told himself that it would be the wisest thing he had done since coming to Florida. The idea suddenly appealed to him.

"You're right, of course," Wade said with a wan smile. "I plan to talk to Angela about that very thing."

"Good, good, my boy," the Major said, patting him on the back as he talked. "She'll be happy, and, well, you know how I feel."

He guided him to the door and Wade left him standing there. He watched as the older gentleman turned and walked back toward the bannister at the edge of the veranda. The Major looked into the darkness toward the river and he seemed satisfied. Wade hoped he understood the Major's expression and that he was not misreading it.

He went up to the third floor and found his room. The next morning, he was checked out and on the boat for home before Angela was even up for the day.

When he arrived at the ranch, Jim was there, but everyone else was at the fence. They had had trouble the night before but Jim waited to tell Wade until he had heard the news of the Major and Angela.

"They'll be coming in on Monday," Wade finished by saying. "You can see for yourself."

"It'll be good," he said, squinting into the distance. "They're like us, Wade. The rest of this bunch aren't."

Wade didn't agree with Jim, but he didn't argue. Jim was not like anyone Wade had ever known—not exactly, anyway. Jim was an individual and sometimes his individuality was not easy to get along with, but Wade also knew that Jim's loyalty was unfailing. Even in his cantankerous moods, he would put Wade and the ranch first.

"So, what happened?" Wade asked, aware that there had been trouble the night before.

"I can't say exactly, 'cause we couldn't find anything, but it was Logan and his bunch, for sure."

"What did they do?"

"Well," Jim began, hesitating as if trying to figure out the best way to explain. "There was this singing," he said. "It was off in the distance and we never could pinpoint the location, but there was also the sound of ground being broken like with a shovel. Singing and digging! We figured Logan was digging up fence posts so Jess and Daniel took off for the fence, riding the line to find them. But Rusty said it wasn't coming from the fence. He walked into the woods—going toward the Clearing— but when he came back, he said nothing was there. He acted right peculiar, though. It was like he was angry with all of us. I think it must have been the lack of sleep. We all missed a bit last night."

The Clearing was what they had begun to call the bare spot

of land near the pine forest, the land where the soldiers were supposed to have been buried and Wade unconsciously looked toward it. He thought he had heard a few things coming from that direction, too, and he was sure Logan and his band had figured out a way to bring the ghosts of Captain Thornton's squad alive just for the benefit of the crew at Wade's ranch. It took some ingenuity and Wade was a little impressed, but at the same time, he was fed up with the pranks the bunch of local boys never ceased to play on them.

"One of these days, I'm going to catch him in the act," Wade said.

"Yeah? And what good will that do? You caught him trying to burn you out and even after the beating you gave him, he came back. It didn't do one bit of good."

"But it did," Wade said. "I've seen a change in attitudes in the community. I've earned some respect."

Jim scoffed at the very idea. "Respect? Who cares what these people think?"

"I do," Wade quickly said.

Jim gave Wade a weary look. "Don't waste your time, Wade," he said. "They'll never accept you. You and I are the Yankees. Ask anyone you like and they'll tell you. And that's all we'll ever be. The war is still alive in this area. That's why Logan keeps coming back. He isn't about to quit. It would be like losing the war all over again."

Wade knew he was halfway right, but Jim didn't understand the people of the area nor did he care to understand them. It was a proud people that populated the South, but even so, they were fair-minded and quick to extend a hand to the man who wanted to join them. If living here meant joining them, then that was what Wade wanted to do.

"Well, we'll see," Wade said. He suddenly began thinking about the twins and the battle they had fought in the spring—the battle to defeat the Yankee scourge. He smiled. It had all been in fun and no offense had been taken, but after Jim's observation, Wade felt a little stricken by their description of him. Children often repeat what they have heard, and Wade wondered who at the Tanner's home had labeled him the Yankee scourge. It was probably Ada. Well, Ada didn't matter, he quickly told himself, but his eyes thoughtfully strayed to the northeast where she lived.

When Rusty came in, Wade met him at the corral. Rusty grinned from ear to ear while at the same time, he looked Wade over, a curious query in his eyes.

"Well, where is she?"

"She's in Green Cove," Wade answered.

"I thought you'd be bringing her back with you."

"No. She wants to buy suitable attire before coming out. I don't think she was prepared for the Florida weather."

"When will she get here?"

"Monday. I'll meet them at Mason's Corner. They're coming in on the train."

Rusty nodded and then Wade turned to the reason for meeting him there. "What happened last night?" he asked and Rusty's expression changed with surprising swiftness.

"Nothing," he said, turning his back on Wade.

"That's not what Jim said."

Rusty turned around. "Then Jim knows more 'n me. I didn't find anything anywhere and if we let Logan do it, he'll have us chasin' ghosts ever' night."

"Were you chasing ghosts?" Wade asked, suddenly aware of a distinctive change in Rusty's attitude.

"No. There ain't no such thing," he said, busying himself with putting up his saddle.

Wade had a feeling he should drop the subject, so he did, but he could not help but wonder if something had happened at the Clearing—something that Rusty didn't want to tell him.

"Come Monday, will you go with me to pick up Angela and the Major?" Wade asked, changing the subject again.

Rusty grinned. "You bet," he said, "If you aren't afraid of losin' 'er. You know when she sees me, you'll be history."

"I'm not worried," Wade said as he turned to leave.

"You should be," he called after him, and then with a grin he added, "Don't say I didn't warn ya'."

"I'm sufficiently warned," Wade said as he kept walking.

Just then Powder Keg stepped to the door of the kitchen. They had built a large room onto the bunk house and it served as both kitchen, dining room, and lounge. He looked out the door and shouted, "Come an' git it, b'fore I throw it to the hawgs!"

Chapter Fourteen

"What's the matter with you, girl?" Mrs. Tanner asked Ada. "You've been draggin' all mornin'."

"I can't seem to get myself movin' this mornin'," Ada admitted.

"Well, if we don't git these clothes on the line, they won't have time to dry b'fore the afternoon rains git here."

She was right. The summer showers had already begun. Every afternoon a shower would move across the land, drawing a white sheet of water that could be seen moving across the landscape. Ada often had time to run out to the line and take down the clothes before the rain reached the house. It was a race she had won repeatedly, and she took great pride in her skill at removing the wash and getting it to the house before the shower could overtake her. The rain, though, was not an antagonist. She loved the showers. They would last only a short while, anywhere from one minute to an hour and after they moved on, everything was clean and fresh and the air was cooler.

Ada picked up a shirt and pinned it to the line and then she reached down for another. Her mother had already put up two before she could get the one finished.

"I'm almost useless today," Ada said with a wry chuckle.

"It ain't got nuthin' to do with that visit from Logan the

other day, has it?" her mother wisely asked. "It seems you've been mopin' around ever' since then."

"Have I? Well, I guess it did bother me some."

Ada didn't want to admit it, but Logan's visit had struck her deeply. She was not thinking the same anymore. Her thoughts were new and somewhat alien, and even though she didn't like the direction in which her mind wandered, she seemed helpless to stop it.

She told herself it was all Wade Thornton's fault. If he had never come, then she and Logan wouldn't be having any trouble. She told herself that she wished Wade would go away and never come back again, but then she would remember the sound of his voice as he spoke her name and the feel of his hands when he touched her, and she felt a quiet softness inside her.

At the same time, the very peacefulness of the thoughts of him brought an immediate reaction that was quite the opposite. She would often snap out of these unwanted reveries with a mental shake of herself and then she would feel the need to throw or to hit something. She had done neither, but if she had given in to her unbridled anger and had taken the action she so desperately needed, she would probably have felt better.

She huffed in exasperation and reached down for another article of clothing which she violently threw on the clothes line. Mrs. Tanner gave her a sober look that was not entirely clueless. Perhaps she knew better than anyone else just what was going on with Ada. Perhaps, she knew even better than Ada herself, but she didn't say anything. She knew the time was not right.

That afternoon Logan came by. He had been hanging around doing much of nothing ever since the beating he had taken from Wade and more and more often he was coming around the Tanner's house.

He arrived just after the afternoon shower. Ada had been prepared and when the rain came thundering down on the rooftop, she was in the living room, folding the clean clothes and smiling smugly at her accomplishment. As suddenly as it had begun, the rain had stopped and the sun shined as brightly as if there had never been a drop of rain in the world. It was then she heard Logan coming down the road and she stopped folding clothes to look outside.

Logan and Fred had been spending more time together than ever and sure enough, when he arrived, he walked straight to Fred and they began talking. There seemed to be something almost clandestine about their meetings even though they were executed right out in the open. Ada looked through the open window and she wondered if it had anything to do with Wade Thornton.

It seemed everything had to do with Wade Thornton anymore—or his gold. Ada popped the article of clothing she held in her hand and with exasperation, she roughly folded it.

Logan made his way to the house just as Ada finished folding the last article of clothing, and she walked outside, meeting him on the porch. "I'm surprised to see you," she said and he simply shrugged.

"I wanna talk to ya'," he said and without hesitation, Ada

stepped off the porch and followed him across the yard.

They went to their usual place and Logan sat on the fence rail while Ada stood beside it. He didn't say anything for a long time even though he had said he had come to talk to her, so Ada didn't say anything either. Logan seemed distracted but finally, he jumped down from his perch on the fence and he pulled her to him.

"Ada, let's go ahead and git married," he said. "I was waitin' on the gold, but I can still git it. I don't wanna wait any longer."

It caught Ada off guard and she didn't know what to say. Funny, two months ago, she wouldn't even have hesitated, but today she felt differently.

"I don't know, Logan," she said and he stepped back, shocked at her answer.

"What d' ya' mean you don't know?"

"I only mean, I don't know if now's the right time. You haven't even got a job. Where will we live? How will we support ourselves?"

Those were questions she wouldn't even have considered before, but Ada was feeling wiser today than she had a few weeks ago.

"We c'n live with my parents until I git the gold," he said without any hesitation or any insight to her reluctance. "After that, we'll live anywhere we like." He grinned with great satisfaction, but Ada only looked at him. The last thing she wanted was to move in with Logan's parents. She had a feeling she would be there the rest of her life, living with his parents, and it was not something she wanted to do.

"Come on, Ada," he said with a frown, seeing she was not sharing in his cheerful observation. "What's wrong with you today? You've been as sour as a lemon-suckin' dog."

"I'm bein' realistic," she said. She put her back to the fence and looked away from him. "What if you can't find the gold—or if there isn't any gold?" She looked back at him and he slowly shook his head in disbelief.

"You can't say that, Ada. It's bad luck."

"Bad luck—my foot!" she said in exasperation. "The gold belongs to Wade Thornton. Let 'im have it!"

Logan's squinted eyes narrowed even more. "Your concern for that Yankee is touchin'," he sarcastically said. "You been seein' him on the sly?"

"What?" she said aghast at his question. "Are you crazy?"

"I promise you," he said, his tone sinister. "I'll wring your neck if there's somethin' goin' on between you."

"There's nothin' between me and him. You know that."

"No, I don't know that," he quickly replied. "You've been actin' pretty queer lately where he's concerned."

"I have not," she insisted. "You're becomin' as paranoid as old lady McMathers."

Mrs. McMathers was the community hypochondriac and overall worrier. She never saw the bright side of anything nor was her glass ever half full. It was always half empty—or worse. Her name had become synonymous with gloom and hopelessness, and Logan needed no other example to understand of what he was being accused.

"Okay," he said, more calmly than Ada had expected. "Prove me wrong," he went on to say. "Let's get married."

"When?" she asked, somewhat reluctantly.

"Next week."

"I can't," she replied.

"What's keepin' you from it?"

"I don't know. I just can't do it next week. It's too soon."

"Then when can you?"

"I don't know."

He looked away from her in thought, his eyes squinted as he looked into the distance. "Next month then," he said.

"You haven't even talked to daddy," she said. "He and mama might have their own ideas."

"I have talked to your daddy," he said, looking back at her. "You know what he said? He said he'd be glad for me to tie the knot with you and the sooner the better. You wanna know why? 'Cause he's afraid you're gittin' int'rested in that Yankee and he'd rather have one of those sorry Hinkleys for a son-in-law than a Yankee. At least one of the Hinkley boys would be southern."

"Daddy would never say that," she vehemently remarked.

"Go ask 'im," Logan said and Ada quickly looked toward the house.

"I will," she said.

"Well, I c'n see I'm wastin' my time here," Logan suddenly said. He looked down the road as if considering his next move. "Do ya' want me to come back, Ada?"

She flashed a startled look at him. "Yes, I do."

"Then you be makin' up yore mind just what you want from me. When I come back, I wan' a' answer."

"Okay," she agreed. He lazily walked away and Ada watched him. He took up the horse's reins and he climbed into the saddle. The horse flipped his tail and sidestepped as Logan turned him toward the road, but just as soon as he was out of sight, Ada looked toward the back yard where she had last seen her father.

He was squatting beside the bench where he cleaned his fish, looking at a brace that needed mending. She walked to him and he immediately smiled up at her.

"Is Logan gone?" he asked and she nodded.

"Yes," she said. "What're you doin' down there?"

"My post here is rottin'. I'm gonna have to replace it." He stood up and placed his hands on the bench. "What's the matter? You've got a grim look in yore eye."

"Logan told me what you said," she said, getting right to the point.

"About what?" he asked with a frown.

"Logan said you wanted me and him to get married just so I wouldn't marry Wade Thornton. You should know that isn't gonna happen."

"Well, Ada, you might not realize it, but you're a good lookin' girl. The only reason all the bucks in the county aren't hangin' aroun here is 'cause of Logan, and I know it. Your sister, Carrie, is a right pretty girl, but you've got 'er beat by a long shot. An' you saw how quick a city man snatched her up."

Ada did see. Carrie was only two years older than Ada, but

she had been married for two years now and was living in Green Cove Springs with her husband, Henson Morley, an important man.

"I wouldn't put it past that Yankee to pick you out as his girl," he went on to say. "Besides, I've seen the look in his eyes when he looks at you. I may be your daddy, but I ain't blind to what men are seein' when they look at you. It'd be a relief to have you married."

"Well, you needn't worry. You won't have him nor any of the Hinkleys as a son-in-law—I understand that was your first choice," she smugly added. "You'd rather have a Hinkley than a Yankee in the family."

"That ain't exactly what I said," he told her. "I said I'd just as soon have a Hinkley as a Yankee. I figure we'd be as happy with one as the other."

That certainly was not saying much for Wade Thornton, Ada was thinking. Not that she cared, or that was what she told herself.

"Did Logan talk to you about me n' him?" Ada suddenly asked, wanting very much to get away from the current subject.

"He did."

"An' you're okay with us gettin' married—even though he ain't got no money nor any place to live?"

"If that's what you want then, I am."

She looked down at her hands and then back up at him. "I don't know that it is."

He squatted down again, and picked up a board that was lying on the ground. He pushed it up under the bench and began working while he talked. "He'll do alright, Ada, if you'll give 'im a chance."

She wondered about that. She wondered if all this time she had been deceived about Logan's true nature and only now was she learning what it was really like.

"I told 'im I'd think about it," Ada solemnly said, and Fred stopped his work to look up at her.

"You might not wanna think too long on it—not if you wan' 'im." That was all he said, but Ada read a grim finality in it.

She left him there and walked back to the house. She stopped at the edge of the porch and stood there thinking.

Ada could hear her mother moving around in the house, humming softly as she worked. It was a comforting sound that set her to thinking about Logan's mother. Did she hum when she worked? Did she move softly around the house, quietly doing her chores and never raising an angry voice? Ada didn't think so. Mrs. Spencer was a captious woman with complaining ways, and besides, there was no one like Esther Tanner.

It suddenly occurred to Ada that she had not seen Paul and Silas all afternoon. She looked around and then she strained an ear for any sound of them.

"What're those two scamps up to?" she said aloud. Her eyes automatically drifted to the trail that led to the spring, but as she looked, she heard a peal of laughter coming from the back side of the garden. Paul and Silas were at the Big Oak.

Ada smiled with relief. Little did she know, it was a false sense of relief. The two boys had simply found a way to get to the spring without arousing suspicions and that's where they had been all afternoon. Furthermore, she had no idea she was the subject of their present conversation, and that a plot was being devised to set a trap for her. Come Sunday, it would take effect, and that's why the boys laughed.

Chapter Fifteen

"Hey, Wade! You ain't forgot, have you?" Paul asked.

Wade had just stepped into the saddle and the surprise of the quiet voice spoken to him from out of nowhere was evident.

"I haven't forgotten," he said with a smile. "Don't renege on me," he said. "I expect a proper rematch."

"You'll get one," Paul said with a mischievous grin. "You have no idea what's in store for you this afternoon."

"I'm anxious to see," he admitted, and he was. He was so much looking forward to meeting with the boys that he hurried through his afternoon with nothing else on his mind, chuckling softly to himself as he thought about what strategy they were planning to use on him, but when he arrived at the spring and no one was there, he looked around in surprise and more than just a little disappointment.

He carefully began unbuttoning his shirt, thinking all the while that they would soon arrive. When he had the shirt off, he sat down and took his boots off and then he stepped into the water. The cold took his breath away just as it had done the week before, but he smiled, thinking that he would have the advantage this time. He would be acclimated to the cold and the twins wouldn't. He held his breath and dunked himself, wiping the water from his face and eyes as he came up.

He looked toward the trail. Still, there was no sign of the

boys. He waited and after a few minutes, he was cold to the bone and decided to get out of the water. He waded out and stood in the sunshine to warm himself.

As he stood there, he looked down the shady path that led to the Tanner's property and because he was impatient for the twins to get there, he began walking toward it. He had only gone about fifteen feet, though, when he heard someone approaching. He smiled with anticipation and then it occurred to him that he could strike the first blow of the battle right here. He stepped off the path and put his back to a nearby tree, thinking that when one of the twins walked by, he would step out and grab him. He could imagine their faces and the thought made him almost giddy with delight.

He waited and the footsteps grew louder, yet they were soft footsteps, almost like only one person coming down the path.

The twins are good woodsman, Wade was thinking as he prepared to catch one of them. He poised himself in readiness and just as the first one appeared, he jumped out and wrapped his arms around him.

"Gotcha!" he said.

But the twins were not the ones to be surprised, but Wade himself. It was Ada who had come down the path and he had caught her in a bear hug that had startled her as much as it had Wade.

"Let me go!" she shouted and then she recognized him and the fright left her. She angrily brushed his hands away and pulled herself back from him. "What's wrong with you?" she demanded with some excitement.

"I thought you were one of the twins."

She was huffing with exasperation and straightening her mussed clothes, but she abruptly stopped and gave him a derisive look.

"First you think I'm one of your men and now you think I'm one of the twins. Maybe you need to get your eyes examined."

"Or my mind," he said sotto voce.

He could not believe his bad luck. He stepped back and wearily shook his head. Maybe there *was* something wrong with him.

"What's this?" she asked him, giving him a mocking look. "What were you doin'? Playin' in the water like a little boy?"

He looked down at himself and then right back at Ada. He had forgotten how he looked.

"Last week, the twins won the battle of the spring. Today was supposed to be a rematch."

His statement prompted an uncontrollable desire from Ada to laugh aloud. Her hand flew up to her mouth to stifle it but it came out anyway. At the same time, Wade felt a tiny amused grin starting at the corner of his own mouth.

They both laughed and Ada had to admit, he was a good sport. She had created an image of him in her mind, that of a stern, hard-nosed, and unrelenting man—and a proper one too, in a stiff, puritanical sort of way. Never would she have imagined him as this boyish, free spirit. It had its own charm and Ada was impressed even though she didn't want to be.

At the same time, she saw the irony of this whole situation.

Logan had accused her of meeting Wade on the sly and here she was, alone with him at the spring. Logan would never believe it had been an accident.

Or was it an accident? Ada suddenly saw the ruse for what it was. The twins had played a marvelous trick on her and on Wade, too, from the looks of things. She was no longer amused and her expression changed and darkened as quickly as an afternoon thunder cloud.

"Why, those little devils," she said, setting her mouth in a hard line. "I'll get them for this."

Wade flashed a questioning look at Ada. What was she saying—that the twins had engineered this whole situation?

"You mean we've been set up?" Wade asked.

Her eyes flashed around, searching the woods. "Yes, and you can bet, they're somewhere out there right now, having the laugh of their life."

Wade looked around, too, but he was more curious as to why they would do such a thing rather than where they were.

"Well, they'll get no more amusement today at my expense," she said, and then emphatically she added, "I'm leaving." She looked at Wade one more time before going and what she saw this time was very much different from what she had seen a few minutes ago. Before, she had seen Wade in a boyishly, playful manner, but now as she looked at him, she saw the man that he was. He was dressed only in his jeans. His body was bare, lean and strong with muscles that she found more than just admirable, his hair was wet, but his face was dry, darkly tanned and more handsome than it had any right to be. "Well, good-bye, Mr. Thornton," she slowly said, suddenly reluctant to leave. She mechanically turned and started walking down the path, hurrying herself along as her thoughts pursued her.

"Wade," he called after her as she retreated down the path. "My name is Wade."

"Sorry . . . Wade," she said. She raised a hand in farewell, but she didn't slow down. She knew better than to even look back.

He watched her until she turned the corner and disappeared from sight, thinking all the while that he wanted to call her back, but then he didn't know what he would say if she did come back. With an exasperated slap on his thigh, he began walking back to the spring.

He told himself it had not gone too badly. In fact, it had been going pretty well until she had figured out what the twins had done. He hoped she didn't think he had had a part in it. That worried him and he glanced around the edge of the woods again, but this time with a more serious consideration. She was right, the twins were a couple of little devils, but at the same time, he could not find it in his heart to be totally upset with them.

He looked down into the clear water, his thoughts as deep as the spring itself, and then with even more exasperation, he turned his back to the spring and sat down on the grass where he had left his clothes. He pulled on his boots and then he picked up his shirt and stood up. He was putting it on when he saw the movement in his peripheral vision.

So, they were out there—gloating, no doubt, at their success. He gave no indication he had seen them, but deftly continued to button his shirt, and then he walked to the bush where he had tethered his horse.

Once he was in the saddle, he looked to where he had seen the movement, but there was nothing there. He smiled at the thought of the two boys. Paul and Silas might be little devils, but they were likable little scamps, just the same. Wade could not stop wondering why they had played such a trick on him and on Ada, too. He was sure they had been looking forward to meeting him at the spring, and yet, they had chosen a prank over the afternoon of fun that had been in store for them.

He turned the horse and had just begun moving when something slammed him forward in the saddle. He heard the shot a second later and then he fell, hitting his head with a ringing jar. With a groan, Wade moved and then his body went limp, and the world blacked out around him.

Chapter Sixteen

Ada had stopped at the fence. Someone had cut it and she was thinking she should have told Wade. She glanced over her shoulder and considered going back and telling him, but she didn't trust herself to do it. He was a better man than she had given him credit for and Ada didn't like to admit she was wrong.

She was standing there thinking about him when she heard the shot. It pierced the afternoon like a clarion call, breaking the spell Ada was under. It had come from nearby and her first thought was a concern for the twins who she knew were hiding somewhere in these woods, afraid, no doubt, to face her after what they had done. Just as quickly, her concern turned from them to Wade and a terrible dread gripped her.

With hurried steps, Ada went back down the path toward the spring. A shot in the countryside was not a novelty, but she knew without knowing that this one had been different.

She saw Wade's horse before she saw him and then all of a sudden, the twins appeared just ahead of her, coming out of the woods at an angle to Ada.

They glanced her way, but then their heads pivoted to the standing horse and then to Wade's still body. Ada lifted her skirt and ran, reaching Wade just seconds after the boys. There was blood all over his back and he was lying so still, Ada just knew he was dead, but when she touched him, he groaned and moved.

"Is 'e dead?" Silas asked.

"No. Take the horse and go get help," she said. "Wait!" she called out as it occurred to her that it was not just any help he needed, but loyal, trustworthy help. "Go to his ranch," she told them, "and if you can, get Rusty."

They left and she gingerly touched Wade. He was lying on his face in the grass and his blood had stained his shirt and the ground beneath him. Anxiously she gripped him, trying to turn him over. She tugged and pulled at him until she had him on his back but when she saw his ashen face, she was afraid. The wound was oozing blood so she placed her hand on it and applied pressure, hoping to slow down the flow.

"Wade . . . Wade . . . can you hear me?" she asked as she knelt over him, pressing his shoulder with her bare hands. His eyes blinked and then he frowned, but he didn't say anything.

"Wade," she said again, more anxiously this time. "Wade, can you hear me?"

"I hear you," he finally said and Ada sighed with relief.

There was blood everywhere and his face was pale, but he opened his eyes and looked up at her.

"What happened?" he weakly asked.

"You've been shot. Lie still. The boys've gone for help."

"I'm okay," he said and then he moved, trying to get up, but he couldn't. There was a throbbing pain in his shoulder and he felt weak, almost giddy. He fell back, panting from the exertion.

"Lie still," she said again. "Wait 'til someone gets here to help."

"Who did it?" he asked once he had caught his breath again, and Ada gave a little start.

"I don't know."

But she figured she did know. Ada looked around, her eyes anxiously scanned the woods for any sign of Logan.

Wade figured the same thing, and he felt uncomfortably vulnerable lying there as weak as he was and with no weapon. What if Logan had seen him and Ada together? He might be angry enough to shoot her, as well.

He moved and Ada pressed harder to keep him still, but there was no need. He blacked out and the next thing he knew, horses were approaching and Rusty was standing over him, the perpetually amused look gone from his eyes.

Daniel and Jess had ridden in with him, but they sat their horses and waited while Rusty approached Wade.

"Boss, you all right?" Rusty asked and Wade grimly nodded. "Well, what some people'll do to get a pretty girl's attention," he then added, looking at Ada.

"Yeah," was all Wade could say.

Rusty nodded to Daniel and Jess and without a word, they rode away, splitting up, each going in a different direction in search of any sign of the shooter.

Powder Keg was coming with the wagon and while they waited, Rusty pealed Wade's shirt back and examined the wound. The bullet had gone all the way through Wade's shoulder, from back to front, just missing the bone.

"Shot in the back," Rusty darkly stated. "He never saw it

comin'."

Ada felt a burning shame inside her. It was bad enough that Wade had been bushwhacked, but it was worse that he had been bushwhacked and shot from behind. No one in the country would condone such a thing.

Rusty was familiar with gunshot wounds and Ada watched as he skillfully went to work on Wade. She didn't like the look of the wound or the smell of Wade's blood and after a few minutes, she got up and walked away. The scent followed her because her hands were covered with his blood. It had dried and it felt tight on her skin. She looked down at it, thinking that his blood was on her hands in more ways than one. She was probably to blame for all this and if he died, it would be her fault. She looked over her shoulder and watched Rusty from a distance and then she slowly walked to the edge of the spring and washed her hands. She could still smell the blood and soberly she looked down at her blouse and her skirt. There was blood on them, too. It made her feel a little sick, but she didn't want anyone to know so she stood up and walked away from the pool, still keeping her distance from Rusty and Wade.

It seemed like a very long time before the wagon arrived. Jim was riding on the seat beside Powder Keg, but Pat and Cody were on horseback, riding beside the wagon. They all jumped to the ground and rushed to Wade.

"He's alive," Rusty said as they gathered around. "It was a low caliber gun that shot him—maybe a twenty-two. That's prob'ly why he ain't dead right now." He casually looked around, but there was nothing casual about his thoughts. "He's lost a lot of blood, but the bullet didn't break any bones. Let's get him to the wagon."

They helped Wade to his feet and he walked to the wagon. Ada watched him from her position a few yards away. He was being supported, but he did it on his own and she was glad. The last thing she wanted was for Logan to murder him.

Daniel and Jess rode back into the clearing just then and Rusty walked to where they sat on their horses.

"What d' ya' find?" he asked.

"The fence's been cut," Jess said. "but whoever did this is long gone."

"I figured as much," Rusty said. His eyes wandered over to Ada and she looked away, unable to meet his gaze.

"How's the boss?" Jess asked and Rusty's eyes swung back to them.

"He'll make it. He was lucky."

"Rusty!" Jim called out. "Wade wants to talk to you."

Rusty walked back to the wagon and looked into the bed where Wade was lying.

"Is Ada still here?" he hoarsely asked, his strength fading.

"Yeah. She's here," he said.

"Tell her . . . thank you—and . . . thank the twins . . . too." He paused, getting his strength and then he added. "I don't know . . . what I'd do . . . without you."

Rusty nodded. "Git 'im home," he said as he stepped back and Powder Keg started the horse to moving. Everyone fell in beside the wagon except Rusty. He stayed behind and watched as they rode away, and then he turned his attention to Ada.

The twins had joined her and they were standing together under the live oak tree, solemnly watching the wagon as it rolled away. Rusty gave her a serious study, and then he walked toward her, wasting no time, but moving with quick, sure steps.

"The boss said to tell ya'll 'thanks'. He's gonna be alright, you know."

"That's good," Ada said, but her worried expression didn't change.

"Who did it, Ada?" Rusty asked.

It was curious that Ada had not noticed the fact that Rusty was armed to the teeth. He was wearing two pistols in tied down holsters, but they looked so natural on him that she had simply overlooked them. She noticed now, and the significance of it was not lost on her.

"I didn't see anyone," she said and Rusty's eyes probed her with such intensity that she had to look away.

"What about you?" he asked the twins and they both shook their heads.

"We heard the shot," Paul said, "an' we come arunnin', but whoever done it was nowhere to be seen."

"Where'd the shot come from?"

"Don't know, but I figure, over there," Paul answered, pointing a bony finger toward the stand of palm trees on the far side of the spring. "Honest, we didn't see nuthin'."

Rusty nodded. "Okay," he said and he even managed a smile for the boys, but when he turned back to Ada, the smile vanished. Curiously, though, the quizzical look was back in his eyes.

The boys ran toward the spring, leaving Ada alone with Rusty and as soon as they were far enough away not to hear, she began talking.

"You think it was Logan, don't you?" she said.

"Yeah," he honestly answered. "I do, but I can't help but wonder exactly what was goin' on here today. Did Logan catch you and Wade together?"

"No!" she said with such force that Rusty was inclined to believe her. "It wasn't like that. I came lookin' for the boys. I had no idea Wade was here."

"An' Logan didn't just happen along and get the wrong idea?"

"No. I never saw Logan. There was nothin' to see anyway," she indignantly added, but then she remembered that had Logan been spying on her, it could have been easy to misinterpret the exchange between her and Wade. Had not Wade snatched her up in his bare arms and when he had turned her loose, had they not laughed like old friends? Well, Rusty didn't need to know all that, she told herself. What was done, was done, and she would confront Logan on her own about it. If Rusty went after him, he would kill him, and in Ada's opinion, there had been enough bloodshed for one day.

"I'm goin' home," she announced. "I'm sorry about Wade—honest, I am, but I don't know any more than you do."

"That's okay," he said. "I'll find out. I'm pretty good at readin' sign. I'll be readin' this sign and if it leads to Logan, well, Wade'll be the last man he ever bushwhacks."

Chapter Seventeen

Ada followed the path back to the house and she was not at all surprised when she saw Logan sitting on the porch talking to her dad. His head turned when he saw her and even from that distance, she could see a strange light in his eyes.

He did it, she said to herself, and now he's proud that he did. She immediately turned and began walking in the opposite direction.

Logan was quick to follow her. "What's the idee?" he said as he caught up with her, stopping her with a rough hand on her arm. "Where've you been?"

"You know perfectly well where I've been," she snapped.

"Yeah, an' I know what you were doin', too."

Ada caught her breath. "No, you only *think* you know what I was doin'."

"Then tell me I'm wrong, an' make it good an' convincin'."

"Of course, you're wrong, an' now if Wade Thornton dies, you'll hang for murder."

Logan suddenly snatched her to him, jerking her up so roughly that her feet almost left the ground.

"So, you were with him. I knew it!"

"Let me go!" she demanded, wrestling out of his grip. "It was a fool thing to do, Logan, an' you're luckier than you know."

His brow creased and his eyes squinted more than usual as he looked at her. "What're you talkin' about?"

"He ain't dead, Logan. I know you think you got him, but luckily, he ain't dead."

For the first time, Logan noticed Ada's dress, all dark with Wade's blood and he took a step back.

"Someone got 'im, then," he said in a musing sort of way. He seemed thoughtful, but not at all upset. "What? They shot 'im?"

Ada was about to tell Logan that he knew perfectly good and well that Wade had been shot when she realized that he appeared to be genuinely surprised. Could it be that Logan had not shot Wade, after all? Ada didn't believe it.

"It was a cowardly thing to do," she said, "shootin' him in the back."

"Yeah, well, I guess whoever done it figured you get a snake anyway you can."

"He isn't a snake," Ada said in Wade's defense. "He's a man, an' you can bet, the law'll be called in on this. Someone's gonna be in a lot of trouble."

"Well, I didn't do it," Logan said. "You can be sure, if I'd 've done it, he'd be dead right now."

Ada was inclined to believe him, but then, how many times had she been fooled by Logan? Looking back, she could see how easily he had manipulated her. She had been led like a child, and now she wondered how she could have been so blind.

In spite of all this, Ada was concerned for Logan. Whether he had shot Wade or not was no longer the issue. The trouble now was that Rusty believed he had, and he would be looking for Logan with blood in his eyes.

"You've started somethin', Logan," she said.

"No, you've started somethin'," he angrily said. "If you'd 've just left that Yankee alone."

"How many times do I have to tell ya', there's nothin' goin' on between me and Wade?"

"I saw 'im huggin' ya'. He wasn't even dressed, Ada, an' you were lettin' 'im make love to you."

"So, you were there! I knew it. I also knew you'd misunderstand what happened. He thought I was one of the twins, an' if you'll think about it, you'll remember that he turned me loose the minute he saw his mistake."

"Well, I reckon a poor excuse 's better'n no excuse atall."

"I'm not makin' excuses. I'm tellin' ya' what happened."

She turned away, but when she realized how easily he had turned the subject to make it work to his advantage, she turned back to him.

"So, that's why you shot 'im."

"I toldja, I didn't shoot 'im. But I wish I had."

"I don't believe you. You were there. You had the opportunity."

"Yeah, well, when I saw 'im huggin' ya', I left. I'll admit, I had murder on my mind. I wish now, I'd 've done it."

"Then who did shoot him?" she asked and a thoughtful look crossed Logan's face.

"Now, that is a question. I'd be right int'rested in meetin' that guy."

He squinted deeply as he looked into the distance, mulling over the thought.

"So, he ain't dead, you say?" Logan suddenly asked.

"No, an' Rusty says he won't die."

"Ya' never c'n tell about these things," Logan said. "What with blood pois'nin' an' all. He might still croak."

A month ago, Ada might have been happy with that thought, but today it left her strangely sober.

"I know you want him dead, Logan, but you better pray he lives, 'cause ever'one'll think you did it."

He smiled, genuinely liking the idea.

"An' Rusty all but promised to kill the man who did this," she added, and the smile left Logan's face in a flash.

"Yeah? Well, it's too bad somebody didn't bushwhack that gunslinger while they were at it. Me 'n him 're gonna meet one day anyway, you can bet."

That was what Ada was thinking, too, and unfortunately, she was afraid Logan wouldn't have a chance—not against that deadly and confident man. She remembered the look in Rusty's eyes and she shuddered with a grim premonition.

No, Logan would not have a chance.

Chapter Eighteen

Wade was having difficulty sleeping. It was not only that his shoulder was hurting, but his whole body seemed to ache, too. He also had a headache, and then, Powder Keg's continual snoring would have made it difficult for the most somnolent of men to sleep.

The house was ready for Angela so Wade had taken a bunk in the bunkhouse. He had hired Della to come and prepare everything for his arriving guests and she had done a marvelous job. She was a local black woman who had come highly recommended and her accolades had not been exaggerated. She was likable and efficient and Wade had been so impressed, he had hired her on for the duration of Angela's and the Major's stay. Wade wouldn't let them put him in the house even when they insisted.

Now, he asked himself about the wisdom of that decision. He tried to roll over, but he couldn't without a sharp pain taking his breath away. He sighed and lay still, listening to the sawing repetition of Powder Keg's snore.

Somehow, Wade managed to fall asleep and it was in the early hours of the morning that he awoke to a silent room. He had become accustomed to Powder Keg's snore and when it abruptly stopped, Wade had come wide awake. The stillness in the room was odd after the night of constant noise. It made

Wade smile into the darkness.

But just as quickly, the smile left his face. Wade heard something else, something far away and so faint that he was not sure at first that he had heard anything. He listened, straining his ears for the sound, and again he heard it, only a little louder now—singing in the night and the sound of shovels digging in the ground.

The next morning, he was not sure if he had heard anything or if he had only been dreaming, but the incident left him a little bit unnerved, just the same. The others had talked about hearing similar sounds in the night, but this was a first for Wade, and strangely, he didn't think it was Logan who was doing it.

Rusty came in and he gave Wade a wide grin as he looked down at him.

"You haven't left yet?" Wade asked, referring to the trip to the depot to pick up Angela and the Major.

"I'm just leavin'," he said. "I wanted to check on you before I left."

"I'm still here," Wade said. "And, thanks, Rusty. You know, I'm depending on you to keep things going for me."

"I'll do it," he said without hesitation. "I'll take care of everything," he added with a soberness that quickly turned to humor. "Includin' yore girl. I'll take real good care of her."

But Rusty's boast took on a whole new meaning when he saw Angela step down from the train. Something happened to him in that moment that had never happened before. He stared in wonder and then in disbelief. Wade's fiancée was the girl of his dreams. He had never been so smitten or so disappointed. The elation drained out of him as the realization of her untouchable reality grew. Rusty was suddenly a very miserable man.

He hesitated, standing back and watching, unsure of himself and reluctant to meet her, but finally, he lowered his head and marched across the open yard to greet them.

"I'm Rusty," he said. "Wade's been hurt and he sent me to pick ya'll up."

Oh, my!" Angela exclaimed and even her voice sent vibrations through Rusty. "Is he all right? What happened?"

"Yes, what has happened?" the major asked.

"He's been shot—bushwhacked," Rusty mercilessly said and Angela's face went pale. She quickly recovered and Rusty saw that she had strength as well as beauty. He was impressed.

"Let's hurry," she said and Rusty was only too ready to comply. He found their bags and loaded them in the wagon and when he was finished, he climbed onto the seat beside Angela. She was waiting there for him, poised with great dignity on the humble wagon seat, and the major was sitting in the back, unruffled by the seating arrangements. He had traveled in a lot worse conditions.

She was more practical than she looked and her personality was very pleasing. Rusty had vaguely hoped that he would find a major character flaw in her that would turn his feelings against her, but by the time they reached the ranch, what had not already been accomplished was completely fulfilled by her charms. He hated himself and he felt miserable and he decided that as soon as he could, he was leaving, going back to Texas where he would never see Angela Wright again, but then, he would look at her and he felt like a man dying of thirst.

Late that evening Wade sent for Rusty. He reluctantly answered that summons, his guilty conscious filling him with dread. He told himself that if he was an honorable man, he would saddle up and ride out without explanation or goodbyes, but at the same time, he felt an obligation that made him uncomfortable about running away. He had almost convinced himself that leaving was in everyone's best interest, however, by the time he arrived at Wade's bedside, but when he looked at Wade, he almost lost his courage.

Tonight, Wade didn't look so well. He seemed lethargic and Rusty wondered how a man could look so depressed with a girl like Angela at his side. They had moved Powder Keg to the room where Daniel and Jess were bunked so she had been there alone with Wade all afternoon, sitting by his bed. She had left only moments before, and then only at Wade's insistence. Guiltily, Rusty feared that Wade could read his mind and he looked away, unable to look into Wade's eyes.

"Boss, I gotta go," he suddenly said. "I gotta leave—go back to Texas, and I gotta do it tomorrow."

Wade jerked with the force of Rusty's words, an uncontrollable groan being the result of the sudden movement.

"Why? What's happened?"

Rusty didn't immediately answer. What did he say in response to a question like that? Did he tell Wade he was in love with his fiancée? Did he admit he was a lousy rat for

164

wanting his best friend's girl?

"I just gotta go—that's all, and you gotta let me."

Wade sighed. "I need you," he simply said and Rusty wilted under the burden of his responsibility. "I can't let you go. It's selfish, I know, but honest to God, I don't know what I'd do if you left."

"You've got Jim and Powder Keg," Rusty pointed out, "and Jess Larkin has shown signs of bein' a top notch hand. You don't need me."

Wade turned his dark eyes to Rusty. "It's Angela," he said, and Rusty stiffened with the guilt of his shame. "I don't trust the others, but I trust you. You gotta stay and take care of her until I'm able."

Rusty had never felt lower in his life. He stared down at Wade and for just a moment, he felt sorry for Wade in his blind, innocent faith. Could he not see that Rusty was the very one who could not be trusted? Could he not see that he was the one who would betray him at the first opportunity? But then, that was not necessarily true. Angela would have to be agreeable for Rusty to actually betray Wade, and Rusty knew she would never give him a second look. It gave him hope that he could fulfill his duty to Wade, but then he thought about Angela and he just wanted to die.

"You hit your head pretty hard when you fell," Rusty managed to say. "An' you ain't thinkin' clear."

"I'm thinking very clearly," Wade assured him.

Rusty stood in silence for only a moment and then he nodded in resignation, accepting his responsibility. "Okay, but just remember, I asked you to let me go. Don't forget that."

He abruptly turned on his heels and left the room, and Wade looked after him wondering what that was all about. Rusty had been acting peculiar for some time, and Wade was sure it had something to do with the strange and unexplainable things that had been going on around here. Rusty seemed to be taking it seriously and Wade could only wonder what had happened to make him so uneasy.

Rusty's mood prompted Wade to think about his dream the night before. He could not be sure if it was a dream or if he had actually heard something, but at the thought, he could almost understand Rusty's behavior. There was definitely something odd going on and Wade decided that as soon as he was able, he was going to find out what it was.

It was days before Wade was able to get up. Angela came every day and sat beside his bed and after a while, Wade became uncomfortable with the arrangement. He insisted Rusty take her for a ride and show her the countryside, but Rusty had flatly refused.

"I won't do it," he had said.

"Please, get her out of here," Wade had begged. "I know I'm asking a lot, but I understand Angela and I know she's only coming here out of obligation. It's really driving her crazy."

"It ain't right, me slackin' when the others 've gotta work."

"They'll understand and who cares if they don't. I'm the boss and I say, do it."

Rusty had lost the argument and he had taken Angela for the ride. The next day, she asked him to take her out again and

Rusty did, but he took a hard attitude toward her which instead of pushing her away, actually drew her to the challenge of making him like her. Little did she know that the challenge was won before it had begun, but Rusty gave no indication that he even liked her, much less that he was dying of love for her.

Every day, she asked him to go riding with her, and every day, he sullenly did his duty. After a week, her curiosity had gotten the better of her and she pulled up beside him and stopped her horse.

"Why don't you like me?" she bluntly asked and Rusty gave her his most severe expression.

"I like you fine," he answered in a noncommittal tone.

"Then why are you so . . . so . . . obtuse?" she asked.

He turned his head slowly, the quizzical look suddenly back in his eyes, and a faint smile on his lips. "Obtuse?" he asked, wondering if she really thought he understood the meaning of the word. He didn't—not exactly, anyway. He knew it didn't mean anything complimentary and that was enough. "You don't really want an answer to that question, do you?"

"I'm afraid, I do," she said, her tone becoming both serious and anxious. "Everyone has been so friendly, but you've been almost hostile. Have I done something wrong? Have I upset you in some way?"

Rusty opened his mouth to promptly reply, but his thoughts were racing around in his head and he closed his mouth before he told her the truth. Yes, she had upset him, but not in the manner she supposed.

"What difference does it make?" he asked. "I'm just the

hired hand."

"It makes a great deal of difference," she answered.

She intended to question him further on the matter, but just then, several shots rang out, the sound coming from the direction of the ranch. Rusty turned with a start and Angela felt every muscle in her body go tense.

"What is it?" she anxiously asked.

"Come on!" was all Rusty answered and he took off for the ranch, Angela immediately following.

They flew into the ranch yard a few minutes later. Powder Keg, Wade, and the Major were all standing in the yard, rifles in their hands. Della was at the open door, looking out, and in the distance, the sound of a running horse was dying away.

Rusty slid to the ground in one easy movement and his horse walked on a few steps before stopping.

"What happened?" he asked.

Both Wade and Powder Keg gave him a sober look. "Some kid," Powder Keg answered. Wade looked too worn out to say anything. "He just opened fire on us and then took off."

"I'll go after 'im," Rusty said, but Wade stopped him.

"No. Let him go."

"Let 'im go? I can catch 'im. We c'n see who it was, at least."

"No," Wade again said. "I know who it was." The rifle was suddenly too heavy in his hands. He leaned it against the porch post and then he sat down. He hated the weakness in him.

"Who was it?" Rusty immediately asked.

"Bud Macon's boy."

"Cory? I thought he liked you."

Wade gave a weary shrug. "Me too."

Rusty looked down the road as he pondered the significance of this turn of events. He heard Angela's saddle creak as she stepped down from the horse and he quickly turned and looked at her.

Rusty had momentarily forgotten about her, but when she walked to Wade and put a comforting arm around his shoulders, Rusty was one hundred percent aware of her again. He clenched his teeth and walked away, taking the two horses with him.

Angela helped Wade to his feet and then she followed him into the room where he was bunked.

"How are you today?" she asked and he heaved a great sigh.

"Better. I just tire out so easily," he said. He gave her a thoughtful look and then he shook his head. "This isn't exactly what I was hoping for while you were here."

She smiled and her eyes lit up. She had small eyes in a face that was more round than oval and Wade caught himself comparing her to Ada without even realizing what he was doing. The two girls could not have been more different. Angela was blonde and very fair with small blue eyes and cheeks as rosy as a cherub's. She was solidly built and rounded in all the right places and she laughed with quiet dignity, her smiles all well-rehearsed with the practiced ease of a debutante. Ada, on the other hand, had dark hair and blue eyes that were so large, a man could lose himself in them. Her face was narrow and oval, and tanned from the Florida sun until no girlish blush colored her cheeks. Her lips were full with natural tones of burgundy that defined their lovely outline, and she was small, but well-shaped, slender, but not skinny and when she laughed, there was no hint of insincerity. Wade had seen those eyes dance with amusement, and just like before, he imagined her as some untamed creature, exotic as a barefoot gypsy girl, but as pure as the spring she loved.

With a start, he realized his thoughts and he snapped out of his reverie.

"You were a million miles away there for a minute," Angela said.

No, only a couple of miles, Wade guiltily thought. He repositioned himself and leaned his head back. He was being a fool and he knew it.

That was when he decided to go back to work. He was going to do it even if he didn't feel like it, but when he walked outside and announced to Jim and Powder Keg his intentions, they both sent him back to the bunk house with Della on his heels to make sure he didn't go astray.

"Dey's right," she told him as he complained to her. "My man knows des t'ings. He worked f'r ol' Doc Weaver f'r more years dan I cares to count. He sez y'u'll be outta work f'r anoder week, at least."

"I'll go out of my mind," Wade declared, but Della shook her head.

"Rest . . . sleep . . . an' stop yore worryin'. Tain't gonna do no good no how."

"I know, but I've got to have something to do. I've never been idle a day in my life."

"Enjoy it!" she said as she backed out the door.

Wade watched her and once the door was closed and she was beyond knowing what he was doing, he picked up a pillow and threw it across the room. He considered something heavier, but he just wasn't up to it.

Logan had been keeping a low profile and everyone suspected it was because he had shot Wade, but one evening just as the men were picking up their gear to return to the ranch, Logan rode up to the fence and stopped about twenty feet away.

Wade's crew looked up in astonishment and then with suspicion. What was he doing here? Jess quickly stepped forward and asked him.

"Hey, Logan," he said, "What y'u doin'?"

"Is Rusty here?" Logan asked and Jess shook his head.

"Naw. He's back at the ranch. Whatcha want?"

Logan stepped down from his horse and every man in Wade's crew tensed in anticipation.

"I ain't here for trouble," Logan said when he saw their caution. "I just wanna ask ya'll somethin'."

"What is it?" Cody bluntly asked.

"Have ya'll seen anything strange around here lately?"

A few men snickered, but most of them remained sober. Daniel Larkin threw down the posthole diggers that were in his hands and he laughed aloud.

"No, cain't say that we have," Cody replied. "What're you

gettin' at?"

"I'm serious," Logan said. "I think there's somebody hidin' out in these woods. I've seen a few things that gives me the clue."

"Like who?" Cody asked.

"A man in a blue suit—or uniform."

"Now, don't start that nonsense," one of the fence builders said. "We've all heard that story. You cain't scare us with that."

"I'm tellin' y'u, I've seen something and I'm tellin' y'u honestly, I didn't shoot Wade Thornton, but I think this man did."

There was silence among Wade's crew. No one said a word, but all of them stared with hard eyes at Logan.

"I checked out where Wade was shot," Logan went on when no one said anything. "Someone stood in the corner of that thicket behind the palm trees and after he shot Wade, he walked to the drop off to Cedar Branch and simply disappeared."

"Maybe he jumped to the bottom," someone suggested, but Logan shook his head.

"I looked. There ain't no sign that anyone's been there."

"So, you're sayin', a ghost shot the boss."

Logan didn't reply. He looked at the unyielding faces and smiled derisively. "No, but I think there's a canny and dangerous man loose in these woods. I don't know why I bothered t' tell ya'll, though."

He immediately turned around and took up the horses's reins. He stepped into the saddle and pulled the horse around, leaving without another word. Everyone watched him in silence until Cody said something.

"Now, what d' ya'll make of that?" he asked.

"Tryin' to turn the blame in a direction away from hisself," Pete said.

"Yeah, well, I'd agree with ya' if I hadn't seen some things myself," Cody said. He turned and looked at the men around him. "Ya'll ain't seen nothin'? Am I the only one?"

No one answered, but they might as well have. Their expressions were all admissions that they had.

"I figure Logan shot the boss," Cody said, "but I also think that what he said oughtta be looked into. There just might be some guy out here and he might warrant our attention."

"I'll go check out the stand o' palms," Jess suggested, "but with the rains, there prob'ly ain't nuthin' to see now."

Cody gave a slight shake of his head. "It might not hurt t' look, but I think you're right. You won't find anything."

"Let's just forget it," Pete said. He picked up the posthole diggers that Daniel had thrown down and he carried them to the wagon. It began the evening cleanup once more and the whole crew began moving. Pete and his two men climbed into the wagon and rode down the line to their camp, but the rest of them gathered up their horses and hit the trail for the ranch. They were only a mile away and it didn't take them long to arrive. They streamed into the ranch yard and went straight to the corral to strip their mounts.

Wade watched them from the porch of the bunk house and it didn't go unnoticed by him that they were all unusually grim.

At supper, they told him what had happened and Wade easily accepted the possibility. Having nothing to do but lie in bed, had given him plenty of time to think, and he had decided that he didn't want it to be Logan who had shot him. If Logan had shot him, then it could be that Ada had scouted things out and set the whole thing up. He moved restlessly, considering that the twins might be involved, as well, but then he remembered Ada's anxious voice and her struggle to keep him alive and he decided that she could not have had anything to do with it—unless it was not supposed to go as far as it had. Wade had considered the possibility that Ada had been sent there to set him up, not to be killed, but for some other purpose, but when Logan had seen them together, he had gotten so angry, he had simply shot Wade down.

If I'm gonna die for something like that, Wade grimly thought, *then, Lord, let me be guilty of it, at least.*

After supper, Wade walked outside with Angela and the Major. They sat together in the warm evening and listened to the Chuck-wills-widows as they sang their short and repetitive song into the night. The locals called them Whip-poor-wills, but, in reality, they were not. The distinctive *chuck* at the beginning of each verse was the give-away, but like everyone else, Wade had begun to call them by their local name.

"Listen to those Whip-poor-wills," he said. "There must be three or four of them out tonight."

"Three, I think," the Major agreed.

"I think they're awful," Angela said with a slight shudder. "They give me a strange feeling."

Wade didn't agree. He loved the sound of them even though their song was rather plaintive. It provoked a feeling of stillness in Wade, a calmness that was also reflective. He often sat and listened to them and his thoughts would wander into areas of his mind less explored and into things long ago and almost forgotten. He suddenly wondered if Ada liked the sound of the Whip-poor-wills and he decided that she did.

"They sound like lost souls," Angela went on to say. She stood up and walked to the edge of the porch and looked into the night. "Don't you get that feeling?"

The Major cleared his throat uneasily. "Now, Angela," he said. "Let's not get dramatic."

She laughed, a lovely, high-pitched sound that carried easily on the night air. "Dramatic? Yes, men always think women are acting when they get too honest with their thoughts." She turned to Wade and smiled demurely. "You've said the most tonight that you've said all day," she pointed out. "I'm glad. It isn't like you to be so quiet."

"Angela, he isn't fully recovered," her father scolded her. "You shouldn't needle him."

"Am I needling you, Wade?" she asked and he gave her a thoughtful look. "Or am I right? You've got something on your mind and I'll bet it has nothing to do with your injury."

"Good Lord, Angela," the major scoffed. "What in heaven's name are you doing?"

"I'm asking Wade what's on his mind, papa. We've known each other nearly all our lives and we understand each other, don't we, Wade?"

"I can't say that any man can fully understand a woman," Wade said with a wry smile.

"Now, don't try to redirect the conversation," she said. "What's on your mind today, Wade?"

"A lot of things," he honestly answered. "You've been there, too."

"Well, I should hope so," she said and she turned her back to the two men and looked across the yard, her eyes peering into the darkness of the surrounding woods. "I thought you had a plan, Wade. I thought you were going to come in here, make your fortune and then go home, a richer and happier man."

Wade stiffened and then he relaxed. Was she referring to the lost gold? Did she believe he had come here only to find it and then get out or was that a vague hope?

"It takes a while to make a fortune," he said, "and I don't think I'll get very rich on these few acres."

"You have five square miles of land," Angela pointed out. "That's a lot of land."

The major cleared his throat again. He had been puffing on his pipe, but now it was clenched between his teeth, totally forgotten. He opened his mouth to speak, quickly catching it up as it dropped.

"It's true," the major said as he brushed at his clothes. "What are your plans?"

Wade had wanted cattle, and he still planned to have them, but there were so many possibilities for making a living on this property that he had given thought to branching out into many different ventures. There were stands of Yellow Pine all over the place and many of them had been slashed for turpentine by the locals. It was a profitable crop and only one of the things Wade planned to do. He told the major that and both he and Angela looked at Wade with blank stares.

"What about me?" Angela finally asked and Wade looked up at her. "What are your plans where I'm concerned?"

The major nervously cleared his throat again and then he carefully replaced the pipe between his teeth.

"Are you ready to get married?" Wade asked. "Or do you want to wait until things aren't so primitive around here?"

"It'll always be primitive around here," she said, scanning the place with solemnness. "I had no idea. I thought it would be like Green Cove Springs or Palatka. I don't know why I didn't understand that it would be like this."

"So, what are you saying?" Wade asked. The Major shifted nervously in his chair and then he stood up.

"This isn't right," he harshly said. "This should be discussed in private. I'll go and let you two talk."

"Oh, papa, he doesn't care if you hear—and neither do I."

"He's right, Angela," Wade corrected her. "We should talk about this privately."

"I'll go," the Major said and without waiting for a reply, he walked away. No one said anything until the door closed behind him and then Angela turned again to Wade.

"Well?" she said. "We're alone. Do you think I'll speak any more freely with papa gone?"

"Maybe not," Wade said, "but he was right to go."

"You men! Well, let's hash it out," she said. "I'll tell you what I'm thinking and then you do the same. It's time we were honest with each other."

Wade was not so sure about that, and besides, he didn't really know what he thought or felt at the moment. Logic told him to marry Angela, but for some reason, Wade had begun to think that in time they would both live to regret it.

"I know why you came here, Wade," she began. "I know what was on your mind and that's why I suggested you buy this property, but I never intended for you to come here and stay. Just like the man you are, though, you've fallen in love with this God forsaken place. You don't ever plan to leave, do you?"

"No," he answered.

"Well, there it is." She slapped at a mosquito and then she looked at her hand as if the slap had offended her. "I hate it here, Wade," she said. "I want you to do what you originally planned to do and go home. We'll get married then."

Wade hesitated before speaking, his heart pounding with a steady, but anxious beat. It was decision time and his whole life would be affected by the choice he now made.

"I came here to make a place for myself—and for my wife," he said. "I thought you knew that."

"You know what I thought," she insisted. "Your family has always bowed under the burden of your father's defeat. This was your chance to redeem your father and give him peace before he died. Isn't that what you've always been thinking— that if you had the chance, you'd fulfill your father's mission?"

"When I was younger, maybe."

"Oh, Wade, can't you see the hand of fate in all of this?"

She looked around as if sizing up the whole world. "This was destiny at work. I mean, what a coincidence that this land would suddenly become available and that your father would suddenly have the money to give you an early inheritance. Is it a coincidence? Ask yourself, Wade, and then consider how many times you've asked God to give you this opportunity. He's doing it. Don't take it lightly."

"Is that it?" he said, smiling wryly. He could see what she was doing and he knew that she would always have to have her way. If he gave into her now, he would be giving into her the rest of his life. "If I agree to do as you say, will you agree to go ahead and get married?" he asked, testing his theory.

"I can't say that I will," she said. "I don't trust you to follow through—oh, don't look so crestfallen. I know you would intend to follow through, but I also know that one thing often leads to another and I'll be stuck here until God only knows when. No, Wade. Have your adventure—fulfill your responsibility—and then return home. We'll get married then, if you still want to."

"We aren't getting any younger, Angela," he said and she made a scoffing sound of derision.

"Oh, pooh!" she said. "How old do you think I am? You talk as if I'm turning thirty next week."

Next week? Wade suddenly remembered that she would be having a birthday the next week, but no, she wouldn't be turning thirty. Wade was twenty-two years old and she was a year younger than he. She would be turning twenty-one.

"I had forgotten," he admitted. "Your birthday is next week. Time sure flies."

"I want a party, too," she said, her tone becoming light and pleasing again. "Can we have a party, Wade? I'd love to have a party!"

Wade nodded. "You can have a party, but I can't vouch for who'll come. It may just be me and my outfit."

"Who cares?" she flippantly said. "We'll invite everyone and if they don't come, well, it'll be their loss."

"Okay, Angela," Wade said. "We'll have a party." He stood up and walked to the edge of the porch where she was standing. She looked up at him with eyes as calculating as those of a fox.

"Do you want to kiss me, Wade?" she coyly asked.

He did. What man wouldn't want to kiss a girl like Angela? But he hesitated, thinking that she was toying with him, playing him as only she could do. She had always used her femininity as a tool—or a weapon. Now was no different. He knew it, but when she lightly touched him and then firmly gripped his arm with a beckoning hand, he didn't care. He pulled her to him and kissed her and he didn't stop even when in his mind she gradually changed and became someone else. It was suddenly Ada he was kissing, but Angela never suspected. Her only thoughts were that Wade had never kissed her with such enthusiasm and passion. It brought a smile of satisfaction to her face. Little did she know, it had nothing to do with her control over him, but actually, it was the very lack of it. Nevertheless, she hummed softly to herself as she returned to the house and prepared for bed. She was good at this sort of game, and she could not imagine that Wade was not totally subdued.

Wade, on the other hand, was beginning to realize what had just happened. He stood alone on the porch and looked across the yard at the light that was burning in the window where Angela was staying. This was not right. He had just pretended that Ada was in his arms and that she was the girl who was returning his kisses instead of Angela.

"You're a crazy man," he told himself. "A crazy and sick man." And with that, he stomped off the porch and went to the empty room where he was bunked.

Not surprisingly, the story of the hidden gold was on his mind. He looked around the empty room and he casually wondered what he should do next. That gold story had caused more trouble than it was worth, and it was worth fifty or sixty thousand dollars.

"That's a lot of trouble," Wade mused to himself. He fell onto his bunk and folded his arms behind his head and then he stared up at the ceiling. It was a lot of trouble and if the truth be known, he was about to step right into the middle of it.

Chapter Nineteen

"So, the Yankee's havin' a party," Fred said. "He's posted invitations all over the place. I picked this'un up at Mason's." He grinned sheepishly at Ada. "It's for his fiancée. He's wantin' everyone t' meet 'er."

"I won't be goin'," Ada frankly stated.

"Ain'tcha curious? I thought women fo'k was always curious about such things."

"Obviously not as much as you men," Ada pointed out as she set a cup of coffee on the table in front of him.

"Maybe so. I'm goin' and so's your ma. I'm right curious as to what he's done to that place. I hear he's been buildin', as busy as a beaver."

Ada could have told him a few things, but she wisely kept her mouth shut. She was eighteen years old, but she didn't put it past her father to tan her hide if he found out she had gone to Wade's place.

"I'm surprised at you," Ada said. "Don't encourage 'im and maybe he'll go away."

"Is that what you really want, Ada?" he asked. The tone of his voice had changed and Ada looked down at him, momentarily startled by the vague implication to which he seemed to be hinting.

"I want peace in this community again," she said as she

pulled off her apron. "An' we'll never have it as long as the war's still on."

She threw the apron down and stomped out of the room, more afraid than angry. She studied her memories and wondered if she had done something that had given herself away. Wade had been incessantly on her mind and her feelings had softened toward him, but then suddenly and quite unexpectedly, a fiancée had turned up. Ada didn't know why that surprised her, but it did. He was a handsome man and could have had the attentions of nearly any girl in the community, but none of them had been of interest to him. Ada had assumed it was because he didn't think any of them were good enough for him, and she still figured that was part of it, but a girl waiting to marry him seemed to explain everything.

It was honorable and Ada admired him for it, but then, she was thinking differently about him these days. Ever since the day he had been shot, she had had softer, kinder thoughts where he was concerned. It was not the injury that had brought this about, but the boyish nature she had seen in him that day, the one that had amused her to the point of outright laughter.

She walked outside and stood on the porch, looking down the road at nothing at all. Everyone was curious about Wade Thornton's place so he would have no trouble getting guests for his party. It was his girlfriend's birthday, Ada had been told, and he was opening up his new barn for the festivities. For no explainable reason, the whole thing made Ada sad.

Paul and Silas ran around the corner of the house and passed Ada, their old yellow dog, Skippy, following along behind them. They ran to the back gate and stopped there, talking about something that had them both engrossed.

"They're always up to somethin'," Ada said aloud. "I wonder what it is now."

She stepped off the porch and walked toward them. The sun was bright and very hot, but a breeze was blowing softly around Ada with cooling effect. She pushed a stray strand of hair away from her face and caught up with the boys just before they opened the gate and went out.

"What's goin' on?" she asked in a genial tone.

"Nuthin'," Paul quickly answered.

"We're busy right now," Silas said. "We gotta go."

Ada smiled. "Busy at what? Makin' trouble?"

"Ah, no, Ada," Paul moaned. "We don't make trouble. It just seems to come t' us."

"I know the feelin'," she admitted. She leaned back against the fence post and sighed heavily.

Paul gave her a sly look. "Y' know, Ada, you got no reason t' feel sad about Wade's party."

Ada flashed him a surprised look that quickly turned dark. "I could care less about Wade Thornton's party," she quipped. "An' I won't be goin'."

"You oughta," Paul said.

"Well, maybe I would if I had somethin' to wear," she admitted.

"You'll outshine ever' other girl even in yore ever' day clothes," Paul said.

"Yeah," Silas added, "You're a whole lot purtier than that

Yankee girl, anyway."

Ada straightened up, her curiosity outweighing her discretion. "Have you seen 'er?"

"Yeah, we seen 'er," Silas said in a conspiratorial whisper.

"What is she like?" Ada asked.

"She ain't so awful purty," Paul said, "but she is good lookin'."

"What about her clothes? Does she wear fine clothes?"

"She does," they both admitted, their tones becoming sorrowful. They knew it was a losing battle where women were concerned. Women put stock in clothes and fashion and Ada would feel awkward in her handmade clothes even if they were new—and they weren't. Ada hadn't had a new dress in more than a year. "But I'm tellin' ya', Ada," Paul went on to say, "Wade don't care about that."

"I don't care what Wade Thornton cares about," she said, pushing out her bottom lip in a little moue. "If I went, it'd only be 'cause I was curious—same as ever'one else."

"Well, you oughta go," Paul reiterated.

"No," Ada said. She leaned her shoulder against the post again. "Logan won't go and I'd feel lonesome."

Paul made a derisive sound in his throat that showed his contempt. "You gotta let go o' Logan," he said.

"Why do you always say things like that?" she asked.

"'Cause it's true. He ain't no good."

"He's a good man," she said, coming to his defense. "You just don't understand him."

The twins gave Ada their wise, but innocent looks. "We

understand 'im better'n you."

"Ada!" her mother called from the house. "I think I see a shower comin'. You better git the clothes off the line."

She was right. The sun was shining brightly, but across the field, a gray wall of rain was pulling a curtain toward them. Ada picked up her skirt and ran across the yard. She was just pulling down the last sheet when she felt the breath of cool air that preceded the shower. It swept past her, cooling her hot face and then she was sprinting for the porch, reaching it just as the rain came thundering down.

"Ha!" She jubilantly exclaimed. "Beat you again!"

Now, she thought, if only she could beat her troubles as easily. Her exuberance was suddenly gone.

What she'd give right now for a new dress!

Chapter Twenty

Wade was dressed in his finest suit. He had given his attire a lot of thought and he wanted to look his best for the guests at Angela's party.

He had feared no one would come, but repeatedly, he had had positive responses to the flyers he had put out. At church on Sunday, almost everyone there told him they would be coming, including the preacher.

The Tanners were coming, too. Wade brushed at an imaginary spot and then nervously shifted inside his coat. He wondered what Ada would think and then he angrily slapped at his pants, telling himself that he didn't care.

It wouldn't be so hard to get Ada out of his mind if he and Angela were not having so much trouble. She was constantly nagging him and that afternoon, they had had an out and out argument. Wade could not understand why she didn't just go back to New Hampshire, but then, at the same time, he thought that it would be best to get this over with now. She and her father coming here may have been the hand of fate dealing another hand in Wade's future, and Wade could see that Angela was not figuring too largely in that future. Perhaps the longer she stayed, the easier it would be for both of them in the end, because Wade could see the end was coming.

He walked out of the bunkhouse and onto the porch. The lights were burning brightly in the barn and he could hear the hilarious laughter of his outfit. They were already in the spirit of the occasion. Wade rolled his shoulders as if bolstering his courage and then he walked with steady, deliberate steps across the yard to the barn.

Angela had spent all day decorating the barn and Wade had to admit, it looked nice. The barn was the largest building on his property and it had a huge open space in the center. The boys had made tables, setting up boards on sawhorses and Angela and Della had worked for more than an hour just on the appearance of them.

Bart and Cody were cooking a pig in an open pit behind the barn and Wade could smell the aroma. It made his stomach growl and he realized that he had not eaten since breakfast. Della walked through with a large bowl of beans and Wade looked longingly at them as she passed him.

"Howdy, Mistah Wade," she said with a grin. "Y'u shore look nice t'night."

"Thank you," Wade said. "And thanks for all your help. I don't know what I'd have done without you."

"Oh, I don't minds," she said. She set the bowl down and turned to leave. "Didja meets m' boy t'day, Mistah Wade? He been he'pin' out—gittin' ready fo de party, y'u knows."

"I did. He seems like a nice young man."

"He's a ha'd worker, Mistah Wade, an' he c'u'd use de work."

Wade quickly considered that. He had no problem with hiring a black man, but he wondered how his crew would take it.

"Tell him to come around tomorrow and talk to me. I'll see what I can do."

"Thank ya', Mistah Wade. I'll do dat."

She walked out and Wade turned to watch her. His eyes caught movement on the road. The musicians were arriving.

There was a steady stream after that. It was almost as if everyone had gotten together at a predetermined location and had come in tandem. The yard was soon full of horses and buggies and people on foot. Walking was a well-used mode of travel in this area and many of the guests came that way. Wade watched them, feeling an anxiety growing in him all the while.

Angela appeared with the arrival of the first guest and, as always, she was the perfect hostess. She welcomed everyone with a graciousness that was easy and natural and immediately, she was well-liked, but Angela was not the main attraction to most of these people, although she ranked high on their curiosity scale. Wade Thornton's ranch was what they had come to see. They were curious about the gold and came looking around as if they expected to see the treasure on display. Their eyes were large and searching and you could see they were disappointed at the fact that they saw no sign of Captain Thornton's gold.

Wade stood beside Angela and no one would have guessed that just hours before, the two of them had had a grievous disagreement. Wade hid his feelings well, but once the party was going and everyone had been properly greeted, Wade left her side. He walked around the room, stopping often to talk with his neighbors, but all the while, he was looking, waiting for something, and when the Tanners walked through the wide open doorway, he knew what it was.

They were here, at last, but just as he caught sight of them, Cody stepped between Wade and the doorway and he lost them.

"The pork's ready," he said.

"Will you tell Angela?" Wade asked, wisely leaving all the arrangements to her. Cody moved away, but Wade could not see the Tanners anymore. He looked around and all the time, he was thinking about something that had been on his mind for days.

Angela was right about one thing, at least. Wade had come to Florida with one thing in particular on his mind. The trouble was, he needed to go to the Tanner's house and have time to follow some clues in order to fulfill his mission. It had not been possible. There had always been someone there. No matter how many times he had checked, he had found someone at home, and after the scare he had had when he had come suddenly upon Ada that afternoon, a few months before, he had not been anxious to go back.

Tonight, though, they were here. If he could just slip away, he could safely go there again. He looked around as if prompted by his own thoughts. Fred Tanner was standing with John Harris and Mrs. Tanner was fussing over one of the twins— Silas, Wade was thinking, but he was not sure. The twins looked too much alike for him to be certain. Where were Ada and Paul? His eyes swung from one end of the barn to the other. They had to be here somewhere.

He could not find them. He continued to look around, but

after a couple of minutes, he became distracted, and the search ended.

Wade casually walked through the crowd and went outside. He stopped in the yard and waited, thinking about what he was about to do. It didn't take long to become motivated and then he turned toward the open corral and took up a rope.

He caught a horse and quickly threw a saddle on him and he was just mounting up when a voice spoke to him from the shadows.

"Goin' somewhere, Boss?" Rusty asked.

"Just for a ride."

"With a party goin' on?"

"Yeah, and you didn't see me," Wade said.

"All right," Rusty agreed. "Want some comp'ny?"

"No. I want to be alone for a while."

"Yeah, I know the feelin'."

Wade gave Rusty a curious look. Rusty had continued with his peculiar actions and Wade was still at a loss as to what had come over him, but right now, Wade was selfishly thinking only about himself. He led the horse to the back side of the corral and stepped into the saddle, quietly walking away. When he was a good distance down the road, he urged the horse into a trot and hurried him along.

The Whip-or-wills were singing again. After getting away from the sounds of the party, Wade could hear them clearly. The night was especially pleasant. There was a bright moon in the sky, lighting the road, and fireflies, or lightning bugs, as the locals called them, were twinkling all around. They decorated the trees and the brush like thousands of tiny stars fallen from the sky, and they floated across open fields, blinking on and off as they flew about.

Frogs were singing and somewhere in the distance, an owl hooted.

Any other night, Wade would have stopped to drink in the beauty of such a night, but not tonight. He hurried, one thought on his mind, and a strange anxiety in his breast.

Wade knew he was near the Tanner's farm when he heard the old yellow dog barking. He came around a corner and he could see the house. There was a light on in one of the windows, and Wade stopped and looked at it.

What did that mean? Would the Tanners go away and leave a lamp burning? It didn't seem reasonable. The threat of a fire was too great.

The only other explanation was that someone was still there and he could guess who it was with some accuracy. He saw a shadow pass by the window and then he knew. It was Ada. She had not gone to the party, after all.

She looked outside as Skippy barked into the night. Wade saw her face appear at a window and then just as quickly, she moved away. The dog stopped barking and Wade could imagine Ada calling him to her, holding him at her side for protection.

He sat his horse and studied the situation. There was nothing to do but return to the party. He could not do anything with Ada here, but Wade didn't move. He kept looking at the light in the window and thinking about Ada, and after a couple of minutes, he urged the horse forward.

Ada heard the sound of the horse long before she could see anything. Wade was right. She had called Skippy to her side and she was holding him there with a hand on his back. He wanted to bark, but she spoke softly to him and he made a rumbling sound in his chest that she alone could hear.

"Quiet, boy," she said, speaking softly. "Quiet, so I can hear."

He was quiet and if Wade had only known, it was a deadly quiet. Skippy was bred for hog hunting, which was not a sport, as the name implied. Hogs in this area were herded just like cattle and it required a special kind of dog to work these dangerous wild animals. Skippy was one such dog. Fred Tanner had several herds of marked pigs, and his mark was registered at the court house just like a brand on cattle. If Wade only knew, Skippy was more dangerous to him right now than a cocked gun.

The horse and rider appeared in the moonlight, but Ada could not recognize him until he was at the gate. Skippy, however, made the recognition right away, and began thumping his tail on the wooden floor.

"Traitor," Ada whispered to the dog as Wade came into view.

He stopped at the gate and sat on his horse, looking toward the house, but not seeing Ada until she stood up.

"Hello, Ada," he said in the quiet voice that set her heart to pounding.

"Wade? What're you doin' here? Haven't you got a party goin' on at your house?"

"Yeah," he wearily said. Ada was quick to pick up the tone of his voice. "But you weren't there."

He stepped down from his horse, and Ada felt every muscle in her body tense. What was he doing here?

"Are you roundin' up strays?" she asked, trying to sound amused even though she was quite apprehensive. "Come to my party or I'll drag you there," she facetiously added, making a joke out of his arrival.

He grinned. "Something like that."

He was standing by the gate, one hand on the post and the other hand holding the reins. Ada squinted her eyes to see him better. He was smartly dressed and it made her feel self-conscious in her faded old skirt and patched blouse. She remembered mending the tear in her sleeve and unconsciously, she put her hand over it.

"Are you alone?" Wade suddenly asked. His hat was pulled low over his wide brow, but Ada could see he was looking around. Her apprehension became more acute. After all, what did she know about him?

"No," she answered. "I've got Skippy here and at least three loaded rifles. They make good company."

He pushed his hat back, his expression wide-eyed and amused. "I'll say," he said and then more soberly he added, "You aren't afraid of me, are you, Ada?"

"No, sir," she said, lifting her chin defiantly. "One word from me, and Skippy would tear your throat out. Nothin' short of a bullet to his head would stop him or save you."

Wade eyed the dog with new respect. "Well, let's not take it that far," he said. He looked across the yard and then back at Ada. "I was out riding to clear my head," he began to explain. "And I saw your light." He tilted his head, trying to get a better look at her. She was standing in the shadow on the porch and he could not see her very well. He wished she would step forward so the moonlight would touch her, but she never moved and the dog never left her side. "I know this is impulsive, but I want to thank you for helping me out the day I was shot. I was hoping you'd be at the party and I was going to tell you there, but you weren't there . . ."

"You should've known I wouldn't be," she pointed out.

He gave her a solemn look. "Should I?" he asked.

There was a lonely sound to his voice that caused Ada to look sharply at him. Her eyes had adjusted to the dim light and she could see him without any trouble.

It was time for him to leave and Ada knew that, but she had the feeling he wouldn't go unless she suggested it. Perhaps he was not as noble as she had given him credit for being. He obviously had something on his mind. Regardless of what he was saying, intuition told Ada he was not here to thank her for helping him when he had been shot. In fact, as unflattering as it was, she had the feeling he had not come there to see her, at all. Just like the day she had caught him here before, she knew he had come, thinking no one was at home tonight.

"You better go, Wade," she said, making the first move to get him out of there. "Before someone catches you here. It wouldn't be good for you—or for me."

Wade unconsciously looked over his shoulder. He

immediately thought of Logan and for just a moment, he again envied the young scamp.

He didn't say anything and Ada waited, wondering what he was going to do next.

"You should hurry," she added when he made no move to leave. "Someone might see you and if daddy finds out, he'll never believe I didn't stay behind just to meet up with you. He'll tan my hide."

Wade gathered the reins in his hand. "I'm sorry, Ada. I wasn't thinking. I don't want to make trouble for you."

"It's all right," she said, "but just get outta here before someone comes along and sees you."

He swung up into the saddle and Ada watched him without a word. Curiously, her heart was pounding and she felt both apprehension and relief at seeing him prepare to leave. He turned the horse but then, he stopped and Ada took an involuntary step forward.

He pushed his hat back and he smiled in her direction. She could see him in the light of the moon, but there was a shadow across his face that hid his eyes. Something like regret swelled up inside her and for just a moment, she contemplated calling him to her. Wisely, she didn't.

"I'm thinking about what you just said," he told her as he paused there. "About your daddy thinking we had planned this meeting. You know, it would be worth the risk of being shot again to have a rendevous with you."

He didn't wait for Ada's response. He knew she would have nothing positive to reply, so he pulled the horse around and urged him quickly down the road. He was halfway back to his ranch before he paused and considered what he had said.

Ada had drawn an apprehensive breath at his remark and had taken another step forward. If Wade had looked back, he would have seen her clearly for the first time that night. She was standing on the edge of the porch and the moonlight was full in her face.

She had watched him ride away and it was not until he was completely out of sight that she realized she was breathing hard and fast as if she had run a long way. She took a deep breath and then let it out, getting herself under control.

But she was not the only one watching Wade Thornton ride away from her house. A lone horse stepped into the road behind Wade and the rider sat still, considering the meaning of what had just happened.

He turned around and rode in the opposite direction, not stopping until he saw the outline of a small cabin that was almost hidden in the dark, under a giant cedar tree. He stepped down from his horse and tied him to a low branch of a tree and then he walked forward, rapping softly on the door when he arrived.

"Who's there?" a voice inside tentatively inquired.

"It's me, Mattie. Let me in."

The door opened immediately and Mattie Hinkley stood just inside, her hand on the door. She was dressed for bed and as she stepped back to let him in, she clutched her gown tightly at her throat. He pushed the door behind him and closed it with his foot and then he drew her to him.

"I need you, Mattie," he said.

"I'm here for you, Logan," she replied. "I'll always be here for you."

Chapter Twenty-one

"Where were you last night?" Angela demanded and Wade leaned back in his chair, giving her an innocent expression.

"What do you mean?" he asked.

"Don't be coy with me," she said. "We both know you were off somewhere last night when you should have been here."

"I had to get away for a while. Something was bothering me."

"I can guess what *that* was," she said and then more calmly she added, "Oh, Wade. What has happened to us? We used to be the best of friends."

"That's the trouble, Angela. We were always just friends."

She looked sharply at him, not wanting to admit that what he said was true.

"Who is she, Wade?" she suddenly asked and he jerked as if she had pinched him. "Who's the girl that's caught your eye?"

He settled down in his chair and ruefully wished he could honestly say there was another girl. "You aren't going to believe this, Angela, but there's no other girl."

"You're right. I don't believe you."

He shrugged indifferently. "Believe what you like."

She didn't immediately respond. She looked at him and thought how dejected he looked. His face was long, his eyes were narrow, and his brow was creased. He was troubled over something and instinctively she suspected another girl.

"Well, if I can find Rusty, I'm going for a ride," she said, suddenly changing the subject. Her eyes scanned the yard and moved toward the stable. "You'll never get out of this mood until you're honest with yourself, Wade, and we can't work things out until you're honest with me."

He looked up at her and wondered what he should say to that. There was no confession to be made. He had done nothing, but then at the same time, he had to admit that the only reason he had not was because Ada wouldn't let him. If she had halfway encouraged him the night before, he would have gone to her. He wanted to—desperately wanted to.

"Enjoy your ride," was all he said and Angela slapped the side of her leg with a finality that was not lost on Wade. This morning, though, he just didn't care.

Angela stomped out of the room and walked across the yard. The sun was already hot, but no hotter than her temper. She looked around for Rusty and found him in the barn. His mood seemed to be no better than Wades and she began to wonder what had come over all of them.

"Rusty," she said, "will you catch a horse for me?"

"Yes ma'am," he said, his tone full of indifference, just as it always was. He walked away and she watched him. She had tried to break that indifference, but Rusty had been less than cooperative. She wondered what it was about his type that made him so stoic and so long suffering. He and Wade were the same in that respect.

She had been cruel and she knew it, but Angela was a hard

minded girl and once she had decided on something, she didn't care who was hurt to further her agenda. The trouble was, in pursuing Rusty's approval, something had happened to her, as well. It was something she had not expected.

She had played Rusty as only she knew how to do. The week before had been especially rewarding. She had seen him weaken on more than one occasion, but with the strength of some unknown power, he had always rallied back again, and she had lost him. She remembered the day she had pretended to hurt her foot, just so he would have to put his arms around her to help her back to the horse. She had used more than one of her feminine wiles on him and he had measurably weakened that day. She had seen it in his eyes, the desire and the longing, but then the hard determination to stay true to Wade had returned. She was thinking that Wade didn't deserve such loyalty, and she was going to see he didn't get it anymore—not from Rusty, anyway.

Rusty brought the horses around and Angela took the reins of the one she always rode. She was a beautiful little horse with no pedigree, but with lines of some forgotten ancestor in her that was surely a thoroughbred. Angela patted her nose and spoke softly to her, thinking that horses were such intelligent creatures—and predictable. Men were predictable too, but not always understandable. Angela had learned how to put a bit in most men's mouths. Rusty and Wade, though, had not been as easily turned as other men. Anyone who knew her, however, knew that would never be a deterrent.

Rusty helped her into the saddle and then he mounted his

own horse, but not without first casting a look of condemnation in the direction of Wade's room. It was a ritual he practiced every time he went out with Angela. He blamed Wade for his misery and he never ceased to be unforgiving in the matter.

They rode out of the ranch yard and turned down the path that had become well-worn from their daily trips. Angela had her favorite places to go and Rusty had automatically started in that direction when she stopped him.

"Let's do something different today," she said and he nodded in agreement.

"Whatever you say."

"What's over to the northeast?"

"Just the Tanner's little farm," Rusty said, giving Angela a quizzical look.

"The Tanners? I think they were here last night."

"Some of 'em," Rusty replied.

"Only some? Who're the others?"

"Just Ada. She didn't come."

"Ada? The pretty young daughter?"

"Yeah, she's pretty, she's young, and she's Fred Tanner's daughter. I didn't think you'd ever met her."

"I haven't," Angela sharply quipped. She had seen Wade ride in the night before and that was the direction from which he had come. Well, the mystery was over, as far as Angela was concerned. It was Ada Tanner who must have won his heart, and the fools were meeting each other on the sly.

The same thought came to Rusty at exactly the same moment and he looked over his shoulder in Wade's direction even though he could not see anything from where he sat. He equally thought that Wade was a fool, but it was for a totally different reason. He looked again at Angela and a feeling swelled up in his heart that almost choked him. Yes, Wade was a fool if he chose Ada over Angela, especially when one belonged to him and the other would never be anything but trouble.

"Well, come on," Angela said, but she didn't go to the northeast. She went due south and she didn't stop until she was at the bank of a ravine that dropped sharply, cutting off her route. It was a twenty foot drop to the bottom where a tiny stream twisted and turned, meandering toward the river. She sat there and looked down at it for some time before she looked back at Rusty.

"This is a strange place," she said. "How do we get across?"

"There's a place further downstream," he answered, "but I wouldn't advise it. It's rough and full of snakes. If you want to go as far as the railroad tracks, you can walk across the trestle."

She reached down and rubbed the calf of her leg. "I think I'm getting a cramp," she said. "Would you help me down?"

Rusty immediately got down from his horse and walked to Angela. He reached up for her and she slid easily into his arms. Her hands smoothly circled his head and her arms wrapped around him, pulling him tightly to her. He caught his breath and looked into her eyes. The look she returned was like a potion and Rusty was intoxicated by it. He sighed with resignation and when Angela pulled him to her, he forgot his promise to be true to his friend. He forgot everything, in fact, including who he was and all the reasons why he should not be doing what he was doing. Weeks of pent up emotion came out in one violent burst of passion and when he finally came to himself and pulled away, Angela had to grip him to steady herself.

"Oh, God, Angela," he said, truly repentant. "What 've we done?"

"We've fallen in love," she answered. "And there's nothing wrong with that."

"The hell you say! There's nothin' right about it. You're engaged to Wade."

"Well . . ." she drawled as she gave herself time to think. "I haven't told anyone, but I'm calling off the engagement."

Rusty visibly wilted. "Does Wade know?"

"I haven't told him, but . . . he knows." She caressed his shoulder and smiled at him. "Can't you see that Wade has other things on his mind?" she asked. "Until today I wasn't sure, but now I know. He's fallen in love with that Tanner girl."

"It sure makes sense," Rusty admitted. "An' explains a lot, but it won't do 'im any good." Rusty paused to consider this new revelation and it brought about a more troubling thought. "Her father'd kill her if she got int'rested in Wade, and then there's her boyfriend, Logan. He wants to kill all of us anyway and one excuse'll be as good as another, as far as he's concerned. Wade's a fool if he's fallen in love with Ada." He suddenly looked down at Angela. "We're fools, too," he said. "We're like the pot callin' the kettle black. We're as foolish as they are."

"No, we aren't, and if Wade wants Ada, well, we'll help them get together."

"You forget one thing," Rusty said. "Ada."

"What about her?"

"She doesn't like Wade. That's the problem, I think. Wade's in love with her, but she isn't in love with him."

"What makes you think that?"

"She's made it quite clear, and she's Logan's girl."

"Oh," Angela sighed, then she sorrowfully added, "Poor, Wade." She stood quietly against Rusty and another thought suddenly came to mind. "Then where was he last night?" she asked, and Rusty's brow creased in thought.

"That's a good question," he said, and immediately, the same thought came to both of them.

"The gold," they said simultaneously.

"It isn't the girl he's after, but the gold," Angela said, but Rusty was not so sure. He considered that and then he shook his head.

"It's both," he said. "He wants the gold and the girl, and one's gonna be as much trouble as the other. But where is the gold? Why doesn't he just go get it?"

"He doesn't know exactly where it is. His father doesn't even know for sure. He was seriously injured and it was his men who hid it. Wade only has some clues."

"What clues?"

"I don't know. He's never shared that information with me or anyone."

Rusty smiled derisively. "Maybe he isn't such a fool, after

all," he said. "Maybe he isn't a fool, at all."

He grinned and pulled Angela closer to him.

"An' maybe Tanner's sittin' on fifty thousand dollars' worth of gold and doesn't even know it. Now, wouldn't that be a kicker!"

Chapter Twenty-two

The major was seriously wondering about more than one topic and none of his thoughts were giving him any peace. Angela and Wade were becoming a disappointment. He could see them drifting apart and that was shooting his plans all to blue blazes.

He puffed on his cigar and looked across the hard packed sandy yard to the trees beyond. It was hot and he was uncomfortable and he was ready to return to New Hampshire, but he could not go with all his plans gone awry.

He had planned to have Angela and Wade united in marriage by now, but neither one of them was being cooperative, and now Angela had told him they were not even getting married.

"Delay it for a while, if need be," he had advised, "but don't call it off."

"Delay it for what reason?" she had asked. "Tomorrow I'll feel no differently, nor next week, nor the next—and neither will Wade. Besides, he's got his eyes on that Tanner girl. Wade'll be okay. You don't have to worry about him."

"You can't be serious," he had angrily said, and Angela had looked at him in surprise. "You have to marry him!"

"Why do I have to marry him?"

"Because I say so!" he had shouted.

Angela's face had turned dark with heated blood. "You know I've never done anything just because I've been told to do so," she had pointed out. "And I'll not do this either."

"You will, or you'll find yourself out on the street, begging for your next meal."

"You'd throw me out? You aren't the man I thought you were."

"No? Well, the truth is, we'll both be out on the street, begging for our next meal."

"What're you talking about?"

"I'm broke, Angela, and I owe Harrison Felder ten thousand dollars!"

Angela drew in a deep breath. Her father had always gambled and had been quite good at it, but lately, he had begun to play with a new group and she had noticed they were much too serious for her liking. She had not suspected anything amiss, however, not as serious as this, anyway.

"How could you, Papa! How could you do such a thing?"

"I'll not make any excuses. I'm weak where cards are concerned, but Harrison is a shrewd man. I had no idea he wasn't playing like a gentleman."

Her admonishment had irritated the Major, but he had gotten his point across. He squinted his eyes and looked through the drifting smoke and contemplated a new plan. Angela had rallied around him after that argument, just like he knew she would. It all hinged on the gold and according to Angela, Wade had not yet found it, but Rusty had an idea, and that idea was what interested the major just now.

If Wade had not found the gold, then it was there for whoever did find it, and unknown to anyone else, the Major knew more about the gold than he was saying. It would have been so easy to sit back and let Wade do all the work. Harrison had given the major a year to make good on his debt and that would have been more than enough time to get Angela married and get a portion of the gold in his hands—or that was what he had been thinking. Not today, however. He was thinking that if he could find the gold, then he would have 100% of it instead of a small portion, and was not all better than some? The major definitely thought it was, but he would still insist that Angela marry Wade—just in case.

He stood up and walked to the corral. He caught a horse and saddled him and then the major rode away. Only Powder Keg saw him leave, and he gave it no thought. People were coming and going a lot around here lately, and he had other things to do. He walked to the bunk house without another thought.

The Major, however, was giving a lot of thought to one thing in particular as he rode unerringly toward the Tanner's farm. It was time to make friends with his neighbors, he was thinking, and to see this young girl who had messed things up between Wade and Angela. He shook his head with disbelief. To outshine Angela would be something indeed.

When he rode up to the fence and stepped down from his horse, he could see Ada. She was standing at the clothes line, an article of clothing in her hands and clothes pins in her mouth, and even at that distance, he had to admit—he could see where a man could lose sight of important things when he looked upon her.

She wore a simple dress, but it did nothing to hide her figure, and there was no hat on her head, even though it was the fashion of the day. Her hair was dark, and pulled back from an oval face and her eyes were large. When she reached up and caught the line so that she could hang the article of clothing, even at his age, the major was moved with renewed and almost forgotten interest.

He suddenly didn't blame Wade. If he had been a young man, he would have been tempted himself—and maybe he was anyway, if he was being honest with himself.

Well, it only made the task more interesting, he told himself, and he was sure that if he gave it some thought, he could work this to his advantage. He chuckled to himself and then he removed his hat just as Mrs. Tanner stepped out of the house and onto the porch.

"Good morning," he genially said, the sly look leaving his face in a flash. "We met at the party, if you recall. I thought it was time to get to know my neighbors. After all . . ."

Chapter Twenty-three

Wade watched as the last fence post was dropped into place and the last of the barbed wire was strung across it. The men gave a hearty cheer with the task of fence building at an end, but Wade felt no jubilation.

He should have. Pete and his crew would be returning to town, and Wade and his men could, at last, get to the job of ranching. For some reason, there was no joy in that thought anymore. Wade felt like a man drifting. He had had a dream, but somewhere along the way, he had lost sight of it. For the first time, Wade was considering leaving all this behind and going home. The thought of the look of disappointment in his father's eyes was the only thing that kept him from it.

"Let's gather all the tools and go home," he said without emotion. It seemed to put a damper on the exuberant delight of his crew and they solemnly set to work picking things up and loading the wagon with the tools.

"Where's Daniel?" someone asked and Wade looked around.

"He was here a minute ago," Jim said.

"Here he comes," Pete said, dipping his head in the direction of a slowly moving figure coming toward them. Pete didn't like Daniel. In fact, few of the men liked the boy as well as they did his brother. The two boys were as different in disposition as if they had no kinship, at all, and Pete was thinking that Daniel had probably been loafing in the woods, just waiting for the job to be finished.

He threw his gloves in the back of the wagon. It was none of his business, but if he was Wade, he would cut Daniel Larkin loose from the crew. There was something about the boy that just was not right but Pete could not put his finger on exactly what made him think that way.

Jim was thinking the same thing, although neither man had any idea they shared the same views on the boy. Jim, however, had no qualms about telling Wade how he felt, and he had done so on a couple of occasions. That was what Wade was thinking about as Daniel sauntered into the circle of men.

"Are you alright?" Wade asked.

"Yeah," Daniel answered. "Why?"

"You've been spending so much time in the woods," Jim interjected, "We thought your stomach was upset or something."

Someone snickered and Daniel turned with a start.

"That's real funny," he said.

Wade gave him a solemn, but interested look. "Cut it out," he said, to defuse any problem, but he was still curious, and a little suspicious. "Mount up and let's go home."

They reached the ranch an hour before sundown and some of the crew gave a whoop of triumph as they rode into the yard. All of them had hated the job of fence building, and it was like them to celebrate its completion.

"Five dollars says we're out puttin' it up again b'fore the week's out," Bart said as he stepped to the ground.

"You'll get no takers on that," Cody told him. "Unless you bet it's sooner 'n a week."

"I'll bet on that," Powder Keg said. "I expect we'll be seein' cut wires within three days."

"Two," Jim said.

"You're on!"

Wade left them making their bets. He walked to the pump and stripped off his shirt. He was hot and dirty and he wanted to cool down and wash up before supper. He had just finished and was buttoning up his shirt when Angela and Rusty rode into the yard.

Rusty's attitude had changed again, and he was almost back to his normal self. Wade deftly slipped the last button into its hole and considered what had happened to make the change in the first place and then to wonder what had happened to turn him back again. He also wondered if he should relieve Rusty of his duties to Angela. He knew how Rusty hated the idea of watching her and Wade was well able now to do the job. He just didn't want to do it.

Wade had thought he and Angela could agree to disagree about the marriage and that they would part ways on friendly terms, but something had happened and after the party, Angela had suddenly become insistent that they reconsider the promise they had made to each other. She was ready to go through with the wedding and all her arguments about going home before they married had changed. Wade picked up his hat and unconsciously beat it against his leg before putting it on.

"Hello, Wade," she said as he drew near. She was standing beside the horse, but Rusty led the animal away and she was left standing in the open yard. "I hear the fence is finished."

"It is," he said.

"So, what does this mean?"

"Nothing, right now. I'll be bringing cattle in as soon as I can arrange it."

She sighed with great weariness. "Can we have a talk right now?" she asked and Wade reluctantly agreed. They walked toward the bunkhouse and Wade opened the door to his room and the two of them entered.

Angela gave the bare walls and the sparsely furnished room a critical examination. Her room in the house was hardly better. She had thought all of this was going to be temporary— very temporary, but her plans had become as topsy-turvy as had Wade's. She no longer wanted to marry him, but Angela understood sacrifice and obligation, and she loved her father better than she loved anyone else. She would gladly sacrifice herself if it would get the major out of trouble.

"Wade," she began, her voice soft and airy. "We both know that buying cattle is going to be a strain on your finances. You'll not see a return on them for a long time. Don't you think you should consider putting off the buying of cattle until after we're married?"

He didn't immediately answer, but instead, he eyed her with great interest. "Do you love me, Angela?" he asked after a long pause. "I mean, really love me—like a girl loves a man she wants to marry."

"What a funny thing to say," she said as she gave him a wry smile. "You know I want to marry you."

"That isn't exactly answering the question," he said. "Do you love me?"

"As much as you love me," she sagely said.

Wade began to smile and then he chuckled. He walked to his bunk and fell onto it, looking up at her with an amused expression.

"Then, come here to me," he said.

"I will not!" she gasped. "How dare you suggest such a thing!"

"I'm not suggesting anything. Just come here and let's see how much we mean to each other."

Angela was furious, but she kept her head. She had no intentions of proving anything to Wade, mainly because she knew she would only be proving that he was right.

"I'll not fall for that," she said and she smiled even though she didn't feel like it. "I'm flattered, though, Wade. It's the first time you've tried anything like that with me."

He sat up and the amused expression was gone from his face.

"The only thing I was trying to do, was to see if you loved me enough to be tempted. You weren't."

"I was, Wade," she insisted. "I really was, but I've got sense enough to know better than to put myself into such a situation. You know better, too."

He shook his head. "Angela," he said. "I don't love you. I

like you. I like you a whole lot, and maybe I do love you, too, but it's the wrong kind of love. Let's call off the marriage."

"I can't, Wade."

He looked up at her, confused by her tone of desperation. "Why not?"

"Because, I just can't lose you," she said. She felt tears stinging her eyes. She was losing the battle and she could not do that. She tried to hold them back, but the tears filled her eyes and fell down her cheeks. Wade stiffened when he saw them, and then he stood up and walked to her.

"Oh, Angela," he softly said as he took her into his arms. "It's okay. Don't cry."

She had not intended to cry and she had not expected Wade to react in such a manner if she did cry, but Angela was quick to take advantage of the situation even though she had not planned it. She held him, and she cried with all the strength and the emotion she could muster, and the whole time, Wade weakened until he was soft and malleable, just the way she wanted him.

"Please, Wade," she said, once she thought the moment was right. "Please, don't tell me it was all a lie. You once loved me. Please tell me you still do. Please . . ."

"I still love you," he said. "I've always loved you."

That was no lie, but Wade felt that it was. Angela and he were never meant to be anything but friends, and he loved her like the friend she had always been. He regretfully wished that he had been wiser when she had suggested they get married. He quickly considered the alternatives and he knew that what he did want was a thing that would never happen. He might as well marry Angela and make the most of it. After all, at least she *did* want him. He could not say the same thing about any other girl. He just felt he was not being fair to Angela. Marrying her would mean living a life of pretense but he knew he could do it if he had to. Maybe if Ada would hurry up and marry Logan, he could do it without any regrets. The thought made every muscle in his body tense until he squeezed Angela too tightly and she pulled away from him with an exclamation of pain.

She read the gesture as a moment of great desire on Wade's part, and she felt her mission had been accomplished. Smugly, she smiled, but she didn't let him see the self-satisfied expression on her face.

He stepped away from her and she let him go, the entire time, thinking that she had won another round with him. If she could have read his mind, however, she wouldn't have been so confident. She took the opportunity, though, to casually pursue the subject that was wholly on her mind. She wiped her eyes and touched her hair, automatically arranging and rearranging herself for best effect.

"Wade, I was wondering," she began. He had returned to the bunk and was lying on his back, looking up at the ceiling, his arms folded behind his head. She walked to within a few feet of him and looked down at his prone figure. He was a handsome man. She had always thought so. It made her wonder why she had never had an attraction for him the way she did for Rusty. Maybe growing up with someone did that to you. "After you buy the cattle, could we fix up the house and make it more comfortable? I'd like some decent furniture too."

He turned his head and looked at her, but at first, he didn't say anything. It was not until he looked up at the ceiling again that he responded.

"No," he answered. "I don't have the money to do both."

"What about the gold?"

His dark eyes sharpened and again he turned his head and looked at her. "What about it?"

"You should have the money to do anything you like with the gold."

He studied her for a full minute before saying anything. She could see the life in his dark eyes and she knew what that meant. She had made the same calculations when she herself had been considering a response to that question, so the expression was completely familiar.

"I can't depend on such a thing," he said. "It may not even exist."

"Oh, but it does!" she exclaimed and she knelt by his bed in her excitement. "Your father said it was here. We could get it, Wade, and we'd never have to worry again. There'd be enough money to invest and to finance your little operation here."

"My father doesn't really know what happened to that gold," Wade explained. "He wasn't with the men when they left the Tanner's farm."

"No, but they told him what they were going to do with it before they left," she insisted.

"You know what he said about that, Angela?" Wade asked. "He told me he was so sick from the gun shot that the whole episode is like a dream. He can't be sure of anything."

"That isn't what he told papa," she said, and then she repented. Wade suspiciously looked at her and she knew she had just made a fatal slip. "You aren't being completely honest with me," she roughly said to hide her mistake.

"It's been a long time," Wade said and he folded his arms behind his head again and looked up at the ceiling just as he had done before. He was not sure why he felt the need for secrecy just now, but he did. "I'll tell you what I think," he went on. "I think daddy's squad had the gold when they left the farm and it was still with them when they were caught and killed. The Confederate soldiers took that gold. They just never let anyone know. Otherwise, why didn't some of them come back looking for it?"

"Maybe they didn't know about the gold."

"They knew. That's why they were out in full force after daddy's squad."

Angela rocked back on her heels, the disappointment obvious on her face. She ran her bottom lip out in a large moue and her eyes narrowed. "It has to be here," she insisted.

"Yeah? Well, it doesn't have to be here, Angela. If you've come here with the hope of finding it, you've probably wasted your time."

Her eyes swung back to him with such quickness and emotion that Wade involuntarily moved away from her.

"I think you're lying to me," she said. It was the truth. She suddenly suspected Wade of purposely delaying the finding of the gold until he could be rid of her.

"Is that what you think? Well, I can't make you believe me."

"You know something. I know that you know more than you're saying."

He eased back onto his pillow and straightened himself on the bunk. "It's nothing to you," he said. He was looking at the ceiling again, but his mind was actively pursuing a thought he had entertained before. Angela and the Major were after the gold and he was just the means to an end. Angela didn't want to marry him any more than he wanted to marry her, but it appeared she would do anything to get her hands on the gold. He had not been deliberately delaying the finding of it, but he decided he would now. If it had not yet been found, the gold would be safe in its hiding place for a little while longer. "Or the gold shouldn't be anything to you," he added with deep feeling.

He turned his head and looked at her and she promptly stood up.

"Wade Thornton," she said with great exasperation. "Of course it's of interest to me. You and I both have heard the story of the gold our whole lives and I'll admit, I was excited about this venture because I wanted you to find it. But I'm sick of this place. I can't understand why you aren't—unless you've found something more interesting to you than the gold. Perhaps, a pretty face with large blue eyes?"

Wade had not expected that. He flashed guilty eyes toward Angela and then she knew.

"Well," she said. "The mystery is solved. No wonder you're ready to be rid of me. You've found a replacement, I see."

It didn't matter that she was guilty of the very thing for which she accused him. The trouble was, Angela had no qualms about marrying Wade and keeping Rusty on the side. Wade, however, was not so inclined. He had a sense of propriety and of loyalty. Whether he loved Angela or not, if they married, Wade would never consider any other woman. He would bear his burden with dignity and with long-suffering.

He made a quick recovery and spoke his thoughts. "You're wrong," he said. There was no lie in that. Wade knew better than anyone that his infatuation was an impossible dream. He had resigned himself to that fact. He was not getting rid of Angela just so he could have Ada. He would be a fool to think that was a possibility. "You have no idea just how wrong you are," he told her, his voice full of bitterness.

"So, the little witch turned you down, did she? That surprises me. I've never seen a girl yet who didn't look twice when she saw you."

Wade didn't say anything nor turn his eyes to her. He continued to look at the ceiling, knowing that Angela was right even though there was no conceit in his thoughts. He had always had the ability to turn feminine heads so he thought it was ironic that when he had not cared, women looked, and now that he did care, the woman he wanted was totally indifferent.

The triangle rang announcing dinner, and Wade slowly sat up. Angela glanced over her shoulder as if she could see, as well as hear, it.

"I still want to marry you," she said. "Regardless of your desire for another woman. I don't care, you know, if you have her, too. Just be discrete, will you? I do hate wagging tongues."

"You're crazy," Wade said, his head dropping. "I would never have a mistress."

"No? Well, just think, Wade. You can have it all. Think about it," she repeated, "and you may find that I offer something very appealing."

He looked up at her and his thoughts were not flattering. Little did she know, Wade was appalled at her suggestion. His estimation of her dropped dramatically, and he wondered why he had not known this about her before. He thought he knew her as well as he knew himself, but he realized for the first time that Angela was an enigma, a mystery he had failed to unravel—or possibly, that he had simply underestimated.

She turned on her heels and walked out of the room, leaving Wade sitting on his bunk, his head drooping and his shoulders sagging. He had lost his appetite, but he knew he should eat. He stood up, pausing only long enough to stretch, the action seeming to renew his energy. He walked out of the room, following Angela's example, but he didn't follow her to the house where he usually ate with her and the major. Instead, he walked down to the end of the bunk house to the gathering room where the men ate and he joined them. No one said a word but their eyes slipped surreptitiously from Wade to the door and then back again.

During the night, it began to rain and when morning arrived, the sky was low and dark, the yard a muddy puddle from one end of it to the other. Thunder rumbled ominously in the distance and the rain fell intermittently, coming down in quick rushes of pounding water that would sometimes stop only seconds after beginning. The men walked around in yellow slickers, seeing to the stock and doing the chores that had to be done whether rain or shine. Bart walked in from the outside, pulling off his dripping coat as soon as he entered. He hung it on a hook beside the door and then he walked straight to the coffee pot, pouring a cupful before sitting down at the long wooden table. Powder Keg turned and looked at him but before he could speak, the door opened again. It was Rusty.

"Hey, what a morning!" he exclaimed as he walked inside. The room was stuffy and too warm, but the smell of bacon frying and coffee brewing gave it an inviting atmosphere. Rusty straddled the bench and sat sideways at the table, propping an elbow on the corner of it as he looked toward the stove. "What's for breakfast?"

"The usual," Powder Keg replied. "Help yourself to the coffee."

Rusty nodded and stood up. He was standing beside the stove, the coffee pot in one hand and a cup in the other when Wade walked in.

"Mornin', boss," Bart was quick to greet him, but Rusty and Powder Keg only looked at him, surprise evident in their expressions. This was the second meal he had taken in the bunk house instead of the house, and the meaning of it was not lost on either man. "We won't get much done today," Bart went on to say, oblivious of the oddity or the reason for Wade's company.

"Well, we deserve a day off," Wade said.

"Yeah. Too bad it's under these circumstances."

"Yeah," Wade agreed. He ate in silence and then as he pushed back from the table, he leaned back in his chair. "I'm going to ride the fence line and see how it faired last night."

"In this rain?" Powder Keg asked and Wade smiled wryly.

"It's letting up, I think."

Doubtful eyes turned to look out the window.

"If you say so," Bart dubiously commented.

"A little rain won't hurt me," Wade then added. He felt he had to get away. Ever since his conversation with Angela, Wade had felt as if the walls were closing in on him. He was almost suffocating with the claustrophobic effect.

"I'll ride with you," Rusty offered.

Wade opened his mouth to refuse, but he changed his mind almost immediately. "You don't have to," he said, "but I'd like the company."

An hour later in one of the lulls of the storm, they rode out together. They went down the road to the gate at the main road and then they turned east. The fence stretched before them in an unbroken line, disappearing behind brush and trees, around curves or over hills, only to emerge a moment later in strung perfection.

"Logan isn't ambitious enough to come out in the storm to cut wire," Rusty offered after a few minutes of following the fence. "But I reckon you know that," he wryly added.

They had pulled up the horses and stopped near the big oak that grew on the line between Wade's property and the Tanner's. It was an open spot with a clear view of the fence for a good hundred feet or more and Wade looked up and down it before saying anything.

"None of this has been checked in over a week, but, honestly, I just wanted to see it up from one end to the other. Besides, I needed to get out of the bunkhouse. It was suffocating me."

Rusty gave him an understanding nod and then he followed Wade as he started his horse moving again.

Wade didn't follow the fence line, however. He turned his horse to the right and walked down a gentle incline that soon came upon a narrow trail. Rusty followed without a word, knowing Wade was going to the spring. It gave Rusty a peculiar feeling, because he knew what was on Wade's mind. He knew and he pitied him while at the same time, he hated himself and inwardly reproached himself for his own deceit. He felt anger, too. He wondered why things could not be simple and straightforward, then he would have Angela and Wade would have Ada and there would be no deception between them, but he knew life was not that just. He didn't understand women, either, for neither Angela nor Ada was making matters easy. Angela was quick to tease him with her promises of love, but slow to tell Wade she wanted out of the engagement. And Ada— well, Ada was a hopeless story. Wade would get nowhere with her.

The rain had stopped again, but the trees were full of water and dripped incessantly on them. They came suddenly upon the clearing as they stepped out of the darkness under the trees to the open sky. The clouds were gray and low, their reflection turning the turquoise water of the pool to a deep blue. The wind was blowing and little ripples rolled across the surface of the water, interrupted occasionally by large drops of water from the limbs of the oak that grew nearby. The golden grasses bent before the wind and the cabbage palms rattled their fronds with a dry sound that was incongruous with the wet surroundings.

Wade didn't say anything. He just sat his horse and stared at the water, and Rusty read the thoughts underneath the facade of calm. It inspired him to make a confession. He wanted to tell Wade about he and Angela and now seemed the perfect time, but just as quickly, he realized the folly of being too honest. For one thing, Angela would never forgive him. That was the deciding factor.

"Wade," Rusty tentatively began, groping for words, afraid he would say something that would inadvertently expose his own guilt. "Why are you doin' this? You're only torturing yourself by comin' here."

Wade looked over his shoulder at Rusty. He misunderstood the concern, thinking that Rusty was referring to the shot that had narrowly missed killing him. "It doesn't bother me—not really. I like this place and I don't want an unhappy event to spoil it for me."

Rusty was momentarily taken aback. He had expected another response and it took him a few seconds to recalculate. "I wasn't talkin' about you gettin' shot. I was talkin' about Ada," he honestly said.

To Rusty's surprise, Wade laughed. Rusty had expected a denial or even an admonishment, but not the joyous outburst that followed his statement.

It was not really joyous, however. It was a sound of irony, although Rusty didn't immediately grasp that.

"Ada," Wade said, her name full in his mouth. "I have no illusions about Ada Tanner. I'd be lucky to make friends with her. It's a challenge I've considered taking, but I don't want any misunderstandings." He looked directly into Rusty's eyes. "I wouldn't want to give the appearance of an impropriety."

"Angela would understand," Rusty said, his thoughts more wistful than honest. "You should tell 'er."

Wade shook his head as he looked again at the ruffled surface of the spring's pool. "No, but then, there's nothing to tell. There's nothing between me and Ada and there never will be."

Rusty was disappointed. If Wade had confessed a desire for Ada, it would have made his own burden lighter. It would also have given him hope, a thing he had very little of these days. He could see the possibility of losing his friendship with Wade—or losing Angela and either way, Rusty was a miserable man.

"I was mistaken, then. I could've sworn there was."

Wade's expression was as dark as the billowing clouds overhead. "No," he said. "I know better than to pursue that impossible venture, but could I be honest with you?" he suddenly added and Rusty eagerly listened even though he was ashamed of himself for being the confidant of the man to whom he was betraying. "I don't want to marry Angela."

Rusty's heart leaped with excitement. He held his breath, afraid to even breathe, afraid that his ears had deceived him and that in the next moment, his folly would be revealed.

"It has nothing to do with Ada, though," Wade continued to confess. "Or maybe it has," he sorrowfully added. "You see, Angela has been my best friend for as long as I can remember. It was she who suggested we get married and at the time, I thought it was a good idea. It's funny how you can look back and see things so clearly—understand things, you know."

"Just tell her," Rusty said.

Wade turned and looked at him. "I have," he said. "She won't release me."

Rusty gave a start. He had dared to hope but now, he felt his high spirits plummeting. It all seemed so simple or it could be. He frowned in confusion, trying to sort out Angela's reason for hanging onto Wade. If she would just give Wade his freedom, then the two of them could be together. He moved restlessly in the saddle, repositioning himself to ease his discomfort.

"But why?" he asked before he could stop himself.

"The gold," Wade frankly said. "She wants me to give her the gold."

"So, you've found it," Rusty said in awe.

"No—maybe there isn't any gold."

"I don't understand," Rusty said, genuinely confused.

"She only wants to marry me to gain possession of the gold."

Rusty shook his head in disbelief. "She isn't that kind of girl," he said in her defense. "You've got her all wrong."

It caused Wade to look at Rusty—really look at Rusty. He

suddenly saw him like he had never seen him before and it was as if a light came on in his brain. What a fool to put the two of them together! Did he not know Rusty wouldn't be able to resist a woman like Angela? He silently cursed himself for a fool and for being a treacherous friend. It was not as if he was upset at the prospect of losing Angela to Rusty. He would have welcomed the idea, but Wade supposed it was a one-sided affair and that Rusty was hopelessly in love with a woman who would never return that affection. Well, the two of them could support each other in their misery, he thought, but it didn't give him any satisfaction to think that.

"Maybe I have," he agreed, although he didn't for one minute believe it. He would spare Rusty, though, and not demonize the object of his love. "She's a complicated girl," Wade went on to say. "And what man can figure out a woman anyway?"

Rusty smiled for the first time. "I'm sure I don't know."

The rain began to spatter around them and then suddenly, it came down in full force. A gray veil settled over everything, and they pulled their slickers tighter against the deluge. Wade quickly left the clearing and sought the protection of the thick canopy in the nearby woods. They found the fence again and took up their original position beside it, riding with greater care because of the rain.

They made the full circle and returned to the ranch just as the skies began to clear. The fence was intact. Not a strand of wire had been cut, but when Wade made that announcement, no one was particularly impressed. They knew it was only a matter of time, and, besides, they had all laid bets to that conclusion.

It was not the fence that was on Wade's mind, though. It was the gold. Critical events were giving Wade an urgent feeling to do something about it, and he was thinking that perhaps finding the gold would be his way out of the engagement with Angela instead of being the reason for it. If she wanted the gold, then he would give her a portion just to be rid of her. He planned to tell her that very thing, but at the same time, he didn't want to be too hasty. For one thing, he feared the treasure was only a myth. For sure, the gold had existed. His father's story was proof of that, but Wade knew how unlikely it was that the gold could still be hidden nearby—that it had not already been found. He still held to his belief that the confederate soldiers had taken it when they had killed Captain Thornton's squad. That was the most logical theory and Wade was afraid it would turn out to be the case.

In spite of this, Wade began to plan. He had put off following certain clues long enough and one way or another, he had to get on the Tanner's farm and do some investigating. He immediately thought of Ada, but just as quickly, he rejected any thought that tried to include her in his plans. She had not been agreeable, and unlike most women, Ada had not been impressed with Wade's good looks nor his apparent prosperity. He was not a conceited man, but it baffled him, nevertheless. He could not remember the time when a woman had not looked once and then looked again at him with favor. It was a bit disconcerting, but not totally unexpected. She was Logan's girl and a staunch supporter of the overall feelings of the south against Yankees. He had always been able to overcome that sentiment, however. Even in Texas, he had found acceptance easily enough, especially among the female population, but the Tanners held a long-standing resentment that he didn't quite understand. Only Mrs. Tanner seemed to soften where Wade was concerned, and he could only guess that it had something to do with his father's convalescence in her home. It had obviously made an impression upon her.

This line of thought was not getting him any nearer to a resolution of his problem so he quickly abandoned it. He cautioned himself to have discipline and to stay focused. It was not that hard. He was ready to concentrate wholly on the finding of the gold and he did.

All evening he worked on possibilities, even making notes that he cautiously disguised in case someone found them and interpreted them. By eleven o'clock, he had a theory. He sat on his bunk and leaned his back against the wall. As he sat there, a sound from outside interrupted his thoughts.

Wade sat up straighter and listened carefully. What was that? It sounded like singing, but it was a great distance away and he was not sure. Quickly, he stood up and then he ran to the door and jerked it open. He was in his sock feet, but he ran down the porch to the corner, stepping into a muddy yard as he made his way to the back of the bunkhouse.

The rain had stopped but clouds were moving swiftly across a dark sky being pushed by a steady wind. There was nothing to see on a night like this, but Wade stood very still and listened. Again, he heard the singing. It was coming from the direction of the Clearing—the land where the soldiers were supposed to be buried. Wade felt the hair on the back of his arms and neck stand up.

A burst of wind suddenly raced around the bunkhouse, catching Wade off guard. He steadied himself, but as quickly as it had begun, the singing had stopped. The night was so still that not a sound was heard anywhere.

Wade asked himself if it had actually been singing. Maybe it was an animal, some night bird, perhaps, indigenous to this area and unfamiliar to him, but then he remembered that Cody, Bart, and Pat, all local men, had been stumped by the sound.

So, what was it? Not for one minute did Wade believe it was the ghosts of the dead soldiers, even though it gave him a strange feeling that set his imagination to work. He stood there only a minute longer and then he returned to his bunk. Unfortunately, the interruption had broken his concentration and he could no longer keep his mind on his plans. He carefully laid his papers aside and blew out the kerosene lamp.

The next morning, Wade found Rusty in the corral saddling a horse before breakfast.

"Where are you going?" he asked, but Rusty only looked at him, his expression serious. "It's early. You haven't had your breakfast."

"It'll keep," he finally said, curtly answering Wade's concern.

"Is something wrong?"

Rusty paused in the middle of tightening a cinch. "No, not

exactly. I just feel like riding out to the Clearing this mornin'."

The Clearing! Well, no explanation was needed.

"I'll ride with you," Wade suggested, turning immediately to catch a horse.

The two of them rode out of the yard together and were at the Clearing in only a few minutes. It was a wide open place, the white sand hard packed after the rain, and only prickly pears — which the locals called pear pads — and bear grass growing on it. The sand was smooth and unbroken except where the rain had made ripples along uneven places. A lizard darted out and scurried across the ground, leaving a trail between bunches of the bear grass, but nothing else moved or showed any sign that anything had ever been there. Wade and Rusty sat on their horses and looked on it with grim fascination.

"So, you heard it last night, too?" Wade asked and Rusty nodded. "Maybe it's the wind."

"Maybe," Rusty reluctantly agreed. He looked around, trying to find a source that could funnel the wind in a way that would make music, but he saw nothing. "It ain't likely."

Rusty got down and walked around, testing the ground as he walked. Wade watched him, thinking that he appeared to be a man looking for a trap door or a loose board that would give way and open up below him. He sat still for a minute and then he too stepped down from his horse.

The sun was low in the sky, just an hour above the horizon. Its brightness seemed odd after the day of rain and Wade narrowed his eyes as he looked into it. Very slowly, he scanned the area.

"Nothin's here," Rusty said after a couple of minutes. "I was hopin' to find sign that would prove it was Logan—or some o' his boys."

"No one's been here since before the rain," Wade agreed.

"Do you reckon this is really the place?" Rusty suddenly asked, looking at the ground with some apprehension. He was referring to the dead soldiers that were supposedly buried here, but Wade needed no explanation to understand that.

He considered an answer before giving one. He didn't know, but it was as likely a place as any. If they had been caught here, out in the open, with no shelter, it would have been an easy job to wipe them out.

"Who knows," he said with some wistfulness. "It would ease my mind to know for sure," he went on to say. "I'd hate to disturb their final resting place."

Rusty nodded. He had taken his hat off, but now, he put it on and walked to his horse. He was just stepping into the saddle when he caught movement in his peripheral vision. His head jerked around, his eyes leveling on the spot where he had seen the movement and he was just in time to catch a glimpse of someone stepping behind a tree in the sapling thicket.

"Don't look now," he quietly said, "but we're bein' watched."

Wade turned with a start. "Where?" he asked, his voice low.

Rusty continued his swing into the saddle and then he took up the reins. "The trees yonder. He just stepped into that pine thicket."

"Let's get him!" Wade said, running to his horse.

Rusty took off before Wade could get set in the saddle, but he was only a thought behind Rusty. They raced across the clearing and pulled to a stop when they reached the pines, sliding to the ground as their horses abruptly stopped.

It was dangerous to ride a racing horse in the densely populated pine thicket. The trees grew very close together so it was safer and faster to go on foot. That's why they both jumped to the ground and dashed into the cool, shadowy interior of the sapling thicket.

They stopped almost immediately and looked around. It was a different world inside the forest of tall straight trees. There was a hush on the place as if Rusty and Wade had stepped into a cathedral, and both of them paused in reverence, awed by the surrounding woods.

There was no sign on the ground. The pine needles made a thick mat that would have hidden an elephant's track. It was a dead-end unless they could see something, but neither Wade nor Rusty saw any movement nor any sign that anyone had come that way. Reverently, they stepped deeper into the forest, separating without a word, and walking cautiously into its depths.

The interior closed around them with a feeling of heaviness. The trees moved and the wind soughed softly in the tops of them making them appear to whisper to each other. In the distance, a woodpecker began pecking, his tap-tap-tap not unlike a code. The woods seemed alive with correspondence, secret messages that only nature could interpret, and Wade felt an unconscious and unexplainable need to draw his gun.

He carefully eased out of the woods and Rusty was not two steps behind him. They stood at the threshold and looked into the quiet recesses without saying anything.

Rusty was the first to speak, breaking the spell that had taken over both of them.

"I didn't see nuthin'. Did you?"

"No," Wade quickly answered. "But I was a little spooked in there," he admitted.

Rusty was, too, but he was not as quick as Wade to admit it.

"I'm ready to ride back to the ranch. What about you?" Rusty asked.

"I'm right behind you," Wade said and both of them hurried to their horses.

They were halfway back to the ranch when Wade began to consider a new idea. The sapling thicket was only a short distance beyond The Clearing and it could be possible that the singing was coming from there. They had all been concentrating so hard on the legend of the dead soldiers that their imaginations let them go no farther than The Clearing, but Wade was at last getting beyond that.

"You know," he began, turning in his saddle for a last look in the direction of the sapling thicket, "if someone wanted to, they could live in that forest and no one would be able to find them. It's sheltered, you leave no tracks on the ground, and there are plenty of places to hide."

"There's water, too," Rusty added, his thoughts in

agreement. "I've been told there's another spring. It's on the other side of that forest, so there'd be game, too. A man could live a long time in there."

"But why would he want to?" Wade wondered aloud.

"Maybe he's wanted by the law or somethin'."

"Or maybe it's just Logan and his friends. It'd be a good place to rendezvous, don't you think?"

Rusty nodded. "That's prob'bly it. I'd like to ride around the perimeter and see what lies on the outskirts."

"That's a good idea."

"I'll do it today—with your permission, Boss."

"You have it."

They rode into the ranch yard and went straight to the corral. They stripped the saddles from the horses, and then they walked together to the bunkhouse. Powder Keg was cleaning up and Jake, Della's son was helping him. Powder Keg never asked a question. He simply set to work warming up breakfast.

"Know anything about that sapling thicket south of here?" Rusty asked Jake as he ate his food.

"Yassah," Jake answered. He was a strongly built young man, short of stature, but well-proportioned, his hair tightly curled and as black as night, and his skin as ebony as his hair. "De's good trees."

"No, I mean, about the place. Do folks hunt in there or hang out? What goes on in there?"

"Deys fo'ks whats goes in dere t' tap de trees. Deys money in de sap."

"That all?"

"Well, sah, de say it's a bad place. Most fo'ks stays clear o' it." His eyes became very large as he spoke—and wary.

"Haunted?" Wade casually asked, thinking that he could almost believe it himself.

"Yassah, dats what dey says."

"Tell me about it," Wade suggested and Jake's eyes grew even larger.

"De says dere's a man what walks to de spring to gits water. He carries a lant'rn and swaings it alon' ez he walks. He got a big, black hat dat he wear and he all in black—like de devil 'isself."

"He ever hurt anyone?"

"Nahsuh, not no more, but de say he be the spirit of de ol' man what onct libed dere. He wuz shore a mean man—beat hiz wife and chil'rens, 'n he'd kill ya' daid if'n the notion struck 'im. Fo'ks wuz skeered o' 'im and dey wuz sum relieved when 'e up 'n died."

"How long ago was that?"

"Twenty—thirty year ago. My ma tells me 'bout 'im onct 'n awhile."

"Did he sing?" Rusty asked and everyone in the room turned to give him a curious look.

"Nahsuh, not dat I knows, but de did say dey wuz a lotta sangin' when de foun' 'im daid."

"How'd he die?" Powder Keg suddenly asked.

"He wuz struck dow' by de han' o' Gawd, sure as I'z stan'in' here," Jake said with great emotion. "Fo'ks sez it wuz lightnin' but it wuz shore de han' o' Gawd!"

"He was struck by lightning in a pine thicket?" Powder Keg dubiously asked.

"Yassah. Dat what dey sez. It struck hiz haid and come out hiz feet an' 'e wuz burnt ez black ez a stump."

"Where d' he live, exactly?" Rusty asked after a short pause to give Jake's narrative the reverence it deserved.

"De ba'k side o' de woods ober near de spring. Hiz house ez still dere, all cubbered ober wid vines 'n t'ings, but it still dere. Onct I cum 'pon it right by acc'dent and ez I wuz lookin', a light suddenly cum on in one o' de winders. I wuz a kid den an' it skeered me so bad, I runned f'r home an' I ain't neber gawn ba'k."

No one said anything, but Rusty unconsciously tapped on the dish with his fork until Powder Keg reached across the table and took it away from him.

It started the move to get up and get out of the room, but before Wade went out, he turned to Jake with one more question.

"Who was this guy?" he asked. "What was his name?"

"He wuz Sidney Spencer, Mistah Wade, Log'n Spencer's gran'pappy."

Chapter Twenty-four

Rusty rode around the sapling thicket that morning and he was not at all surprised when he found that the Spencers lived on the edge of it. He rode wide of their small farm, but he could hear the dogs barking as he made the circle.

Their place was just a run-down house on a few acres of land, surrounded by two open fields waste high with corn and peas. Rusty gave it a serious study as he hurried past it, not slowing down even though he wished for a better look. He was thinking that this made a lot of sense and explained a few things, but it didn't ease Rusty's mind about everything. He began to wonder, though, if through some freak condition, sound from as far away as the Spencer's farm could somehow make it as far as Wade's ranch. He had heard of crazier things and he was not ruling anything out, but he doubted that theory, especially when he considered Logan's singing voice. If it was an example of the other Spencers then Rusty knew there was no way it could be them. Logan's voice would irritate a screech owl.

When Rusty returned to the ranch, he had nothing of significance to report to Wade. The location of the Spencer's farm was of interest, but like Rusty, it was no surprise to him. It did give Wade a better topographical understanding of the area. It had been on his mind to do more scouting. Riding to his neighbor's homes with Jess and Daniel had acquainted him with a great deal of the countryside, but Wade was interested in seeing it all. Given time, he wanted to have it all mapped out in his mind.

Not a lot happened in the next week. The sun shined bright and the ground dried out and the roads filled with white sand that cut into ruts.

It was hot. Wade sat on the porch and looked across the field, his thoughts on the cool water of the spring. It was Sunday afternoon and he wondered if the twins were there, playing in the water. He had not gone back except that one time with Rusty since the day he had been shot. He hadn't wanted to go, but today, he could not shake the desire that at last had him walking toward the corral to catch a horse.

He rode without care through the woods, but as he approached the spring, he became more cautious. He emerged from the tree line and the sunlight stabbed him in the eye as it reflected off the turquoise water. The scene before him never ceased to fill him with awe. Its beauty never became tiresome or trite. He enjoyed it each time he saw it as much as he had the first time. Today was no different. He sat on his horse and was looking at the glade, savoring the quiet scene, when he saw movement under the oak tree to the left of the water.

Two towheaded boys were squatted on the ground, intently looking at something before them. One of them turned and held out his hand and then they both laughed.

Wade smiled. He wondered what they were up to. He slid off his horse and tied the animal in a shady spot, and then he approached the twins on foot.

They were head to head when Wade drew near and not wanting to frighten them, Wade called out a greeting before he was very close.

"Hello, boys," he said and both of their heads came up. "What're you doing there?"

"We're doodlebug fishin'," Paul said.

Wade knew their propensity to play tricks on him and he figured this was the beginning of a scenario to trap the gullible Yankee once more.

"Catch any?" he carefully asked.

"Shore! You wanna see?"

Paul stood up before Wade could answer and walked to him, holding out his hand as he approached.

Wade looked into a palm filled with white sand and he mentally patted himself on the back for not being taken in by this ruse. He decided to go along with him, though, just to see where the prank would lead.

"Uh-huh," he grunted, approvingly. "I see there. You've got quite a few."

Paul wrinkled his brow and then he turned up his lip in a scowl of disdain. "Are you crazy?" he rhetorically asked and then he disturbed the sand in his hand with a finger, shaking it a little to show Wade what was beneath it.

The sand began to move and a little dimple appeared.

"See!" Paul excitedly exclaimed and Wade looked closer, not believing his eyes, and then, at last, recognizing the little creature for what he was.

"It's an ant lion," he said with delight.

"An ant lion?" Paul said, pulling back with disgust. His face was wrinkled with the biggest scowl he could make. "Only a Yankee," he said. "It's a doodlebug."

"You're right," Wade agreed. "How did you catch him?"

"I fished 'im out."

"Really?" Wade asked, still not certain he was not being fooled again.

Silas suddenly made a triumphant sound and then laughed as he held up his hand in victory. "Come see!" he said. "I got the gran'daddy uv 'em all. Just look at this big feller."

Wade and Paul hurried to him and they looked with keen interest. Silas was holding a stick, not more than a twig, and on the end of it was a length of spider web that hung down to make a fishing line. On the very end of the web was a tiny bug that Silas expertly removed and held in his hand.

"Git some sand," Paul quickly advised. "Boy, you're right! He's a big 'n, all right."

"You caught him!" Wade said, as caught up in the excitement as the boys.

"You wanna try?" Paul asked and Wade laughed outright as he took the tiny 'fishing pole' and squatted down.

"Here, you gotta hold it like this," he said, turning the twig in Wade's hand. "Now, put it over his hole and drop it down to 'im."

There were several cone shaped holes in the sand, each of them looking like hollow, upside down pyramids. Wade chose one, but Paul quickly admonished him.

"No, Wade. You gotta git one that you c'n see the doodlebug in. Look, see the black spot in the bottom? That's his pinchers. He's gotta be showin' 'em if you wanna ketch 'im."

"Okay, I've got it," Wade said and he daubed the spider web on top of the unsuspecting doodle bug only to have him disappear under the sand at the bottom of his hole. "What happened? Where'd he go?"

"You gotta be gentle," Paul said. "Just barely touch 'im. Easy—you gotta have a light touch an'----! Hey, you got 'em! Pull 'im out!"

Wade was so excited that he jerked the web out and he lost his catch. The web twisted hopelessly around the tiny stick and stuck to the back of it.

"Ah! Too bad," Paul moaned and when Wade touched the end of the web to straighten it, he was given another admonishment. "Don't touch it—oh, too late. We'll have t' find another spider web."

"Why?" Wade asked.

"'Cause it ain't sticky no more," Paul explained. "When ya' touch it, it loses its stickiness. It won't catch the bugs. See? They don't git caught no more."

Paul held it to the doodlebugs again, but he was right. Not one of them was captured with the contaminated web.

"There ain't no good webs around here," Silas reminded him. "We'll haf t' go back t' the house."

"What do you do with the bugs?" Wade asked as he watched their catch move around in a sandy box they had brought for the purpose. "You don't hurt them, do you?"

"Nah. We just play with 'em for a while an' then we let 'em go. They're happy anywhere as long as they got sand, so we turn 'em loose beside the house."

"Why did you come way down here to catch them if there were doodlebugs by your house?"

"It's more fun and mama always finds somethin' f'r us to do if we play too close to the house."

Wade smiled at their simple honesty. It was hot and he could feel the sweat beginning to run down the side of his face. He removed his hat and fanned himself as he looked at the cool water of the pool.

"Whew! It's a hot one today. I came to swim in the pool. Wanna join me? We never did get that rematch, you know."

Their eyes lit up. "Last one in the spring's a rotten egg!" Paul shouted as he and Silas dashed for the water, leaving their catch of doodlebugs behind. They stopped at the bank and began pulling off their clothes and Wade quickly joined them, realizing without malice that he was going to be the 'rotten egg'.

Sure enough, he was just pulling off his boots when the twins jumped into the water.

"Wade's a rotten egg-g! Wade's a rotten egg-g," Silas sang out in his singsong manner.

Wade stood up. He was smiling when he eased himself into the water. The chill was like a shock to his system. He shivered and then he quickly went under to completely wet himself. He didn't know why, but it always helped take away that initial icy feeling that almost hurt.

The twins wasted no time. They attacked simultaneously

and Wade went under again, but he caught one of them by the arm and dragged him down, too. The other one jumped on Wade's back and he fell over splashing water all the way to the bank. They played like this until all of them were so exhausted that they could hardly drag themselves out of the water. They crawled to the grassy spot in the sunshine and threw themselves down on the lawn. All three of them were panting as they lay there looking up at the sky.

"Well," Wade said after he caught his breath, "I think it was a draw. We'll have to have another match to break the tie."

"Sure looks like it," Paul agreed with mock consternation. "We cain't let the Yankee scourge go free, you know."

Wade chuckled softly. "After I've lived here fifty years, will you still think of me as the Yankee scourge?"

"Not us!" Paul said with some impatience. "We don't think of you as no scourge—but you are a Yankee. You can't help that."

Wade smiled. He folded his arms behind his head and wondered who they were repeating.

"I guess it was a member of your family who coined the phrase, then."

Paul sat up and then he turned his back to the sun, lying down again on his stomach. He propped his chin in a cupped hand and with the other hand, he plucked at a blade of grass. "Yeah, I reckon it was," he admitted.

"Your sister?"

Wade didn't see the look that passed between the two boys. He was looking at the clouds, thinking that one of them looked very much like a beautiful horse, racing in a cloud of dust which billowed around him as he stretched his neck to the finish line, but as the wind moved the clouds, his horse slowly transmogrified into a hideous dragon that grew wings and spouted fire. Curiously, Wade liked the dragon better than the horse. It seemed to reflect his mood much better and he smiled thinking maybe that was why he fancied he could see a dragon, at all.

"Nah. Ada didn't say it. I'll tell ya' somethin' if you promise not to tell Ada I told y'u," Paul said, his youthful voice taking on a serious tone.

"I promise," Wade said, his heart suddenly pounding.

"She's been sayin' good things about you. I don't think she hates you no more."

Wade was so excited, he found it hard to speak. "I'm glad to hear it," he said. "I've always hoped we could be friends."

"Well, she would be your friend, I think, if it weren't for daddy. He's still pretty set in his ways. You gotta remember, he fought in the war and he don't like no Yankee. It ain't personal, in his case. It's just that he cain't forget."

"I understand," Wade said. "But I had hoped to win his approval, too."

"It ain't gonna happen," Paul sadly admitted. "But you could win Ada," he said. "If ya' wanted to."

"Could I? Well, friendship should just happen," Wade said, thinking that anything he did would be construed as inappropriate. He wished again that Angela would agree to call off the wedding and then go back to New Hampshire. "That's the way it'll happen with me and Ada. We'll just one day realize we're friends."

"Maybe," Paul said. "Ada's different. You gotta remember that."

"Yeah, and she's Logan's girl," Wade said, suddenly sitting up and then coming to his feet. "You have to remember that."

Wade reached down and picked up his shirt. He put it on and then he began buttoning it up, not saying anything else.

"There's things I could tell ya', but I ain't gonna," Paul said as he too came to his feet. "Just don't give up on 'er, okay?"

"A man can never have too many friends," Wade said with a derisive smile. "I never give up on anyone."

He sat down and pulled on his boots, leaving a few minutes later in a somber mood. The twins, however, were grinning as they watched him ride away.

"He's hooked," Silas said and Paul agreed.

"It's just like doodlebug fishin'," Paul said. "You gently bait 'im and then you carefully pull 'im in. He'll think about what we said and his 'magination'll do the rest."

"Now, comes the hard part," Silas said. "Ada. We gotta convince her she's in love with him when she don't even like 'im."

"She likes 'im," Paul wisely said. "An' somethin' tells me this ain't gonna be as hard as we think."

"What about Wade's girl? What we gonna do about her?"

"Nuthin'. She ain't even in'rested in Wade. I seen her with that gunslingin' cowboy o' his and it took no 'magination on my part to see what's gonna happen there. I ain't worried atall about her."

"But Ada . . ."

"Yeah, well, she'll come around. We just gotta start the ball a rollin'."

"Maybe if it weren't f'r daddy," Silas said, looking glumly toward the path leading home. "Ada sets store by what he thinks. He wants 'er to marry Logan. I heard 'im say so."

"She won't marry 'im," Paul positively said. "If she starts t' do so, I got an ace up my sleeve. When she hears what I gotta say, she'll never marry Logan Spencer."

"Then just tell 'er," Silas impatiently said.

"Not yit. I gotta wait until the time's right. Remember, this is like doodlebug fishin'. If we strike too heavily, she'll retreat and there'll be no way to get to her. We gotta have a gentle touch an' pull back real careful like."

"Hey! What about our doodlebugs?" Silas suddenly said, looking in the direction of the oak tree.

"I forgot about 'em! Come on! Last one there's a rotten egg!"

Chapter Twenty-five

Ada loved and hated the garden. She loved the summer vegetables, especially the peas and corn, but she hated the work it took to get them from the field to the table. That's why she was grumbling as she picked the peas.

It was early. The sun was only a couple of hours high in the sky, but it was already hot, and Ada's back was already aching from bending and stooping. She put her hand to it and straightened up, looking toward the house as she rested a minute.

Her daddy had left early that morning for the river and he wouldn't be back until noon or later, but it was he that Ada was thinking about as she stared at the house.

Inevitable events had taken a turn after that afternoon when Wade Thornton had been shot, but unfortunately for Ada, they were falling back into place. Logan had come the day before, just like he always did on Sunday afternoon, and he had again pressured Ada to set a wedding date. The trouble was, this time, Fred Tanner had supported him, telling Ada that it was time she did the right thing and marry Logan.

"A pretty young girl's more trouble than one hen in a coup full of roosters," he had said. "Marry Logan b'fore I have t' start killin' off the roosters."

"What roosters?" Ada had indignantly asked. "The only men I see are you and Logan. The two of you see to that."

"Is that what's botherin' ya'? Not havin' enough men hangin' 'round here a squabblin' over ya'? I thought you were different th'n that. But I reckon women 'r women. I ain't seen one yit that didn't wan' the men a fightin' like cock roosters over 'er."

"That isn't true, daddy, and you know it. It's just that I feel diff'rent about Logan lately. It's not the same as it used to be."

"If it's cause uv that Yankee, you c'n forgit it," Fred Tanner had frankly said and her face flamed red with anger.

"You can't be serious!" she had said. "I hardly know Wade Thornton."

"Is that so?" he had mildly asked.

"Besides, he's engaged to be married. I ain't crazy."

"Maybe so, but hear me out anyway."

"I know what you're gonna say, but it ain't necessary."

"Well, just listen anyhow."

Ada had stood there and let Fred talk and what he had said cut deeply because she knew he was right.

"He ain't like us, honey," he had said, his voice soft and compassionate. "He's differ'nt, with differ'nt ways th'n ours. Now, don't look at me that way," he had said when a look of incredulousness and some exasperation had crossed her face. "You think I'm wrong, but I'm tellin' ya'—a Yankee might think he wants ya' and he might think he'd be happy with ya', but onct the honeymoon's over, he'll want ya' t' be somethin' that ya' just cain't never be. It's got nuthin' t' do with anythin' 'cept that he'll expect it and you cain't give it to 'im 'cause you just don't know how."

"This look isn't what you think," she had said, pointing a condemning finger at her face. "This look is sheer disbelief! I can't believe you'd think that of me."

"Think what? That you couldn't fall in love with a handsome young rich man? Well, that is unbelievable."

Ada shook her head as she remembered the conversation. She had gotten unreasonably angry with her father and now that she was being honest with herself, she knew it was because she had felt guilty. More and more, she had been thinking about Wade Thornton even though she had told herself it was a waste of her time. But she could not help remembering the things he had said to her, the things that set her heart to pounding with hot blood. Rendezvous—really! And being with her instead of playing war games—how bold! Was he so naive? Or was everything he said a calculated strategy to lure her in, just like a seasoned fisherman with an unsuspecting bass on his line?

She gave herself too much credit, she supposed. He probably never gave her a passing thought. Like most men, he couldn't resist the opportunity to flirt with her, and just like most men, it was probably only for some ignoble end. Men were not above casting a line, and if it caught something, he was lucky. If it didn't, he was not out anything—or that's what Ada was thinking just then.

Paul and Silas were two rows over from her and Ada looked their way before bending over the pea patch again. Peas and corn were grown together and the corn stalks were higher than her head so she could not see the boys, but she could hear them. They were laughing and she could not imagine what there was to laugh about in the pea patch.

"My bucket's almost full," she called to them. "I'll be goin' in soon. How're ya'll comin'?"

"We're almost done," Silas called back to her.

She filled her bucket and then she picked it up, swinging it at her side as she walked to the house. They now had to be shelled, but Ada didn't mind that. She sat down on the porch and she pulled the bucket to the side of her chair and an hour later, she had reduced her bucket of harvest to a bowl full of black-eyed peas.

It rained again, and not just an afternoon shower. Fred had just made it in from the river when the sky grew dark and thunder crashed nearby. The rain came down with a rush and it rained all afternoon. It suited Ada's mood, which was a little stormy. It was definitely dreary and in that, she felt a kinship with the rainy day. By sundown, the storm had passed and the sun came out for a showy display in parting, but Ada's mood didn't leave with the rain. She found herself moping around and even though she realized the uncharacteristic humor, she didn't care to change it.

Two days later, she was still in a foul mood when the twins brought news to her that, despite her vows of not caring, stirred her with an inkling of gladness.

"Ya' know what we heard?" Paul asked. They were standing under the white oak tree in the back yard and Ada was sitting on her 'reading' stool, an open book on her lap. "That girl—you know, the one that's over at Wade's place."

"Angela," Ada interjected to help him. "What about 'er?"

"She ain't gonna marry Wade, after all."

"How do you know?" Ada asked, her heart beginning to beat harder.

Paul furtively looked around as if he feared he would be overheard. "Ya' won't tell anyone, will ya'?"

"What?" she asked, suddenly very interested. "No, I won't tell. What is it?"

"I seen 'er with that gunslinger. They were huggin' and kissin' like nobody's business!"

Ada felt her face turn red. The little scamp! Did he think tellin' such a lie would endear him to her?

"I should tan your hide!" Ada said as she came to her feet. The book fell unnoticed to the ground.

"What for?" he demanded. "I swear, I ain't lyin'!"

She suddenly believed him and her thoughts went immediately to Wade.

"Poor, Wade," she said with great empathy.

"Well, it ain't like he really cares," Paul slyly said, planting a seed that he hoped would grow. "He put 'em together a purpose."

Ada had been blankly staring into the distance, but her eyes jerked back to Paul, alive with interest and curiosity.

"What 're you sayin'? Wade wants 'em together? Where'd you get such an idea?"

"From them," Paul assuredly said. "I he'rd Rusty tell 'er if

Wade hadn't purposely put 'em together then none of this woulda happened. An' she said, Wade didn't care—that he wanted 'er to go back to New Hampshire, but she couldn't go jest yit—especially not no more. She was meanin' about him 'n her."

"Are you shore that's what you heard?" Ada asked.

"There ain't nuthin' wrong with my ears," he sarcastically said. "I he'rd 'em plain as day."

"What does it mean?" she asked to no one in particular.

"Ain't it plain?" he impatiently asked. "I tell ya', Ada. Wade's got other things on his mind."

"How would you know what he's got on his mind?"

"Well, 'cause I c'n see, for one thing," he sheepishly said as he guiltily looked down.

"What? Have you been goin' to the spring again? Pa'll whip ya'," she insisted.

"Who said I'd been goin' to the spring?" he asked, but then he quickly walked away before she could question him further.

He and Silas ran to the big oak and then they laughed with delight. This was more fun than anything they had done in months! They put their shaggy heads together and began to plan their next move.

Ada, on the other hand, was seriously considering what Paul had said. She knew he was not above lying when the notion suited him and she was afraid he was doing that just now, but it was such a fantastic story. How did a little boy make up such a thing?

Strangely, she felt sorry for Wade. Even if he had put Rusty and Angela together and on purpose, too, she still saw him as the slighted partner. How could she do that to Wade? Ada angrily asked herself that and then she almost laughed aloud when she realized what she was thinking.

Her thoughts were interrupted by the sound of a wagon coming down the road. It would be her daddy returning from Mr. Harris' farm. She walked out from under the white oak tree for a better look and sure enough, the old wagon was lumbering down the road, but oddly, there were two people on the front seat. One of them was Logan.

Ada sighed just as her mother walked onto the porch nearby, wiping her hands on her apron as she stood looking at the wagon.

"Do they have the boar?" she asked and Ada moved first one way and then the other to see.

"I think so—yes ma'am. They're goin' to the loadin' chute."

Fred had a sow he wanted to breed and Mr. Harris had the finest boar in the county. He had made a deal with John and when the litter came, it would be split between them for payment.

The arrival aroused some excitement. The twins ran in from the big oak and Ada and Mrs. Tanner walked from the house to the side of the pen. They stood beside the rails, watching as Fred expertly backed the wagon up to the chute. Logan had jumped down and he was holding up a hand that he signaled with, guiding Fred in his endeavor.

The hog was a big Yorkshire boar and he began to grunt and squeal as Fred and Logan prodded him into the chute. He didn't like the closeness of the narrow aisle they forced him into and he squealed all the more. Logan let down the rails between the chute and the pen and without any coaxing, the boar escaped the chute and ran into the open pen.

It was a large pen—not a small smelly sty. One corner had a trough and a muddy spot where the hogs liked to cool off, but today there was only the sow there. She didn't even stand up when the boar entered her domain.

"They don't seem too in'rested in each other," Logan said as the boar ran around the pen, checking it out as he continued to grunt excitedly.

"They will be," was all Fred said. He walked back to the chute and checked to see that the rails were properly back in place before he climbed onto the wagon seat and moved it away. Logan glanced toward Ada and then he quickly walked to her. She watched him come without comment or feeling. He had once excited her with his approach, but not anymore.

"Hello, Mrs. Tanner," he genially said, removing his hat in her presence.

"Hello, Logan," she said. "It was nice of you to help Fred."

"Yes, ma'am. I wasn't doin' anything else today, so it was no problem."

You're never doing anything else! Ada quickly thought, but she said nothing.

"I made a blackberry doobie this morning," Mrs. Tanner said. "If you'd like to come to the house and have some."

"Yes, ma'am," he said with a wide grin. "I would."

"You comin', Ada," he said when he began to follow Mrs.

Tanner but Ada didn't move.

"I will in a minute," she replied, wishing she could go away until he left.

"Suit yourself," he said and he continued to accompany Mrs. Tanner to the house.

Ada had stepped up on the bottom rail of the hog pen and was standing, leaning over the top rail. She stepped down and watched Logan as he walked away. It was an odd relationship he had suddenly taken up with her parents although Ada was not sure how her mother really felt. Mrs. Tanner was a complex woman with deep feelings. Everyone liked her, but few people really understood her. That was what Ada was thinking as she moved away from the fence. She was also considering what she would do about Logan.

When she entered the kitchen a few minutes later, she was no closer to a decision than she had been before, but the sight of Logan sitting at the table, eating doobie with Mr. Tanner, softened her heart.

"Where ya' been, Ada?" her father immediately asked and she shrugged before answering.

"Just wanderin' around," she airily said and Logan gave her a look that was both smug and amused. It made Ada wonder what the conversation had been before she walked in. Her soft spot quietly began to harden.

"Come 'ere. I wanna talk t' ya'," Fred suddenly said.

Ada obeyed. She walked to the side of the table where he was sitting and she stood beside him. He pulled out a chair and she silently sat down. Something was in the air and Ada was afraid she knew what it was.

"Now that I got you and Logan t'gether, I wanna talk t' ya' about somethin'," he said in a genial manner. He pushed back in his chair and smiled at her, and then he put a fatherly hand on her shoulder. "Look," he began, "I understand y'u got some concerns about gittin' married, especially when you ain't got no place of yore own t' live, but you know the folks around here. We'll all pitch in an' build ya' a house. Don't let that keep ya' from settin' a weddin' date. We'll see ya' got a home and Logan'll find some kinda work t' do. He c'n always go t' fishin' if nuthin' else." He glanced at Logan as if for approval, but Logan's look was as blank as a slate. "There's lots of things he c'n do to make a livin' for ya'," Fred went on. "So, I wancha to set a date and the sooner the better. Go ahead an' do it, so we c'n git started on y'ur house."

Ada didn't say anything for a few seconds. She stared at Logan and then ever so slowly, her eyes moved across the room to Mrs. Tanner. Esther was looking at her, but if there was a message in those dark eyes, Ada couldn't read it.

"It isn't that," she finally said. She could feel a blush of embarrassment creeping up her neck.

"Then what is it?" Fred demanded. Logan's eyes locked onto hers and she read his look quite easily. It was obvious he and Fred had been talking. Otherwise, Mr. Tanner wouldn't have known about Ada's concerns about living with the Spencers. Did he think it would be so easy? Did he think he could simply build her a house and solve the problem between them? It was not a simple matter, but Ada could see that Logan assumed it was.

"I—I ain't ready t' git married," she said, stumbling over her words in an effort to get them out. "I ain't—I mean, I don't want t' git married."

"Is that it, Ada?" her father asked. He leaned forward in his chair and his overall mien changed from genial to serious business. "Or is it that the right man ain't asked ya'?"

Logan moved so suddenly that his chair scrapped on the floor. Fred held up a hand as if to caution him and Logan settled down, easing back in his chair.

"If you're thinkin' about that Yankee, you'd better reconsider," Fred sternly said. "Even if he wanted ya', I'd have second thoughts about lettin' 'im see ya'. I've toldja how I feel."

Ada felt her whole body tense and then she began to shake.

"An' I've told ya' I have no interest in him," she angrily said. "Why do you continue to accuse me?"

Fred eased back in his chair. "'Cause I seen ya'll together, Ada," he frankly said. "An' I know he was here the night of the party. You ain't done somethin' foolish, have ya'?"

Ada caught her breath and stood up. How did Fred know Wade had come here the night of the party? An' where had he seen them together? The times had been few and brief, but which ones had Fred witnessed? Ada found herself on the defensive and it was a position she didn't like. She could not explain—not to their satisfaction, anyway, and she didn't feel inclined to try.

"No," she simply said and without another word, she calmly walked out of the kitchen.

Chapter Twenty-six

"Supper's ready," Mrs. Tanner softly called at Ada's door.

Ada had cried until her nose was stopped up and her eyes were swollen. She didn't want to come out for supper.

"I ain't hungry," she said.

"May I come in?" Esther quietly asked.

The door had no lock. She could have come in if she had wanted, but she had a way of showing courtesy and respect even to her children. It was an endearing quality and one that immediately gave Ada a desire to let her come in. Ada sniffed loudly and dabbed at her eyes, and then she answered. "Yes ma'am. You c'n come in."

Mrs. Tanner opened the door and paused on the threshold before entering. The room was very small with only a few pieces of furniture crammed into it—a bed, a table with a kerosene lamp on it, and a small dresser. Ada was sitting on the bed, her hands folded in her lap and her head hung down. Mrs. Tanner sat down beside her and pulled Ada's head to her shoulder.

"Tell me what's goin' on with y'u, girl," she softly said.

"Oh, mama!" Ada cried and she began to sob again. "I don't wanna marry Logan. I just don't love him no more."

"There, there," she crooned as Ada cried. The stormy mood finally passed and Ada pulled away from her mother. She sat quietly for a few minutes and then she nodded her head.

"I'm okay, now," she said. "I don't know what came over me."

"You wanna talk about it?"

Ada shook her head. "There ain't nuthin' t' say 'cept I don't wanna marry Logan. I don't have to, do I, mama?"

"No," Mrs. Tanner was quick to answer. "But you might give yore daddy a better explanation. He believes you're seein' Wade on the sly and he ain't the only one. Folks are beginnin' t' talk."

"Are they?" Ada asked with true astonishment. "Why, that's crazy!"

"Wuz 'e here the night of that party, Ada?"

"He was," she honestly answered, "but he never even came inside the fence. I stood on the porch an' talked to him an' I held Skippy real close t' me."

"Why was he here, then?" Mrs. Tanner wondered aloud.

"It wasn't t' see me. I don't believe he even knew I was here. It ain't the first time he's been here either," Ada admitted. Once the confession began, she felt like telling her mother everything. "He came here right after he moved in and he was snoopin' around when he ran into me under the white oak tree. He was sure surprised."

Mrs. Tanner thought about that and she suddenly sighed. Ada looked at her in wonder.

"Well," Esther drawled, "I have to admit, I was rather hopin' it was you and not the gold he was after."

"Mama!" Ada gasped. "But he's a Yankee!"

Esther's head came up with a start. "An' what does that

mean? He's a good man an' that's all I care about. His daddy was a good man, too. I c'n shore see 'im in Wade," she wistfully said. "Listen to me, Ada," she suddenly said, her tone changing. "you could do a lot worse than marryin' a man like Wade. Maybe it's just the gold he's after and maybe it ain't, but I'd be proud t' have 'im in the family."

"He ain't int'rested in me, mama. Oh, he flirts, but all the boys do that."

"Then you ain't been seein' 'im? Logan says he was huggin' you down by the spring one day."

Ada laughed despite the seriousness of the conversation. "He grabbed me—said he thought I was one o' the twins comin' down the path, an' he turned me loose just as quick as he saw his mistake. He was as surprised as I was."

"Was he?" Esther coyly asked.

"He was, mama. I could see it in his eyes."

"Then ya'll weren't laughin' and carryin' on?"

"I guess we were. He'd been playin' in the spring like a little boy and it struck me funny. I teased him about it, an' I'll have t' admit, he was a good sport. But that was all."

Ada dropped her head, thinking about the times she had been alone with him and the hints he had given her that would indicate things could be different. Was he seriously testing the waters to see if he had a chance with her or was he simply trying to see how far he could go without any strings attached? Ada wondered, but in the end, she came to the same conclusion she always did. He was not sincere. In fact, Ada was convinced it was the gold he wanted and that was why he kept coming around. She said as much to her mother.

Esther nodded with resignation. "Well, girl," she said in her endearing way, "I think you underestimate yoreself. Maybe 'cause you don't know about all the boys Logan's run off since he got int'rested in y'u. He's a big man and he's won ever' fight he's had."

"Not every fight," Ada reminded her. "Wade whipped 'im real bad."

"So, he did," Esther said with smug satisfaction. "Wade's full o' surprises, it seems. That's why I wonder if we have even more surprises in store f'r us where he's concerned."

Ada knew what she meant. It was a hope that Ada found curious coming from Esther Tanner, but it really was not a great surprise. Caring for Wade's father had done something to Esther. She spoke very little of the incident, but when she did, it was with a warmness and an unmistakable fondness. He had made a great impression on her and Ada suddenly wondered if that was part of Fred's attitude toward Wade. Ada looked at her mother with new eyes. Had she hidden feelings for a wounded man she had cared for so many years ago? The thought startled Ada and she gasped, in spite of herself.

"Esther!" Fred's voice boomed through the wall. "Where're you women?" he curiously demanded. "Supper's gittin' cold."

"Come on, Ada," her mother said. "Show yore dad what you're made of. Dry yore eyes and come to supper. He'll see things straight one o' these days."

Ada took her mother's advice and when she walked into the dining room, she held her head high. Fred cast a curious look her way, but he didn't say anything.

"Where's Logan?" Ada asked.

"He left," Fred answered. "Sit down and let's eat," he added and that was the end of the conversation.

Chapter Twenty-Seven

"Angela, we gotta tell Wade the truth," Rusty said. She was clinging to him, spent after the way he had hugged and kissed her. "I cain't go on like this."

She tightened her arms around his neck and looked up at him. Rusty had no idea what was going on between Wade and Angela. He didn't know that Angela, following her father's orders, was trying desperately to get Wade to the altar. If she told Wade about Rusty, she would never get him there.

"No," she said. "Not yet."

He pulled away from her and leaned forward, resting his hands on his knees as if he needed help catching his breath. "This is so wrong," he said. "Wade's my friend. I cain't keep doin' this."

"You wanna call it off?" she asked and his head came up in an instant.

"I cain't," he admitted. "I'm a lost soul, Angela. I cain't let you go and I cain't face Wade no more."

"Just a little while longer," she said.

"He'll let you go, Angela. I know he will."

"No. I won't be pushed away like an old piece of garbage!"

Rusty stood up straight and he gave Angela a curious look. "What does that mean?" he asked. "We lost our pride when we kissed for the first time."

"It's more than pride," she said, being honest for once.

"Then what is it?"

"Well . . . there's papa to consider. You know how he feels. He has his heart set on having Wade for a son-in-law."

"He'll get over it."

"Yes, but he's my father," she insisted. "I love him very much."

"More'n me?" Rusty asked and Angela gave a little shriek of dismay.

"Never!" she said, throwing her arms around his neck again. It was all that it took to win the argument. Rusty could not resist her no matter how hard he tried.

They rode into the ranch yard a few minutes later and Wade was standing beside the bunk house watching them. Rusty guiltily read suspicion in his eyes even though it was not there. In all honesty, Wade was hoping Angela had taken a liking to Rusty. His thoughts were running down that avenue of thought, but then he wearily dismissed it as he considered Angela.

"Enjoy your ride?" he casually asked as Angela stepped down from the horse and approached him.

"It was wonderful! Did you know, there's a lovely spring about a mile from here? I've never seen a more beautiful spot. Wade, you chose the wrong site for your house. It should've been there."

Wade jerked as if he had been stung by a hornet. It was Ada's spring and Angela being there was almost a sacrilege. He wanted to tell Rusty not to take her there again, but he knew it was too late for that. Angela had found it and now she would never let anyone keep her away.

"Be careful if you go there again," he sternly said. "Snakes like the water and so do alligators."

"I won't be in the water, Wade. I'll just be near it."

"Neither snakes nor alligators stay just in the water," he warned her. "We heard Mr. Maraquette killed a sixteen foot alligator in his back yard just a week ago."

"Well, I'll keep my eyes open," she said, not at all concerned by his warning. She waved a hand before her face to move the air in an effort to cool herself. "Whew, it's a hot one today, isn't it? I'm going to the house. Is Della there? I'm ready for lunch."

Wade nodded. "She's there," he answered, "but wait, Angela. I want you to know that I'm leaving for a few days."

She had begun to walk to the house, but she stopped and returned to him. "Where are you going?" she asked.

"There's a man on Fleming Island that has cattle for sale. I'm going to look at them and see if I can make a deal."

"Oh, Wade!" she exclaimed. "I thought we'd been over this and you had agreed to wait."

"No, I never agreed to wait."

"But you did," she insisted. "There are so many things that are more important than your stupid cows."

"Not here, Angela," he said, looking around to see if she had been overheard. "Let's keep our disagreements private."

"Oh, pooh!" she said with an impatient wave of the hand. "Everyone knows, anyway. What do I care about the hired help anyway?"

Rusty had just come around the corner of the building as she spoke and he stopped in his tracks. He had an inferiority complex where Angela was concerned. It was a fear that had him always on guard even though she came willingly to him. He imagined her as royalty and himself as a humble slave whom she took pleasure with whenever it suited her and her statement stopped him as surely as if he had run into a brick wall.

"Well, I care even if you don't," Wade roughly said. He took her by the arm and led her to the house. Rusty watched, his teeth clinched tightly and his eyes squinted in anger. He had mixed emotions just then. On one hand, he was stricken with grief over Angela's slip of the tongue, and on the other hand, he wanted to confront Wade for manhandling her. He looked down at his feet and mentally reprimanded himself. What had become of him? Maybe it was time for him to leave, and this time, he wouldn't tell Wade. He would just get on his horse and go.

He turned on his heels and walked away. His mind was made up. Tomorrow, he would arise early and before anyone was up, he would saddle up and leave. It was time.

But before Rusty could get as far as the barn, Cody rode in on a fast moving horse.

"Hey, Wade!" he called out and Wade appeared on the porch at the house. "The fence huz been cut. Ever'thing from the southwest corner to the back of Mr. Dover's farm. Three miles or more of fence!"

Wade stepped down from the porch, his face grim. Angela

stepped down beside him, but she was not unhappy. In fact, she fought to hide the smile that crossed her face.

"Well," she softly mused, speaking so that only Wade could hear her. "I suppose this takes care of the problem with the cattle."

He flashed her an irritated look, but then he quickly turned back to Cody.

"Let me get my horse," he said. "I want to see."

Rusty joined him, suddenly forgetting his misery in the face of this new development.

"I'm comin', too," he said, and the three of them rode out together a few minutes later.

Angela and the major watched them go and neither of them could hide the smug look of satisfaction on their faces. The major pulled a cigar from his front coat pocket and casually lit it while he slyly looked down the road.

"How fortuitous," Angela said. "I should like to thank Logan Spencer. He has become an unwitting ally."

"Not Logan, my dear," the major said, "but he shall be blamed."

Angela gave her father a dubious look. "What do you mean, papa?" she asked.

"Never you mind," he said. "The less you know, the better."

She laughed. "You are devious. I've become a regular villain myself," she added. "Aren't we a pair?"

"Blood is thicker than water," he said. "But I do feel sorry for Wade. I've always liked him. It's too bad, but self-preservation is a powerful motivation." He removed the cigar from his mouth and looked at Angela, squinting through the smoke that drifted between them. "By the way," he added, "I've seen your rival and I have to admit, she's an opponent to be reckoned with."

"Oh?" Angela said with great curiosity. "Wade's backwood's Juliette?"

"She's more than that. If I was a few years younger, I'd been tempted myself. Perhaps, I was anyway," he said with a coy smile.

"Oh, really. Well, now my curiosity *is* piqued. I'll have to meet this alluring creature."

"Yes," he absent-mindedly said. "Rightly spoken," he went on to say. "Rightly spoken, my dear. She is quite alluring."

Chapter Twenty-eight

Wade sat on his horse and looked down the fence line. The wire had been cut and then the posts had been pulled up. A horse had been used to do the job and it had been done over a period of time. This was the line farthest from the ranch and the one least checked, so this could have been going on for days—or weeks.

Wade stepped down and walked to the place where the fence once stood. He looked down the line, his hands on his hips and his hat pulled low over his face. He would put the fence back up. There was no question about it, but he didn't know if he would have enough money to support himself if he put the fence up and bought cattle. He had plans to get odd jobs to bring in money, but everything took time, and Wade was running out of money as fast as he was running out of time.

"What d' ya' say, Boss?" Cody asked as he joined Wade. "Do we put it back up?"

"We do," Wade grimly said. "But maybe not yet."

He was thinking that he could bring the cattle in and let them roam free until he could get the fence up again. Everyone did it. There were cattle on his land right now that didn't belong to Wade, but the fence was more than just a way to keep in his cattle. It had become a statement that said Wade Thornton would not be run out. If he let it lay, he would have lost something he didn't know that he could retrieve.

"I have a notion to go see Logan Spencer," Wade suddenly said.

"I'll go with you," Cody offered with enthusiasm.

"Not just yet, though," Wade said as he walked back to his horse. He gathered up the reins and swung up into the saddle. "I'm going to ride the line."

He started the horse down the line that had once held the fence and Cody and Rusty rode with him. Here and there, a fence post stood in place, but most of them were lying sideways or flat on the ground. The barbed wire was twisted and coiled, cut in many places and sometimes piled in a heap along with the posts. The farther Wade rode, the angrier he became until he was boiling mad when he at last came to the uncut line.

The unspoiled fence began at the gate to Mr. Dover's homestead and disappeared as it dipped into a low place just over a rise in the ground. Wade stopped and studied the ground. This had been the most recent scene of activity. Unlike the southwest corner, you could see sign of both horses and men. Wade could not tell how many. The ground was too torn up and used, but Rusty gave it a serious and thorough going over, reading things Wade could not see.

"There wasn't but one or two men here," he said after a while.

"I guess it didn't take but one, if you come right down to it," Wade said, his face set in hard lines.

"Logan's lost a lot of his prestige in the community," Cody said, pushing his hat back on his head as he spoke. "He ain't got as many followers as he used to have. People 'round here like a game man, and you've proved to be one. They might not accept ya', but they won't fight ya', either."

"That's why the fence has got to go back up," Wade said.

"I figured as much," Cody admitted.

There was a brief silence and then Rusty spoke up. "We might be able to salvage some of the wire and most of the posts," he said. "You want us t' check it out?"

Wade turned with hope in his eyes. "Yes," he readily answered. "Do that." He had been resting his arm on the saddle horn, but now he sat up and gathered the reins to himself. "I'm going to Mason's Corner."

"You think that's wise?" Rusty asked, afraid he knew what Wade was looking for. As mad as Wade was, if he found Logan, he would pick a fight, and if he picked a fight, Logan would need a doctor when he was through.

"Maybe not, but I've got to show them I'm not whipped— not yet anyway."

"I'll come with you," Rusty suggested, but Wade shook his head.

"No. You and Cody check on the fence. I'll be alright."

Cody and Rusty reluctantly turned their horses and rode back down the line. Wade watched them go and then he turned his horse's nose east and began walking him toward Mason's Corner.

Wade heard a dog barking before he could see the buildings at Mason's Corner. A minute later, a train whistled in the distance. He rode to the gate and opened it, going through and closing it without getting down from the saddle.

The little community was quiet and no one was in view when Wade rode up to the steps of the store and stepped down. He looked around while he tied his horse, but the only living thing he saw was a hound dog, lying in a freshly dug hole under the corner of the porch. Wade walked inside, removing his hat as he came into the shadowy interior of the store. Mr. Mason was sitting at the back corner, fanning his face with a paper fan. The back door was open wide and a breeze was drifting through it. Mason looked up when Wade stepped inside and then he called out his usual greeting.

"Howdy! Shore is a hot one today." He slowly came to his feet and walked to the counter. "C'n I help ya' with somethin'?"

"No," Wade answered. "I'm lookin' for Logan Spencer. You seen him lately?"

There was a pause before Mason answered and the moment was charged with meaning.

"No. I reckon I ain't."

"If you see him, will you tell him I'm looking for him?"

"Trouble?" Mr. Mason asked.

"Yeah. Three miles of fence is down. I want to ask him if he knows anything about it."

"Whew!" A whistle arose from the back corner. Wade turned. It was Pappy and he was rubbing a grizzled chin as he sat over his keg of checkers. He suddenly laughed, but it was a derisory laugh, with no humor in it. "You blamin' Logan?" he asked.

"No. I just want to talk to him. It can be friendly if he likes or otherwise if he doesn't."

"That's plain enough," the old man said. "He's been over at Tanners a lot lately. I hear him and that gal of Fred's is gittin' married any day now."

"Oh?" Wade said, his face feeling hot, but it was a heat that had nothing to do with the weather.

"Looks like it," Mason said. "An' it's about time. They've been hangin' around together long enough that Logan's whipped ever' boy in the community over her." He laughed at his observation only to stop short as he remembered the beating Wade had given Logan. He cleared his throat and changed the subject. "You gonna need supplies? I'll have to order wire and such, but I c'n git it."

"I might. We're salvaging what we can. I'll let you know."

"Shore thing," Mason said and then he watched as Wade walked out of the store.

Pappy stood up and walked to the counter. "That's a tough man," he said as Wade stepped into the saddle and turned his horse around. "I'd hate t' know he wuz huntin' me."

"Yeah, well, Logan ain't no coward, but I don't imagine he'll relish the idea either."

"Whatta ya' think?" Pappy asked, rubbing his chin again. "Do ya' reckon he's got the gold on his ranch or has he moved it?"

"I haven't seen any indication that it's been moved. It's probably still there."

"You oughta ask Della. I bet she'd know." He looked out the open door in thought. "Or that boy o' her'n. She's purty tight-lipped, but the boy'd tell if he knew."

"I don't know," Mason said. He was looking out the door, too, but he was not thinking about Della or her family. He was thinking about the fence and Logan Spencer.

"I don't think Logan pulled his fence down," he suddenly said. It took Pappy a few seconds to catch up with the change in subject. He turned and looked at Mason, his brow furrowed.

"No? Well, I kinda agree with ya', although," and here he paused to consider, "Logan swore it'd never stay up."

"Yes, but that was before someone shot Thornton. Logan's been layin' low since then."

"Prob'bly figured the law was gonna git 'im," Pappy said.

"He swears he didn't do that either," Mason said. "An' I believe 'im."

"Who then? Nobody else had a reason."

"Are you sure? I heard that girl of Fred's has been sneakin' around meetin' Thornton on the sly."

"All the more reason for Logan t' shoot 'im."

"Yeah, well, you know how her daddy feels about Yankees. I wouldn't put it past him."

"That's a thought. It shore is." He rubbed his unshaven chin and considered that. "Ya' know, I ain't one t' gossip, but I heared Fred and Esther had trouble when he come home from the war—somethin' about that Yankee she took care of—Wade's daddy."

"Esther's a good woman, so don't believe everything ya' hear. Besides, he was shot nearly t' death. There was no love affair, 'cause he weren't able."

"Love ain't always physical," Pappy pointed out. "Sometimes there's just somethin' there and two people know it. An' Esther wuz a right purty woman when she wuz y'ung."

"She's always been a lady," Mason said. "An' she'll always be a lady. If there was somethin', no one'll ever know."

Pappy nodded. Of that, they could both agree.

It might have been good if Wade had heard the conversation between Pappy and Mr. Mason, but he didn't. He rode out of Mason's Corner and rather than go home, he rode the fence line all the way to Tanner's property. He stopped his horse at the well-worn trail that led down to the spring and he sat there simply looking at it, not saying anything nor really seeing it either. He was thinking about Ada and the fact that she was about to marry Logan Spencer, but more than that, he was thinking how much that hurt him.

He jerked on the reins, turning the horse with a suddenness that startled the poor beast. He cut across his property and came out on the back side of the sapling thicket where the Spencer's small farm sat against the background of tall pine trees.

A dog began to bark and Wade scattered chickens in every direction as he rode up to the house.

It was a small two story wooden house, faded and worn with age. A woman stepped to the door as she heard him approach and she shielded her eyes with a hand over her brow as she looked out at him.

"Light n' set, stranger," she said as he stopped in the yard.

"I'm looking for Logan," Wade said. "Is he here?"

"No. He's helpin' Fred Tanner." She walked onto the porch and it was then she recognized Wade. She dropped her hand as a dark look crossed her face. "What y'u want with my boy?" she harshly demanded. "Ain't y'u done enough?"

"I don't want any trouble," Wade said, but that was really a lie. He was mad and hurt and he wanted nothing more than to beat the daylights out of Logan Spencer. "My fence is down," he explained. "An' I ain't saying Logan did it. That isn't why I'm here. I want to ask Logan about the man he claims to have seen hanging around these woods."

"Ain't no claim. He seen 'im."

"Well, I'd like to talk to him about the guy."

She hesitated. "I toldja where he is," she slowly said. "Don't start nuthin' there or Fred Tanner'll have yore hide." She proudly lifted her chin. "Logan's gonna marry Fred's girl, ya' know."

"Yes, I know," Wade said. He wondered why everyone kept pointing that out to him. He didn't know, but Mrs. Spencer, like many other people in the community, had heard the rumors that Wade and Ada were secretly meeting. It gave her a great amount of satisfaction to point out that Logan would beat him in this challenge, if no other. "Thank you, ma'am," he said with a tip of his hat, and then he turned and left. He knew he shouldn't do it, but he rode straight to the Tanner's farm and stepped down from his horse at their front gate.

Paul and Silas came running around the corner of the house as he opened the gate and let himself into the yard. Skippy began to bark and Mrs. Tanner appeared at the door, holding a broom in her hands as she looked out.

"Hey, Wade!" Paul excitedly shouted. He and Silas were grinning from ear to ear, plainly happy about his arrival. "Whatcha doin' here?"

"Hey, boys," he said, giving them both a brotherly grip on the shoulder. "I was out riding and I thought I'd like to see your doodlebug holes."

"Ah, you're jokin'," Paul said with a wave of his hand. "You're lookin' for Ada, ain'tcha?"

Wade pushed his hat back and the genial look left his face. "No, boys," he soberly said. "I'm looking for Logan Spencer."

"He ain't here," Silas said. "He and daddy went to the river t'gether."

"Howdy, Mr. Thornton," a voice spoke from the porch. Wade turned, seeing Mrs. Tanner standing there. "Come in," she added.

He removed his hat and walked to the steps, stopping to look up at her. "Hello, Mrs. Tanner," he said. "I was looking for Fred and Logan," he quickly explained.

"They aren't here," she said, "but you're welcome to come in and wait."

Wade hesitated but not because he didn't want to accept. He weighed the consequences and considered what would happen when Logan returned and found him sitting there waiting for him. Wade was not afraid, but he didn't want to be at a disadvantage when that time came. He knew, however, that he was going to accept even before his foot moved up to the first step.

"Thank you," he said, and he followed her into the house.

The room was square with another door that opened onto the walkway to the kitchen. It was a humble room, but everything was clean and neat. There was a table in the middle of the room with a large kerosene lamp on it and a fireplace on the wall to the right. Two wooden chairs were against one wall and a worn couch was against the other. Hand crocheted antimacassars covered the threadbare arms and the back of it. Wade wondered if it was the same couch his father had reclined on as he recuperated from the gunshot wound, and he quickly decided that it was. An odd feeling came over him at the thought.

Mrs. Tanner gave him a sapient look as she paused in the room. She seemed to look right through Wade, seeing his heart and reading his mind. He nervously shifted his feet and he was glad when she offered him a cup of coffee. "I was just makin' a fresh pot when you rode up," she explained.

"Thank you," he said and he followed her out the door and down the walkway to the kitchen.

This room was large and very welcoming, serving as both kitchen and dining room. A large wooden table was the focal point, but the gingham curtains at the windows were the first thing that caught Wade's eye. It reminded him of his mother's kitchen and a warm, nostalgic feeling immediately came over him.

"This is nice," he said, really meaning it.

"Have a seat," was all Mrs. Tanner said. She poured him a cup of coffee and set it on the table before him.

He looked around, wondering where Ada was, and just as the thought came to him, he heard her outside, singing as she approached the house.

She sang a few words of a song and then she hummed the rest of the tune, oblivious of the fact that Wade was there. He sat back and listened, smiling as he heard her soft footfalls on the porch. There was a distinctive thump as she set something down and he looked intently at the door, completely forgetting that Mrs. Tanner was watching him.

Ada came straight to the kitchen and opened the screened door, removing a large straw hat as she entered. Wade slowly came to his feet and when she saw him, she abruptly stopped on the threshold, her hat in her hand.

"Wade!" she exclaimed.

"Hello, Ada," he said, smiling at the surprise he made.

She immediately cast an anxious look over her shoulder. Wade knew what that meant. She was looking to see if Logan and her father were returning, but the road was clear. She cautiously stepped into the room, letting the screened door close behind her.

She was self-conscious again, the way she always was when Wade Thornton was around. She was consciously aware of her faded skirt and her mended blouse and the old shoes that were community property. She and her mother both used them. They were for messy chores and Ada was just then returning from the field. She was hot and a little sweaty, and her hands were dirty. She unconsciously rubbed them on her skirt as she stepped deeper into the room.

"I suppose I'm the last person you expected to see just now," Wade stated.

"Yessir," Ada admitted. She offered no other comment but warily looked at him as she crossed the room. Wade knew without being told that she was escaping, leaving because he was there.

"Where're the beans?" Mrs. Tanner asked and Ada quickly answered.

"They're on the porch."

"You've been picking beans?" Wade asked, trying to engage her in conversation so she wouldn't leave. "Is your garden doing well?"

"Yessir," she said, "an I've gotta clean up. You sit down an' finish yore coffee," she said as she reached the back door. "It'll git cold."

She walked out and Wade watched her. He was still standing when he heard water being dipped into a basin and the splash of water as Ada washed her hands and face. Mrs. Tanner said something about getting the beans and she walked out, leaving Wade alone in the room. He stood there for a moment only, and then he followed Ada.

Ada heard the door open and close, and she knew without looking that it was Wade. She turned to him and the facade she had used for her mother's sake was gone. She showed no pleasure at seeing him.

He had stopped just outside the door and he took in the whole scene before him in one quick glance. Ada was standing beside a bench that stretched from one post to the other. There was a bucket half full of clean water at one end and a silver dipper hanging on a hook beside it. A white enamel basin with a tiny red ring around the top was in front of Ada and a bar of soap was lying on the board beside it. She had a towel in her hands and she was slowly drying her hands on it.

"What're you doin' here, Wade?" she plainly asked.

"I want to talk to you," he said.

"You're gonna get us both in trouble," she said as she pushed past him. He caught her by the arm and stopped her.

"I don't want to get you in any trouble. I just want to talk to you about Logan."

"An' you don't think that's trouble?" she said.

"For me, maybe."

"Are you blind and deaf? Can't you see what's goin' on around you and hear what people're sayin'?"

He gave her a puzzled look. "What're you talkin' about?"

She pulled her arm away from him. "Daddy knows you were here the night of your party—Logan told him."

"How did Logan know?" Wade carefully asked.

"He was either spyin' on me or followin' you. Either way, the rumor's out that we're secretly seein' each other. Folks're talkin', and daddy don't trust me no more. You gotta get outta here b'fore he gets back."

Wade gave her a startled look that gradually changed to realization. No wonder everyone was telling him about Ada and Logan's upcoming nuptials. They were probably morbidly fascinated with the reaction that a secret lover would give to such an announcement. He wondered if he had given them

284

sufficient satisfaction, but being neither guilty of the accusation nor aware of the rumor, he imagined they were rather disappointed.

He suddenly laughed, sardonically and a bit bitingly. How ironic to be accused of the thing he had dreamed about—and he *had* dreamed about it. More than one reverie had had Ada meeting him—willingly and not by accident. Was he now to be punished for those dreams?

"If he was watching," Wade pointed out, "then he knows I didn't even come inside the gate."

"He saw us down at the spring, too—the day you were shot," she hesitantly added. "He tol' daddy you were half naked, huggin' me. Daddy was ready to go find you and finish what the shooter hadn't accomplished."

Wade jerked with this new piece of information. So, Logan had been at the spring that day, which meant he had had the opportunity to shoot Wade — and a motive, too, in his eyes, anyway.

Later, that would be important to Wade, but right now, he could not get his mind off the current problem.

"That explains a few things," he said, looking intently at Ada. She had a fresh look about her from the water and her hair made a damp outline around her face. Wade lost his train of thought as he looked at her, immediately going back to what she had just said. It painted a provocative picture in his mind that he only wished was true.

"You gotta get outta here," she repeated, disturbing his reverie. "Daddy'll never believe you came here to find Logan.

He'll think I've lied to him, for shore."

"If I leave without seeing Logan, it'll look bad," Wade pointed out.

"No one'll tell him you were here. Daddy'll never know."

Wade simply stood there, mute and more than just a little crestfallen. He frowned as he thought about the injustice of prejudice. It meant that no matter whether Logan Spencer or Angela Wright were in the picture or not, he wouldn't be allowed to come here, calling on Ada, and the sad thing was, there was nothing he could do to change that fact. That's the way prejudice was.

And she was prejudiced, too . . .

"I'll go," he said, "but only to save you trouble. I didn't know—"

A sound interrupted him. Someone had entered the kitchen by way of the other door. Ada gasped and Wade looked up with concern until he heard the patter of four little feet.

"It's the boys," Ada and Wade said in unison and with great relief.

Wade opened the door and Ada went through it. He was right behind her, somehow sensing the urgency in the boys' arrival.

"Daddy's comin'," Paul said as they came through the door. "He's five minutes down the road."

Ada looked up at Wade. "You've got time," she said and he nodded with resignation.

He took up his hat and hurried to the door. Ada and the twins were right behind him.

"Thanks for the coffee, Mrs. Tanner," he said as he crossed the walkway to the living room door. "And good-bye."

He didn't wait for her parting endearments, but he heard her say something. He ran to his horse and pulled at the reins. He swung up into the saddle, and in less than a minute, he was out of sight.

Ada stood on the porch with the twins and they watched him go. Mrs. Tanner was nearby, snapping beans, but no one said anything until Wade was gone and the dust had settled.

"How d' ya know daddy's on his way?" Ada asked.

"We went down the road lookin' f'r 'im when Wade got here. We figured he'd wanna know."

"Then we run back here when we saw 'im pass the ol' sour orange grove," Silas added.

"Thanks, boys. I'm in enough trouble without daddy thinkin' Wade Thornton was here to see me."

They ran off after that and Ada stood silently on the porch, saying nothing until her mother spoke.

"He was here to see you," Mrs. Tanner stated. She never looked up from her task. She snapped the end off the green bean in her hand and then she picked up another.

Ada solemnly looked at her mother. It had not gone unnoticed that Mrs. Tanner had conveniently disappeared when Ada had arrived.

"There's nuthin' goin' on between me and Wade Thornton, mama, regardless of what people 're sayin'. He was lookin' for Logan, an' I can just bet you, it's because he's had trouble again."

"Have the boys let Ol' John out and run 'im down the road," Mrs. Tanner said. "An' do somethin' with Wade's cup, will ya'?"

Yes, that was the thing to do. Hide any evidence that Wade had been here and pretend it had never happened. Ada was surprised at her mother, but she wasted no time with useless words. She did as she suggested and erased any sign of his visit.

"Silas needs to hurry," Ada said to Paul as she anxiously watched for her father. Five minutes had come and gone and Ol' John, their mule, was still out of the pasture.

"I musta miscalculated," he said. "But don't worry. We'll just tell daddy, Ol' John got out ag'in. He does it all the time, ya' know."

"Yes, I know," she absent-mindedly said. She felt as guilty as a thief with all this deception, and with a wag of her head she considered how easily the twins and her mother had become accomplices.

It opened Ada's eyes to something she had not seen before and the wonder of it made her look over her shoulder to the woman sitting in the chair, snapping beans. She was unruffled by her part in the deception, it seemed, undisturbed, and as innocent looking as a newborn baby.

In just a few minutes, Fred arrived. He pulled the wagon to the side of the house and jumped down, casting a glance toward the pasture gate where Silas was just then closing up.

"Ol' John git out ag'in?" he asked.

"Shore did," Paul lied without a hint of conscience. "But we got 'im back in."

Fred went about moving the bucket of fish from the back of the wagon and toting it to the scaling bench, but Logan got down carefully and he looked down the road as if he suspected something. Ada guiltily watched him and every move he made convinced her he was aware of the visitor who had come and gone while he was away.

He was not aware, however. He had things on his mind that caused him to look down the road, but he had no idea that Wade had been there looking for him.

Wade had things on his mind, too, and had Logan known, as he looked one way down the road, Wade was looking the other. He had stopped his horse at the turn to his ranch and was sitting in the saddle, staring in the direction from which he had come. He could not see very far because of the trees and the brush that grew right up to the narrow, rutted road, but he was not looking to see anything anyway. He was contemplating his next move, and it had him in a deep quandary.

His head slowly turned and he looked toward home. He told himself he should be hurrying, but it didn't prompt him to move. The horse took a tentative step on his own and it was enough to finally motivate Wade. He pulled himself up in the saddle and urged the horse forward. There was a lot to do and he was no nearer a solution when he arrived at home than he had been when he left.

Angela met Wade in the yard as he rode in. He stepped down from the horse and Pat took the reins, leading the horse as he walked toward the corral.

"Well?" Angela said, standing arms akimbo, looking at

him. "We've been wondering all day what's going on. Is the fence down?"

"Yeah," Wade lazily answered. He walked beside her to the house and met the Major there.

"What does it mean?" she asked.

"It means we've got a lot of work to do."

"Where's Rusty?"

"He and Cody are seeing what they can salvage of the fence."

"So, you're putting it back up," Angela said. Her eyes surreptitiously shifted to the major and then right back to Wade.

"I am."

"Is that wise, my boy?" the major asked. "I mean, it's none of my business, but, darn it, Wade, you're like a son to me. I hate to see you make bad choices and throw your inheritance away. Ask yourself what your father would think about all this. I believe he would tell you to move on with your plans and forget about the fence."

"That's the trouble," Wade said. "The fence is my plan. I can't let it go. No one in this community would ever let me forget it if I did."

"Of course, they would. They don't even like the fence. They'd be happy if it never went up."

"You're right—and you're wrong. They hate the fence, but they'd hate me if I started something I couldn't finish."

"They hate you anyway," Angela pointed out.

Wade's back stiffened with the blow of her words. She was

right. Had not he thought the same thing less than an hour before. There was so much prejudice in this small community— and deception. Wade knew that the seemingly friendly neighbors that smiled to his face, often spit in his tracks when he walked away.

Deep down inside, most of the people in the community liked Wade, but there were not just scars left from the war on these people, there were open wounds that didn't heal. Fred Tanner was a good example.

The sound of approaching horses interrupted his thoughts and they all looked up with interest, the fence momentarily forgotten. A small group of men were riding in. They were not typical of the neighborhood. Their horses were too well bred and their outfit too fine. They stopped in the yard and a heavyset man of forty stepped down from a fine stallion. Everything about the man spoke of money and success and Wade curiously walked toward him, giving him a friendly greeting as he approached him.

"Hello," he called out. "Welcome."

"Hello, yourself," the man said. He pulled a soft glove from his smooth hand and reached out to give Wade a shake. "I'm Rich Macon," he said as he looked around.

"Wade Thornton," Wade said and then he immediately turned and introduced Angela and the major. The men on horseback were just then stepping down.

"Take care of the horses," Rich brusquely ordered his men and without a word, they filed away in the direction of the corral. "I just heard about you," he went on. He placed a brotherly hand on Wade's shoulder and without waiting for an invitation, he began walking toward the house. "My family and I have been out of the country for a few months. We just returned a week ago or I'd have been here sooner."

"You've got a place nearby?" Wade asked.

"Have I got a place? You should see it," he bragged. "It's up in Putnam County, just north of Rice Creek. I've got a house that, well, frankly, you could lose this tiny place inside of."

He laughed and patted Wade on the shoulder.

He had a distinctive Connecticut brogue and he was a boastful, overbearing man. Wade immediately disliked him, but the major seemed to take to him, graciously inviting him into Wade's humble home and quickly ordering Della to bring something cold to drink.

"I can see you've got a lot of work to do here," Rich said as he looked around. "Are you planning to build a bigger place? I can tell you, there's good houses to be had without all the work. I know just how to get you into a fine old southern house. You pick it out and, well, I've got connections. You'll get it."

Angela saw the look that crossed Wade's face and the way that his eyes turned dark and feral. She had seen that look before and she knew that Rich Macon was in dangerous territory. She quickly joined the conversation, turning it before Wade lost control.

"I do so want to go to Palatka," she said. "Do you live near there?"

Rich looked at her with the same expression he might give a horse he was considering buying. "Yes, I do. My place is north of there," he said. "You'd do well to take the time to visit Palatka. Stay at the Putnam House and tell them Rich Macon sent you. You'll not be sorry."

"I'd love to," she said, casting a doleful look in Wade's direction.

"And then come to Wisteria Acres—that's my place. You can stay with us. My wife would enjoy your company. She gets so little proper companionship. These people around here are, well, you know," he said, raising his eyes to the ceiling with exasperation. "She'd love to see someone of her own kind."

Wade stiffened and then his body took on a threatening posture, but Angela put a hand on his arm that checked him.

Rich continued to look around, his expressions as easily read as a book. He disapproved of the house, but he approved of the tea Della served. He was totally oblivious to Wade's reaction to him, but he liked what he saw in Angela. It was all there in his eyes and Wade took it in, weighing it for what it was worth.

"I'd be lying if I didn't tell you I was expecting more," Rich said as he looked around. "I heard you'd come into a big inheritance and an even bigger windfall," he continued with smug understanding. "You should have put it into an existing plantation, but then, I guess you had your reasons for choosing this particular piece of property," he knowingly added.

Wade was surprised and very much dismayed. The story of the gold was out, it seemed. If Rich Macon had heard about it all the way to Rice Creek, then it was dangerously spread out.

"I'm not a farmer—not even a gentleman farmer," Wade

soberly said. "I'm a rancher and this property will do fine for what I want."

"For you, yes," Rich said, "but what about your wife? I can see in her eyes, she wants better things than this. Am I right?" he asked, smiling at Angela. "You come to Wisteria Acres and get an idea of what you can do—and I'll help you. Like I said, I've got connections."

"I'd love to come for a visit," Angela quickly stated so that Wade could not say anything just then. She knew if he had the opportunity to talk, he would probably order Rich Macon out of his house. She could see the signs of his mood all over his face and she could not understand why Rich could not see it, as well. "But you are mistaken on one point. I'm Wade's fiancée," she said with a demure smile. "I hope that won't change anything or be reason to withdraw your invitation. I was just thinking that, maybe your wife and I could make a trip into Palatka. What did you say is her name?"

"Beatrice—but we call her Bea. And, sure, she'd go with you. In fact, she made me promise to get a definite acknowledgment from you on that matter before I left today— that is, if you turned out to be the right kind of people."

He was digging a hole that just kept getting bigger and bigger. Angela didn't know how much longer she could keep Wade from pushing him into it and filling it in.

"Is it far to your place?" the major asked.

"About fifteen miles," Rich said. "But I would recommend you go by way of steamboat. They make regular trips to Palatka and you could hire one to bring you right up Rice Creek to our landing. Everyone knows where it is."

"It sounds marvelous," Angela said, and she really meant it. Wade had not said anything. He was quietly letting the conversation pass him by. "Bea could help me with my trousseau."

Wade suddenly stood up. It startled Angela and she stood up, too, the major following shortly behind.

"I don't mean to be rude," Wade said and Angela gripped his arm in a gesture that pleaded for his patience. "I've got a problem that needs my immediate attention. I was about to take care of it when you rode in." Angela's grip on his arm kept him steady and he successfully controlled the desire inside him to bodily throw Rich Macon out. "Stay as long as you like," he added. "Angela and the major, I'm sure, would be happy to entertain you, but I've got things to do."

Rich had come to his feet along with everyone else. He looked a little perplexed. Angela wondered if he was at last getting the idea that Wade Thornton was neither impressed with him nor even liked him.

"Is there a problem?" Rich asked. "I mean, I could help if you're having trouble."

"No, it's nothing you can do."

"But thank you for the offer," the major quickly intervened. "It's so kind of you to offer."

"Yes," Angela said. "Isn't it, Wade?"

"Yes," Wade said, his voice a lifeless monotone. He picked up his hat and started for the door.

"I hope you'll come to Wisteria Acres," Rich threw at Wade

as the door opened. "Bea would like to meet you and I'm anxious to show you my place."

"I'll keep that in mind," Wade said as he slipped his hat on his head and walked out the door. An awkward silence filled the room and it was Angela who broke it. She laughed merrily and then she took a couple of steps nearer to Rich so that she could grip his arm much the same as she had Wade's.

"Isn't he a terror!" she said. "So serious," she added with a frown and a playful moue on her lips. "Don't mind him. He's always that way, but he'd been horrified if he thought you didn't feel welcome. Come—sit here beside me. We'll plan that visit to Wisteria Acres. What a lovely name! I know it must be a reflection of your home. I can't wait to see it."

She was babbling, but it impressed Rich Macon and he sat down beside her. He cast a sorrowful look at the door and it was obvious he was somewhat disappointed. He had come to see Wade Thornton and it was not just to deliver an invitation. Rich Macon had other things on his mind. He had not gotten where he was by being a gentleman or by being a good businessman, either. He was a man who had an eye for opportunity and he usually stampeded in and simply ran roughshod over everyone and everything until his objective had been obtained. That is what he had done after the war. He had come south with nothing more than the clothes on his back, a glib tongue, and youthful good looks. In those days, it had been enough, and in his success, he had forgotten where he had come from—a poor man without two nickels to rub together. He was an important man now, successful, rich, and in his eyes, respected.

Wade walked outside, straightening his hat as he stepped off the porch. He didn't even give a backwards glance as he walked across the yard and went straight to the corral. He caught a horse and was putting on the saddle when Pat and Bart joined him.

They approached quietly and with an air of secrecy, throwing cautious glances over their shoulders.

"Hey, Boss," Bart said, "you know who that feller is?"

"Rich Macon," Wade answered.

"From up around Rice Creek?"

"Yeah. That's what he said."

"He's bad news," Bart said, speaking softly so that only Wade could hear.

Wade looked over the back of his horse toward the house, considering what Bart was saying. He had the same feeling.

"You've heard of him?"

"Yeah, and nun uv it's good."

Wade tightened his cinch and then he paused to think about this. It was the gold. Wade knew that was what must have brought Macon, but then he wondered why. Surely Macon didn't think Wade had the gold lying around and he could just snatch it up. He leaned his elbows on the side of the saddle and wondered what was on Rich Macon's mind.

"Where's the men who rode in with him?" Wade asked.

"In the lounge," Pat said. "They're askin' a lotta questions about our spread."

"What kind of questions?"

"Usual things—and some things about you. Like, what

kinda boss you are and how the pay is."

"They don't seem real happy," Pat added. "Seems like Macon ain't no good to work for."

"Well, that doesn't surprise me," Wade said. "I wouldn't work for him."

Both men grunted an affirmative.

"What's he want?" Pat asked.

"I don't know," Wade said. He imagined it was the gold, but he was not going to admit that to Pat and Bart. "He said it was a friendly visit to welcome me."

"Don't believe 'im," Bart said. "He's up to somethin'."

Wade pushed away from the horse and took up the reins. "Well, we'll wait and see."

"Where ya' goin', boss?" Pat asked.

Wade cast a glance toward the house as he swung into the saddle. "To the fence," he replied.

"We'll come with ya'," Pat said.

"No," Wade stopped them as they turned to catch a horse. "Do me a favor. Stay here and see what you can find out about Macon. Maybe his men will talk."

Bart opened the gate and Wade rode out of it. He galloped across the open field and disappeared into the woods on the east side of the ranch. Pat and Bart watched him until he was out of sight and then they turned and slowly walked back to the lounge.

Wade made his way across the flat ground under stands of indigenous trees. He hurried because the day was quickly waning and he wanted to reach the fence before Rusty and

Cody left it.

He pulled up beside the broken fence and stopped, looking down the line but not seeing anyone. He urged the horse forward and followed the line, coming upon Rusty and Cody less than a quarter of a mile from Mr. Dover's farm.

He stepped down and let the reins trail.

"How's it comin'?" he asked and they stopped their work to meet him halfway. They had a stack of posts neatly piled in a clearing and the twisted wire cut away from it. They had done a lot of work in the few hours since Wade had left them.

"It's comin'," Rusty answered.

"Quit for the day," Wade said. "An' we'll send a whole crew out tomorrow. Cody, you head it."

"Yessir," he said.

"Cody, you can go back to the ranch. Rusty, I want you to come with me."

"Where're we goin'?" he asked after they had left Cody and started down the line toward Mason's Corner.

"Lookin' for Logan," Wade replied. He suddenly cut away from the fence line and started north across his property, his direction going straight toward the Tanner's property.

Rusty didn't say anything more, but there was an uncharacteristic, grim look in his eyes as he rode beside Wade.

They crossed the fence at the northeast gate and came up to the Tanner's farm from an unexpected angle. A dog barked vigorously as they approached and Fred Tanner appeared on the porch, solemnly watching the two riders.

"Hello, Mr. Tanner," Wade courteously said as he came to a

stop beside the house. He looked around, quickly surveying the place where he had been only a little while before. There was no sign of Ada—or the twins. Wade wondered where they were and then he wondered about Mrs. Tanner. She was nowhere in sight either.

But his eyes were looking for more than the Tanner family. Wade was looking for Logan and the green-eyed dragon of jealousy slowly consumed him as he considered that Logan was probably with Ada.

"My fence is down," Wade went on to say, not waiting for Fred to say anything. "Logan was telling my men about someone he'd seen hanging around and I wanted to ask him about him. Is Logan here?"

Fred was smoking a pipe and he removed it from his mouth before speaking. "Shore," he said, "but I'll ha'f t' find 'im. He's off somewhere with my girl."

He grinned with meaning and Wade's face burned. He hoped it had not turned red. He didn't want Fred to know how that hurt him.

"If he's busy, just tell him to get in touch with me," Wade said, his voice calm in spite of his emotions. "Tell him no one will harass him if he comes to the ranch. It'll be peaceful terms as long as he comes peaceful."

"I'll tell 'im," Fred said, still grinning.

He did that on purpose, Wade thought as he turned his horse and eased away from the gate. He began to wonder if Logan was even here or if Fred had just said that to rub in the fact that Ada was Logan's girl. He decided that Fred probably had not lied. Logan and Ada were probably there together. After all, they were getting married soon. What did he expect?

"You alright?" Rusty said after they had gone a short way in silence.

"Yes," he said, but he didn't take his eyes off the road before him. "Let's stop and wait here," he suddenly said. "We'll see if Logan comes along. I have a feeling he will."

They waited and Rusty was thinking that it was a waste of time when suddenly he heard a horse approaching.

It had not taken long for Logan to get the message and leave the Tanner's farm. He came down the road, riding fast. When he came around the curve and saw Wade and Rusty sitting their horses in the middle of the road, he stopped so quickly that his horse reared up and sat back on his haunches.

"Hold up, there!" Rusty said when Logan gave the indication that he would turn and run. He and Wade pushed their mounts forward and were in strategic positions around Logan before he could get his horse under control.

"Whatcha want?" he demanded as he worked to calm his nervous horse.

"No trouble," Wade assured him. "We want no trouble. I just want to talk to you."

"Well, talk, then. I got things t' do."

"You came to my men and said something about seeing a stranger in the woods. Tell me about him."

Logan looked at Wade through squinted eyes, full of suspicion. "We been hearin' things," he finally said. "I figured it was yore men tryin' to scare us, but several times now, we've seen someone lurkin' about. Don't know who he is, but he ain't any o' my men and I don't think he's one o' yourn.'"

"We've been hearing things, too," Wade admitted. "Singin' and diggin'.'"

Logan's eyes lit up. "Us too."

Wade looked around. This put an interesting spin on things and having Rich Macon show up just now seemed more than coincidence.

"You know, Logan," Wade said. "Maybe someone's playin' us."

"Maybe," he halfway agreed. He didn't trust Wade and even if he did, he wouldn't have admitted that he did. He hated Wade Thornton. "It don't matter," Logan added. His horse had calmed down and he was sitting still, carelessly holding the reins in his hand. "I ain't losin' no sleep over it."

Funny he should say that, Wade thought, because everyone at his ranch had lost hours of sleep. He figured Logan was lying.

"Did you know my fence had been cut again?"

Logan grinned. "No," he said, "but I ain't sorry."

"I didn't figure you would be, but I thought you might find it interesting."

"I do," Logan admitted. "I do find it int'restin'. But I didn't do it." He grinned again and a look came into his eyes that was not so different from the one that had been in Fred's eyes just a few minutes before. "I been too busy to care what you do, Mr. Yankee." He swaggered a bit as he continued. "I'm gettin' married in a few days and I've been busy makin' love to my girl. You know, gettin' a head start on things."

Rusty tensed, expecting Wade to explode, but when no immediate reaction came from him, he cast a curious look his way.

Wade's expression was bland and his voice calm, but Rusty saw fire in Wade's eyes and knew that Logan was skating on thin ice. "Where I come from, we don't talk about our women in any such manner," he carefully said. There was an edge to his voice that was almost sinister.

"Where I come from, too," Rusty added to take the advantage away from Wade. "Her daddy might take offense, if he knew."

"Fred knows," Logan said, but the smile left his face. He took up the reins and gave indication that he wanted to leave. Wade eased his horse back, not trusting himself to keep his calm if Logan stayed there any longer.

"He's lyin'," Rusty said after Logan had galloped away.

"So what if he is?" Wade said. "It's none of our business."

Rusty looked askance at Wade and then he turned completely in his saddle for a closer look. "I feel sorry for Ada," he said. "I don't think she's gettin' a square deal."

"It's too bad," Wade roughly said. "But I have a ranch to run. I don't have time to worry about things I can't change."

Rusty studied him as he turned his horse. "I gotta know somethin', boss," he said and Wade pulled his horse to a stop. "It's about Ada."

"What about her?"

"I always wondered why the two of you were at the spring the day you were shot and now, everyone's sayin'—well, everyone's sayin' you two are slippin' around, meetin', an'. . ."

He stopped talking and Wade just looked at him for a moment without comment. "And what?" he finally asked, seeing that Rusty was embarrassed to continue.

"Honestly? Well, they're sayin' that's why this weddin's bein' hurried up. Logan's marryin' her, 'cause . . ."

He hesitated again and Wade frowned. He drew his horse around and pulled it up beside Rusty. "Spit it out," he roughly said.

"Well, ya' gotta know," Rusty said. "They're sayin' she's in a family way and it's because of you."

Wade's face turned red and for just a few seconds, he could not say a thing.

"It's a lie!" he finally said. "There's been nothing between us."

"I thought so," Rusty said, but he was suddenly thinking about Angela and what had happened between the two of them and he was feeling a little sick.

"Besides," Wade said, "Logan wouldn't have her if she was—I mean, with my—" He couldn't bring himself to finish the sentence. "He'd kill her but he wouldn't marry her."

"He might marry her," Rusty pointed out. "Just to spite you."

"He might, at that," Wade thoughtfully agreed. He was suddenly thinking about the many people who had pointed out Ada's wedding plans to him. He understood their comments now. Logan's snide remark even made a little more sense. Perhaps, he believed it was true, too.

"There's nothing I can do about it," Wade said. "I can't disprove them."

He suddenly remembered what Ada had said to him when he had made the call at her house earlier that day, and just as quickly, he wanted to curse, but oddly, it was the thought of Mrs. Tanner that calmed him. He curiously wondered about her and her still, even disposition in the face of such a bold rumor about him and her daughter. If she believed the rumor, she had given no indication of it when she had invited him in—or had she? She had conveniently left them alone. He knew that had been no accident. It had been carefully orchestrated to give him time alone with Ada. He wearily shook his head. "I feel like I ought to do something," he said. "But I don't know what to do."

"There's nothin' you can do," Rusty said. "Unless it's true and then you and Ada could just run away together."

Wade had been looking at nothing in particular, way off in the distance, but he suddenly whipped around and gave Rusty a hard look.

"I ain't sayin' it's true," Rusty quickly said, holding his hands up in a defensive manner. "I only said, *if* it was true—but I know it ain't, so," he paused and wagged his head, "why am I continuing to talk when I should just shut up?"

"That's a good question," Wade said.

"You're right an' I'm shuttin' up."

"You've brought up a good point, though," Wade said. "Why wouldn't we just run away together if it was true? Why doesn't anyone see that that would be the logical conclusion to this scenario—not this convoluted rumor that's going around."

"Two reasons—Angela and Fred."

"Not Logan?"

"No, it's Fred," Rusty assured him.

"You're right," Wade acrimoniously agreed. "I've been told by everyone I've come in contact with today about Ada's upcoming nuptials." He stopped and smiled sardonically. "I wonder what perverse pleasure they got from that, and what they expected from me." He again looked far away, seeing nothing as he thought. "I guess they wanted a show. I wonder if I gave them what they were looking for."

"I wonder what Angela'll do when she hears," Rusty suddenly mused.

"She'll hit the ceiling," Wade said with a derisive chuckle. "But not because she cares. It's the scandal that will upset her."

"What about you and her?" Rusty carefully asked. "What's goin' on?"

Wade looked at Rusty. "I honestly don't know."

"Do you love her?"

Again Wade smiled sardonically. "Yes, I love her."

Rusty's heart fell to his feet and he dropped his eyes as the pain of regret stabbed him.

"But I've found it isn't enough," Wade continued and Rusty's eyes looked up again. "She and I have been friends for as long as I can remember. Do yourself a favor, Rusty. Don't ever think you can marry a friend. It's the wrong kind of love."

"Does she know how you feel?"

Wade nodded. "Yes."

"You gotta let 'er go."

"I know and I've tried. She's got something in her head and she won't let go of it. It isn't like her."

Rusty considered that and his conclusion left him cold. He was going to have to let her go, too, but he didn't know how to do it.

"Come on," Wade said, turning his horse again. "Let's get back to the ranch and see if Rich Macon is still there."

He was. Angela had steered him to the bunkhouse, giving him and his men a couple of rooms for the night. Wade and Rusty rode into the corral and were stripping their mounts when they were told the situation. They both looked over the rumps of their horses, no gladness on either face.

"What d' ya' suppose he's up to?" Rusty asked after a few seconds.

"I don't know," Wade lied. It was the gold. Somehow, he just knew it was the gold.

They finished their chore and walked to the lounge at the end of the long straight building. Powder Keg was just then calling the men to supper so they joined them.

The table was large enough to seat eight people comfortably and ten by squeezing in two more chairs so several of Wade's crew dished up their plates and walked outside to eat. Rich Macon and his crew of four sat down and Wade, Rusty, and Jim sat with them. The arrangement seemed to annoy Rich. He had expected better, but he was diplomatic enough to hide his true feelings. Besides, he had Wade's attention and that was what he wanted.

"You got potential here," Rich announced between a bite of

stew and biscuits. "But there's opportunities all over the south for a man who's smart enough to take advantage of them."

"This is enough for me," Wade said.

"Yeah, well, you've got a uniquely interesting situation," he casually mentioned and then went on before Wade could respond. "I'm telling you, there's real profit here, but you're going in the wrong direction. There's no money in cattle — no big money. I can steer you right and show you the ropes."

"Thanks, but I'm content with what I have."

"Yeah," Rich drawled with meaning. His eyes slipped around the room as if he was looking for the lost gold. They came back and rested on Wade, a calculating look in them. "This country has a way of eatin' up your reserves. You might think you've got enough to sustain you but you have to be careful. You need to invest, and that's where I can help."

Wade pushed back in his chair and took a deep breath. He had wondered why Rich Macon was here and now, he was beginning to understand. "It takes money to invest," Wade carefully said. "And, honestly, I've put all my available cash into the building of this ranch."

Rich nodded. "That's my point," Rich said. "If you invested instead of just spending, you'd have something to live on the rest of your life."

"No offense," Wade said, "but I don't know you, and I don't discuss my business with strangers."

Rich's face turned red, but he didn't give up. "No offense taken," he lied. "And you're right." He eased back in his chair, too, and reconsidered his approach. "It was just friendly advice.

I hate to see a newcomer go under because he didn't understand the way things run down here. And, there's no reason for us to remain strangers. You come up to Wisteria Acres for a visit and get to know me. What do you say? Can I tell Bea to expect company?"

Wade didn't trust Rich Macon, nor did he have any plans of visiting him at his place on Rice Creek, but he saw an opportunity to get Angela off his hands for a while and the idea appealed to him so greatly that he consoled Rich with an acceptance.

"Sure, that would be fine."

Rich beamed. "Now, you're talking!" He reached across the table and shook Wade's hand as if they had just made a business deal. "When can I expect you? And, don't put me off. I want you up right away."

"Next week?" Wade asked and Rich grinned with delight.

"Perfect," he said.

The next morning, Rich and his men left, and Wade, Angela and the major stood in the yard, watching them go.

"I'm surprised at you, Wade," Angela said as her eyes followed the departing riders. "I didn't think you liked Rich." She turned her head and looked at Wade. "And here, you've accepted an invitation to Wisteria Acres. I'm puzzled."

"You wanted to go, didn't you?"

"Yes, but—"

"Well, I did it for you."

"Oh, Wade," she sighed, gladness coming into her eyes. "Thank you."

But a week later when the time came to leave, Angela wasn't thanking Wade anymore. He waited until the last minute and then he explained how he was not going. She and the Major could go and be the diplomats for the Thornton Ranch, but he was not going.

"I can't leave now," he said when she pressed him. "Can't you see that?"

"No, I can't," she angrily quipped. "You're the boss, for heaven's sake! Give the order to these men and leave them with it."

"I can't do that," he said.

"You mean, you *won't* do that."

He nodded. "You're right. I won't do that."

"Fine! I'm going anyway and I'm going to Palatka while I have the chance. I can see you aren't going to take me."

"No, I'm not," he admitted.

"Well, you might, after all," she said, her tone suddenly changing. "When I get back, Wade, I'll be ready to get married. I expect you to honor your commitment and then you can take me to Palatka for our honeymoon."

Wade stiffened and his face burned. "I feel like a yo-yo," he said. "You and I need to get on the same page about this wedding."

"The only page you need to be on is the one where you get the preacher and then say 'I do'."

"You can have the gold, Angela—if there is any. If it's that important to you, then take it and leave, but give me my freedom."

310

"Where is the gold?" she breathlessly asked.

He looked sharply at her. "I don't exactly know."

"Give me the clues and I'll find it."

She probably would, Wade was thinking as he hesitated. He turned his face away and reconsidered. "When you come back from Wisteria Acres," he stated with finality.

Angela thrilled with excitement. The Major would be delighted and soon she could go home and get out of this damnable heat, and she could live in style, just as she liked.

"That's fine with me," she said.

"Only one thing," Wade said as she turned to leave. They were standing alone, inside the house and no one could hear them. "What about Rusty?" he asked.

Every muscle in Angela's body seemed to contract. She was holding a small satchel and she let it drop with a heavy thud.

"What about him?"

Wade stared deep into her eyes. "He's in love with you, isn't he?"

She considered an answer before responding. "It isn't my fault if he is."

Wade threw down the hat he was holding and slumped into the nearest chair.

"It is your fault, Angela — and it's my fault." He shook his head with regret. "Rusty's my friend and I've not played fair with him." His eyes suddenly jumped up to Angela. "But you haven't played fair with either of us."

"You're both grown men," she pointed out.

"Yes, but Rusty's as innocent as a new born baby where

women like you are concerned."

"Women like me!" she indignantly said. "What about friends like you? And how dare you piously sit there acting like you haven't done anything. I know all about you and that backwoods Tanner girl. "

Wade came to his feet. "It's all a lie," he said.

"Really?" She had him on the defensive and she planned to keep him there. "You've been caught, Wade, and you can't talk your way out of it."

He shook his head. "I haven't been caught, because I haven't done anything. Ada doesn't even like me." He sorrowfully looked away. "She and Logan are getting married any day now. If there was something between me and her, do you think I'd stand for that?"

Angela's expression changed and so did her attitude. She gently touched Wade's arm. "Oh, Wade, I'm so sorry," she said. "You're really in love with her, aren't you?"

He shook his head and denied it.

"Look at me," she said. "This is Angela you're talking to. We've been friends too long for you to try to fool me. I know what's going on with you whether you admit it or not."

He looked at her and his attitude softened, too. "Lord, Angela!" he exclaimed. "We're arguing like we did when we were twelve years old."

They both laughed, but it was a mirthless laugh, full of irony.

Wade took Angela into his arms and he embraced her in a tight bear hug. "God, I love you," he said and she gripped him just as tightly. "It'd be a shame to get married and destroy how we feel about each other."

He was right and Angela agreed with him, but she didn't know how she could get out of the situation she was in. She felt as if she had painted herself into a corner.

But, then, didn't she have the promise of the gold? That was all she wanted from Wade. He could have his freedom.

"Admit you're in love with Ada Tanner and I'll call off the wedding."

Wade laughed. "That would be too easy," he said and then he became serious. "What about Rusty?"

Angela gritted her teeth. "He's been fun," she admitted. "But I could never marry a guy like him. I'd be stuck in a place like this the rest of my life."

"I thought that's how you would feel," Wade soberly said.

"Well, are you taking the easy way out, Wade?" she asked when he grew silent.

"Yes," he said. "I'm in love with Ada Tanner. Are you satisfied? Now, Rusty and I can commiserate together."

"The wedding's off," she casually said, but then more soberly she added, "but don't forget. You've already promised me the gold."

"Okay," he said. "When you come back from Macon's, I'll give you the clues."

She picked up her bag, the relentless, calculating attitude back again. "And don't try anything while I'm gone," she said.

"Don't worry," he said. "A bargain's a bargain."

She paused for a moment. "Wade," she finally said. "Have

313

you told Ada how you feel about her?"

"No," he flatly replied. "It isn't like people are saying," he went on to explain.

"You should tell her."

"No," he replied again.

"Well, wallow in your misery, then," she roughly said and he cast her a hard look. "If you never tell her, then you'll never know what could have happened."

He shook his head again. "No," he said for the third time. "She's made her choice. I won't make a fool of myself."

"Very well," Angela said and this time, she turned and walked out of the door, leaving Wade alone in the house.

Bart and Cody loaded the wagon and when they were finished, Wade walked outside. He helped Angela onto the wagon seat and then he and the major climbed up beside her. Wade took them to the dock and waited until the steamboat pulled away, watching until it disappeared into the southern horizon and then he rode home alone. He was rather melancholy, but, at the same time, he felt a burden lift from him. He was out from under the obligation to Angela, but he had sold his freedom for the price of the gold.

He didn't really care, but then, at the same time, he realized what this would mean. He had put too much faith in the gold. Even though he was not sure it was here anymore, it had been like a security, an insurance he kept mentally tucked away in the back of his mind, and as a result, he had spent his available money freely. He had to get some things going to bring in income or he would lose everything.

It was dark when he arrived at the ranch. The lights were on in the bunkhouse, but the house was dark. Wade pulled into the yard and Cody met him as he jumped down from the wagon.

"Welcome home, boss," he said. "You look beat."

"I am."

"I'll take care o' the horse and wagon. Powder Keg's holdin' your supper."

"Thanks," Wade said and he walked straight to the lounge.

The windows were all open, but it was still hot inside. Wade fanned his face with his hat as he stood inside the door looking around.

"Did ya' get 'em off?" Powder Keg asked as Wade stood there.

"Yeah, they're gone."

Powder Keg grunted a reply. It was well known by Wade that everyone was glad to see them go — everyone except Rusty, that is. Which brought up the question of where Rusty was just now, and Wade was quick to voice the query.

"Don't know," Powder Keg replied. "He took off about an hour ago. Don't know where he went."

Wade sat down. He wondered what he should do about Rusty and he decided he would say nothing. Rusty need never know that Wade was well aware of his affair with Angela. If there had been a chance for Rusty to win her, then Wade would have gone to him and confessed so that he could then give him his blessing on the situation, but there was no chance, and Wade was not even going to bring it up.

He had just finished eating when Bart walked in. He pulled up a chair and straddled it, so that he was looking over the back of it at Wade.

"Saw somethin', boss. I thought I oughta tell ya'."

"What?" Wade asked.

"I saw a man walkin' across the Clearing. He was goin' straight to the saplin' thicket."

Wade sat up in his chair. "Who was it?"

"I don't know. He was a spooky-lookin' feller. He had on a big black hat and he wore a black coat. He was carrying a pail, it looked like, and he was walkin' fast."

"Sounds like Jake's ghost," Powder Keg interjected.

"It does," Bart agreed, "but I figure he was real enough."

"When did you see him?"

"Last night."

"What were you doing out there last night?" Wade asked.

"I thought I heard somethin', and I went to see. I didn't want to bother you with it this mornin'. You had so much on your mind already."

Wade nodded. "Well, tomorrow, we'll go look for sign."

But during the night it rained and by morning, there was nothing to see. Wade stood in the Clearing, his hands on his hips and his face grim. There was something going on here that worried at his brain like a feather tickling his nose.

He turned back to the ranch and when he rode into the yard, Rusty rode in from the opposite direction.

"Where have you been?" Wade asked as they both stepped down from their horses.

The quizzical look was back in Rusty's eyes. Wade had not seen it there in weeks, but it was there this morning, along with a mischievous look of boyish delight.

"We gotta talk," he said and he quickly led his horse toward the corral. Wade followed, his curiosity hurrying him along.

Rusty looked around as he stripped the saddle from the horse's back, then furtively, he began to talk.

"Did you hear that Ada's gettin' married next weekend?"

Wade stiffened. The last thing he wanted to hear just now was anything about Ada and Logan.

"No," he gruffly answered.

"Well, it's a lie," Rusty said. Wade's expression changed and his eyes went wide. "You wanna know where I've been? Well, I've been out talkin' to the twins."

"They'll lie to you," Wade warned.

"Yeah, I know, but just listen. Paul said his daddy's the one pushin' Ada into this marriage and that Ada has threatened to run away from home if he keeps pushin' 'er."

"She won't," Wade said.

"She might. Paul says she's makin' herself a stash out by the big oak so she can get to it when she runs. I checked. It's there."

Wade frowned. "Where will she go? What will she do? She can't just up and run. She'd be at the mercy of a cruel world."

"I know. I thought maybe you'd like to talk to her."

Wade turned to Rusty with a question in his eye. "What good would that do?"

"Well, I don't know, but I thought you might like to try."

Wade smiled and then he chuckled. It was a wry chuckle that reflected his outlook on this subject.

"What about Logan?" Wade suddenly asked. "Why would he insist on a marriage with a girl that doesn't want him? That doesn't make any sense."

"He's been talkin'," Rusty soberly answered. "He's bragged that you want her, but she's chosen him. He can't lose her now without losing face. She's become a pawn in all of this."

Wade cursed and then he stepped away from Rusty, ashamed at his reaction.

"I've messed things up for a lot of people," he said. "I wish I could go back and do some things differently."

"Don't we all!" Rusty exclaimed. "We cain't go back, but sometimes we can change things."

Wade shook his head. He didn't think anything he did at this point was going to help Ada.

"Paul said Ada's been goin' to the spring ever' afternoon. He said she's just been mopin' around like she was waitin' for someone. I thought you might like t' know that, too."

"Paul's a little devil," Wade pointed out. "I can't trust him."

"Well, whether you can or not, the fact is, Ada's at the spring ever' afternoon, if you wanna talk to her."

Wade looked around with hope in his eyes. "Maybe I will," he said, but then just as quickly, he felt a dread come upon him. It might be unwise for him to go there looking for her.

"I'll stand guard, if you want," Rusty said as though he read Wade's mind.

"We'll see," Wade said. He had already changed his mind.

He had no intention of going to the spring, not tomorrow nor the next day, but when morning came again, Wade was not so sure of himself. In the light of a bright new day, things looked differently, and for once, Wade was honestly considering his true feelings. He wanted to see Ada. He wanted to see her so badly that he ached, and so when the sun began to fall toward the west, he took up his saddle and put it on a horse, and then, he rode northeast, going directly toward the spring.

Chapter Twenty-nine

Ada saw the carriage coming down the road and she laughed with joyous surprise. It pulled into the yard and Ada was the first one out of the house. She raced to the carriage and jumped into it before her sister, Carrie, had time to get out.

"Oh, Carrie!" she exclaimed. "Oh, Carrie, I'm so glad to see you."

They gripped each other and laughed and hugged until Carrie's husband, Henson, teased them with a mild rebuke.

"See here," he said. "I'm about to be offended. Don't you have a greetin' for me, too, Ada?"

"Oh, Henson, yes! Welcome and so good to see you." She gripped his hand as she continued to smile. "I can't believe it! What a wonderful surprise."

"Surprise?" Henson curiously asked, but Carrie admonished him with a look of caution and he stepped out of the carriage, coming around without another word.

By that time, the twins and Esther had arrived and the hugs and kisses were passed around once again.

"Where's daddy?" Carrie asked when she didn't see Fred.

"He went to Mason's Corner. He'll be back soon."

It was an hour later when Fred arrived and by then, Ada had come to the realization that she was the only one surprised by Carrie's visit. The reason didn't really matter to her, although she correctly guessed that it was about the vile rumors being circulated.

After lunch, the two sisters walked outside and casually strolled around the yard, coming to a stop near the white oak tree where Ada's reading stool sat.

Carrie leaned her back against the tree and she looked across the way, sighing softly and rather wistfully. "I miss being here," she said. "I often wish Henson and I could live close by so I could be near you and mama."

"I wish you could, too. I miss you so much."

Carrie turned her face toward Ada, a soft look in her eyes. "I especially wish it now."

Ada stiffened. She imagined she knew why Carrie was here, but she had hoped she was wrong. "Why now?" she asked anyway.

"I'm going to have a baby."

Her announcement took Ada by surprise. She had imagined Carrie would say something about the rumor circulating about her and Wade and when she didn't, Ada stared for a few seconds before she could get her thoughts straight in her mind.

"A baby!" she finally said. "Oh, Carrie! That's wonderful news."

"Are you happy for me?"

"Happy? Of course, I am."

She suddenly threw her arms around Carrie and hugged her tightly, laughing all the while. They stood there for some time, just laughing and talking, both of them animated by the news, but then Carrie drew a deep breath and leaned against the tree again, fanning her face with her hand.

"Whew! It's hot today. I think I already feel the effects of the pregnancy. The heat bothers me more every day."

"Does it?" Ada said, wistfully looking in the direction of the spring. "At one time, I would've just gone to the spring to get outta the heat, but those days are gone forever."

"So I've heard," Carrie said.

Ada's eyes quickly swung back to Carrie. "So, who told you?" she asked.

"Mama wrote to me."

Ada nodded as if that was what she had figured and then she frowned. "So, mama believes it, too?"

Carrie saw Ada's pain and she sighed as she leaned toward her. "Oh, Ada," she said, "tell me what's goin' on."

"I wish I knew myself," Ada replied. "Mama says one thing, daddy says another, and Logan says something altogether different."

"From what I gather, daddy and Logan are sayin' practic'lly the same thing."

"Yes. Daddy wants me to marry Logan."

"Well, isn't that what you want?"

"No."

"The last time I saw you, you told me you were going to marry Logan."

"Did I?" Ada asked, looking at Carrie in surprise. "Well, a lot's happened since the last time I saw you."

"So I hear."

"What have you heard?" Ada asked.

Carrie fanned her face a few times while she contemplated an answer. Her hand suddenly stopped moving and she gave Ada a serious look. "Tell me about Wade Thornton, Ada."

Ada blushed and she didn't know why. Perhaps her thoughts of him made her feel guilty or perhaps the idle gossip about him embarrassed her. Either way, Carrie was sure to misread her reaction. She wanted to explain, but she didn't know what to say.

"Is it true then?" Carrie breathlessly asked.

"No!" Ada said, finding her voice, at last.

"You can tell me," Carrie said. She pushed away from the tree and gently touched Ada's arm. "You know you can tell me. What happened, Ada? What happened between you and Wade Thornton?"

Ada stared with her mouth open and her eyes full of disbelief. She had lost her voice again and it had the same effect on Carrie as a moment before. Carrie inhaled deeply and then she gripped the arm tightly that she had so gently touched a few seconds before.

"Did he do somethin'? Did he force himself on you?"

"No," Ada said in horror. She pulled her arm away and continued to look at Carrie in disbelief.

"You wouldn't lie to me, would you?" Carrie said. "It wouldn't be your fault, you know. I understand he's a big man and he's strong. No one would blame you."

"Is that what you were told?" Ada asked. "Have you seen Wade Thornton?" Carrie shook her head so Ada went on. "Well,

I'll tell ya', he's a right good lookin' man—even if he is a Yankee. I don't imagine he would have to force himself on any girl nor would he try. Daddy 'n' Logan are crazy."

"Is that what happened, then? You lost your head over him and one thing led to another."

"No," Ada emphatically stated. "Wade Thornton wouldn't waste his time with me—nor I with him. I can't believe daddy would tell you such a thing."

She was angry. She was so angry that she almost wished she had been with Wade Thornton. It would serve them right, she told herself.

"It wasn't daddy, Ada. It was Logan."

"Logan!"

"Yes," Carrie said with a nod, "but daddy confirmed it. They both have a lot to say."

"It's a lie!" Ada hissed. "What's come over daddy?" She paused to catch her breath. She was suddenly having trouble breathing. "Logan wants Wade dead and I guess daddy does, too, but I never expected them to hatch such a lie."

"Daddy believes it, Ada. He doesn't think it's a lie."

"It is a lie, I tell you."

"Okay," Carrie softly said. "Just tell me everything."

"It sounds like you know more than I do," Ada pointed out.

"I don't know the truth."

"Well, I don't know that I do either—not anymore."

"Have you been seein' Wade—meetin' him somewhere—at the spring or over at his place?"

Ada turned with a start. "Who told you I'd ever been to

Wade's place?"

"Logan."

"Logan? When have you seen Logan?"

"He came to visit us in Green Cove a couple of weeks ago."

"Oh!" Ada exclaimed, turning away from Carrie in exasperation. "That dirty, lousy, no good—"

"Then it's true?" Carrie asked, interrupting Ada's tirade.

"Logan sent me there," Ada said. "I went for him."

"And Wade caught you."

"Well, yes," Ada reluctantly admitted. Her temper cooled and quickly turned to anxiety as she found herself on the defensive.

"What happened?"

"Nothing . . . nothing happened. He was quite the gentleman—even though he had every right to throw me off the place."

"Logan said you came home with hay in your hair and on your clothes. His words were, that ya'll had took a romp in the hay together."

"Is that what he thinks of me? How long have I gone with Logan? A year? I've been his girl for all that time and he thinks I would just go play in the hay with another man. I wouldn't even do that with him, much less with a man who is practically a stranger." She turned, hurt by Logan's accusations. "Well, now you know why I won't marry him."

"Was there hay in your hair and on your clothes?" Carrie asked and when Ada flashed guilty eyes toward her she continued, "How did it get there?"

"I fell down in the shed," Ada said and then she quickly amended that, not wanting to be false with Carrie. "Wade knocked me down. I was wearing daddy's old hat and he thought I was one of the men who'd been causin' trouble around his place."

"Is *that* what he said?"

Ada's eyes went wide. "It's the truth. You would've had to've been there to understand. He couldn't see anything but the hat and it was dark in the shed. He was horrified at what he'd done and then he was angry at me and Logan. He could've taken advantage if he had wanted to—the opportunity was there for him, but he graciously and with more kindness than I deserved, helped me up and then let me leave. That's all that happened."

Carrie let out a long sigh and slumped against the tree. "That story is just crazy enough for me to believe it," she said with a tiny laugh.

"It is kinda crazy. You c'n see why I've kep' it to myself."

"I guess I can," Carrie halfway agreed. "It wouldn't convince daddy, that's for sure—nor Logan."

"Maybe not even mama. She thinks Wade has his eyes on me. She's wrong, you know."

"Is she? She's pretty sharp."

"She's wrong."

"What's he like, Ada? I've only gotten the men's account and, well, you know how they feel. What is Wade Thornton really like?"

Ada considered that and she wondered just how she should

answer that question without giving herself away.

"I don't really know him," she truthfully answered. "I've met him a couple of times and he's been okay. I think if everybody would just leave him alone, he'd be a good neighbor."

Carrie smiled. "I didn't expect you to sidestep a description of a handsome man, Ada."

Ada smiled back. "Well, in all honesty, Yankee or not, you can't deny he's quite pleasin' to look at."

"An' you haven't been tempted?" Carrie asked.

"I ain't crazy," Ada said. "He's engaged. His girl is right there at his ranch—her and her father. He gave her a party a few weeks back."

"Yes," Carrie said. "Which brings me to another question. What was he doin' here when there was a party goin' on at his house?"

"I don't know, but I'll tell you what I think. I think he came lookin' for the gold."

"The gold," Carrie sighed. "Is it real, then?"

"I think it is."

"Daddy always called people fools for lookin' for it. He swore the army took it when they took Captain Thornton away."

"Obviously Captain Thornton tells a different story."

"You know, I never wondered before because daddy had convinced me there was no gold, but he wasn't even here at the time. Mama was, though. I wonder what she has to say. Has anyone asked her?"

"I always figured daddy was repeatin' what she'd told him, so I never wondered, but daddy's changed his attitude since Wade arrived. Strange, mama hasn't said a thing."

"She probably doesn't know anything," Carrie said, musing a bit as she thought about how it must have been for her mother back then. When the enemy had taken over her home, Esther had been a woman alone except for a little girl and a baby. She must have been afraid—no, terrified! Carrie unconsciously touched her abdomen. Now that she was pregnant, she could better understand a young mother's concern. She wouldn't have been as much afraid for herself, as for her children. Carrie shivered at the thought of facing such an ordeal.

"She was lucky," Carrie said. "I guess she realized it and that's why she's never spoken an unkind word about Captain Thornton."

"Yes, and why she feels about Wade the way she does."

"How so?"

Ada shrugged indifferently, but she felt anything but indifferent. "She likes him. She's hinted that she wouldn't mind him comin' here to see me."

Carrie looked toward the house. "Really? Well, that does say somethin' for the man."

"No, I think he just reminds her of Captain Thornton."

"Maybe so—and maybe that's daddy's biggest problem. It always bothered him that a Yankee captain convalesced on our couch. I was so young when he came home from the war that his return is more like a dream than reality, but it seems I can remember one thing and only because it was so odd. It was him draggin' the couch outta the house and threatenin' to set it on fire."

Ada looked toward the house, too. "I never knew that."

"Well, maybe it was just a dream," Carrie said. "The couch is still here and no one ever said anything about it. I guess it was just a dream."

Perhaps, but Ada wondered.

"Let's go back to the house," Carrie said. "I'm hot and tired. An' I brought some things for y'u," she added. "Would you like a few hand-me-down dresses? My waist line has already outgrown them."

Ada beamed with excitement. She would love to have Carrie's hand-me-downs and she told her so, but then she thought, if only they could have arrived a few weeks earlier, then she would have had a new dress to wear to Wade's party. It was a moot point, but still, she wondered how differently things might have turned out if she had just gone to the party that night. She shook her head and followed Carrie to the house. It didn't matter. The rumors had already started and the wagging tongues would probably have made accusations whether she had gone or not.

But if she had just had a new dress . . .

Chapter Thirty

Wade arrived at the spring in mid-afternoon and the sun was unbearably hot. He tied his horse in the shade and walked to the head of the spring where the cool air rose up from the water.

He removed his hat and sat down, throwing the hat aside as he leaned against the trunk of the giant live oak tree, and then, he waited.

A long time later, he stood and looked toward the path that led to the Tanner's property. It was empty. A blue jay scolded him from a low limb of the tree and a wren sang noisily from an overhead branch somewhere down the trail, but there was no sound of approaching steps, nor any sign of Ada.

He reached down and picked up his hat, smiling derisively at being so gullible. He slapped the hat against his leg and then he walked toward his horse. Well, he wouldn't be caught so unsuspecting again, he told himself. He put the hat on his head and took up the reins, swinging into the saddle a second later, and riding away.

A few minutes later, Paul and Silas appeared on the trail. They ran into the clearing near the spring, and Esther Tanner would have washed his mouth out with soap if she had heard Paul's language at that moment.

"It would've worked," he angrily exclaimed as he looked in the direction Wade had gone. "If Carrie hadn't come home and kept Ada from comin', our plan woulda worked."

"He's shore hooked," Silas agreed. "He came just fur her. There ain't no other explanation."

"Well, dad-blast-it!" Paul said as he kicked at the tall grass. "He'll think we lied, for shore. We'll never get 'im back."

"Humph!" Silas grunted. "A lot you know. He's hooked, ain't 'e? Well, I bet he comes back on his own. We ain't gotta do nuthin', 'cept make sure Carrie don't stop Ada the next time."

Paul calmed down. "Hey, maybe you're right. He shore is hooked. There ain't no doubt about that." He suddenly laughed. "He shore is hooked!" he repeated and Silas joined in the laughter.

Had the boys known, they need not have worried whether Carrie would keep Ada away from the spring, because the next morning, she got up with news that she and Henson were going home that day.

After breakfast, Henson loaded the carriage and while he did that, Carrie pulled Ada aside and talked seriously with her before leaving.

"I talked to daddy," she began. She wagged her head with regret and Ada knew what was coming. "He won't budge on what he thinks. He says Logan knows more'n me and you'd lie for Wade, anyhow."

Ada hissed with indignation. "Well, at least you and mama believe me."

"I do, anyway. I don't know about mama."

Ada looked at Carrie in alarm. Surely her mother understood what Logan was doing.

"I think mama hoped you and Wade would get together and now that it doesn't look like it'll happen, well, she's afraid, Ada."

Ada looked over her shoulder toward the house. There was no one in sight, but she pictured her mother standing in the kitchen.

"Poor mama," she said, but had Carrie known, it was not because Ada regretted her mother's lost hope. She regretted what she was planning and how it would hurt her mother.

"I've got things ready," Henson announced and Carrie gripped Ada's arm.

"It's not the end of the world, Ada," Carrie assured her. "Mama and daddy both love you. Just remember that and ride it out."

It was not very good advice, or that was what Ada was thinking as Carrie rode away. Maybe if Carrie had known what was on Ada's mind she would have come up with a wiser bit of advice, but as it was, Ada was left to her own devices, and there was no wisdom in that, at all.

She watched the carriage until it was completely out of sight and then she walked back to the house.

There was a hush on the place that Ada had not noticed before. It was as if Carrie had taken the joy with her. Esther stood at the stove, making coffee, and Fred was sitting at the table, a sour look on his face. As Ada walked through, his eyes followed her.

"I thought maybe your sister could talk some sense into yore head," he said.

"Well, I thought she might talk some into yours," Ada replied.

Esther turned and looked at them, her mouth set in a hard line.

"Don't disrespect your father," she told Ada.

Ada bit her tongue. "Yes, ma'am," she replied. "I'm goin' outside."

She turned to go, but Fred stopped her. "No, you ain't. You come back here and sit down."

Mechanically, she walked to a chair and sat down.

"Now," he said. "Since no one can git to the bottom of what's goin' on with you, I wanna hear it straight. Am I gonna be a grandpa once or is it gonna be twice, Ada?"

She felt an awful rebelliousness rise up inside her and she honestly considered lying to him. It seemed that was what he wanted to hear anyway. He was not going to believe the truth.

"I'm gonna kill that Yankee," he said when she remained silent. "But first, I'm gonna teach him a lesson about messin' with our women."

Ada cast a startled look in his direction. "You don't want to hear the truth, daddy," she said. "Wade Thornton's been more uv a gentleman than Logan has. I would think if you believed this about me, you'd figure it was Logan to blame."

"Well, I c'n keep an eye on you and Logan, but I cain't that sneakin' Yankee."

"Oh, Fred," Esther finally said. "Ada's all right. I'd know if she weren't."

"Yeah, and you'd lie for both uv 'em." He cast an accusing look her way. "An' I reckon I know why."

Ada instantly remembered Carrie's dream-like memory. She had a feeling it was not a dream, at all. The look in Fred's eyes said a lot.

"Come Sund'y, the preacher'll be here. You and Logan are gettin' married," Fred said. Ada looked across the table at him, and in her eyes was a silent pleading. "An' don't look at me that way. You're lucky he'll have ya'. That oughta tell you something about the kinda man he is."

"It does, daddy," she solemnly said and he took her meaning in an instant.

"Well, somethin's gotta be done before we're disgraced outta house and home. This is the right thing to do and one day you'll thank me for it."

Ada slowly came to her feet. "May I go, now?" she calmly asked. Her very stillness upset Fred more than had she yelled at him, but he eyed her suspiciously and only nodded.

Ada turned and went to her room. She closed the door and walked to her bed and once there, she sat down. She sat there for a very long time and then she laid her head on the pillow and stared up at the ceiling.

"I ain't gonna marry Logan," she said to herself. "So, tonight's the night."

Chapter Thirty-one

Powder Keg heard the horses coming and he walked onto the porch for a better look, shotgun in hand. Everyone had left early that morning and he was alone on the ranch, except for Della who was working at the house. When the seven horses streamed into the yard, she came to the door and looked out, too.

Powder Keg immediately recognized Logan and his face went pale. He was glad he was holding a shotgun, especially when he saw the mood of the group was grim.

"Where's Thornton?" Fred Tanner demanded.

"Out at the fence," Powder Keg readily answered even though Fred's tone was anything but friendly. "The whole crew left early this mornin'."

"Is she in the house then, or is she out there with him?"

"Who?" Powder Keg asked, plainly confused.

"Ada!" Fred snapped.

Powder Keg was genuinely surprised. "She ain't here," he said. "An' we ain't seen her."

One of the men on a horse behind Logan pulled his rope off the saddle and began uncoiling it. Powder Keg lifted the barrel of his gun and pointed it directly at the man's stomach.

"Put the rope up," he warned him.

Della suddenly stepped outside and quickly walked into the

yard. She knew all the men in that group and they knew her. She was just a small, black lady in her fifties, but she was well liked and respected. No one wanted to cross her.

"Howdy, Mistah Fred," she said. Her voice had a calming effect and they all turned and looked at her. She walked right up to them and shielded her eyes against the morning sun. "Dey's trouble in yore eyes, dis mawnin'."

"It's Ada, Della. She's gone. I figured she was here."

"Naw, suh. She ain't 'ere. She neber cums 'ere."

"Are you sure?" he hotly asked and Della nodded.

"I ain't neber seen 'er 'ere, an' you knows I don' lie, Mistah Tanner."

"I know it," he admitted. He pulled on the reins and turned his horse. "We'll be goin'. I gotta find her."

"Gawd 'elp you!" she called after them as they rode out of the yard.

"There's trouble if I ever saw it," Powder keg said. "I wish I had time t' warn Wade. They're goin' after 'im, for sure."

Della nodded in agreement. "An' fer what, I haz t' ax? De way dey's actin', you'd t'ink Mistah Wade wuz one of dem sorry Hinkley boys."

"Yes, ma'am," Powder Keg said, eyeing Della thoughtfully, "An' I reckon he'll get just about as much consideration."

Powder Keg was right. Fred and his friends rode straight to the fence line and began riding down it, coming upon the work crew as they topped a rise in the ground. Cody heard them coming and ran for his rifle. All the rest were quick to see his example and follow it. When Fred's group came to a stop,

Wade's crew was armed and spread out behind him.

Fred slid off his horse and walked right up to Wade. He stopped before him and before anyone knew what was happening, he hit Wade, knocking him back against the fence post behind him.

Every rifle leveled and every hammer cocked, and Wade threw up a hand and shouted.

"Hold it!" he yelled. If someone started shooting, it would be a bloodbath and Wade knew it.

"Where is she?" Fred demanded, his voice low and full of meaning.

Wade wiped the blood from the corner of his mouth as he pushed himself away from the fence post. He had expected the trouble to originate from Logan, and he was still a little shocked by the turn of events.

He knew it was Ada to whom Fred referred. She must have run, he was thinking, as he straightened up and squared his feet. He didn't want to hit Fred, but he knew he was not going to take a beating from him either.

"Back off," he warned Fred in a low, hard voice. "If you're talking about your daughter, maybe you should ask Logan."

Fred glanced over his shoulder and then he swung his attention back to Wade. "I'm askin' you, Yankee. You're the one what got 'er into this mess."

Every muscle in Wade's body tensed. "I hardly know your daughter, but I've heard the rumors," he admitted. "Surely you don't believe that about your own daughter."

"Ya' shamed 'er," he stated. "An' now she's run off, afraid t' face her family with the truth."

Strangely, Logan had not moved or said a word. He was sitting on his horse, his hands folded and resting on the saddle. He was looking at Wade. His eyes were narrowed and his lips were set, but there was no hint of deep passion on his face. He was surprisingly calm. Wade wondered what was going on behind his well-placed facade.

But he was worried about Ada and standing here arguing with Fred was not getting her found. He swallowed his pride and also the knot of anger welling up inside him. "Let's lay our differences aside until Ada is found," he said to Fred. "My men and I will help you find her, if you'll let us, and after she's found, then you and I can have this conversation in private. Ada's name has been dragged through the mud enough."

"Humph!" Fred snorted with contempt, but surprisingly, he nodded his head. "I reckon you could find her, at that," he said. His nostrils were flared with anger, but he spoke calmly enough. "An' you c'n just bet, we'll continue this conversation onct she's safe."

"Put the tools away," Wade said, speaking over his shoulder so that his eyes never left Fred. "An' mount up. We're going back to the ranch for fresh horses," he then said to Fred. "You're welcome to join us there or we'll strike out on our own."

Wade was thinking that he knew where to start. He and Rusty would go to the big oak tree that separated his property from the Tanners, but he could not tell that to Fred. There was already too much suspicion between them.

"We're goin' to Mason's Corner," Fred said. "I don't reckon

338

I trust ya' to check the train or the steamboats. We'll do that."

Wade was happy to let him, but then, he wondered if that was what Ada had done. That would take money, though, and Wade didn't think Ada had any money. Fred didn't think so, either and if she had bought a ticket, they were sure to think Wade had given her the money.

Well, he could not let that distract him. He led his men back to the ranch and they streamed into the yard, going straight to the corral.

Powder Keg joined them, and relayed to Wade what had happened there.

"I need someone to stay here," Wade said after they had exchanged information. "Just in case she comes here." The idea worried him, but he tried not to show it. "You wanna do it, or should I ask Bart?"

"I'll do it," Powder Keg said. "Ya'll just find her," he then said, his voice deep with concern. "She's a good kid, but she's been drove t' this. I blame Logan. No man oughta talk about his girl like he talked about her. He's the one that oughta be ashamed, not you."

"I'm not ashamed," Wade quickly pointed out. "I've got a clear conscious where Ada Tanner is concerned. I can look any man in the eye and say that."

"I figured as much," Powder Keg said with a nod of his head. "An' not jest 'cause I know you. She's quality even if she is Logan's girl."

Wade eyed him. "She isn't. She hasn't been Logan's girl for a while, I'm thinking, and maybe that's half the trouble."

"Maybe so," he agreed. "Ya'll just find her before her pa does. It's gonna be bad, I'm afraid—real bad."

Wade thought so, too. He caught up another horse and was throwing on his saddle when Rusty stopped beside him. He was already on his horse, ready to go, and he waited while Wade secured the saddle in place.

"What's the plan, Boss?" he asked.

"Get the men together. I want Jess and Daniel to make two groups—Jess take one and Daniel the other—and set out looking in the most likely places. Except for you," he added. "You and I are going to the big oak. We'll start there."

Rusty nodded. He urged his horse forward and rode out of the corral. He found the men waiting in the yard beside the bunk house and he delivered Wade's orders. They divided and rode out of the yard, separating as they cleared the gate and then Rusty sat there until Wade joined him.

They rode straight to the big oak and both men climbed down from the saddle and walked under the spreading limbs of the giant tree.

As they stepped into the shady interior, movement caught their eyes and then the twins cautiously emerged from the back side of the tree trunk.

Wade was glad to see them, but Rusty cautioned them to be careful and not to disturb the ground. He hoped he could read something in the sign Ada had left behind.

Paul stepped up on one of the rough, gnarled roots of the tree and carefully avoided putting his bare feet on the ground. Silas did the same thing and they waited as Rusty went over the whole area, starting where Ada had left her stash.

"She picked up her stuff," he said as he moved along, "an' then she walked this way." He slowly walked across the open, sandy expanse beneath the tree's canopy. "She moved this branch aside. See where it brushed the ground—and then she went out. She's headin' toward the spring."

"Let's go," Wade said.

The twins ran down to the spring, but Rusty and Wade rode their horses. They all arrived at approximately the same time, but the twins held back, knowing not to approach the spring until Rusty had time to examine the ground.

"She was here," Rusty said after a few minutes.

Wade stood by the pool of water and looked into it, wondering what had been on Ada's mind when she had come to the spring in the middle of the night. His eyes drifted across the swimming hole to the runoff that funneled the water east toward the cypress pond in the distance and he prayed she had not been desperate enough to do anything foolish.

Rusty put his hands on his hips and then he reached up and pushed his hat back as he looked across the woods. It was overgrown and thick with trees and vines, a tangle of jungle that was not inviting. "An' that's where she went," he said, much to Wade's relief.

They all walked in that direction, Wade and Rusty leading their horses and the twins running along behind. Wade apprehensively looked into the tangle, but Rusty was quick to recognize sign of her passing.

"She went in right here," he said.

"How c'n ya' tell?" Paul quickly asked.

"Stand back an' look," Rusty said. "See the way the brush is moved aside. It almost looks like a hole in the woods."

Paul eyed it and then he smiled. "I see it," he said. "She went right through there."

Wade could see it then, too, but it didn't relieve his anxiety. It was a bad place to be traveling and he wondered why she had chosen such a dangerous and difficult route.

"She don't want t' be followed," Rusty replied when Wade asked that question. "She's taken the hardest route, thinkin' everybody'll be lookin' for her on the trails."

"She's right, too," Wade said. "God! What is she thinking!"

"I'll tell ya'," Paul soberly said. "She'd rather be dead than married to Logan. You oughta know that," he said, looking right at Wade, his expression full of meaning.

"Don't believe everything you hear," Wade carefully said. "It isn't true what they're saying about me and your sister. She's a good kid."

"I know that," he said with great exasperation. "But she's in love with you. Any fool oughta be able to see that."

Wade jerked with the force of Paul's words. His eyes immediately jumped to Rusty's face and Rusty smiled and simply shrugged.

"Any fool c'n see you're in love with her, too," Silas added. "So I guess I don't understand why all this hubbub. Why don't you just marry 'er?"

Wade could not say anything. His mouth dropped open and he stared in wonder at Paul and Silas.

"From the mouth of babes . . ." Rusty facetiously quoted and Wade frowned at him.

"Well," Wade said, playing for time as he tried to think how he should answer that. "It isn't that simple." He squared his shoulders and looked into the thicket. "Look," he began, "you boys go back to the house so we can get back to work. Time's important."

"We c'n help."

"You've helped," Rusty said, his habitually amused look in his eyes. "Now, run home and help your ma."

"He's right," Wade said. "You'll slow us down from here on out. An' if Ada returns home, your mother will need someone to bring that news to the searchers. That's where we need you."

"Okay," they agreed and they quickly scampered off in the direction of home.

"Any fool . . ." Rusty sang out as Wade turned back to him. It brought a smile to Wade's lips even though, at the same time, he felt like he wanted to hit Rusty for teasing him.

"Yeah, well, I bet I've got company," he said, and Rusty immediately lost his smile.

"I reckon you do," he admitted. "I gotta tell ya', Wade. I'm in love with Angela."

"I know," Wade said. "And you've got my blessings."

"Whew!" Rusty exclaimed in animated relief. "D—! It's been killin' me. I've wanted to come clean for weeks. An' I wouldn't blame ya' if ya' beat the daylights outta me right now."

"If I did that, who'd find Ada?" he wisely pointed out.

The confession had finally come out and Rusty was

relieved, but Wade was not giving it any thought. He was looking around, wondering how they were going to get the horses through the tangle ahead of them.

He scanned the woods and then he looked back toward the Tanner's property. He had never stood at exactly this spot, nor looked back at the Tanner's property from this angle but he immediately saw the profit in it. He smiled and thought to himself that once Ada was safe, he would be back. His daddy's clue was no longer a mystery.

"We'll lead the horses," Rusty said as Wade voiced his concern. "It'll be slow going, but not that hard. Come on. She's left an easy trail. Let's go get 'er."

But an hour later, Rusty was not so confident. They were standing at the edge of the sapling thicket and Ada's trail was gone as surely as if it had never existed.

"Why, Ada, why?" Rusty mused in his peculiarly witty way. "Why would you go in there?"

Wade wondered the same thing. It was a strangely sobering place in the light of day, but at night, it was an ominously spooky wood.

"Maybe she's going to the Spencer's farm," Wade said, thinking that it was on the other side of the pine forest and the shortest route was right through here.

"She's tryin' t' get away from Logan," Rusty said. "Not go to 'im."

"Is she?"

"Well, yeah. Didn't she run away 'cause of him?"

It didn't make any sense and Wade was not sure he was

understanding everything properly.

"We're wastin' time," Wade said. "Come on. Let's go."

"Go where?" Rusty asked. "There ain't no way to trail 'er in there."

He looked up at the sky, checking the time. It was nearly five o'clock. In three hours it would be dark—even sooner in the dark recesses of the pine forest.

Wade hesitated while trying to decide what to do. If Ada was in there, then it was possible she was lost. It was easy to get lost in such a place. Wade was concerned for himself on that matter.

"Can you get in and out of there without getting lost?" he asked Rusty.

"I think so."

Wade nodded. "Okay, let's do it."

The horses were no good to them at this point and they didn't know how long they would be gone, so they stripped them and turned them loose. The horses trotted off a few yards, stopped and began munching on a patch of grass. Rusty and Wade stowed the saddles nearby and then they walked to the edge of the forest.

"Well, here goes," Rusty said and he led the way inside. Wade followed without a word and the two of them were soon out of sight under the tall trees.

A moment later, a dark figure leaned over the saddles and carefully fingered the leather. Then silently, he glided into the forest and mysteriously disappeared into the shadows.

Chapter Thirty-two

Ada was frightened—no, she was terrified. She had long since given up trying to climb out of the well where she had fallen. The muddy walls broke and came down every time she tried to get a handhold and after the last nearly endless avalanche, she was afraid to try again, afraid she would be buried alive.

She was standing knee deep in dark water, and her feet were sunk into ankle deep rocks that she struggled to wade through. She was exhausted, but she had nowhere to sit down and there seemed to be no way out.

She looked up. All she could see was the round opening of the well far above her. The sky looked strangely close and oddly out of place and she wondered if it would be the last thing she ever saw.

She had fallen in the well early in the morning. She was making her way to the old Spencer's house hidden deep in the sapling thicket. It was the only shelter she could think of where she could hide until she could make other plans, but she had not known about the old well, covered over years before with boards that had become soft and rotten.

She had seen the house and had paused, apprehensive about going inside once she had found it, but as she had taken a step toward it, something had given way under her feet and with a loud crack, the boards had broken and she had fallen, catching herself on the rim of the well.

Ada had clung there, dangling over the abyss until her hands could no longer hold on. She slipped and then her hands lost their hold, and she had slid down the side of the well, falling into the water beneath her amid a shower of dirt and mud.

She had called out until her voice was all but gone, but there had been no one to hear. No one ever came into this forest, especially not near the Spencer's old house. That's why Ada had thought it was a good place to hide out. Now, she wished she had never heard of it.

She leaned against the side of the well to rest. It didn't help much, but it was all she could do. The rocks shifted under her weight and the side of one of them cut into her ankle. She pulled her foot up and then repositioned it, wishing she had a solid floor beneath her.

Oddly, time meant little as she waited. It seemed never to change. There was never a moment when she could say it was noon or when she could tell that evening had come nor the night that followed. It was always dark in the well and the sky was always bright. She could see stars all the time.

She began to cry and then she hoarsely called out again.

"Help!" she cried. "Anybody! Somebody! Help me!"

She waited, breathlessly listening, but there was no sound.

And then suddenly, a shadow fell across the opening. Ada had closed her eyes, but she sensed the change in the light overhead and she opened them again.

She felt as if she was upside down and she literally touched her face to be sure she was looking up. The sky was gone and she gasped, thinking that she had been sealed inside the well.

"Help!" she called out again. "Please, help me."

The shadow moved and the sky looked down upon her again, but now, Ada was really afraid. What was up there? Could it be that a wild animal had found her? She began to imagine a bear prowling around the perimeter of the well, trying to figure out a way to get to her—or a panther. Maybe even a giant alligator. There was a stream nearby. It was not impossible.

She began to tremble but she also became very quiet, hoping whatever it was would give up and go away. She strained her ears, listening for evidence but she heard absolutely nothing, at all.

And then, she did hear something. Shuffling footsteps were approaching. Something was lumbering its way to the edge of the well, sniffing as it moved along. Ada leaned back and tried desperately to hide by pressing her body into the muddy walls of the well. She was breathing quick and fast and before long, she was light headed. Her vision was as narrow as the opening in the well. She felt faint and she closed her eyes, hoping she wouldn't give out just now.

The sniffing stopped. It was an animal and it whined with eagerness when it found her scent. Ada heard it claw at the ground around the edge of the well and then suddenly, it barked.

"Skippy!" she cried out with relief, and then she began to

cry.

Chapter Thirty-three

Rusty and Wade had not gone far when the same oppressive feeling came over Wade that he had had the last time he had entered this forest. The weight of the trees seemed to press on him and the hush of nature's cathedral awed him. He hesitated even to speak as if it was irreverent in such a place.

Rusty held a knife in his hand and every so often, he would put a mark on the side of a tree. They walked and they looked, but neither of them saw anything.

If they had walked straight across the forest, they would have come out of it in just an hour or so, but they were searching and stopping a lot just to stand and listen, and after an hour had passed, they were not very far into the interior.

"Why did she come in here?" Rusty wondered again. He had stopped and pushed his hat back, and he was looking around, a perplexed look on his face.

The trees grew close together and it was hard to see a very far distance. Ada could have been twenty feet away from them and if she had not wanted to be found, she could have easily eluded them. Rusty was thinking that very thing when he began walking again.

After a few minutes, the trees suddenly thinned out and the forest took on a different feel. It was actually rather pleasant here in this spot. The trees were older. They were very tall and had large trunks, and they were separated from each other far enough to give a long line of sight.

The trouble was, it was getting dark, and both Wade and Rusty knew they should turn back. There was nothing they could do in the dark.

"We gotta go back," Rusty said and Wade nodded.

"I know," he said. "Just a little longer, okay?"

Rusty didn't say anything, but he began moving again. They crossed the field of old trees, taking their time and constantly looking, hoping to see something that would tell them Ada had been there, but by the time they came out of the old growth trees, they were both discouraged.

"We might as well go back," Rusty said. "We can start fresh in the mornin'."

Wade nodded an agreement. "I wonder if she's even in here," he said. He looked over his shoulder as he considered that. "What if she just went around the edge of this forest, using it to cover her while she slipped away."

"Then we've wasted a lot of time," Rusty admitted.

"Tomorrow, let's ride the perimeter of this forest and see if we can find a place where she came out."

"That's an idea, at that," Rusty agreed, but as he turned to leave, something flashed in his peripheral vision and he quickly swung back for a better look. He caught it again, a light moving through the trees.

"Wade!" he hissed and Wade quickly turned and looked. Rusty pointed and they both stood very still and watched.

It was a dark figure. He seemed to move in a straight line although with the thick growth of trees, Wade and Rusty knew it was an illusion. He wore a huge black hat and his clothes were dark and hanging loosely around him, and his light winked in and out as he moved through the trees.

"Come on!" Wade whispered and they both ran toward the disappearing figure.

They lost him, but caught sight of the light a few seconds later. They altered their course and ran to catch up only to lose sight of him again. They stopped and looked around, the light appearing for a few seconds to give them direction and they were off once more, running through the thick stand of pine trees.

The light was gone, but they kept going and then out of nowhere, a dog began to bark.

Rusty skidded to a stop and Wade almost ran into him.

"Listen!" he said, holding up a hand in warning. They listened and Wade heard it, too. It was a dog, anxiously barking and from the sound of him, he was not far away.

"It's Skippy," Wade said with hope.

"Skippy?"

"The Tanner's dog. He's barked at me enough that I ought to recognize him. I tell you, it's Skippy."

They were too excited to say anything. They just took off again, running through the darkening woods, following the sound of Skippy's bark.

They came suddenly upon an opening in the forest. The pine trees thinned out and were now mixed together with bay trees, sumac, and oak, and across the clearing was an old house, vine covered and broken down, but still standing, and there to one side, barking at the ground, was Skippy.

He wagged his tail when he saw Wade and then he danced around and whined.

"What is it, boy?" Wade asked as he approached, and then he heard a faint voice call out.

"Help me," it said. "Please, someone, help me!"

Wade ran to the hole in the ground and dropped to his knees. "Ada!" he called out and she answered. "Get something!" he shouted at Rusty. "We have to get her out."

Rusty looked into the well. "Ada, are you all right?"

"Yes, but I'm exhausted. I don't know how much longer I can stand here."

Rusty was hoping he had time to run back to his saddle. He had a good, strong rope on it, but it was not going to be an option. He looked around for anything he could use.

"I'm going down there," Wade suddenly said and he reached down to pull off his shoes.

"No!" Ada called up. "I've tried to climb out. The wall crumbles and falls. You'll be stuck, too."

"She's right," Rusty said. "I need you up here. If you go down, we may lose both of you."

Wade paused with his hand on his boot. "What will we do, then?" he asked.

"I see something by the house. I'm going over there and see what it is. Maybe I can find something we can use."

He ran to the house but Wade leaned over the rim of the

well and looked down. "Hold on, Ada. We're going to get you out."

Rusty kicked around the junk left outside the old house but he didn't find anything. There was a ladder, but it was rotten and fell apart in his hands. There was rope, but it shredded like dry straw. He looked through a window and for just a few seconds, he stared in disbelief. The room inside was clean and well organized and leaning against the wall was a new ladder.

Rusty rushed to the door and pushed his way in. Someone was obviously living here. The evidence of habitation was everywhere, but Rusty took no time to wonder. He ran to the ladder and as he laid his hand on it, he saw a coil of rope on the floor. The ladder was too short—he was sure of that, so he grabbed up the rope and ran out of the house.

"I got a rope, Ada," he called down. "I'm gonna tie a loop in it and send it down. You sit in it and we'll pull you up."

"Be careful," she warned. "The sides of the well want to fall in."

"Is one side more stable than another?" Rusty asked.

"Maybe," she answered.

"When I throw down the rope, I'll walk around the perimeter. You tell me to stop when I get to the side that's the most stable."

"Okay," she called up and the rope dropped down beside her. "There!" she said to stop him.

"Tell us when you're ready," he said.

Ada threw the loop over her head and settled onto the rope as best she could. "I'm ready," she said and she felt the rope begin to tighten.

Wade and Rusty took up the slack in the rope and when Ada's weight hit the end of it, the rope dug into the ground. They pulled harder and Ada's feet slowly rose out of the water only to drop back down under a shower of dirt as the rim gave way and began to crumble.

"I'm okay," Ada called up at their shouts of concern. They repositioned the rope and began pulling again.

The rope tightened and cut into Ada, but she made no complaint. Her feet rose out of the water again and soon she was halfway to the top.

And then, the side of the well began to cave. It started with the tiny movement of sandy gravel shifting down the side of the well in a fine shower, but it quickly cracked and broke, large pieces of the ground coming off in chunks that dropped like lead weights. The side of the well caved in under the rope and Rusty and Wade fell forward with the change of balance.

Wade stopped pulling, but Rusty shouted to keep going. "Don't stop!" he yelled. "Pull faster! Pull faster!"

Wade had stumbled, but he jumped up and pulled with strength he didn't know he had. The well was enlarging as the crack opened up and the wall fell away, but Rusty and Wade pulled back from it, almost running backwards in an effort to stay ahead of the enlarging hole.

Ada's head suddenly appeared and they dragged her, pulling her out of the well and then away from the opening. She turned loose of the rope and turned over and Wade ran to her, snatching her up in his arms as he fell to the ground beside her.

"Oh, God, Ada!" he exclaimed as he hugged her to him. "Oh, God! Tell me you're alright."

"I'm alright," she readily answered him, "but I wouldn't 've been. I was about ready to drop."

Skippy stuck his nose in between them and Wade laughed as the dog licked at Ada.

"Good, Boy," Wade said, giving him an affectionate rub.

Rusty stood over them, coiling the rope in his hands. Now that Ada was safe, he was considering a lot of things that he supposed Wade wouldn't be able to calculate in his present state of mind.

"Boss, I gotta go get the horses," he pointed out. "An' we need to get her farther away from that well. I don't trust the ground here."

Wade cast a cautious look toward the gaping hole and without a word, he got up. He picked Ada up and she didn't protest when he carried her in his arms away from the old well.

Ada was filthy, and even though she was near exhaustion, she brushed at her arms and wiped at her face. There was mud all over her and she looked up at Wade, self-conscious once more.

"Somebody's livin' in the old house," Rusty said as he followed Wade to the side of it. "But I'd take 'er inside anyhow. Git those shoes off o' her, too, before they start dryin'."

"Is there a lamp inside?" Wade asked as he set Ada on the ground by the wall.

"I'll check."

Rusty went inside and in a couple of minutes, a soft glow

radiated at a window.

He came out again and much to Ada's delight, he had brought with him a bucket of water and a rag.

"I thought you might want this, Ada," he said with a grin. "You're as filthy as a field hand."

She smiled. She was not one bit offended by his observation. She took the cloth but she was so tired that her hands trembled. Rusty set the bucket beside her and then he and Wade talked in hushed tones as she cleaned her face and hands.

"That's about all I'm good for," she announced as she leaned back, too tired to sit up.

"I'm going to take you inside," Wade said to her and she gave him no trouble as he picked her up and carried her inside.

"Here, Boss," Rusty said as they came into the room where he stood. "Put her here."

There was a cot against the wall and Wade carefully deposited Ada on it. It was smooth as glass, not a wrinkle in it, and it looked clean. Ada was so tired, though, that she didn't notice. She simply sighed and lay there, limp and exhausted.

"I'm goin' after the horses," Rusty said. "I'll be back as soon as I can."

"Okay," Wade said. He walked to the door with Rusty, closing it behind him before returning to Ada's side.

"I'm going to take your shoes off, Ada," he told her.

"Thanks, Wade," she softly said, and he knelt down beside her. "There's a stone or somethin' in my right shoe that's killin' me," she went on to say. "I'll be glad to git it out."

He smiled as he took her foot in his hand. He worked at loosening the shoe and finally he got it off. The offending stone fell out. Wade looked at it, studying it for a minute before actually picking it up. He closed his hand around it and then he dropped it into his pocket.

"You gonna keep it as a souvenir?" Ada asked.

"I thought I might."

"There were a million of 'em in that old well," she said. "I kept sinking in 'em and wadin' through 'em. If it had been a solid ground, I don't think I'd be so tired right now."

"You just rest," he said. "I'm gonna stay right here beside you."

Wade sat down on the floor beside the bed and he leaned his back against it. Neither of them said anything for a long time and then it was Ada who spoke.

"What now, Wade?" she asked and he pushed himself forward so he could look at her.

"Tonight, I'll take you to my place," he said. "Tomorrow, I'll take you anywhere you say."

"I botched this, didn't I?" she calmly said. Her voice was a monotone and Wade was beginning to think it no longer stemmed from her exhaustion. It was her mental state at this point.

"Why did you run away?" he asked.

She didn't immediately reply and when she did, it was with a slight shrug of her shoulder.

"Ada, you've got to know something."

She turned her large eyes toward him and he just stared

into them for a few seconds.

"I didn't start the rumors about us."

"I know," she interrupted him. "That ain't why I ran away."

"I didn't start the rumors," he repeated, "but I wish to God they were true."

Her eyes flashed with surprise and then with a look that Wade could not interpret.

"What 're you sayin', Wade?"

He turned away from her and put his back against the bed again. "You did something to me," he said. "The first time I saw you, it was like nothing I ever felt before, and it's only gotten worse." He paused to brush at an imaginary spot on his shirt sleeve. "It's taken me a while to admit it, but I'm in love with you."

He expected a long silence or maybe an immediate rebuke, but he never expected her quick response.

"Then what're you doin' down there on the floor?" she asked him. "I've been waitin' for you to kiss me ever since you pulled me outta that blasted well."

Wade turned with a start and then he laughed. "Yes, ma'am," he said, throwing his hat across the room as he came to his knees. He scooped her up and kissed her and they were still hugging and kissing when Rusty returned with the horses.

"Well, you look better," he said to Ada when he had stepped inside the house. "You got your color back."

She looked at Wade and they both laughed and then Rusty grasped the truth and it was he who blushed.

"Well, excuse me for hurrying back when I thought I was

needed," he said. "I c'n leave again an' come back later, if you like."

"No, sir!" Wade said. "We've got to get Ada to my place."

Rusty put a hand on Wade's arm and a frown crossed his face.

"You ought not t' do that," he said. "Take 'er home."

"There ain't no way," he said, falling into the Texas lingo.

"You've got the support of the community right now, but if you take her home with you, you'll lose that."

"He's right, Wade. I gotta go home sooner or later. I might as well do it tonight and git it over with."

"What about Logan?" Wade asked Ada.

"Did you mean whatcha said a while ago?"

"I did."

"Then for better or worse, Wade Thornton, I'm yours. Logan ain't got no hold on me atall."

"He thinks he has."

"No, he knows better. It's a matter of pride with him."

They stood there just looking at each other and Rusty nervously shifted his position while he waited.

"I'll take you home," Wade finally said. "I promised your daddy I'd see him tonight anyway."

"Don't do anything stupid, Wade," she cautioned him.

"I won't, but you better believe, this isn't over."

They left the old house, but not before Wade turned and looked at it, giving it a final study. He picked up his hat and as he did, he wondered who lived here, but at the same time, he had a crazy idea that he thought he knew.

They rode out of the sapling thicket, coming into the Clearing around midnight. All of them were exhausted, but no one complained. They rode across Wade's property and crossed into the Tanner's property by way of the northeast gate. Skippy had beat them home and he bayed as the horses stopped at the gate and Wade got down.

Fred appeared on the porch. He was holding a kerosene lamp high and it spread a light all around him. Esther crowded in behind him and the twins looked out a window.

"So, you've brought 'er home," Fred soberly stated, but then he saw Ada's condition, all filthy and dirty, and his belligerent attitude dropped in an instant. "Ada!" he gasped.

"She fell down a well at the old Spencer place in the sapling thicket," Wade explained. "Skippy led us to her."

Esther came forward and gathered Ada to her, pulling her inside without a word, but Fred stood there, holding the lamp and frowning at nothing in particular.

"I knew you'd know where t' find 'er," Fred finally said, his tone full of meaning.

"I didn't know where she was," Wade told him. "No more than you did."

"I should've killed you dead when I had the chance."

"Did you have the chance?"

"I reckon I did—onct."

That was a sobering admission, and Wade was afraid he knew what he meant. He had always suspected Fred of being the one who had shot him.

"You can kill me, but it isn't going to relieve you of the

guilt."

"Yeah, well, if this was a shotgun instead uva lamp, you wouldn't be talkin' so smart."

"No, I suppose I wouldn't," Wade admitted. He swung into the saddle and picked up the reins. "But I'm not afraid to face you. It's when I turn my back that I worry."

A slap in the face would not have had any greater effect. Fred moved with the force of Wade's words and for just a second, Wade thought Fred would throw the lamp at him. He didn't. He stood on the porch, too angry to speak and Wade rode home, concerned that at any minute he would hear the sound of a shot that would knock him out of his saddle.

The next morning, Rusty disappeared before breakfast and when the men went to work, he still had not returned. It was the next afternoon when he rode in and he wasted no time before going straight to Wade.

The door was open, propped back to let in a cooling breeze, so he walked into the house and paused just inside. Wade was sitting at a makeshift desk, making notes in a ledger. He looked up when Rusty stepped inside.

"Where have you been?" he quickly asked.

"A lotta places," he said, but then, he quickly added, "Ada's gone. I thought you'd want to know."

Wade stiffened and then he slowly came to his feet, his eyes narrowing as he considered the meaning of Rusty's news.

"Her pa put 'er on the train today. I saw 'im. It was north-bound."

"Northbound? Where's he sending her?"

"Anywhere away from you, I'm thinkin'."

Wade grimly nodded. "Did she go willingly?" he asked.

"It looked like it, but she caught my eye once she was on the train and it looked like she wished she could say something to me."

"The twins would know where she is," Wade said and Rusty nodded.

"I thought about that," he said. "I thought I'd go lookin' for 'em tomorrow—with your permission, Boss."

Wade thought about it and for a fleeting moment, he considered going himself, but then, he reluctantly nodded, knowing he should not go to the Tanner's property right now. "Okay," he said. "You've got my permission."

After breakfast the next day, Rusty rode away and Wade stood in the yard, watching him. It was a long day for him and when Rusty arrived at the ranch late that evening, Wade was pacing with impatience.

"She's gone to stay with her sister in Green Cove," Rusty said. "I don't know when she'll be back."

"Then Fred agreed to call off the wedding," Wade pondered aloud.

"No, I don't think it was Fred. I think it was Logan."

"Logan?"

"Yeah, and you ain't gonna like what I'm about to say."

Wade's dark eyes flashed with concern. "Don't tell me he's started something new."

"He has. It's pretty vile what he's sayin' about him and her—and you and her. He said he's done with her and you c'n have his leavin's."

"I'll kill him!" Wade vowed through clenched teeth. He swung at the air with a fist of anger. "I'll kill him for this!"

"I know somethin' else," Rusty said. "Paul told me."

Wade was wound up, tight as a drum, but he cast an anxious look at Rusty. What else could that scamp be saying?

"You know who the Hinkley's are, don't you? They're that sorry bunch down at Scratch Ankle that nobody has anything much to do with."

"Yeah, I know who they are."

"Logan's been seein' Mattie Hinkley for nigh onto a year."

"Well, isn't he the little hypocrite?" Wade wryly said. "What did Fred think about that?"

"I don't know that he knows. Paul told me."

"Does Ada know?"

"Yeah, Paul told her, too."

The sound of an approaching wagon interrupted their conversation and both Wade and Rusty looked outside to see who was arriving. The wagon rode right into the yard and a man stood up as it came to a halt.

"It's the Major!" Rusty exclaimed and Wade quickly pushed past him on his way outside.

Angela was sitting on the wagon seat but the Major had jumped down by the time Wade got to them. They looked tired, but Angela also looked sadly repentant.

"Major! Angela!" Wade said in surprise. "You're back so soon. Is something wrong?"

Angela stood and Wade walked to her and helped her down

from the wagon seat. It was she and not the major who answered.

"Everything, I'm afraid. You were right about Rich, Wade, and I have to admit, I should not have gone."

By that time, Rusty had joined them. He had taken his time, sauntering slowly out of the house, but he was there by the time Angela made her announcement.

"What happened?" Wade asked.

"He's a brute!" She looked around as if she didn't want anyone to hear and then she tilted a head toward the house. "But let's talk inside."

It was then her eyes fell upon Rusty. He had been staring at her the whole time, but she was just then getting around to looking at him. She found it sobering that she had actually missed him. When she looked at him now, she was equally surprised that she was glad to see him.

"Hello, Rusty," she said and he nodded a solemn greeting.

There was no time for more than that. Wade hurried Angela and the major inside, but Rusty didn't go with them. He stood in the yard watching them, but he never said a word.

Angela sat down on the only chair in the room and the major leaned against the wall.

"We're beat," the major said, "but glad to be here."

"What happened?" Wade asked again.

"Rich Macon wants your gold—no, he needs your gold. He's got quite a place south of here, but it takes a lot to keep up his lifestyle. I found out real fast that he's borrowed to his limit and he isn't a man to work for a living. He's gotten everything he has by swindling honest people."

Wade eyed Angela curiously. Just how honest were she and the major? They had come to Florida with one thing in mind and that was to get the gold. He wondered how they justified that while condemning Rich Macon.

"You're about to drop, Major," Wade said. "Let's talk about this tomorrow."

It was a well-received suggestion and by morning, they were all in a different mood. The rest seemed to have softened Angela's opinion of Rich Macon and she no longer wanted to talk about him. He was playing a game of confidence and that was all she would say, and the major followed her example, saying very little.

Wade didn't pressure them. As long as Rich Macon left him alone, he didn't really care what the man did, but Angela and the major were a great concern to him. He had made a bargain with Angela and now, the time was here to fulfill it but he hesitated to give her the clues. He knew things he had not known before he had made that deal. Things were different and he struggled with what he should do in order to keep his honor.

By noon, Angela and the major had learned about the local drama and about all they had missed while visiting at Wisteria Acres. Angela approached Wade just after lunch, putting a comforting arm on his shoulder as she consoled him.

"I'm sorry, Wade. I heard about Ada."

She seemed truly regretful.

"It's not all bad," he said. "I took your advice. I told her how I feel."

"And she was ready to hear it, wasn't she?"

Wade nodded. "She was."

"See? I'm not all bad."

"No. I've never thought you were bad, Angela."

She suddenly gave him an intense look. "No? Well, you may want to change that statement when you hear what I'm about to say. I want the clues, Wade. I want to get the gold and get out of here. I've had my fill of this place."

Wade moved so that he could look more closely at her. "You don't need the clues," he said. "I think I know where dad's squad hid the gold."

A flush of excitement briefly lit up her face. "You've seen it? It's there?"

"No, but I saw something a few days ago that made sense of what dad has been saying about all this."

"What was that?"

"Well, if you remember, dad was hurt real bad. He said everything was like a dream—a bad dream so he wasn't sure what he had been told about the gold. It was something about a slingshot and he kept thinking he was told to hold one in the palm of his hand and knock down the oyster house, but that makes no sense, at all."

"No, it doesn't," Angela agreed, suddenly thinking that if that was the clue, then they could forget about the gold. No one was going to find it with that direction.

"I saw a strange thing the other day," Wade said in a musing manner. "I saw a palm tree that instead of having one straight trunk with fronds on top, it was divided with two heads of fronds—just like a slingshot."

"Oh, Wade! That's it. That must be it," she amended. "But what did your daddy mean by holding it in the palm of his hand and knocking down the oyster house?"

"I told you he was delirious. The palm is the slingshot and I'm guessing that somewhere near it is something that will explain the rest."

Angela was not so sure, but she was eager to explore the possibilities, anyway.

"Let's go now!" she said.

Wade hesitated. "It's on the Tanner's property," he said.

"Oh," Angela sighed. "This could prove to be awkward, especially since you've outraged Fred Tanner."

"We might pull this off without him knowing," Wade suggested. "Or you could offer him a portion of it in good faith."

"Hardly!" Angela exclaimed. "That could be a disaster."

"Okay. There might not be anything there anyway. We can go have a look if you want to."

"You know I do," she immediately replied.

Wade and Angela walked to the corral and caught two horses. Rusty saw them saddling up and he walked to the fence, resting his elbows on the top board as he watched them.

"Goin' somewhere?" he asked after a few minutes.

"Just for a ride," Angela quickly said.

He looked at her and there was hunger in his eyes—and disappointment. Wade pitied him.

"We'll be back soon," Wade said as he stepped into the saddle. "One last ride between old friends."

Rusty nodded and then he opened the gate, closing it after the two riders had cleared it. They rode out of the yard and across the field, going northeast toward the spring. The sun was dancing on the water as they arrived and a soft breeze was moving the grass beside the run-off stream. Wade stopped his horse in the shade of the oak tree and stepped down. Angela was looking around, studying every palm tree she could see as she followed his example.

"Where is it?" she demanded when she saw nothing like he had described.

"You can't see it from here. You have to be at exactly the right angle. I was standing over there when I saw it." He pointed toward the woods on the other side of the spring. "I could just see the top of it, but come with me and I'll show you where it is. Quietly!" he cautioned her. "No talking from here on."

She obeyed without any protest, following Wade as he walked down the trail leading to the Tanner's property. They crossed the fence and continued to follow the path until they were close to the Tanner's house. Angela heard a rooster crow and the bawl of a cow somewhere nearby. To her left was a field of corn stalks, and straight ahead, the back side of a barn.

Wade left the path and waded through golden grasses that were almost waist high to Angela. They were going away from the Tanner's farm, moving in a direction that appeared almost to take them back toward the spring. It didn't. The tree was in a direct line between the house and the spring, and Wade could only imagine what it must have looked like nearly twenty years ago. Probably this had all been cleared land. Except for the palm tree and a few others, all the trees were young.

Wade stopped and Angela came abreast to him and stopped, too. There was the tree, divided like a slingshot, and at its base was a mound of debris, covered over with dirt and weeds.

"Is that it?" she whispered and Wade nodded.

The debris was the broken walls of a small building. It looked like stone, but it was a type of material made from oyster shells and mud, a tabby house—the oyster house.

"Someone's been here before us," Wade quietly announced and Angela tensed, every muscle in her body going taunt.

At the base of the broken slabs of the old wall there was freshly turned earth. Someone had dug under the debris and then covered it over again. Angela ran to it and fell to her knees.

"It can't be gone!" she exclaimed, digging at the dirt with her hands.

Wade followed her. He knelt down beside her and put his hand on her arm. "Stop it, Angela," he said.

"It can't be gone," she said in disbelief. "It has to be here."

"No, Angela. Now, stop," Wade said and he put his hand around her wrist. He pulled her arm back and she obediently let him stop her. "We'll come back with shovels and see what we can find."

"I'm not leaving," she announced. "You go get the shovels— and papa."

"I can't leave you here. What if whoever has been here comes back again?"

"Then you stay. I'll go get Papa and the shovels."

Wade looked around. His eyes went immediately toward the Tanner's house. He could not see it, but he knew it was just beyond the overgrowth and too close for comfort.

"Let's go together and come back together. Nothing's going to happen in the next hour."

"You don't know that," she insisted, speaking louder than Wade liked.

"Quiet!" he warned. "If you keep arguing, the Tanners will hear us and then you can kiss whatever is left here goodbye."

She caught her breath and flashed a startled look in the direction of the Tanner's farm.

"Please, Wade!" she begged in a hoarse whisper. She suddenly gripped his shirt and pulled him closer. "I have to have this gold. Papa's in trouble. He owes gambling debts that he can't pay."

"So, that's it," Wade testily said. He pulled her hands away from him and then he stood up. "Get up, Angela!" he demanded, and oddly, she stood up without a word of protest. "The two of you are quite a pair. Well, I hope the gold is here and I'll be glad to see you take it and go."

"Don't hate me, Wade."

"I don't," he said. "But you're probably going to hate yourself one day. All the gold in the world isn't going to solve your problems."

She dropped her chin in a dejected way and her blue eyes sadly looked up at him. Wade felt sorry for her. He wearily shook his head and then he slipped a brotherly arm around her shoulders.

"Come on," he said. "Let's hurry and get this done before it gets too late."

She reluctantly followed him back to the horses and then they quickly rode back to the ranch, flying up to the house at an alarming speed. The major was standing on the porch as they arrived and Cody and Pat were standing in the opening between the house and the bunkhouse. Everyone turned and looked and Bart came out of the lounge as they sped into the yard.

"Somethin' wrong, Boss?" Cody quickly asked.

"You ain't bein' chased, are ya'?" Bart added as he looked down the road.

"No," Wade replied. "We were just racing a little." He turned then and looked at the major. "Major, you want to join us in a ride? We thought it would be a good idea, seeing as you'll be leaving soon. It might be our last ride together."

Something in Wade's tone and also in Angela's eyes tipped him off and he readily accepted, coming off the porch with eagerness.

"I'd like that," he said.

"What about the shovels?" Angela whispered as the major went for a horse.

"Leave that to me," he said and then he walked away.

A few minutes later, they were riding out of the yard together. Wade circled back and picked up two shovels he had thrown over the back fence and then they rode quickly to the spring.

The afternoon was waning as they arrived, but it was still

hot. The turquoise water of the spring was inviting and Wade looked at it, remembering the battle of the spring. He suddenly wondered where the twins were and he cautiously looked around, letting his eyes scan the woods.

"So, you've found it!" the major excitedly said as he tied his horse to the tree.

"We found where it was," Angela said. "It looks like someone else has found it, too."

The major frowned. "Too bad," he said. "That is too bad."

Wade took the shovel in his hand and began walking. "Let's see if it's still there," he said. "Maybe we'll be lucky."

They walked fast, each of them anxious. Everything was just as Wade and Angela had left it, so without delay, Wade began digging. The hole opened up quickly. There was very little dirt at the opening and once it was cleared away, a tiny cave revealed itself under a large slab that was once a wall.

"There's something here," Wade said, pulling a rotten bag out of the dark. Gold coins scattered on the ground, catching the light and shining for the first time in nearly two decades.

"Oh!" Angela exclaimed, falling on her knees and touching them. "Is there more?" she asked, turning hopeful eyes to the dark opening. "I think I see more."

They pulled out all they could see and then Wade enlarged the mouth of the cave to get a better look inside. They found very little more and both the major and Angela ceased to hide their disappointment. They would be lucky to have enough money here to pay off the major's gambling debts, let alone, to have anything to live on.

"Someone took it!" Angela hissed. "It's been stolen before we could get to it."

"Maybe there was no more," Wade pointed out. "The amount was always in question."

It mattered very little. The fact was, this was all that was here and so the scheme to get it now seemed a hopeless endeavor. All the way back to the ranch, Angela and the Major bickered, and Wade was glad to put some distance between them. He was even happier when he put them on a train two days later and sent them back to New Hampshire.

Rusty, however, was not so glad to see them go. He secretly followed them to the station and then he watched as Angela boarded the train, knowing it would be the last time he would ever see her. He had known from the beginning that this would be the end result of their relationship, but still, he was not prepared. He rode away that morning without a word to anyone and when Wade came home, Rusty was gone.

Wade looked around without any surprise. His only regret was that he had not had the chance to say goodbye.

"Well," he said aloud as he stood alone looking down the road, "Good-bye, old friend, and good luck."

Chapter Thirty-four

"What the devil was that!" Bart exclaimed.

Everyone had gotten up and were standing at attention, alert and listening. It was a sound, strange to the night, that had brought them to their feet and each man listened with great care. The sound was not unlike an animal in great pain. It hoarsely cried in the night, making a long wail of anguish that lingering long after the cry had ended.

Wade had stood, too. He looked around in wonder. "What kind of animal is that?" he asked.

Cody wagged his head from side to side. "That ain't no animal I ever heard before," he was quick to say.

"Me neither," Bart said.

It cried again and the hair rose on Wade's arms. "Whatever it is, it's moving. It's closer now."

Chairs scraped on the floor and boots pounded as all of them moved at one time, going for the door. It was dark outside, but they all crowded onto the porch and looked into the distance.

"It's a man," Pat calmly said. "He's mighty hurt — or awful mad. Either way, we oughta be careful."

Bart and Cody quickly went back inside and when they came out again, they were armed with rifles. Powder Keg had a shot gun in his hands. He had been ready, all along.

Something loomed darkly on the edge of the yard. Bart jacked a shell into the rifle's chamber and at the same time, they all spread out.

"Good Lord!" Bart declared. "It's Jake's ghost!"

"It's mine!" the ghost cried as he leveled a rifle. The shot rang out and the bullet scattered splinters from the front post.

He was nothing more than a black spot against the white sand. He wore a long black coat and he had a floppy old hat on his head. He was easily seen even in the darkness, but Wade's men were at a disadvantage. They were trying to protect themselves and getting off a shot at the easy target was not so easy, at all. He fired again as he staggered forward and someone finally returned fire.

"Give it back!" he screamed. "Give it back!"

He stumbled and almost fell, but he caught himself and fired again, this time narrowly missing Powder Keg.

Wade and his men were crouched on the porch. Cody and Pat were scrambling for the corner of the building and they made it just as a bullet clipped wood over their heads. They quickly took a stand behind the protection of the wall and Cody fired.

The ghost went down.

An ominous silence fell over all of them. For just a few seconds, no one moved, but then, Wade slowly stood up and Cody and Pat ran out from their protected place. Cautiously, they walked toward Jake's ghost.

His hat had fallen away from him and he was lying on his back. He was not dead. He moved, reaching up to grip his chest as they approached. His rifle had fallen away from him and Cody picked it up.

He was an old man. His face was lined with wrinkles and his eyes were tired with age, but as Wade knelt down beside him, the old man's eyes came alive.

"Ah!" he cried out. He suddenly reached up and gripped the front of Wade's shirt. He had more strength than expected and Wade was pulled forward before he could wrench away. "Cap'in!" he hoarsely whispered just as Jim and Bart pulled Wade free.

"No, wait!" Wade said as they pushed the old man back. He rolled to his back again and his arms flung wide. Wade pulled away and then he fell to one knee beside him. "Who are you?" he quickly asked.

The old man tried to lift his right arm, but he could not. He tried twice and then he wagged a weary head. "Sorry, Sir," he said. "Can't . . . salute . . ."

"It's alright," Wade said. He looked around, trying to find Powder Keg. "See if you can help this man," he ordered.

Powder Keg gave his shot gun to Cody and then he stepped forward, squatting down beside the old man. He pulled the coat back and then he stopped in amazement. Beneath the long black coat was a uniform, old and threadbare, but clean and well cared for.

"I can't help 'im," Powder Keg said and Wade flashed a hard look at him. "He's dead," he went on to explain.

He was dead. No one said anything right away, but finally Bart broke the silence.

"Well, I'll be," he said. "How d' ya' explain that?"

The question began a debate, but Wade didn't join in. He knelt in silence beside the old man as he worked out a scenario in his mind that he felt was all too true. This was the last of his father's squad. He had survived that last battle and had been guarding the gold all this time.

"Find a place in the shed to lay him for tonight," Wade said, interrupting the conversation still going on around him. "Tomorrow, we'll take him to the Clearing and bury him."

The next morning, Cody set out for Mason's Corner to make a report of what had happened. The rest of Wade's crew handled the solemn task of digging a grave and burying the old man. Before they took him to the Clearing, Jim and Powder Keg had a better look at him, going through his clothes at the same time, hoping to find some identification. There was a letter in one of his pockets addressed to Corporal Lauren Harris and they brought it to Wade.

"I guess this is who he was," Powder Keg said, handing the letter to Wade. "Somethin' funny, too," he went on to say. "He musta been shot in the head a long time ago. There was a deep scar across the side of his head just over his left ear. Maybe he wasn't quite right anymore. You know what I mean?"

Wade nodded. He had not been quite right and Wade was sure of that, but there at the end, maybe he had had some clarity.

"Thanks," Wade said as he turned the old, faded letter in his hand. He would get the letter to his father. There was a return address in the upper corner and Wade knew his father

378

would want it.

They buried the old man in the Clearing, digging a hole in the very center of it and placing a makeshift marker at the head of his grave. It was a wooden cross made by Bart. He had burned the name Lauren Harris into a slab of wood and then had nailed it across a flat piece of wood to make the cross. It was Powder Keg who drove it into the ground and it was a solemn moment even though no one had known the recipient of it.

Wade remained behind after everyone else had gone. He stood over the old man's grave and wondered about a few things.

He looked up and his eyes followed an imaginary line from north to south, moving straight from where the gold had been hidden to the sapling thicket. Wade was sure it was Lauren Harris who had been living at the old house in the woods, and it was he who had been mistaken for Old Man Spencer's ghost. Wade figured a few other things, as well, and as he thought, his hand slipped into his pocket and he fingered something he had dropped there days before.

He pulled the object out of his pocket and it shined in the early morning light. He rubbed it between his thumb and finger as he considered what he was going to do. He looked down at it, and he smiled wryly. So much pain — so much grief — and now, so much to gain, if what Wade imagined was true.

He slipped the gold coin back into his pocket, but before he turned away, he lifted his hand and saluted the grave.

"Well done, Corporal Harris," he said and then he walked

away.

Chapter Thirty-Five

"When will you be back?" Jim asked as Wade stepped onto the train.

"In a few days."

"Isn't there any cattle for sale closer than Hibernia?" Jim asked, giving Wade a knowing look.

Wade smiled. "Just keep things running while I'm gone and don't worry."

"That'll be a trick," Jim dryly stated.

The train whistled. Wade waved a goodbye and then he climbed the steps and disappeared into the nearest car.

He settled down on one of the seats and stared out the window as the train pulled out of the station, northbound. He had one thing and one thing only on his mind and that was Ada. He had no idea where she was nor even her sister's name, but he was going to find her if it took him forever.

The train pulled into the station at Green Cove Springs just after four o'clock in the afternoon and it was shortly thereafter that Wade found himself standing, bag in hand, looking around. The Clarendon Hotel was near the river and he began walking toward it. A few minutes later, he had a room that overlooked the sulphur spring that gave the town its fame. He looked out his window, seeing the river in the distance and the spring much closer. He wondered if it was as pretty as Ada's spring and then he smiled wryly, thinking that he would go and see. An hour later, he was standing beside it, looking into its depths, curiously satisfied that it was nowhere as beautiful as Ada's spring.

It was larger—much larger, but it lacked the wild beauty of a wilderness spring. Instead of an oak tree, the hotel loomed large nearby sending out steps instead of roots down to the spring, and instead of the shiny runoff stream, there were bathhouses around it. In the distance, there was no cypress pond, but a pier on the St. Johns River and a dock for the steamships.

Wade walked down to the river for a better look and he was amazed at the activity. People were coming and going, workmen were bustling around, and children were playing nearby. There was one figure, however, that seemed out of place among all this movement. It was a dejected looking man with bronze-streaked blonde hair, hatless in the afternoon sun, his hair blowing in the steady wind. He was looking across the river, his arm resting on a post and his chin propped on his arm. He appeared to be hypnotized by the scene before him for he neither reacted to any stimuli nor spoke when spoken to. Wade recognized him and his heart swelled up with both pride and pity for he loved Rusty Gavin as if he was his brother.

Wade approached him and stopped about ten feet away. "So, this is where you ran off to," he said.

At first, there was no reaction. It was as if Rusty had not heard Wade, but then he slowly turned his head and squinted into the western sun.

"Yeah, well," he said, pausing for just a few seconds before continuing. "I ran outta money after three days of a binge and this is as far as I could go without a job."

"You've got a job."

Rusty nodded apathetically and then he turned and looked back across the mile-wide St. Johns River.

"Did you come all this way lookin' for me?"

"No," Wade honestly answered. "I figured you were gone for good. I'm looking for Ada."

Rusty smiled. "That shouldn't have come as a surprise."

"But it did?"

"No, not really," Rusty said. He pushed himself away from the post and turned to face Wade. He took a deep breath and then he stretched as if his body needed to uncoil after the prolonged position.

He looked thinner—gaunt, even, in Wade's opinion.

"How long since you've eaten?" he asked.

Rusty looked around as if considering that and for just a moment, the once ever-present look of amusement came back into his eyes. "Eaten? What's that?"

Wade smiled. "Come on," he said. "I'm hungry and I hate to eat alone."

Rusty rubbed his chin. He had a three days growth of beard on his face and his hair and clothes were disheveled. "I don't imagine any decent place would allow the likes of me. I look like a bum."

"I'm staying at the Clarendon. Come on. We'll go back there and you can clean up."

Rusty was not adverse to accepting. He went with Wade and after he took a bath and shaved, he put on a clean pair of clothes that he borrowed from Wade. He was his old self again, or almost. There was a new look in his eyes and Wade wondered if Rusty would ever be the carefree, full-of-life man with the humorous disposition he had once been. Angela had stolen it from him and it was a loss not only to Rusty, but to anyone who knew him.

Over dinner they talked and Wade explained his problem with finding Ada.

"I don't know her sister's name," Wade said. "So, I don't know where to begin looking."

"Well, you sure came prepared," Rusty smartly stated and Wade smiled, thinking that this sounded like the old Rusty. "Lucky for you, you found me. Her sister's name is Carrie Morley and they live right over there on Oakwood Drive."

Wade felt a moment of excitement that dulled to a steady pounding heartbeat. He was actually afraid now that he knew where to go.

"I guess I'll go over there tomorrow."

"Why wait? Go this evenin'."

Wade hesitated to respond. What if Ada didn't want to see him? Or what if Carrie's husband ordered him to leave? Maybe Fred Tanner had given them that strict order concerning Wade. He didn't know what he would do in that case.

"Stop worryin'," Rusty said, seeing Wade's expression. "You know Ada wants you. All you gotta do is let her know you're here. She'll see to the rest."

"I hope you're right. I'm afraid Fred Tanner has prepared everyone for this scenario and I don't imagine I'll be received."

"Ada'll receive you. That's all that matters."

Wade was not so sure, but he was going to give it a try. After dinner, he got a room for Rusty and then the two of them went out. They walked down Walnut Street toward the river and turned left onto Oakwood Drive. About four blocks down, Rusty pointed out the house.

"There it is," he said. The house was large and white with a picket fence around it. There were windows all the way across the front and two gables overlooking the street. Several trees shaded the yard and bright blue hydrangeas bordered the front steps.

It was dark under the trees, but a soft glow of light came from the house. Wade stood with his hand on the gate for such a long time that Rusty finally opened it and pushed him in.

"Good luck," he said and he walked away. Wade watched him and then he took the first step toward the house.

The second step was easier and so were the next few steps. He seemed to gain momentum as he approached the house, and by the time he knocked at the door, Wade was confident and full of self-assurance.

It was an attractive young woman who opened the door and if Wade didn't miss his guess, there was no surprise on her face.

"You must be Wade Thornton," she calmly stated.

"Yes, ma'am," he said as he removed his hat.

"Please, come in," she said as she opened the door wider.

He stepped inside and quickly looked around. The Morleys were doing well. He could see it in the large rooms and fine furnishings, but none of these things were of interest to him. He was looking for Ada.

He didn't see her, but his ears picked up the sound of feminine laughter. It was a delicate laugh followed by conversation and although it didn't belong to Ada, her voice followed closely behind it.

"My husband is on the back porch," Carrie said. "He likes to sit out there after dinner and smoke. You could join him if you like."

Wade gripped his hat tighter. "I want to see Ada," he said without hesitation.

The voices in the nearby room stopped with amazing abruptness and Wade anxiously looked in that direction. Ada appeared at the door, followed by a young woman about her own age.

"Wade!" she exclaimed in obvious surprise. He quickly walked to her and they stood looking at each other for a moment without saying anything.

"Why did you leave?" Wade finally asked as he took her hands in his.

"Daddy said I had to go," she quickly explained. "Mama sent me here."

"So, you've been kicked out because of me," Wade said with sorrow.

"No, Wade. You didn't start all those rumors. Daddy'll get over it in time. He always does."

"Give him time to see the truth of it," Carrie offered. "He's a fair man. It just sometimes takes him longer to arrive at the truth than other people."

Wade looked over his shoulder at Carrie. "He wants to kill me," Wade said. "I hope he arrives at the truth soon or I might not live to see it."

The girl beside Ada laughed aloud, but it had a pleasant sound to it, nothing crass or inappropriate.

"Uncle Fred won't kill you," she said. "Hello, Wade Thornton," she added, extending her hand toward him. "I'm Maggie, Ada's cousin. I can see she isn't going to introduce us, so I'll take the initiative."

She was a bold girl, her blue eyes full of laughter. Her dark blonde hair was pulled up and she had a slim face that had a striking resemblance to Carrie's. She smiled sweetly and gave Wade an appraising look that left nothing out.

"Well," she drawled with approval, "Ada's description hardly did you justice. Do you have a brother, by chance?"

Wade returned her smile. "No, I'm an only child."

"Too bad," she said as she walked away. She stopped beside Carrie and then she slipped her arm around Carrie's, linking elbows with her. "It's a bit stuffy in here," she said with a wave of her hand. "I could use some fresh air. What about you, Carrie? Want to join me on the lanai?"

They walked away and Wade turned his attention back to Ada. She was looking up at him, her big eyes wide with excitement, and he gave her a quick study, thinking she had never looked so lovely.

She was dressed in a simple dress that was of much better quality than her usual attire and her hair was pulled up much the same as Maggie's had been. She looked more mature and ever so alluring. Wade pulled her to him and kissed her without any thought of what was appropriate.

"Wade Thornton!" she said after a minute of deep passion. She pulled away from him, but there was a smile on her lips that told him she approved.

"Let's get married, Ada," he said, but to his surprise, the smile left her face.

"I want to," she seriously said, "but my name's been shamed and it'd be a blight on you if we got married."

"No, it wouldn't. It would show everyone that my intentions were always honorable."

"You're naive to think that," she said with a frown. She took a step away from him and folded her hands before her chest. "I gotta prove 'em wrong, but I don't know how. I thought if I waited then time would show 'em. It'll prove me right if I c'n hold out that long."

Wade took her by the shoulders and turned her so that she had to face him. "I don't care what anyone thinks. I love you and I want to marry you."

She nodded. "I love you, too, but it'd be no good if I wouldn't be accepted. I couldn't live that way."

"No, you couldn't," he agreed, and a deep emotion stirred in him. It was more than anger. Ada was innocent and there was nothing to prove, but he understood her need. It was that prejudice again, the thing that made people act irrationally —

the thing that Ada had no more control over than Wade had with the prejudice against him. It was different with a woman, especially this kind of shunning. It had to be made right and Wade suddenly had an idea that he knew what to do.

He dropped his hands from her shoulders and looked away as he thought about it.

"I'm leaving," he stated and she gave a start that caused her whole body to jerk. Her large eyes looked up at him with apprehension.

"Don't go, Wade," she said, but he had already turned and was walking toward the door.

"I'll be back," he promised her. "We're going to straighten this out and then if you want, we'll get married."

"That's what I want," she assured him.

"Then make your plans. I've got some plans of my own to make. I know what I've got to do."

"What is it?" she breathlessly asked.

He paused at the door, thinking about a response. "I'm going back to my ranch. I'll leave tomorrow. May I see you before I go?"

She nodded, but her eyes were still anxious. "Don't kill Logan," she said. "They'll hang you and then I'll die, too."

He smiled with mild amusement. "I won't kill him," he said. "He isn't worth the pain that would cause."

Ada sighed with relief, but then just as quickly, she tensed with apprehension. "What are you gonna do?" she asked.

He smiled again. "Don't worry," he said as he slipped his hat on his head. "I'll see you tomorrow."

Ada stood very still and looked at the closed door. She *was* worried. His easy manner didn't fool her. She knew he was planning something bold and maybe even outrageous and his reassurance didn't give her peace.

"I guess I know what I gotta do, too," she said to the empty room. "I gotta stop this before Wade does something stupid. I love him," she said with a wag of her head, "but after all, he's still a Yankee."

Chapter Thirty-six

"I'm going home," Wade told Rusty.

"When?" he simply asked.

"Today. I'm taking the afternoon train."

"Things not go well with you and Ada?"

"Things went okay," he replied, "but we both know what's got to happen before she and I can have any peace—or respect."

Rusty took a deep breath and let it out as he narrowed his eyes, looking into the distance as if he was seeing the future. "Yeah," he agreed. "Mind if I sorta ride back toward the ranch?"

"I told you, you still have a job."

"Thanks," Rusty said. "I'll ride that way."

They were in Wade's room and he was throwing his belongings into a black satchel he had brought with him. He stopped long enough to reach into his pocket and pull out a few bills.

"Here," he said, "You left without your pay and you're going to need something until you get home."

"Thanks," Rusty dryly said as he took the money. He stepped back and watched Wade finish his task and then, they walked downstairs together.

Rusty led the way, and as his foot touched the bottom step, he stopped so abruptly that Wade bumped into him.

Two girls had appeared in the open doorway on his left,

coming out of a sitting room where they had been waiting. One was Ada. The other was a girl Rusty had never seen before, but one that immediately caught his attention.

He had sworn never to love again, vowing that no girl but Angela could ever win his heart, but as he looked at Maggie, every thought he had ever had of Angela left him in a flash. He thought he had been smitten when he had first seen Angela, but it was nothing to the way he felt looking at Maggie. He thought he had never seen anything so beautiful in all his life and when she smiled, he was sure of it.

"Hello, Rusty," Ada greeted him, but he had to swallow before he could reply.

"Ada," was all he said.

Wade suddenly pushed him to move him out of the way and it was enough to wake him from his trance. Rusty moved aside and Wade stepped off the stairs, going straight to Ada.

"I'm glad you came," he said. "My train leaves in an hour. Hello, Maggie," he then added. "It's nice to see you again."

"And you, as well," she said. She cleared her throat and smiled. "And your friend?" she asked.

"Oh," he said with a smile. "Maggie, this is my foreman, Rusty Gavin."

Rusty gave Wade a curious look with the obvious promotion, but he made no comment to him. He gave the proper response to Maggie and then he eased back, almost melting into the woodwork behind him.

"I thought if you didn't mind, we'd walk to the station with you," Ada said.

"I'd like that," Wade said. "We have time to walk down to the spring, though. You want to do that now?"

She did. He touched her gently on the arm, guiding her to the door and Maggie and Rusty fell in step behind them. They walked down to the spring and Ada looked around with haunted eyes.

"It's not as lovely as your spring," Wade said, seeing her reaction.

"My spring?" she said. "Why, Wade Thornton. That's your spring."

"What's mine is yours — or will be."

They were talking to each other, giving no mind to Rusty or Maggie and it was not long before they realized they were all alone. It was a consideration that Wade appreciated and he took full advantage of it, but the time went by too quickly and he soon had to leave. They all walked to the station together and Wade left them standing on the platform.

"What's he gonna do, Rusty?" Ada asked, but Rusty shook his head.

"I don't know. He didn't tell me."

"Why didn't you go back with 'im?"

"My horse is here. I'll be riding out in the mornin'."

"I won't be far behind you," Ada soberly announced. "I'm goin' home."

Rusty's eyes ran down the rails, looking south in the direction Wade's train had just gone. "Is that a good idea? Maybe you should give Wade some time."

It was Ada's turn to wag her head. "No," she replied. "I

have a feelin' I should be there. Maybe I can keep him from doin' anything stupid."

"I don't think you have to worry. If I don't miss my guess, Wade Thornton is gonna shake things up, but when he's finished, he'll have the respect of the community."

"Then you do know what he's plannin'."

"No, but I know him and he's anything but stupid."

"Well, I guess I wanna see it," Ada said. "I'm still goin' home."

"I have a feelin' you may be right," Rusty solemnly said. "I wanna see it, too."

"I don't suppose I could go along and see, as well?" Maggie asked and both Rusty and Ada answered her at the same time.

"Yes!"

It broke the tension and they all laughed.

"Rusty, will you get word to my folks that I'm comin' home and that Maggie's comin' with me?"

"Shore," he answered. He turned with excitement. Maggie would be at the Tanner's farm and that would be so close to him. "Let's check the schedules and I'll give 'em an exact time. What day're you plannin' this move?"

"The day after tomorrow," Ada stated. "That'll give you time to get back and to deliver the message."

"Okay," he agreed. He felt jumpy inside and he was not sure whether it was because of Maggie or because of a premonition about Wade that suddenly loomed over him. He looked at Maggie and was startled to think that perhaps the premonition was for himself. Did he dare to think that Maggie could ever be interested in him? Would it be another situation like the one with Angela and would he find himself thrown aside once she had had her fun? He didn't think so. He had known from the beginning what to expect from Angela—he had simply chosen to ignore that fact, but Maggie . . . well, she was a lady. Too bad he could not say the same thing about Angela.

They checked the schedules and agreed on a time. Rusty made a mental note of the girls' arrival time and then, without realizing what he was doing, he took Maggie's hand and turned her around so that she was facing him.

"May I call on you, Maggie, while you're at the Tanner's?" The words jumped out of his mouth before he could stop them.

She smiled and her eyes danced with excitement. Rusty suddenly cringed. Was she laughing at him? Did she find his request amusing? He dropped her hand and closed his mouth, his jaw setting as he clinched his teeth.

"If you don't," she replied, "I'll be *very* disappointed."

It took a few seconds for her response to filter through the fog that had momentarily clouded his brain, but as the words took meaning, he smiled and then his eyes lit up. The dark cloud disappeared and suddenly, Angela was no more than a dream. It was as if the entire episode with her had faded away just like a dream does with the waking of a new day, and Rusty was energized again.

He looked south down the rails and felt anxious to go home. Had he known, Ada felt the same way. If she could have left right then, she would have, but there were things to do and it took time to do them. Oddly, they were all three ready to leave the station and so they hurried away from it.

Rusty returned to his hotel room, but he was too jumpy to relax. He paced the room and went to the window a dozen times just to look outside. Finally, he picked up his meager belongings and walked out.

He found the stable where he had left his horse and saddled up. An hour before sundown, Rusty was riding south toward Wade's ranch.

A couple of hours later, he was sitting on the edge of the yard, curiously reluctant to enter. Powder Keg stepped out of the lounge and stopped with his hand on the porch post. He saw the dark figure sitting alone in the shadows and his hand dropped to his side as he stiffened with alertness.

Rusty eased forward and Powder Keg relaxed as he recognized him. He stepped off the porch and walked across the yard, intercepting Rusty.

"Wal," he drawled, "Glad t' see you're back."

"I had somethin' t' do."

"Figured."

"Is the boss here?"

"Yeah. He just got here, though."

Rusty looked toward the house. The lights were on and the windows were open.

"I know," he said and Powder Keg gave him a curious look.

"I'll care for your horse if you like," Powder Keg offered and Rusty stepped down, ready to accept the help.

"Thanks."

Powder Keg led the horse toward the stable and Rusty

made his way to Wade's house. He knocked on the door and Wade called out a gruff, "Come in."

Rusty carefully walked in, easing the door back and looking around. Wade was sitting at his desk but he was not reading or looking at papers. He was sitting back, his chin resting in his hand in a musing manner. When he saw Rusty, he leaned forward.

"I came on home, Boss," he said.

"You must've read my mind," Wade said. "I was wishing I had told you to beat it back here and here you are."

"I guess I did," he agreed. "I had a feelin' you were gonna need me."

"You're right."

"Whatcha plannin'?"

"I'm going to call Logan Spencer and Fred Tanner out in public."

Rusty whistled, long and low. "That'll shake things up."

Wade nodded in agreement. "I have to let the community know that Logan's a liar. I'm going to call him one to his face."

"He'll deny it."

"I hope he does. That'll give me an excuse to beat the daylights out of him."

"And Fred?"

Wade thoughtfully looked away. "I don't want to, but I've got to call him out, too."

"He'd expect no less," Rusty said. "He'd never respect you otherwise."

Wade was not so sure about that, but he trusted Rusty's

judgment. He turned and looked at his friend and he fleetingly wished he had the ease and self confidence that Rusty would have in this kind of situation. He was a warrior at heart, a Spartan, in many ways, and he would be well equipped to pull off this sort of deal.

"I know I don't have to ask, but watch my back. Don't get involved. Just keep any of Logan's friend's off of me."

"When is this shindig takin' place?"

"When the time's right. I'll know when it happens."

Rusty understood. Timing would be all important and if Wade pulled this off correctly, he would walk away a hero.

Rusty left Wade and walked across the yard to the bunkhouse. He turned in early and the next morning he was riding toward the Tanner's farm before anyone knew he was gone.

The dog announced his arrival and Rusty stopped at the gate, sitting his horse while he waited. Fred appeared on the porch, rifle in hand. It was something Rusty could appreciate. He was armed, as well. He wore two pistols in a tied down holster, he had a rifle in the boot of his saddle, and unknown to anyone else, there was a knife in a special case that lay down the back of Rusty's shirt in easy reach. He sat straight in the saddle and eyed Fred.

"Whatcha want?" Fred asked.

"I saw Ada in Green Cove. She asked me to bring you a message."

"Spill it and ride," Fred curtly remarked.

"She and her cousin, Maggie, are comin' in on the three

o'clock train tomorrow."

Fred grunted a response and then he added, "I mighta knowed. Does Wade Thornton know this?"

"Not yet."

"If you're smart, you'll keep it to yoreself."

Rusty chose not to reply to that. "I'm ridin'," was all he said, and he turned his horse and started back toward the ranch. About halfway there he stopped and looked over his shoulder. He had a funny feeling and he didn't know why. Maybe it was because he imagined he felt the sights of Fred's rifle bearing down on him with every step his horse took, but then he never once saw Fred tip the weapon in his direction. He had stood with it at his side, pointing it to the floor the whole time Rusty had been there. It was another premonition. Rusty had a feeling it was a precursor of things to come and with it, came that jumpy feeling again.

He rode into the ranch yard just seconds before Wade stepped outside. The sun was bright and already hot and Rusty wiped the sweat from his brow as he stepped down from his horse.

"Where you been?" Wade quickly asked.

"The Tanners."

A dark look passed over Wade's face. "Why?"

"Ada asked me to give her pa a message. She's comin' in on the three o'clock train tomorrow."

The dark look turned to surprise and then to curiosity. "How did he take it?"

"He didn't look too happy," Rusty said. He pushed his hat

back on his head and looked around. "But then, he wasn't too happy with my arrival and his expression didn't change a whit." He turned back to Wade. "You gonna be there?"

Wade gave that some thought before answering. "Yeah," he finally said. "I will."

Rusty nodded. "So will I."

It was early afternoon the next day when Wade and Rusty left the ranch. They rode east to the newly made road that led to Mason's Corner. When they arrived, they were both surprised. Mason's Corner had never been so busy. There were several wagons scattered about and a few lone horses. A band of children ran across the dusty street, playing a game, and people were busily going here and there.

Wade swung down from his saddle and carefully looked around. Rusty sat on his horse, taking his time as he took advantage of the high vantage point. He could see across the yard and down the road. Another wagon was coming into view on the horizon.

Pop appeared on the porch of Mason's store and he stopped there, his hands on his hips.

"Hey, what's going on, Pop?" Wade asked.

"Wal," he drawled as he reached up and scratched his chin, "that is a question. It 'pears as if Logan brought his friends with 'im to meet his girl. She's comin' in on the afternoon train."

Wade looked toward the tracks and then right back at Pop. He considered arguing the point, but then he thought better of it. No use showing his hand this early in the game.

Rusty finally stepped down from his horse and he and

Wade walked to the shade of the nearest tree.

"He's right," Rusty softly said. "Most o' these folks are Logan's friends."

"What does it mean?" Wade asked.

"I think Logan believes you won't start anything in a crowd. He's afraid of you."

"Well, he's wrong there. I want a crowd. I want witnesses around when I call him a liar."

"Hey, look," Rusty suddenly said. He was looking down the road toward the north and a tight bunch of riders were coming into view. "It's your crew."

Wade turned with a start. There were Powder Keg, Cody, Pat, Jim, Bart, Jake, and Jess coming down the road to Mason's Corner. Daniel was nowhere to be seen, but then Wade was not surprised. He had never wholly won Daniel's loyalty. They rode right up to him and Jim stepped down from his horse.

"What are you doing here?" Wade asked.

"I gave the order—I hope you don't mind. We heard there was going to be trouble and we came to even up the odds."

Wade looked up at them. They were a fine looking group of men and he was proud of them.

"I don't mind, at all," he said. "In fact, I'm glad to see you. I never expected this."

"Well, just do what ya' gotta do and don't worry about nuthin' else," Powder Keg said. He leaned forward in his saddle and then he eased back, repositioning the double barreled shotgun he always carried. "We gotch yore back."

"You always have," he stated with pride.

The men all stepped down from their horses and they tied them in the deepest shade. One by one they walked away, each of them going in a different direction.

Some children ran by, noisily playing a game, and then in the distance a train whistled. It was too soon to be Ada's train and anyway, it was coming from the south, but it caused Wade to stiffen with anxiousness.

"Take it easy," Rusty said and Wade smiled. He was as jumpy as a rabbit. The train came in and stopped and after a short pause, it left again.

"You know," Wade said, "This is what I've been waiting for—witnesses. I'm going to find Logan and call him out."

"They're witnesses," Rusty agreed, "but they're Logan's friends."

"I know," Wade said with a nod of his head. "The only fly in the ointment is Fred. I need him here, too."

"Well," Rusty drawled, "you may just have gotten your wish. Here comes the Tanner's wagon."

Wade jerked and his body stiffened with a moment of anxiety. Slowly, he relaxed. He looked down the road to the northwest and sure enough, the Tanners were coming. Wade recognized Fred and then Mrs. Tanner sitting beside him, and in the bed of the wagon, Paul and Silas suddenly stood.

As if on cue, Logan stepped out of the blacksmith's shop. He didn't seem to notice Wade. He was looking toward the Tanner's wagon and nothing else appeared to interest him. He stood there with a casual attitude, unconcerned about anything, at all.

Wade began walking toward him before he even realized what he was doing. He stepped out of the shade and the afternoon sun hit him with full force. It was hot, but he was not thinking about that. His whole focus was on Logan. He could see the man's eyes, squinting as they looked down the road, and the insulant smile that turned the corners of his mouth. He saw the sweat on Logan's forehead and the move of his hand as he reached into his pocket to remove some tobacco, and then, he saw the attitude change and caution touch his mien. He dropped the tobacco and turned, stiffening as he recognized Wade.

Logan didn't say anything. He stared and then he slowly relaxed as a couple of men followed him out of the blacksmith's shop.

"Logan," Wade began. His voice was soft and not very loud. He spoke only for Logan to hear, but it brought others out of the shop. Behind Wade, Pop and Mason appeared on the porch of the store and down the road, the Tanner's wagon was coming closer and closer. "You're a low down lousy excuse for a human being, but that isn't what I've come to say. You've lied on me and you've lied on an innocent girl and for that, I'm calling you out."

Logan looked Wade up and down before answering and then, he sneered. "I ain't armed, but I c'n see that don't mean nuthin' t' you."

Wade was wearing a pistol, but he quickly removed it, throwing it on the ground without a thought of what the dusty sand would do to it. Logan's face blanched and the belligerent smile left his face. He knew Wade could whip him. He remembered only too well the beating he had taken before. He was not anxious to fight with him again.

"You c'n beat me, Yankee—that's a fact, but it won't change nuthin'. You cain't erase yore sin with my blood."

Wade had to hold himself in to keep from reaching out and snatching Logan by the collar and dragging him into the street.

"You're a liar, Logan Spencer," he said, his voice cutting like a crack from a whip.

You could have heard a pin drop in that crowd. It was almost as if no one even dared to breathe. They were all tense and listening, wondering what Logan would do. He could not let such a challenge go. No man could live in this community without disputing this kind of accusation.

But Logan was afraid. He didn't want anyone to know that, so he summoned all the bravado he could muster. He stood up straight and he looked Wade in the eyes. After all, he had his friends to back him up and they were all around him. He smiled and looked over his shoulder to reassure himself.

His false confidence left him in an instance. He saw something on their faces he had not expected. They were looking at him, their expressions hard and somber and none of them were looking very friendly. Logan's body tensed and then he angrily threw something away from him. It looked like a straw he had been chewing on, and the wind caught it and whipped it away.

"I won't take that from no man," he growled in anger. He sidestepped as he talked, moving to his right, getting the sunlight out of his eyes. Wade turned his head, his eyes following Logan's movements, but he held his ground.

"Then take it back," Wade said.

"I won't!" Logan said, his anger overriding his better judgment. "You're a skunk and she's a sl—"

He had no chance to finish that sentence. Wade hit him right in the mouth and Logan went down. He sprawled out on the ground, his arms flung wide, and blood all over his chin. He shook his head and then he wiped his mouth with the back of his hand. It was bloody and he looked at it in confusion.

Just as quickly, he came to his senses and then, he jumped to his feet. He had given a lot of thought to the beating Wade had given him before, and he realized he had gone into that fight underestimating his opponent, but he wouldn't make that mistake again. He quickly analyzed that fight and he wondered if maybe he could beat Wade Thornton, after all. Cautiously he circled, looking for an opening. It came and he stepped in, swinging hard and fast with his fist, aiming for Wade's exposed mid-section. Wade turned and the blow hit him at an angle, sliding off his body and sending Logan off balance. He fell past Wade and hit the dirt again.

Suddenly, his friends were cheering him on, encouraging him to get up. He sprang to his feet and charged Wade, making contact in his onslaught that actually sent Wade down. He fell backwards and hit the ground, as surprised as Logan.

Logan gave him no time to get to his feet, he fell on him and pinned him there, trying to hit him in the face. One blow caught Wade on the ear and he saw stars, but mostly Logan was beating at nothing, wearing himself out in the effort.

Wade caught Logan's arm and pulled him aside, hitting him at the same time. Logan fell back and Wade sat up, quickly coming to his feet before Logan could get set again. They came together then and slugged it out, each one beating at the other until Logan went down. He was no match for Wade and he quickly lost his stamina.

He raised his head and looked around, sucking in the air that he seemed unable to get enough of. His friends were no longer cheering. There was silence all around him. Wade was standing a few feet away, bent forward, breathing deeply, as well.

"Well, I'll be doggoned if you ain't beat me," Logan said in surprise. He had briefly entertained the idea that he would win this fight, but he could see it was not going to happen. He sat in the dirt, admitting defeat, not wanting another beating like the last one he had taken.

"Do you take it back?" Wade asked.

"I reckon I do," Logan said as he wiped blood away from his mouth. He gently shook his head, trying to clear it. "I'll admit, I shouldn't've said those things, but I really thought it was true about you and her."

Wade held out his hand to Logan. "Can I help you up?" he asked and everyone cheered.

Suddenly men were all around them, patting Wade on the back and pulling Logan to his feet. They were laughing and talking, satisfied with the turn of events, but Wade was not finished. He looked around, trying to see through the crowd and at last his eyes fell on Fred. He was still in the wagon, sitting, looking at the commotion, and the look in his eyes could have meant anything.

The twins jumped out of the wagon bed and Mrs. Tanner said something to them, but Wade was concentrating on Fred and he didn't hear her words. He was staring at Fred and Fred was staring back at him. Their eyes had locked across the way and although no one seemed to notice, the afternoon drama was far from over.

"You're next, Fred!" Wade suddenly shouted and the crowd went silent. Fred came to his feet, looking unusually tall on the wagon.

"I suppose I deserve this," Fred admitted with a solemn nod of his head. He was still holding the reins and in one hand, he held a buggy whip. "I ain't the fighter you are, but I ain't afraid of you."

"I know that," Wade agreed, suddenly wishing there was another way. He wanted to like Fred. In spite of his aggravation with him, Wade wanted to be friends with him, too. He couldn't think about that right now. He had to stay focused, so he quickly added, "But you've helped perpetuate a lie. I've got to call you out."

Fred again nodded his head, agreeing with Wade, and suddenly admiring him so much that he regretted ever having animosity toward him.

"An' rightly so," he said. "I'll publicly apologize if that'll be enough. If it ain't, I'll take my medicine."

Wade was so relieved that he actually wilted, but then he

thought it wise to take advantage of the situation.

"It isn't!" Wade exclaimed and Fred visibly stiffened. His face went white and then it darkened with hot blood. He carefully laid the whip and the reins down. "You admit that the malicious gossip about Ada is a lie?"

"I do," Fred said, his expression hard and calculating.

"My intentions have always been honorable," Wade went on. "I've asked Ada to marry me, but she wants your blessing. Do you give it?"

"I reckon I do, even if you are a Yankee."

Someone in the crowd let out a whoop of delight and then everyone cheered again, the tension broken.

"Now's the time to say, 'drinks 're on me!'," someone else exclaimed and the whole crowd laughed.

It was a jolly crowd that met the train a few minutes later and Ada and Maggie were astonished and confused at the carnival-like atmosphere. Wade was at the front of the group and he held his hand out to Ada as she paused on the train steps. He was disheveled and a blue welt had appeared on his left cheek, but he was smiling, his dark eyes dancing with delight.

"What's this?" she asked as she stepped down and the whole crowd whooped again.

"Your father has just given us his blessing to get married," Wade said and Ada anxiously searched the crowd for Fred, thinking that Wade had beaten it out of him. "He's alright," Wade went on, seeing Ada's reaction. "But Logan might need a few days to recover."

"What've you done?" Ada anxiously asked.

"Nut'in' a man wouldn't do if'n he is a man," Aubrey Callahan assured Ada.

Just then, Ada saw her mother and she reached out to her. Mrs. Tanner stepped forward and took Ada's hand and it was the cue that sent everyone drifting away. The entertainment was over. It was time to return to normal things and let the Tanners have their privacy, but everyone was sure they would never forget what Wade Thornton had done that day. More than one man wagged his head with delight and exclaimed repeatedly, "Now, there's a man!"

Chapter Thirty-Seven

Wade was in a quandary. He had something to do and it was going to be dangerous, but he hesitated to ask anyone to help him. More than once, his eyes ran across his crew in contemplation. They finally came to rest on Rusty.

Rusty's ironical expression had returned to his eyes and these days he was back to his old witty self. Everyone knew it was because of Maggie. She was a girl that had made more than one of the men look once and then look again, but despite this, they all admitted, she was the perfect match for Rusty. It has been said that opposites attract, but even though the two of them were very much alike in temperament, it seemed no two people had ever been more right for each other.

Bart was ribbing Rusty as Wade approached and everyone else was backing him in good-natured fun.

"You might not oughtta marry that girl," Bart was saying.

"What makes you say that?" Rusty asked, his eyes cautiously amused.

"Ain't no tellin' what kinda children ya'll have," Bart wryly said and everyone snickered.

"The usual kind, I imagine," Rusty said, knowing Bart was teasing, and wondering where he was going with this.

"Ain't no way," Bart insisted. "I hear she out-shot you at target practice an' she out-wrestled ya', too. Now, just think about that f'r a minute and you'll see what I mean."

"I let her win," Rusty insisted, knowing Bart was referring to the Indian wrestling match he and Maggie had playfully had.

"Uh-huh!" he exclaimed. "Wal, just the same, she hit that target, bulls-eye ever' time, and maybe you let 'er win at wrestlin' and maybe you didn't, but I shore wouldn't take the chance with children."

Everyone laughed and Rusty smiled along with them. He didn't care if they teased him. He would have done the same to any one of them if the shoe had been on the other foot. Besides, he was so much in love with Maggie, it didn't matter what anyone said.

"Okay," he said, drawing out the word for effect. "You've had your fun at Rusty's expense," he continued with a smile, "but I know what you're really thinkin' an' I feel sorry f'r all of y'u."

"Yeah, well, we feel sorry f'r y'u, too," Bart said, wagging his head as if he was grieved. "What ya' reckon, boys? Should 'e chance it?"

"I don't know," Pat said. "Maggie might need a man with a milder disposition — just f'r the kids' sakes."

"I'm mild," Rusty insisted.

"Yeah, like a tornado."

"I'm perty mild," Bart said. "I gotta right easy-goin' disposition. I might be just the feller to tame a wildcat like Maggie."

"In your dreams!" Rusty said.

"Well, it's just because we're your friends," Bart said with

411

pathos. "We'd make the sacrifice f'r y'u only because we're your friends."

Everyone was still laughing when Wade stepped through the door.

"Whatcha say, boss," Bart sang out. "Ya reckon it'd be safe f'r Rusty and Maggie to have offspring? Don't ya' think that's a bit scary, given their mutual tendencies?"

"I don't know," Wade said, playing along. "They might raise an army of Titans."

"Wal, I don't know what that is," Bart said, rubbing his unshaven chin as he thought, "but if it's something big and tough, I bet you're right."

"I need to talk to you, Rusty," Wade said, changing the subject and interjecting a serious note into the conversation. It reminded everyone that it was time to get to work and they quickly got up and went out the door—all except Powder Keg. He had taken over the job of cook and janitor and he spent most of his time right there, so Wade and Rusty followed the rest of the crew outside. They walked across the sandy yard and stopped in the shade of a nearby tree.

"What's up, Boss. You look down-right serious," Rusty said.

"I've got a job for you, but you can refuse if you like and no hard feelings."

"I'll do it—whatever it is," he assured Wade.

"Then I want you to gather up a few things, saddle a couple of horses, and be waiting for me in half an hour."

"Okay. What do I gather?"

"Rope," Wade began, carefully considering what they would need, "a couple of buckets, and some gunny sacks."

Rusty eyed him curiously, his interest piqued by the odd request. "Any partic'lar kinda rope or just haulin' rope?"

"That'll do."

"Okay," Rusty agreed without any more questions. A half hour later, he was waiting in the corral, standing beside two saddled horses and one pack horse. "I threw in a shovel just for good measure," he stated as Wade joined him.

"Good thinking," Wade said with approval. They quickly mounted and rode out of the yard, leading the pack horse between them.

Wade led the way. He rode straight to the Clearing, but he passed it, giving Corporal Harris' grave a long, solemn look as he went by. They came to the edge of the pine forest and Wade didn't even hesitate. He rode directly into it and set a course for the Spencer's old house. Rusty followed in a curious silence.

The house came into view as Wade and Rusty rode out of the thickest part of the forest. Everything seemed the same. It had been Corporal Harris' home all this time and now that he was gone, no one had been here to disturb anything.

Wade stepped down from his horse and looked around. Rusty did the same. It was quiet — very quiet.

"What're we doin', Boss?" Rusty asked. He pushed his hat back on his head and carefully studied the place. It still made him feel uneasy.

Wade turned his head and looked at Rusty. "I thought you'd figured it out," he said.

Rusty considered that. "Well, I know that Corporal Harris was Jake's ghost," he said. "He was the last of your daddy's soldiers, wasn't he?"

"Yes," Wade answered.

Rusty pushed his hat back and looked around.

"I thought the Major and Angela got the gold," Rusty said, suddenly realizing what Wade was thinking.

"No, only part of it."

"I'm surprised she would leave any of it behind."

"She didn't think she had," Wade said and at Rusty's questioning look he went on to explain. "The gold was hidden beneath the floor of an old shed on the Tanner's property. It was one of those little tabby houses you see around—the one's made from mortar with oyster shells in it," he clarified before going on. "They buried it and then they pulled the walls down over it to mark the spot. You could see the shed from the Tanner's house back then, but over the years, things have grown up around it. It was well hidden, but Corporal Harris knew where it was.

"For some reason that he alone knows, Harris began moving the gold. He dug under the slabs of the old wall and removed the gold, one bucket at a time, and he brought it here."

"That's what everyone's been seein'," Rusty said with a dry chuckle. "Jake's ghost."

Wade nodded and then Rusty asked, "So, how d' y'u know this?"

"I'm guessing, but I'm willing to bet I'm right, because I found the gold. It's here."

Rusty whistled and then he looked around. "Where?"

"Where do you think?" Wade asked. He reached in his pocket and pulled out a gold coin. He handed it to Rusty and then he smiled. "This was in Ada's shoe when we pulled her out of the well."

"Well, I'll be dad-burned!" Rusty exclaimed. "He threw it in the well! That's crazy, but anyone could see, he wasn't in his right mind."

"No, I guess not," Wade agreed. They were both looking toward the well and without a word, they simultaneously began walking to it. They stopped beside it, hands on their hips, looking down into the abyss. The walls were uneven where they had fallen in and it was going to be a difficult operation, but neither man doubted the ability to bring up the gold.

They worked all that day and part of the next. When they finally called it quits, they had more than forty thousand dollars' worth of gold recovered from the well.

"Ten percent of this is yours," Wade told Rusty. "Is that fair?

"Good Lord!" he exclaimed. "That's more money than I could make in a lifetime."

"You've earned it."

Rusty looked at Wade with wide-eyed realization. "I can marry Maggie," he solemnly stated, and then with more enthusiasm, "I can marry Maggie!"

They both laughed and then they shook hands to secure the deal. They rode back to the ranch and secreted away the findings of their labor, never telling anyone what they had done. Two months later, Ada married Wade Thornton, the Yankee from New Hampshire. Maggie's mother required a longer engagement in Rusty's case, but a year later, he led Maggie to the altar and then they settled down on property near Wade and Ada.

Paul and Silas looked on all of this with the philosophy of a poet. They felt they had stirred the embers of romance in Wade and Ada and without a doubt, they knew they should be credited with the success of the whole outcome.

"I toldja," Paul said to Silas. "It's like doodlebug fishin'. We patiently baited 'em and gently coaxed 'em, and well, we ketched 'em, didn't we?"